Books in This Series

By Death Series

Touched by Death

Haunted by Death

Chilled by Death

By Death Books 1–3

DALE MAYER

TOUCHED BY DEATH

BOOK ONE OF BY DEATH SERIES

About This Book

Digging up the dead isn't the best way to lay ghosts to rest …

Anthropologist Jade Hansen had been touched by death once before. While in Haiti one year ago, she'd lost her unborn child, and the devastation nearly took her sanity in the time that followed. Getting back to work means facing the grief that's all but destroyed her. Determined to be strong, she returns to Haiti with a mortuary team to recover the bodies of an American family from a mass grave, following a devastating earthquake.

Dane Chester is an independent contractor, who willingly puts his life on hold to help rebuild the sleepy town of Jacmel, after the natural disaster all but razed it. He's staying with his sibling while Dane volunteers his services in the group effort, but finds himself put off by his brother's pregnant wife and her relatives. Wanting to do good for those who lost so much from the quake creates a tug of war within him, given the unexpected family strife. Selfishly he wants nothing more than to go home, … until he meets Jade, who, at first sight, makes him realize what's been missing in his own life for so long.

Jade's mortuary team begins work, but, from the start, everything that can go wrong does. As anthropologists, they've all faced the very human horrors of situations like this before. But something else is at work at this mass grave site—something malevolent that none of them can explain— yet equally can't shake the communal disquiet. Rather than laying her ghosts to rest where she suffered such loss, Jade finds herself confronting death all over again. This time her grief is mingled with an unnerving dose of terror—and this incredible man Dane, who unexpectedly awakens her heart to love again, is somehow right in the middle of it all.

Sign up to be notified of all Dale's releases here!
https://geni.us/DaleNews

Prologue

IN PERFECT SYMPHONY the clouds swayed in the sky, wrapping the moon in protective cotton wool, as the ground shook and trembled beneath the sleepy town of Jacmel in the south of Haiti.

Mother Nature growled and raged, over and over again.

As if she knew the secrets long kept hidden in the hills behind the small town.

As if she knew about the injustices done.

As if she knew this had to stop.

She gave one last mighty shove, and the earth cracked open.

Trees toppled, their roots ripped from the ground in hapless destruction. Large rocks tumbled, as their foundations were wiped out from below. Everything fell to the force of Mother Nature—at long last exposing old secrets to the light.

When the clouds moved from their protective stance, the moon glared upon the result of Mother Nature's game of fifty-two-card pickup with the Devil. The lunar light shone on bones long picked clean—now newly exposed to the sky.

The ground undulated one last time. The surrounding hillside shuddered, sending a light dusting of earth and rock to rebury the gruesome evidence.

As if the sins of man were too much for even the moon

FIVE DAYS LATER, a tractor with a bucket on the front—hastily called into service—groaned, as it carried yet another load of the town's dead to a large grave. Herman, the tractor driver, was beyond pain and grief and death. He focused on the gritty details of plain survival. Five days of heat and exposure hadn't been kind to the dead—or to the living. Survival had become a grim business, and rotting bodies needed to be buried, or disease would crush them further. So many dead. No money. No time. No help.

No choice.

His neighbor, John, lifted the last small corpse from the dump truck's deposit on the ground to the loader's bucket. He pulled off one work glove, straightened the makeshift mask tied around his mouth and nose, and shouted, "Good to go!"

Herman popped the gear shift forward, then swore and prayed that Bertha would survive the job given her. He trundled forward. "Come on, girl." He patted the stick shift in his hand. "I need you to get it done. If you quit on me, I ain't gonna make it through this." And that was no joke. He knew for damn sure that he wouldn't if ol' Bertha didn't. *Bad business this.* He had respect for the dead. Every one of his family and friends had received a proper send-off, a decent burial—as was fitting. Until this earthquake.

Pain clutched his heart and squeezed. So many dead.

He'd lost his wife, one son, and two grandkids this last week. Sex and age hadn't mattered here. Mother Nature hadn't cared. She'd wiped them all out.

John, the only other person who'd stepped up to help,

had been lucky. His young wife and her family had survived the devastation. Living out of town had helped. That also contributed to his motivation to help out. This mass grave butted against his wife's family's land, so it made sense for John to ensure this grave was closed over, right and proper.

Many people could be trekking here on All Souls' Day, as families came to honor their dead. Then again, complete families had been buried together. There might not be anyone left to mourn.

Herman would come and visit. Too many people remained here to forget.

HERMAN TUGGED AT the old T-shirt tied around his nose and mouth, his sun-blackened skin blending with the poor light. Nothing kept the smell out. He'd already gone through a half-dozen pairs of gloves. But, without the makeshift bandanna, each breath caught in his chest, making him gag. His clothes would have to be burned after this. No way to rid them of the smell of death.

Bertha struggled forward. Darkness hid the evidence of what they were doing. What he'd done. He only hoped he wouldn't have too many more loads to haul.

In the aftermath of the earthquake, everyone had been numb, in shock, or frozen with grief. No one could make decisions. No military arrived to take care of the problem. The government buildings and staff had been as decimated as the rest of the population.

Herman refused to leave his people lying exposed like that. Determined to do what he could, he'd taken command and had done something. Something so awful that he couldn't close his eyes without seeing the stares of the dead—blaming him.

So far, close to sixty people had gone into this pit. The natural depression, a ready-made burial spot, was a godsend to the desperate survivors, a fast answer to the bloated dead rotting on the sidewalks. Herman didn't know how many more were to come, maybe hundreds. Later, much later, if someone cared, they could open this mass grave and do the right thing. But not now. Now they had to get on with the business of survival.

Mother Nature was a bitch.

Chapter 1

One Year Later ...

JADE HANSEN TWISTED in her sleep at her Seattle, Washington, apartment, while a nightmare across the ocean took over her. Her sweaty panicked body searched for a way out of the endless nightmare of bloated bodies, desperate people, and cries for help—pleas that would never get answered. She turned in the fog as one more person, caught among the fallen rocks, cried out to her. Jade came face-to-face with a woman—blood congealed in her hair and streaked down the side of her face, a chunk of concrete crushing her legs. She begged for Jade to find her son.

Screaming, Jade took off to the safety of the tent, the tent filled with the dead ... and the living who searched for their families.

She couldn't help them all.

She couldn't help any of them.

She couldn't even help herself.

With tears streaming down her face, Jade woke in a panic, as if the demons of her nightmare had followed her into the present.

Shuddering, she recognized the hanging lamp overhead as the one in her apartment. The Aztec print couch she'd fallen asleep on was hers, a gift from her brother. And she finally understood that the evening's in-depth television coverage of a recent small earthquake in Haiti had been the trigger for her nightmare.

Jade curled into a ball, pulling her throw higher up on her neck. She winced at the images still flashing on the news. Another earthquake in Haiti. Only a little one this time. Not that the size mattered. The memories of her one and only humanitarian trip to that area, after the major earthquake almost one year ago, had etched themselves permanently into her brain. A horrible time, a praying-on-your-knees-for-help kind of horrible time. In Haiti, nightmares had destroyed her sleep. The shortage of food for those suffering had destroyed her appetite.

She'd lost weight over there, but nothing compared to the pounds that had slipped off after her return home. Sure, that had been almost one year ago too. It didn't matter. With the nightmare fresh in her mind, it felt like only days.

So much pain and suffering. *So much torment.* She couldn't stop it. She couldn't even begin to make it right. There'd been nothing she could do to help—or so little relative to the scope of the problem that it might as well have been nothing. If she'd been offered a ride out of that hell on any given day, she would have jumped over her colleagues to grab it.

She wasn't proud of that.

In fact, it made her feel small and ashamed. Her colleagues had done so much better.

She'd wanted to be better. She'd tried to be better.

She'd failed. Failed her colleagues. The victims. And herself.

The memories still haunted her.

She had had her nice safe lab job in Seattle. She drove to work every day in a nice car and returned home every night to her clean, safe apartment with running water, heat, and electricity. All the comforts denied the Haitians still struggling through the devastation from twelve months ago.

After she'd locked her front door behind her that first day home, the tears had started to pour. It seemed she'd been crying ever since.

Her life had gone from bad to worse for a while, before she'd picked herself up—somewhat.

And now another earthquake.

If a small one like that triggered Jade's memories, what was the reality doing to all those poor people still living the horror?

Her phone rang.

She ignored it.

It wouldn't quit. Finally she couldn't stand it, so picked up her cell. She didn't even bother to check the caller ID. Duncan called every night at nine. "I'm fine, Duncan."

"Hey, kitten." Her brother's pet name for her made her smile, as he'd probably intended. She used to be like him. Upbeat, funny, and carefree. Until life had dumped her on her ass at the top of the slide and had given her a hard kick downhill. She wasn't sure she'd hit bottom now either.

"I've got a job proposition for you."

His cheerful voice made her want to smile. The job proposition didn't. "I don't want to hear it."

He laughed, a buoyant sound that rang around the room. He never failed to raise her spirits. The effect just didn't hang around after his calls. "Maybe you don't, but maybe you do. How will you know if you don't hear it? It's a good one."

His wheedling tone made her smile in spite of her horrible mood. "Not if I don't want to hear it."

"You don't know what you want."

Jade groaned. "If I don't know, then how do you?"

His laughter pealed again.

She shook her head and felt the lightness—the joyful spirit that was her brother—ease the ache in her soul. "I know you keep trying to save me, Duncan, but I'm fine."

The laughter and joy cut off suddenly. Duncan's voice, sober and sad, whispered, "No. No, you're not."

Tears choked her. She rubbed her eyes. She wouldn't cry, damn it. Not tonight. Not *again* tonight.

"This has to stop, Jade. You'll collapse, and I don't want that to happen." Love slipped through her phone, making it harder to hold back the tears. Jade didn't trust herself to speak. She sniffled ever-so-slightly.

"I know you're hurting inside. I feel it, and I hurt for you."

"I know," she whispered, starting to shake, knowing she had to stop—only she didn't know how. And once again couldn't deal with it. "Look. I'm really tired. I need to get to bed. I'll talk to you tomorrow."

She didn't give him a chance to say goodbye and disconnected instead. And the tears rolled. Hot and steady, they streamed down her cheeks. She snuggled back into the couch and let them run.

The point of stopping them was long gone. Besides, she no longer knew how.

"HEY, DANE, THAT guy phoned again," John called out.

"Yeah, which guy?" Dane walked over to stand beside his stepbrother, who'd stopped by the hospital construction site for a visit.

"The guy about the grave," John said.

Dane tugged off his hard hat to wipe the sweat running down his forehead. Christ, it was hot and humid here in Haiti. He surveyed the construction site in front of them. Not bad at all. They were ahead of schedule, but completion of the new wing was still months away. Jacmel hadn't recovered from the last big earthquake, and, with smaller ones continually causing setbacks, the country would be years getting back on its feet.

It had taken weeks to convince John to let Dane come over after the big quake. When he'd realized how badly in need the town was, Dane had stepped in to help. John's small engine repair shop had been decimated in one of the smaller, more recent earthquakes, yet he refused to let Dane repair it. John had said he wanted to fix things himself.

John added, "Remember? They called before and want to open the mass grave to retrieve some guy's family?"

Dane glanced at his brother. Only the two of them were left in the family. Both stubborn. Independent. And family oriented. It had only taken that one phone call with something odd in John's voice to catch Dane's attention. He'd put his Seattle construction business in the hands of his capable foreman, an old school friend, and, without his brother's invite, Dane had flown to Haiti two days later. That had been months ago.

Shielding his eyes from the hot sun, Dane said, "I have to admit. The never-ending sunshine and warm, dry weather is hardly a hardship. Of course we haven't hit the humid summer season yet."

"See? Isn't this much better than the wet misery of the coast? Seattle is probably still buried in snow—even in March." John grinned, with satisfaction.

Dane couldn't argue that. His foreman had been complaining of just that in their last phone call. "Not everyone hates the rain like you do."

"Come on. Admit it." John smacked Dane's shoulder. A cloud of dust rose, making him step back hurriedly. "You love it here."

"I love visiting you, and, of course, I adore Tasha." Dane grinned over his white lie. Tasha obviously adored his brother, so that was good enough for Dane. It had, after all, been the call of family that had brought Dane here.

John had a terrible history with relationships. His longtime high school sweetheart had walked out the door of her home one day, just weeks before graduation, and had never returned. A few years later, John had married the witchy Elise. That marriage had been a walking disaster right from the wedding reception. Dane couldn't stand the woman, and the feeling had been mutual. John was just a big teddy bear, who attracted unscrupulous people.

Unfortunately Elise died in a car crash.

After that fiasco, John disappeared for years, before finally setting up housekeeping with Tasha in Haiti. Dane's antennae went off at that, and, given John's past, Dane could be forgiven for worrying about his brother. Only John appeared to have stabilized, flourishing even. Dane had been delighted.

The major earthquake had changed all that, sending John back into the same morose, angry man as before. So Dane was happy to see the joking John appear at times.

"Hey, are you in there?"

Dane started.

John smirked at him, a sign his lighthearted kid brother was showing through the more cynical angry one of recent years. "What's the matter? Felice getting to you?"

Heat washed over Dane's neck and face. Felice was too hot, too willing, and way too young. She was also the daughter of one of Tasha's friends who'd visited yesterday. He didn't know the specific laws in Haiti relating to that sort of thing. Still, he was pretty damn sure he'd get jail time back home, and that was deterrent enough for him. "She needs to be locked away for a few years."

"Not here. Girls her age are often married and pregnant." John added thoughtfully, "And not likely in that order."

Dane shook his head. "As long as it's not to me."

John changed the subject abruptly. "What should I do about the call? … About this guy's request for help at the mass grave site? Sounds crazy to me."

Easily following the lightning shift of his brother's mind, Dane asked, "What's to do? He's a grieving man. His request isn't unreasonable. And it's done all the time."

John visibly shuddered. "I never expected to feel so strongly about it, but, after that earthquake last year? … I don't know, Dane. I saw too much death. More than I should have—more than anyone should have. It seems wrong to dig up those poor earthquake victims again."

"You've been living here too long. Some weird Haitian beliefs are rubbing off on you."

John snickered, making Dane laugh. "Or not long enough. According to Tasha, Mother Earth claimed them, and she won't be happy if she's forced to give them up again."

With a sigh of disgust, Dane said, "That's crazy talk. This guy lost his family. He wants to take the three of them home to Seattle and to bury them properly. He needs closure. That's all. What's so wrong about that?"

John kicked a stray rock in the dirt. "I don't know that anything is wrong with it. I guess if it were me and mine, I'd want to take them home too. However, it's a mass grave. There are other bodies to consider, other families who will be hurt."

"Really?" Dane stared at him. "Like *how mass?*"

John shot him a look, before grimacing and staring off to the horizon. "I stopped counting at sixty. We did what we had to do. The dead? ... They were everywhere. Herman, our old neighbor, used his front loader to transport them. ... Christ, it was bad."

Dane scrunched his face.

John rushed to explain. "I saw children playing beside bloated bodies. They'd become dulled to them because there were so many. Oh, don't blame the children. They stayed close to the people they knew because they had no one else. That a dead mother or sibling lay within a few feet didn't seem to matter. Even dead, they were a comfort."

Dane closed his eyes, as terrible images flooded his mind. He couldn't imagine the horror. "I wasn't judging. I just can't envision what you went through. And to think of children sitting there, so lost and alone? ... Well, ... it's a terrible thought."

Shadows darkened John's brown eyes.

Dane was sorry for what John had been through. "That's the thing about family." Dane patted John on the shoulder and noticed his brother cringe.

"So you think this guy should be allowed to come in and remove his kin?" John wasn't backing away from this one.

"I don't have any say in this. I wasn't aware that you did either. I'm sure this man has already gone through the authorities. I'd suggest that you accept that this will happen, whether you want it to or not. The team of specialists should be here soon. When they arrive, be nice to them. Helpful. They will probably be there for a day or two, a week or two max. Then they'll be gone, leaving the others to rest in peace."

"It's not that easy."

"I know. Other people's loved ones are in that grave. Maybe someone should suggest that all the victims be identified." Dane pursed his lips and nodded his head, pleased with his idea. "Reburied properly. This guy has money. Maybe some of it should be put toward assisting the community to help them deal with the disaster. Granted, that will take more time."

John shook his head. "You don't understand the full scope of the problem here. Hundreds of bodies could be there. We just kept putting them in, then piling dirt and rocks on top to ensure they weren't disturbed. We probably went overboard on that part."

Dane blanched. "Hundreds?" He swallowed heavily. "Okay, so maybe the team will need a little longer. Still, something could be done for the other remains." Dane winced. "Or at least for the remains they can find and identify, while they search for the ones they are shipping back to Seattle."

John stared at him and gulped. "That's not helping."

"Yeah. I know. Sorry about that."

The two men stared at the half-completed hospital building in front of them. Dane took an involuntary step back. Right now the damn thing resembled a skeleton, reaching out of the ground.

Chapter 2

JADE GROANED AND closed her eyes. A Saturday, and still she'd awakened early. What was the point of having a morning to sleep in if her body didn't get the memo? Sometimes life just sucked.

Surprisingly she drifted back to sleep.

The phone woke her hours later. She stretched out an arm, trying to find her cell, all without having to disturb her comfortable position. "Hello," she mumbled.

"Jade, I let you push me off last night but not today." Duncan spoke hurriedly. "This guy with the job wants an answer, and he wants one now. It's important. Are you awake?"

Jade huddled deeper under the covers. "No. I don't want to hear it. Leave me alone."

"Won't happen. I'm coming over," he said firmly. "Get up and have a shower. I'll bring the coffee. Be there in twenty." The call cut off.

Jade rolled over on her back and stared at the ceiling. *What the hell?*

Twenty minutes later, she slipped on socks, just as the doorbell rang. Opening the door, hairbrush in hand, she frowned. Her brother wasn't alone.

A thin man of average height and wearing coke-bottle-thick glasses stood beside Duncan. He had an overstuffed folder in his hands.

Damn it. She glared at her brother, snagged one of the coffee cups out of his hand and turned her back on them.

"Don't worry about her. She's always grumpy in the morning." Duncan motioned the stranger inside. "This is Tony Maholland. Tony, my sister, Jade."

Jade shot her brother an irritated look. Good manners dictated she at least smile politely at the man standing awkwardly behind Duncan. Exasperated, she said, "Oh, come in and sit down, for heaven's sake. You're giving me a kink in my neck."

"Jade, be nice. Good thing I warned Tony about you."

"Why?" she shot back, leading the way to the small kitchen. "You aren't being nice to me."

Duncan pulled out a chair for Tony, who stood uncomfortably beside them. He twisted a second one around and sat on it backward to face her. "Everything I do is because I love you. We don't always know what we need in life, and sometimes loving someone means making the hard choices for them."

She sat with a *thump*, glared at him, her instincts on high alert. She wouldn't like what was coming. Duncan never backed away from a fight, and he'd always been the kind of brother to lead her down the right path—whether she wanted to go there or not.

"Jade, I need to talk to you. And I need you to *listen*."

"I don't think I want to."

Compassion filled his eyes, and her brother leaned toward her. Instinctively she pulled back slightly. Wary. Duncan was a counselor—helping people was his passion. He couldn't help himself. She loved him but hated when all that do-gooder energy was turned her way.

"I want you to return to Haiti. And Tony will help you get there."

Jade's heart dropped, her stomach clenched, and tears welled in her eyes. "No," she whispered. "I can't go back."

"I'll even go there with you."

Wordless, Jade stared at her beloved brother. *He would too.* She knew he'd drop everything to help her get through this.

He placed his hand on her knee and squeezed gently. "You have to deal with this. Only then can you move on."

"Haiti? But that's where it all started." She stared down at her clenched fists. How did going back make any sense?

Duncan caught and held her hands in his. "I know."

His words, so simple and so powerful. And so not helpful.

"Excuse me." Tony leaned forward, his gaze shifting between the two of them. "Duncan, I can see this is personal, and I can't begin to understand what's really going on here, but I'm not sure she's the right person for the job. We need someone who can handle themselves down there—not people carrying personal baggage."

Jade agreed with a slight nod.

Duncan, however, grinned at the stranger. "Well put, Tony. However, remember this. *Everyone* has baggage. At least with my sister, you will know up front what the problem is. So this is the scoop. My sister went down to Haiti as a part of the Disaster Mortuary Operations Response Team. She was there precisely three weeks. She endured physical attacks on her person, unbelievable emotional trauma due to the massive number of deaths she had to deal with, and her spirit took a major hit. The experience changed her. It was as if she'd been touched by

Death himself."

With an apologetic look at Jade, Duncan continued. "She was pregnant at the time. When she came home, her fiancé couldn't deal, and he bolted. About three weeks after his departure, she lost the baby."

Jade winced. Duncan hadn't said anything wrong; he hadn't exaggerated or minimized the truth. However, laid bare like that, even she could see how, although life had certainly been shitty, it was something she should have and still could recover from.

If she cared to.

Her soul was weary. That was close to explaining the way she felt. She'd been unprepared for the horror and devastation in Haiti. The need and desperation of the people. Her inability to fix … any of it.

The normalcy of her existence after her return home had only amplified it. Her guilt. Her failure. Her life.

"She's always a professional. That won't be an issue. Haiti, itself, wasn't the problem. It just started the problem. She has to face Haiti, before her depression declines into something more than she can deal with. Besides, she's got the perfect skill set and experience, as you well know. Plus, she's available on short notice."

Depression? She stared at Duncan, her attention snagging on that one word. That was it. One simple word? Then she remembered a period in Duncan's life, just after their father had died. She'd been away in college several years by that time, buffered from the emotional element, but Duncan had been there, taking the full blast of guilt from their father's suicide.

"Is that what you felt?" She hadn't known. Not really. How could she have? To understand such darkness, such sadness in others, she had to experience these emotions first herself. *Shit.* So typical. Was everyone blind to what didn't immediately affect them? Duncan had had it hard then too, and she hadn't noticed.

"Oh yes. The thing is, sis, you can honor the grief you feel for the loss of your child and for the horror you felt for all those people in Haiti, but you can't let this beat you. You need to pick yourself up and to grab hold of the reins of your life. Reacting to a stimulus is one thing—wallowing is another thing entirely. When you know what you're doing and choose to do nothing, then …" He sat back, his gaze warm and caring. "Whereas Tony is offering you a chance to step up and out of this place … and to move forward."

Tony leaned forward. "Uh, *maybe* I'm offering this chance."

Duncan and Jade ignored him.

Jade traveled from one realization to another, as they slid through her, lighting all the dark places she'd clung to in her mind. Her grief *was* real and *was* valid. Her distress was also justified. She had a right to feel the way she did. Validation was empowering. Her anger at her fiancé wasn't something she had a problem honoring. … Still, not doing something about this hollowness inside? … Duncan was right.

That was not acceptable.

She sat back, as understanding dawned. "And—now that I do know, … and don't do anything about it—it's self-pity?"

He grinned, pride and love shining at her. "Exactly. And now that you do know, you can't continue on the same path. And by your own words …"

She winced, hearing her voice from past conversations. *I don't do self-pity.* She closed her eyes and dropped her head back. "Not fair. I don't know that I can do Haiti again."

"Maybe this time you could see the healing. The people who have turned their lives around and moved on. You could find the positive and let that heal you too."

She groaned. "You're so into that New Age mumbo jumbo."

"It's me."

She couldn't argue that. Abruptly she turned to face Tony. "What's the job?"

Surprised, and looking a little disturbed, he answered, "My client wants to retrieve three members of his family from a mass grave and bring them home. The team leader on the project is Dr. Bruce McLeod."

"Mass grave?" That didn't bother her. She'd done those before. It was true; she knew she handled death well. She just didn't handle the *people dying* part so well—especially on a large scale. "How mass?"

He peered over the rim of his glasses. "We have it on good authority that close to one hundred people are buried in a grave outside of Jacmel."

Jacmel. She racked her head for the little geographical information she'd allowed to rattle around inside. The opposite side of Port-au-Prince, where she'd been last time. Where her life had been flattened. "Is his family Haitian?"

Tony tilted his head, a curious look on his face. "Yes. Does it matter?"

"No. Identification would be easier if we're looking for three Caucasians in a mix of dark-haired Haitians, for example. After a year, hair will likely still be attached, making identification easier."

"My understanding is that the grave contains mostly locals, with a few tourists who were there at the time."

She nodded. She liked the idea of doing something to help someone. This could work. Close to—but not the same as—what she'd been through before. She'd been stronger going into it back then. But she'd also been unprepared. She'd be neither of those things this time. "How long?"

"As long as it takes to get the job done. My client isn't worried about the cost, within reason, and he's willing to have the other bodies in the grave identified and processed along with his family. The team will leave the information with whatever officials are in place to help identify those victims. The local families will then have the choice of what to do."

"That's generous. What about reburial of the others for the families with no money?"

Tony grimaced. "This is obviously a sensitive issue, and we're working toward a happy resolution for everyone. It may not be possible to identify everyone, and it's quite possible that many, if not all, of those people will be reburied in the same grave. And though he's generous, the expenditures must fit in his budget."

Duncan leaned back and shoved his hands into the front pockets of his faded jeans. "Whew. That'll be some job."

Shooting him a mocking look, Jade asked, "Still willing to come with me?"

He brightened. "Absolutely. I can travel and socialize, while you work."

Her leg shot out and connected with his ankle.

"Hey, I was just kidding." He shifted out of the way, sending her an injured look.

The happy relief in his eyes made her realize just how much he had been hoping she'd come around to his way of thinking. "You'd better be."

"If I could give you a few more details," Tony interrupted. "You'll leave in one week. The plan is to give it three months and reassess. We've been assured this is a decent time frame for our needs. Some adjustments may come down the road, depending on the progress." He glanced at his notebook. "Of course, ... as I said, a budget is in place. So ..." He narrowed his gaze at her. "We'll work out many of the details over there."

"I have a job here. Remember? I'd have to give notice, ... not to mention I'd have no job when I return home." She frowned. She couldn't walk out on her boss on such short notice like that. Neither could she afford to be jobless when she returned in three months. Relief swept through her. No way she could go. She opened her mouth to say just that, when Duncan spoke first.

"Now don't get mad, Jade. However, I've spoken with Gerard already, after Tony and I discussed the issue in greater depth."

"*You what?*" Her voice came out as an incredulous squeak. "You called my boss? Are you nuts? I'm lucky he didn't fire me yesterday."

Duncan grinned. "On the contrary. And don't forget. He and I go way back. He actually liked the idea. He thought this placement might just do the trick for you."

Now her astonishment turned to anger. Like a too-old rubber band, her emotions seemed to stretch thin and snap easily. "I don't like you talking about me behind my back."

"Then don't act in such a way that the people who care about you feel they need to get involved secretly."

"Whatever." She shot him a fulminating look. Why did big brothers only come in arrogant, high-handed models? Her anger flowed, until he spoke again.

"He cares, and so do I. The bottom line is, you can leave for three months, and your job will be here when you get back."

Her protests died on her tongue. She was too weary to continue the fight. A fight she knew he'd win. Her brother did love her. It was hard to argue with her self-proclaimed savior. Besides, he was right. She couldn't continue on the same self-destructive path. Someone had to do something.

That someone had been him.

Now it was up to her.

DANE WALKED TOWARD the main house, tucking his T-shirt into faded jeans, admiring the play of the sun on the bright trumpet-like flowers bouncing in the breeze. Haiti had a lot to offer. At least this area. The countryside was green and lush, the rolling hills and white beaches some of the nicest he'd ever seen. The people were wholesome and strong in faith, even after the disasters they'd faced. He'd loved his time here.

It was coming to an end; he knew that. His future didn't lie here. He knew he'd wake up one day and know it was time to go home. He hoped it would be after the birth of his niece or nephew.

"Aren't you up early today?" His brother's voice came from the vicinity of the patio.

"Look who's talking." Dane grinned at his brother, unshaven and tousled, huddling over a large mug of coffee. "Bad night?"

"Tasha said the baby was playing soccer with her bladder all night. She must have gotten out of bed a dozen times."

Dane barely held in his laughter. "Ah, the joys of impending fatherhood." He walked toward the kitchen door. "Did you leave any coffee in the pot?"

"I left some. I don't know that Tasha did."

Dane grimaced. Tasha was pretty reasonable most of the time, but he'd been witness to a few of her *I'm pregnant, don't mess with me* moments. And they seemed to be more frequent now. He stuck his head inside first, gauged the small room to be empty, and strode over to the coffeepot, where he quickly grabbed a cupful and made a fast exit.

Back outside, his brother chuckled. "Made it, I see. She's gone back to bed anyway, so I imagine you're safe enough."

"You could have told me that before I went in there, thinking I was risking my life." Dane pulled over the second wooden chair and sat down to enjoy the morning.

"*Nah*, if I have to risk my life, you might as well too."

"There's a brother for you." The two sat in companionable silence. Dane marveled at a location where the weather every day remained a comfortable seventy-five to eighty degrees. He knew it fluctuated sometimes, but, during his stay, it had been remarkably consistent.

Suddenly Tasha stormed outside, the door slamming behind her. Dane took one look at the building fury on her face, blinked, and turned slightly away. John would have to deal with this one.

"They can't come. You tell them that they can't do this. It ain't right." She shifted into a spat of guttural Creole, making Dane grateful for his less-than-rudimentary understanding of the language.

John closed his eyes briefly, then opened them and faced his Haitian wife, while Dane looked on. "Now, honey. We've been over this. Just because I say they can't come won't stop them."

"Why not? That property is ours."

"No, it's not." John's weary voice went over ground that he had obviously covered many times.

Dane took a sip of coffee and tried not to show any interest. Tasha's black hair stood on end; her face was puffy, her dark skin splotchy. Her large belly, covered by an old stretched-out T-shirt that hung low, covered the bulk of the goofy boxer shorts she wore. Dane had been around other pregnant women, just none that reacted like Tasha. The longer he stayed, the more he worried about his sister-in-law's mental and emotional health. John never seemed to notice. Love had to be blind.

"Honey, I've told you before. That land borders the family land, but it's not ours."

"It's land we've used since forever. It should be ours." She pouted and collapsed on the arm of his chair beside him, the tempest over for now. "We think of it as ours."

John grinned and tugged her closer. "Except it isn't. I know you think it's wrong. However, you might want to try to see their point of view for a moment. If that were your family thrown into a large pit in another country, wouldn't you want to bring them home? Have a place where you could visit them? Talk to them? Grieve for them?"

She frowned. "I understand that. I'm not heartless. I feel sorry for the family. … I do. What about all the other people buried there though? Some of them could be friends. Family. I don't know who's buried there. I do know it's bad luck to wake the dead. We need to honor their souls and let them rest."

"Maybe we can do something for the other people too. And no one is talking about waking the dead. We're hoping to give the dead—and the living—peace. We've gone over this. It's in progress, and we can't stop it."

"I still want to."

Dane buried his smile in his thick ceramic mug. She sounded more like a truculent child now. He could see her point, but his brother was right. The process had already started. By this time next week, the grave would be open.

She'd see then. Nothing bad would come of this.

Chapter 3

T HE HEAT HIT her first. Jade had forgotten how strong and heavy the air smelled. Being March, the humidity shouldn't be bad until they were almost finished with the job here. Jade stepped out of the airport in Port-au-Prince and walked the tarmac toward the waiting vehicles. Now she almost wished her brother was beside her, but she had arrived with the rest of the team. So Duncan and she had both decided it would be better if he came in a month or so.

She took a deep breath. Christ. She was really here.

The team consisted of seven members. A smallish-enough group to get to know but big enough to get the job done.

Besides Bruce, the leader, and Jade herself, there was Dr. Mike, a forensic anthropologist, but with more degrees than she had herself. Plus Meg Pearce, who had some social anthropology degree and a psychology degree, if Jade remembered correctly. Two other men—Stephen and Wilson—would double as computer nerds and would work at the grave site. A third female rounded out the group, Susan, but Jade had forgotten the details on her.

It wouldn't take long to get to know each other, Jade hoped. Meeting new people wasn't normally an issue for her, but this last year of hermit living hadn't been productive in that sense. She was nervous. And that was stupid. She was good at what she did. She wanted to help on this project. She could do this.

And she'd almost convinced herself.

Taking several deep breaths, she allowed herself to really look at the area. The last time she'd flown in with the army. She'd been whisked in and whisked out and had worked most of the time behind tight security. This time the team had taken a commercial flight. When they landed, no army, no police—no security of any kind—met them.

Intense blue skies smiled down on her. She almost believed everything would be all right.

Almost.

Her gaze wandered the surrounding areas, as her team made their way to the rental vehicles. Some things hadn't changed. Collapsed buildings still dotted the terrain; abandoned vehicles had been dragged off the main roads to clog fields and side roads. The biggest differences were the lack of bodies decorating the landscape and the roads were now passable.

It took a good ten minutes—with her gaze darting from side to side, searching for bodies and hoping not to find them—before Jade finally believed that death wouldn't plague her every step. She breathed a sigh of relief, feeling the almost unbearable tension draining from her system.

Haiti was obviously in recovery mode.

Thank God.

They planned to stay outside of the city center for the night to wait for gear, supplies, and mainly the paperwork. They would continue on to Jacmel in the morning.

"Come on, Jade. Stop gawking. We'll get time to sight-see later." Meg, one of the forensic anthropologists on the team, grinned at her. Tall, slim, and energetic, Meg's initial friendliness had enfolded Jade, easing the uncertainty of her decision.

Meg waved toward the three SUVs leased for the duration of the job. The team climbed into the vehicles and, within an hour, were booked in at a small and homey hotel. It appeared to have survived the earthquake unscathed. Complete streets were ripped apart in other parts of the city. Some portions were buried under collapsed buildings while others were perfect. So much of the city had been leveled. but there were pockets, like around the hotel, that appeared untouched.

The tent cities were new. The garbage lining the streets, the alleys, the sidewalks still remained the same. It was as if many people were stuck in a time warp, unable to move forward and to leave the disaster behind.

Mother Nature had a hit-and-miss hate thing going on.

After dinner, Meg and Jade stood outside the hotel and surveyed the streets for signs of progress. Stores were open, doing a brisk business. Port-au-Prince had been a thriving metropolis at one time. Jade didn't think recovery had restored that level of economic progress and stability. Poverty had always been a major part of life here. It looked to be the same. Not that she'd spent any time sightseeing on her last trip. There'd been nothing nice to see back then.

"Wow. Looks like the area still needs time to recover economically. Although I guess it's better than it was a year ago." Meg sat on the stone fence, her long jean-clad legs swinging loose. She ran a hand through her short brunette hair. She glanced over at Jade. "Are you ready for this?"

"Ready for what?" Jade asked absentmindedly, her focus on the surrounding scene, so similar and yet so different from before. She leaned against the stone fence and looked at her colleague.

"This life without electronics—although I did bring my phone. So, if you ever wanted to make a call, let me know."

"And I brought my laptop, so ditto," Jade added.

Meg nodded. "So, are you ready for the job we're here to do? It's not likely to be much fun." Meg pointed to the wreckage of cars heaped off to one side, surrounded by tall weeds. "I didn't expect to see this level of refuse strewn about. It's easy to be unaware of what's required in a country's recovery, unless you're actually on location."

"True enough. No, the job isn't likely to be much fun, but it'll be meaningful." Jade smiled, her heart lighter already. Her words had been instinctive, coming from her heart. The job had purpose, not as necessary for the masses as her previous one to Haiti, but still important. And not the same urgency or panic to this second visit. That helped to keep Jade calm and focused.

"Come on. We need to go to bed, if we want to get an early start."

They wandered into the hotel, saying good night to the other team members. At their rooms, Jade was pleasantly surprised to see she had a room to herself. Three women and four men were on the team. The others seemed normal and upbeat; Jade found herself relaxing and looking forward to her time here.

She said good night to Meg and opened her door. A maid in the hallway glanced at her shyly and handed over several towels.

Jade really was back in Haiti—where it all began.

MORNING DAWNED BRIGHT and sunny. Jade opened her

eyes, staring at the same ceiling she'd stared at for over half the night. A heavy knock sounded on her door, followed by a bright, cheerful Meg calling out, "Rise and shine. It's a whole new day. We're pulling out in an hour. Get moving, and you'll have time for a shower and food. Otherwise you'll have to choose."

Jade heard her new friend bouncing down the stairs. At least one of them was in a good mood. Still, Meg's excitement was infectious. Twenty minutes later, after a fast shower and dressing, Jade poured coffee for herself in the small dining room. The rest of the team was boisterous and chewing through their meals.

"Good morning, Jade. Did you sleep well? Lovely rooms, aren't they?" Dr. Mike Chandler smiled at her, as he served himself fluffy scrambled eggs. Thankfully he didn't appear to need an answer. "Take a seat. Take a seat."

She grabbed the empty chair next to him. He looked to be in his sixties, with white hair and an aura of ageless wisdom, as if he'd seen a lot of life, and yet still found something to smile about. He looked to be someone she'd enjoy getting to know.

The waitress came around bearing food, generously heaped on her plate. "French toast? I thought we'd be eating fried bananas—or is it plantains here?—and orange juice-soaked French bread?"

"You can have that another time, if you want. I ordered this for everyone. You won't get much work done on a fried banana or two."

"I've never tried them," Jade protested, reaching for her knife and fork.

"And you won't today either. Better eat. We're rolling in ten." He finished his meal and stood to leave. Several other members followed.

Alone with only Meg at the table, Jade said, "Wow, everyone is in such a good mood."

Meg grinned at her. "Now if only we could cheer you up."

Jade sat back and gave her a sheepish smile. "I'm feeling better. Don't worry."

"Feeling better, yes. Feeling good, no. We'll fix that." She motioned to Jade's empty plate. "If you're done, let's go."

Caught in the general mood of everyone else, Jade found her doubts and worries from the night before drifting away. She raced after Meg and the others.

DANE AND JOHN watched the vehicles park outside the picket fence. Dust billowed behind them. Three SUVs—heavily loaded from the look of them.

The doors opened, and several smiling people hopped out and approached the brothers.

An older man with a beard said, "Excuse me, we're looking for Peppe or Emile Jacinte."

John pursed his lips, studying the newcomers. "They are my father-in-law and brother-in-law. Are you the mortuary team?"

Several people gathered around the speaker. The older man winced. "Yes, that's one way of putting it. I'm Dr. Bruce McLeod, and this is my group of specialists." He motioned to the rest of the group.

"Right. Well, Peppe is, ... well, he's not quite the right person to talk to, and Emile is at work already."

Dr. McLeod frowned. "We were hoping to get specific

directions to the grave site, so as to evaluate the equipment we've brought with us."

A tall, lean, cheerful brunette in the group spoke first. "Could *you* show us the way to the site perhaps? We understand it borders this property."

Dane glanced over at John to see him glancing at the house. If Tasha found out John had helped them, well …

"I'll take them, John." Dane turned to the strangers, ignoring the look of relief on John's face. "I'm Dane Chester, and this is my brother, John. His wife is Peppe's daughter. The grave site borders the family property."

The group broke into smiles and introductions as he approached them. Better to go now before Tasha saw them, though she'd have to deal with this sometime. It might be easier on her if the team had already settled in, before Tasha was forced to face them.

"It's in this direction." As they turned in the right direction, he considered the problem of parking. "Let's walk from here, and you can assess a clearing down the road a bit for parking and unloading. There isn't a road, but the path is wide and well-traveled."

They fell into a group and walked beside him.

Dane added, "John's wife's family isn't used to this many foreigners at once. How many of you are there?"

The same tall brunette spoke. "Seven on the team."

The oldest-looking man of the group walked beside Dane. "Plus one or two from the company will probably go back and forth from the States to check on our progress."

"*Progress*. Right." His lips quirked. "You do realize that not everyone is happy about what you're doing?" He felt their surprise more than saw any signs of it.

The brunette spoke again. "We hoped that people would

understand."

Dane nodded. "Some will, though many more may be against having the grave opened—or *waking the dead,* as they'd call it."

"Are you Haitian?"

Dane spun around to gaze at the small blonde with a serious, almost haunted look on her face. His skin got plenty of sun with the work he did, yet he figured the locals deemed him a foreigner easy enough. He studied her for a moment, then answered, "No. I'm from Seattle, Washington. I own a construction company there, thankfully now manned by a very capable foreman." He shrugged self-consciously. "So, when I came to visit my brother and saw the destruction, I had to stay and help out."

Several people made comments in response. Dane ignored most, his gaze locked on the tiny blonde with such a serious look, who'd walked up beside him. Somehow he needed to see the reaction on her face. Her gaze stayed shuttered, but her lips quirked.

She murmured, "It's hard to *not* do something."

He was glad she understood. He wasn't sure of the undercurrents in her voice but felt like he'd said something right.

It took close to twenty minutes to get to the clearing. He pointed out the vast area to the others. "This is the best place for parking and unloading."

His gaze landed on the blonde again. She stilled at his words. Or was it from his gaze? Everyone else continued to talk around him. There were only seven of them, and he'd heard their initial introductions, but it was hard to keep them all straight. He didn't bother trying to remember names. Except for one.

Her name was Jade.

Several team members wandered the space, talking among themselves about logistics. He listened with half an ear. Jade stood quietly at his side.

He cast around, searching for something to say. "What brings you here?"

Her gaze, deep and dark, never shifted. She answered, "Sometimes you can't run away and hide. No matter how hard you try."

With that cryptic remark, she moved off to join the others, leaving him to stare after her, intrigued.

JADE STRUGGLED AGAINST the onslaught of emotions, while she stood and watched the team. She was really here.

Their guide had been a surprise. Tall and rangy, he reminded her of the lean cowboys she'd grown up with in Montana. Her family's move to Seattle hadn't erased the memories of weathered men, who loved the long hours they worked outdoors. Dane appeared to be—at least at first glance—of the same breed.

She wandered the clearing, listening, waiting for the next step. That had little to do with her.

"Anything to add, Jade?"

She glanced over at Meg. "Nothing until we actually see the grave site and understand what we're up against."

Dr. Mike agreed. "You're right. We need to consider the whole picture." He turned to Dane. "Can you show us, please?"

Moving off in that long-legged style, Dane led them to a well-worn path through the rocks and brush—one she hadn't noticed before. The group followed in single file. She fell into the last place.

Tall spindly trees grew on either side. The path was almost wide enough to drive on, and that was something to consider, although she was pretty sure the locals wouldn't appreciate that level of damage to their site. She didn't doubt they considered it their place.

She rounded the last corner and almost walked into Meg and Dr. Mike. She stepped around them, their silence seeping into her thoughts.

Oh, no.

She stilled and stared.

They'd been told that a cave-in had presented a natural depression and that the men had used the surrounding rocks and dirt to finish the job. The hilled area stretched for what appeared to be one hundred feet, crossing the path and ending at a large pile of rocks and stones at the base of a hillside. Strategically placed rock steps allowed friends and family easy access when they visited.

No one had said anything about the large cross or the many wreaths on display—or the wildflowers strewn across the area. Some of the flowers appeared to have been deliberately planted, and others appeared to be gifts from Mother Nature. Wild roses also grew rampant.

This wasn't a deserted mass burial ground. This was a well-tended and beloved grave site.

"This could be a problem," Jade noted.

The other team members murmured their agreement.

Dane asked, curiosity in his voice, "Why?"

Jade answered, "There's a difference between a mass burial ground and a beloved grave site. This place is beloved." She felt his hard gaze, wondered at it, then dismissed it as not her problem. She had her own issues to deal with.

"You didn't expect this?" Dane asked.

"No," Dr. Mike answered. "Not really. We've all seen large grave sites. Not all of them are a place of worship. Obviously people here, … at least one person, comes on a regular basis."

"Possibly. I've never seen anyone though. Not that I've been looking."

Several of the team members stared at each other and then at him. "Are there other ways in and out of here?"

Dane shrugged. "Presumably. There's a lot of country here. I don't know all the access points."

"Have you heard anyone say anything against us coming here? We've tried to be low-key about our work but …" Dr. Mike opened his arms expressively.

"Not everyone understands. My sister-in-law is one of those, but then she's pregnant, and everything appears to upset her lately."

Meg nodded in commiseration. "And she probably knows some of the people buried here."

"And, if she's Haitian," Dr. Mike said, in his professor voice, "her beliefs could be very strong about disturbing the dead."

Dane grimaced at both comments. "Both of those apply here. For myself, I understand. If my family were in here, I'd want to take them home too."

Bruce waved his clipboard to gain everyone's attention. "Right. Okay, everyone. I think we have a good idea of logistics. What we need to do is plan a workspace and see if we can get that much established." He turned to Dane. "Any idea who buried these people here? It would be helpful if we had some idea of how far down or in we need to go."

"If this is full, we may not have enough supplies." Bruce

jotted down a few notes. "We can get more, if necessary. I'm concerned about getting mobile labs. It would be less disturbing if we could work here on-site. Otherwise we should look at moving the bodies closer to town."

Dr. Mike wandered the area. He studied the size and scope of the grave. "We've got several sites in town scoped out, depending on our needs. And we may need to use all of them. Depends on the number of bodies. After all this time, the skeletons *should* be clean. But we won't know for sure until we open the grave."

Jade suggested, "I don't know how feasible this would be, but one or two reefer trucks could work well. We don't want to disturb the locals any more than we have to. The temperature can be adjusted as needed, and it's a lockable mobile storage solution. If the bones are clean—and we won't know until we start—then storage won't be a problem. The remains can be kept in boxes in the reefer."

Bruce considered the options. "Tony has ordered body bags over boxes, considering the unknown state of the bodies. The clearing is tight but not impossible. At least one truck could be backed in there."

Body bags were more expensive, but, as cost wasn't an issue, she'd be happy to have them. Honestly, Jade could work with either. "Our labs could be along the same lines. ATCO trailers come to mind."

"That's what they used in Katrina," Meg said, her hands on her hips, considering the issue.

Bruce glanced at the clipboard in his hands. "We do have the use of a lab trailer used by past medical teams."

Knowing she had little to do with their setup's where and how, Jade clambered over the rock pile to read the inscription on the huge cross. Her French sucked. Meg hopped up beside her and translated it. "*To those who have gone this road before*," she read aloud. "Weird."

"Different, certainly." Dane climbed the rocks to stand on a large boulder and to survey the rubble. "You'll need some heavy equipment," he noted.

"That could be fun. The town is strapped as it is." Jade wandered past several wreaths to another cross with the same inscription. Dane stayed where he was, but she felt his gaze on her back as she wandered.

"True, except equipment is available, if you know where to look."

She glanced at him. "Like from you? I believe you said you're in construction," she said politely. Jade turned around to see Stephen and Wilson, the lab techs who doubled as computer geeks and laborers, walking back toward the path.

Bruce joined them. "I think the question was lost earlier, so I'll ask again. Do you know who buried these people?" Bruce asked.

Dane fisted his hands on his hips. "Herman, a local, ran the front loader that made the trips here from the clearing, and my brother helped as well. Herman committed suicide a month later, and my brother's had a hard time ever since and refuses to talk about that time of his life. I'd like to avoid bringing him in on this, if possible. As I mentioned before, his wife is very against this project."

"Would you know how deep they buried them?"

Dane shook his head. "No. If I'd done it, I probably would have started at the path and worked in from the side. The original cave-in couldn't have been too deep or too big."

"That means there's probably no organization in the grave," Bruce muttered.

Jade hunched her shoulders. The bodies would have

been tossed and crisscrossed as they landed. They could be dealing with one to ten at a time. "If we work in from one spot, instead of trying to expose the top of the grave, we might have better control on how many are exposed at one time."

"Except they'll just keep coming, ... and we'd have no way to know whether we were gaining enough ground or if another year could be required. In fact, I think Tony—our boss back in Seattle—anticipated some sort of organization to the burials. Men to one side, children with mothers, ... that sort of thing."

Dane grimaced. "Not from the little bit of information I've managed to get out of my brother. It was tough. The bodies were collected throughout town by trucks, then brought here, loaded in the tractor bucket, and dumped."

Jade nodded. "That's fairly typical. The town was lucky to have those two men take on the job. It's a hard thing for anyone to do."

Bruce put away his clipboard. "Let's head back to town. I need to make some calls and to see what we can do to get this moving forward. Jade, what about you? Any thoughts?"

"I think, if possible, we need to leave the space as close to the same condition as we found it. It won't be possible to replicate placement of the rocks and the flowers that will be destroyed. If I photograph the area before we begin, we can replace any items when we're done."

"Once we get into this job, everything will look different. Pictures would be helpful," Meg piped up, studying the grave.

"They are necessary actually. We always document everything—before, during, and after." Bruce motioned to the grave. "I'd appreciate it if you'd do the photography, Jade, as it would save me a job. Try to be methodical and do several panoramic photos so we can lay the photos out and see everything displayed at once. We might use the digital ones for mapping a grid even."

That made sense. Jade unpacked her Canon SLR and set about checking the light. She'd been into photography for years. Her hobby might help her get through the coming days.

The two team leaders left in one SUV; the others stayed on-site.

Jade lost herself in her art. *Click.* Twisting and turning. *Click.* Turning slightly again. *Click.* She regulated her movements and took shot after shot, as she systematically covered the burial site. The cross. The wreaths. Another smaller wreath off to one side—older and mostly destroyed by the weather.

She went closer. *Click.* Walked close enough to lean over it and took a picture of the inscription, recognizing it as a repeat of what was on the others.

For all those who have gone before. Again. Now how weird was that? Maybe it was a common saying over here. It wasn't one she recognized, although it reminded her of an old *Star Trek* saying from TV. She grinned at her fanciful thought and continued to shoot the area.

"Are you done?"

Startled, she spun around and lost her footing. She ended on her backside, landing on a pile of small rocks. "Ouch."

"Sorry, I didn't mean to scare you." Dane stood above her, a large capable hand outstretched to help her to her feet. "Are you okay?"

"I'm fine." She scrambled up, ignoring his hand, and gave him a reassuring smile, as she stepped onto another rock, slightly farther back. "Rough ground, that's all."

"Plus, you were focused on your pictures. Did you find anything interesting?"

"Another cross, although it's older than that one." She pointed to the big one ahead. "Or made out of older wood?" she guessed.

"True enough. Supplies being as short as they were, I'm sure everything was commissioned into use."

She watched Dane bend down and read the inscription. "Interesting saying. I can ask Tasha, my sister-in-law, if she knows it. It might have special meaning to the region."

"Better ask someone else. She might get a tad upset, considering it's on this grave."

Dane winced. "Her brother works for me. I'll mention it to Emile."

Jade finished taking the pictures. She'd snapped her way through several hundred, without even thinking about it. Chances were, she'd only keep a couple dozen or crop out portions of some others. Thank heavens for the digital age.

Finished, she clambered down the rocks to where Dane and Meg were now talking. Jade swiped her cheeks and forehead on her sleeve. The heat would take some adjusting to. "I think that's got it."

"Good. Let's get to the hotel and check in. The others left already."

"Isn't it lunchtime soon?" Jade complained, her stomach rumbling on cue.

"Yes, and we'll need hours to set up and to consider how we want to establish a grid. We can check in, grab lunch, and come back later, if need be."

"Good. Hopefully they'll find a small loader. At least to take a layer off the top and to open one side. That's probably the best way to start, but—"

"That's in an ideal circumstance—which this isn't. A secondary grave is another option. I'll mention it to Dr. Mike and Bruce."

"It would be cheaper, if the numbers get out of hand."

Dane walked beside them to the SUV. "Tell Bruce, if he can't find a loader, I can rent him one of mine for a couple days—to get started."

Meg smiled. "Thank you. That's very helpful." She hopped in and closed the driver's door. Jade walked around, giving Dane a wide berth, and opened the passenger door. As she jumped in, she realized she'd lost her lens cap. She looked back frantically, as Meg started the SUV.

Dane held it out. "Here. You dropped this."

"Thanks." She closed her door and reached her hand through the window.

He dropped the cap into her palm. Their fingers brushed together ever-so-slightly. Energy sparked, like a static shock.

Startled, she pulled her fingers back and stared at him in surprise.

He grinned. "See you later."

Meg reversed the SUV and turned it around, then headed back into town.

Jade refused to look over her shoulder at him as they drove away.

But she wanted to.

Chapter 4

"**J**ADE? HEY, ARE you okay?" Meg poked Jade's jean-clad leg, as Meg drove the SUV away from Dane.

"I'm fine." Jade gave her a wan smile, hating the tiredness sliding through her body. She needed her strength back fully to deal with the job ahead. And she knew stress from the thought of coming back was the root cause. Food would help. And a good night's sleep. "I got a shock from his hand, when he gave me the cap."

Meg, her gaze back on the road, gave a half snort. "Not surprised. He couldn't take his eyes off you."

Jade snickered. "I doubt it. He was just being polite."

"*Uh-uh*. No way. That man is seriously hooked on you. His reaction was badass."

"Wow." Jade laughed, her spirits brightening. "I'd expect to hear something like that from a teenager. Sounds a little odd coming from you."

Meg relaxed slightly, the smile on her face natural and cheerful. "That's my inner child. Actually I can probably blame my nephews for corrupting me. They're all of thirteen and fifteen, and are they a handful."

Sinking deeper into the SUV cushions, Jade smirked. "Sounds about right. Kids are good for your soul."

"True enough. I'm just not ready to stop gallivanting around the world long enough to have any of my own. What about you?"

Jade's heart froze. A question she hadn't expected—but should have. Any one of the team might have asked this personal question, and Jade should have prepared an answer. Coughing slightly to cover her pause, she tried to joke about it. "No father to donate."

"I hear you. Who wants to be a single mother in today's world?" She tossed a wide grin at Jade. "I'm thinking Dane would be interested in that position."

Shaking her head, Jade let Meg ramble into a tale about her sister's first marriage that ended in divorce.

This area of Haiti was new to Jade, but it resembled every other part she'd visited. The same broken buildings dotted the landscape; the same weeds crept between fallen chunks of cement, and people navigated around as best they could. The same poverty coated the country, even here. So accustomed to the devastation, most people no longer noticed the state of their lives.

Sad but also reassuring. Life did carry on—in spite of everything. "People are resilient, aren't they?"

Meg glanced at her curiously. "That they are. Haiti is slowly recovering." She pointed to a group of laughing teens standing beside a broken wall. "Look at them. They're moving forward, finding a new normal in spite of what they've been through."

"*Hmm.* I found it hard enough to deal with life after being here last time. I came over on a mortuary team after the big quake. I thought long and hard before taking this job."

Meg smiled in understanding. "It would have been harder to adapt to the abrupt change from one situation to another. Staying here day in and day out, this would have quickly become 'normal.' For you, however, the contrast would have been unbearably hard to deal with."

"You have so got that right. What are you, a shrink?"

"Not really. However, understanding human psychology is paramount in my work." Silence filled the cab for several minutes, as Meg pulled the SUV into the hotel parking lot. "Coming here was probably one of the smarter things you've done, you know?"

Gathering her purse and camera, Jade paused to look at her. "How so?"

"Because you'll find closure this time." With that parting shot, she hopped out of the SUV and slammed the door.

Jade followed slowly. Closure would be good—on many fronts.

DANE STRUGGLED TO like his sister-in-law. He could give her some leeway because she was pregnant. A little more leeway for being upset over the current set of events with the grave, but how much leeway did she get before she came under the heading of disgruntled witch?

He was trying, honestly he was. He'd wanted to love her, to feel secure about John's future with her. Right now, every minute Dane spent with Tasha, she grated on his nerves something awful. He should move into town, give them more space. Living in the cabin at the back of the property and even having coffee with them was too close—for everyone.

Knowing Tasha and John wouldn't notice, Dane grabbed his coffee and slipped out to the patio to enjoy the cooler evening air. The sounds of their argument followed him.

"I don't care how logical it is. I don't want you to have anything to do with it. It's not safe. For you or for me."

"Tasha, I've gone over this several times. Nothing is dangerous in what they're doing. It's perfectly safe."

"Waking the dead is dangerous. This isn't just about you. You're putting me and the baby at risk—not to mention Peppe and Emile."

John, weary but so patient that Dane had to give him kudos for his superhuman effort, said, "I'm also not helping them. Dane will rent them a piece of equipment. That's all."

"And that's too much," she complained.

Dane turned and strolled down to his cabin. He'd heard enough. She could argue all she wanted, but he had no plans to rescind his offer to Bruce. Yet Dane understood the pain and the trauma on both sides. That wouldn't stop the job from happening, so he might as well help, so it could be completed faster. Then everyone would get what they wanted.

The deal would be done.

Besides, Dane wanted to get to know Jade better.

FOUR DAYS OF running around, trips back and forth, problems and tech trouble, and finally, it was the day.

Jade stood off to one side and watched as Dane navigated his smallest loader through the small spindly trees to the grave site. He'd wanted to be the one driving, in order to minimize the environmental damage. He had a good crew working for him. However, he insisted this location required his delicate touch.

It took two tries to navigate one corner to avoid cutting down a tree. Trees were no longer an abundant resource in

Haiti, and so every remaining one was precious.

Dane backed up and wiggled the large machine in degrees, and, as delicately as diapering a baby, he maneuvered it to the right angle and swung right, onto the straight path.

Nice.

Jade watched him carefully take the machine to where the rocks met the path before shutting it down.

"Are we ready?" he asked, without getting out. "Has everything been logged, photographed, and removed?"

Bruce walked over and hopped onto the machine to speak to Dane, their heads bent together, as they discussed the plan of attack. Jade knew it would take the bulk of the day to remove the top layer off this portion of the grave. At that point, Dane would open a ten-foot-wide working space from the path side, and they'd work left to right until they ran out of bodies. At which point they'd move into the hill to look for the rest of them.

She knew all that, but it didn't settle her nerves at this point. Four of the team were scheduled to have the day off, but no one had taken it. They'd all showed up for this symbolic beginning.

Dr. Mike climbed on top of the grave, as high as he could stand against the hillside and started work on the project with a prayer. Everyone bowed their heads. Jade found herself repeating his words quietly in her head. *Amen.*

Dane started the loader.

It took almost an hour for him just to get a few buckets off the top. Meg wandered over to where Jade stood. "I'll head into town for lunch. How about joining Susan and me for a girls' afternoon of sightseeing and shopping? Nothing we can do here. Not today and most likely not until late tomorrow—if then."

It was a good idea. A little light relief before the real work started tomorrow. "Now that sounds great."

With a wave of her hand to the men, Jade followed Meg and Susan. Jade could really use some lightweight work clothes. She'd forgotten how badly the heat affected her here. T-shirts and shorts were the uniform of choice; a half dozen of each would be perfect.

The women headed for the Iron Market and the few shops open along the way. The elegant mansions and townhomes spoke of days gone by. Once glorious in their regal bearing and bright colors, these buildings had taken a major knock from Mother Nature. Still, even with the damage from the earthquake, Jacmel was a tourist destination like no other. At least here, obvious revitalization attempts to get the city back on its feet were seen.

The afternoon zipped by at a rapid pace—full of shopping, laughter, and fun as the women ran from shop to shop and stall to stall, buying a few items to make their job a little brighter and more comfortable. Jade was delighted to find several brightly colored T-shirts and cotton pants in a beige-khaki color. They would withstand a lot of wear and tear. At one brightly festooned stall, she found several hair clips, big enough to hold her heavy blond hair off her neck.

If she'd had a little longer to prepare and to pack, she'd have gotten a haircut. As it was, the clips would do for now. She could always get it cut here, if she couldn't stand the heat. Meg's short brunette curls looked perfect. And Susan's fine black bob that stopped at her chin also looked comfortable.

"Now that has to feel better." Meg patted Jade's hair clip. "Nice. Now I almost wish I had long hair myself. Almost." She grinned and picked up several clips. "I bet my sister would love a couple."

"Later, when it's time to go home. Too much to pack this early."

"You're right." Meg put it back with a sigh. "Too bad though."

As they headed back to the SUV, Susan stopped at another brightly colored stall, one festooned with odd-looking handmade dolls. An old short and squat woman—wearing so many necklaces, they almost obliterated the sight of her red blouse underneath—worked at the booth. The woman's black gaze latched onto Jade and never let go.

Jade moved to the other side of Susan in an effort to get away from that piercing stare. And came too close to the weird-looking straw and cloth dolls. She noticed the papier-mâché looking ones painted in black with weird markings … and many other items she couldn't begin to recognize. "What are these things?"

"Vodou paraphernalia."

Jade shuddered and took several steps back. "Not for me, thanks."

Susan shook her head vigorously. "No. You don't get it. This stuff is for good luck. Used to ward off bad spirits."

With a second shudder, Jade moved several steps back, shaking her hands in front of her. "I still don't want one."

Susan grinned and plucked her choice off the top of the stall. "Well, I do. Just what we need for the grave work."

The transaction was done in silence. The old woman accepting the money never took her eyes off Jade. Unsettled, Jade did everything to avoid her. She wished Susan would hurry.

Finally they were done, and Jade turned to leave. The old woman moved off her stool so quickly that Jade never would have believed it possible, if she hadn't seen it herself. Before Jade could back away, the old woman grabbed her by the arm.

"Danger stalks you. You see it, but you don't understand it. Careful. Or you will join those who have gone before." She dropped Jade's arm and returned to her stool beside her cart.

Jade froze. So shocked and horrified by the crone's touch, Jade hardly understood what the old woman had said.

Meg grabbed her arm. "Come on," she hissed. "Forget about her. Let's get back to the SUV."

Susan snagged Jade's other arm, so the three walked back, linked together.

"That was too weird," Meg said. "I'm glad you got a doll, Susan. Good luck is just what we need."

JADE HAD HOPED the odd event would be over once they'd left the market, only Susan mentioned it at dinner that night.

"No way. She actually used *those* words?" Wilson stared at Jade curiously.

"Yeah," Meg confirmed, with a delicate shudder. "That so upped the freaky factor."

"This old lady never said a word to me the whole time I was buying that thing, and she never looked at anyone except Jade," Susan complained.

Dr. Mike studied Jade, his gray eyes serious. "She didn't bother you, did she? The Haitian culture is full of various superstitions. Their belief system is littered with them."

"It was kinda weird, although nothing I can't handle," Jade said casually, cutting a piece of fish, hoping her nonchalance satisfied their intense looks.

"We need to find out what that phrase means."

Marie, the hotel night manager, walked in to ensure everything was all right and to see if they needed anything. Bruce brought up the old woman at the market and her prophecies.

After quickly crossing herself, Marie stared at Jade. "Magrim. She is very well-known. She is very wise. Very accurate. Ms. Jade, you need to be careful." Crossing herself again, she almost ran out of the dining room.

Silence filled the room. Not a person clinked a fork or spoke. Everyone stared at Jade.

She was compelled to break the uneasy silence. "*Great*. I always wanted to be famous. Hadn't planned on it happening this way."

"Well, I don't believe in that stuff. The old woman was just trying to scare you into buying one of her dolls."

Jade brightened at Bruce's words. That actually sounded reasonable, as street sellers would do anything for a sale. Everyone resumed talking at once. Thankfully several different conversations took flight, and the awkward moment passed.

Dinner finished with coffee outside and an update on the day's progress at the burial site.

"So we should be ready to get started by about ten. We have one reefer trailer set up to receive bodies already. The lab trailer is to be delivered early in the morning. If the weather is cooperative, we might do some work outside. I presume you've determined a system of some sort for working through the numbers?"

"Somewhat," Meg answered. "Although that'll be a work in progress."

Susan asked, "What about DNA testing? I know we'd hoped to find a lab here—"

Bruce shook his head. "They can't handle it here. We'll ship the samples back to Seattle for testing."

Sinking farther into her chair, Susan winced. "I'd hoped we'd get results faster than that."

"We can only process the bodies as fast as we can. Then it's up to the lab. At least they'll go to a private lab."

"Does Haiti have a database of survivors' DNA? Some way we can test the dead against the living?"

Stepping in, Dr. Mike said, "No. They don't have that capability or the resources. Bruce asked the local authorities to put out the word that anyone interested in locating their loved ones needs to come and give samples at our local clinic we will set up soon. We'll have the samples shipped to Seattle, typed, and the results entered into our own database, hopefully to match with that of family members."

"If we rebury all of them before we have the results, they may have to be dug up again. That's not good."

Bruce nodded. "We'll give Jade's suggestion to give reefer trucks a try first. The decomp should have the bodies down to just bones and teeth by now, but it's never that clean."

"Even then, decomp inside the bones will continue beyond a visual examination. So we're better off with refrigeration capabilities." Jade smiled apologetically. "As a backup, an alternative burial site would be good."

She took a sip of water, thinking. "Because we're processing everyone in that grave, it'll take time. It would be much easier if we were just looking for say, ... an adult female and a female child. Then the others could be moved to one end of the grave as we sorted through them all. As we're processing everyone, well, it'll be more complicated."

His grin flashed.

Jade hadn't noticed how personable Bruce was. That head of red hair and beard surrounded a smile that offered quick praise. A nice man. She grinned back.

The discussion moved into logistics. As they returned to their rooms for the night, the old woman crowded her way back into Jade's mind. What had her words meant?

She walked over to her bags and pulled out her laptop. She turned it on and opened a Word document. She realized something was beyond prophetic about Magrim's words. Repeating them aloud, she typed. *"Danger stalks you. You sense it, but you don't understand it. Careful. Or you will join those who have gone before."*

Scary shit. She sat back and studied what she'd written. Just what did Magrim mean by them? No doubt in Jade's mind that the old woman thought she had seen a vision of some kind. Or she was a very good fake.

What danger stalked Jade? And was it a coincidence that Magrim had used some of the same words that were carved on the crosses at the mass grave?

Chapter 5

THE NEXT MORNING Jade immersed herself in work in the lab trailer. She set about organizing a viable production line plan. DNA samples needed to be taken, along with photos, and then identifying marks must be charted, plus measurements and dental impressions. She could hope the work on each case would take approximately two hours, though possibly twice that long would be required. Really no way to know until she started. They would also need help moving the bodies from the grave site to the lab trailer and to the reefer or from the reefer to the lab trailer, if the team became backlogged.

Had Bruce considered labor—as in hiring a couple young men to help with the physical moving of the body bags? She wasn't expecting them to be heavy, but they needed to be held together as much as possible. She'd have to remember to ask him.

They had ninety body bags stored under the trailer. It was anybody's guess whether that was enough or not. If the body count were higher, and the bones completely clean, then the surplus skeletons could be packed in boxes. She wasn't expecting them to be that clean though.

Finally, as organized as she could be, she stood in the lab trailer and surveyed her workspace. There wasn't much. No air-conditioning. No heat. No power. No running water—

that was an issue. Antiseptic smells permeated the space after her major scrubbing session. No microwave or coffeepot. Even she'd been perturbed by that. Everything else needed for a lab was here.

This was definitely a case of making do with what they had. What she needed now were bodies.

She walked to the front steps and stood outside. The forecast for heavy rain hadn't come through. Thank heavens. Things were rough enough now, but hurricanes, floods, or another earthquake would shut them down—not to mention what it would do to the Haitians who were barely surviving now.

"Jade, they're getting close," Meg called to her from the path.

"Coming." She locked the trailer—without knowing why—pocketed the keys and raced over. Two security guards were posted today, just in case the locals decided to lodge an on-site protest. So far only Dane was here, working the tractor.

Good. She wandered in closer. Dane had sliced the top off the burial mound and had taken a good ten-foot-wide chunk out at the path. He'd also gone in a solid six feet.

He waved, nimbly backed out the machine to one side, and shut it off. Opening the door, he hopped down.

Bruce walked over to Dane, and Dr. Mike joined them.

Meg nudged Jade, and the two women headed over to see what the discussion was.

Several men, locals from the look of them, came out of the woods with shovels in their hands.

"What's up?" Jade asked.

"Dane says it's time for shovels." Dr. Mike walked around the backhoe and returned with two shovels in each hand.

Jade grinned and put her hands behind her back. "Never did find a shovel to fit my hand," she explained.

"Well, you could always try one of these. … However, I'm sorry to say, I don't have enough to go around." He laughed and handed out shovels to Bruce, Stephen, and Wilson. Dr. Mike kept one for himself. "The hired help are only here for today to help us cut down the top. Then we're on our own."

Jade walked over to the newly dug space. Uneasiness rested heavily on her shoulders. Her gaze landed on the cross laid carefully off to one side, until they were done. Magrim's warning came to mind. Jade shivered, her apprehension growing about this massive grave that she hadn't felt before.

She'd worked for morgues and labs for years. She'd seen plenty of Death's work. Too much.

On every project an initial sense of awe, a respect for the dead, was recognized at the moment just before starting work. This respect was healthy and comforting.

Today was different. When Jade thought about the task at hand, instead of awe, her feelings resembled dread. She didn't know why. She only had the old witch woman's words to blame.

"Ready?" Dr. Mike stood beside her, surveying the rocks. The odor creeping out of the ground told them what they would confirm within minutes.

"Sure. Why not." She stepped off to one side and took a closer look at the pile in front. She frowned.

Red. Just a small amount tucked between rocks on the left.

"What's that?" She stepped forward and bent down.

"Here, let us in. We've got the tools." With gloves on,

two men stepped forward to move boulders, while two others used shovels to move the smaller stuff out of the way.

It took a good ten minutes to open the space.

They'd found their first set of remains.

Everyone stopped, and heads bowed for a moment of silence. Then, in unspoken accord, those in the business of identifying the dead began their work.

The portable stretcher stood nearby, with an unzipped body bag on top. The red was a T-shirt, holding a set of ribs more or less in place. The rocks were removed completely, before the body was shifted. Even then the hips and leg bones separated inside the crumbling shorts. The skull—tufts of black hair plastered into the dirt—sat nearby. For the most part, Mother Nature had done a decent job. Most of the bones were bare. A few ligaments and tendons vainly tried to connect the bones, and the odd clump of tissue was exposed.

"Glad to see the condition this one is in. Won't help with identification, however."

"Yeah, I didn't expect much would be left by now in this climate." Bruce slipped a hard plastic sheet under a foot in a fairly successful attempt to keep its bones together. He moved it carefully to the body bag and came back for the second one. "The first one is always the worst."

"*Hmm.*" Jade couldn't agree more and was relieved to know the general condition of the bodies they'd be working with. Much easier to detach emotionally and to get on with the scientific duties when decomp was this far along.

"There, I think that is it."

Bruce already had a second body bag out for the next that lay directly under the first. And it went that way for hours. Body upon body upon body. Even standing at the open slash in the earth, Jade could see no less than seven skeletons exposed, or partially exposed, in the open air.

Nothing to do but continue to dig in.

She came to a stop several hours later, when a bottle of water was shoved in her face.

Jade straightened, groaning at her screaming muscles. "Oh, thank you."

"We have to drink lots of liquids. We're not used to the climate here." Meg was sweating profusely, as she took a long drink of bottled water.

Jade sat down on a large rock to unscrew the sealed top and tried to settle her queasy stomach. She drank half the bottle in her first drink. Wiping her mouth, she grinned at the look on Meg's face. "I just streaked dirt-turned-mud across my face, didn't I?"

"Absolutely." Meg's face shone through a layer of dust. "You look like the rest of us."

"And we all look like we've been playing in the sand-box."

"At least we've gotten a good start this morning." Meg sat down beside her. "Bruce has gone to town to pick up lunches for all of us. He's planning for the hotel to provide bagged lunches, if possible, starting tomorrow."

Jade shrugged. "As long as there's lots of it, I don't care where it comes from."

"You do like your groceries, don't you?" Meg shook her head and laughed.

"Yep." Speaking of which, she reached into her pocket and pulled out a badly melted chocolate bar. She ripped it open and took a decent-sized bite, licking the melted chocolate off her fingers. Meg just stared. Jade offered the bar to her.

"No, I'm good. Besides, lunch is on its way."

"Just not fast enough." Jade alternated chocolate with her water, and, by the time she had reached the end of both, her stomach felt better. She'd been fine for the first hour; then the smells had hit. The queasiness grew after that. Add in the heat … and she had a problem. Meg's water break had been timed perfectly.

"Ready to do a bit more?"

Jade tilted the bottle for the last few drops and stood. "Yes. Let's get this last one over to the trailer. Enough people are here that we could start in the lab this afternoon."

They walked over to the men, where Dr. Mike zipped a body bag closed as they arrived. "Hello, ladies. This is a small one. Can you move it?"

"Absolutely. When you say small, are you saying a child?" Jade refused to look down on the bag, her gaze locked on Dr. Mike's dirt-smeared face. He looked ready for a break too.

"Yes. The third one so far. All three females."

Jade pursed her lips. What ages were they looking for again? Tony had mentioned something about it back in Seattle, but she hadn't been the most clear-headed then. "And we're looking for a six-year-old female, correct?"

Dr. Mike nodded. "Yes. And the mother was twenty-eight and the father, thirty."

Jade tucked away that information for later. She bent down and lifted one end of the stretcher. Meg grabbed the other end, and they headed to the reefer, as the call came that lunch had arrived.

JADE WIPED THE sweat from her forehead. The sheer

physicality of the job wore her down. After lunch, she'd returned to the burial site to help with the excavation. Many bodies were falling apart, as the team sifted through the pile, and the most important thing was to move the exposed ones.

Another three must be moved before they could close off the area again. In theory, the best approach would be to finish the bodies they already had in the trailer, before digging up more.

"Another hour with any luck." Bruce grinned at the look on her face. "I'm hoping we don't find more spare parts at the bottom."

Jade shook her head. "I know. That last couple appeared to be a lot of puzzle pieces and not a whole lot of cohesion. It won't be easy to find and match all the corresponding parts."

"We can only do the best we can." Bruce carefully laid out another body bag and started to place the uppermost skeleton inside the bag. "At least this one appears complete. I think the last one is still missing the right hand."

"We'll find it."

They worked companionably for the next hour. Finally they opened what should be the last body bag of the day. At least she hoped it would be. She was more than ready for a hot shower and something to breathe other than the smell of death. Her back ached from the constant bending. The end of this workday couldn't come fast enough.

Digging deeper into her reserves, she helped Bruce pack the last exposed set of bones. The two of them carefully lifted the rib cage and carried it to the waiting body bag. Straightening, she couldn't hold back a slight moan.

"Long day, huh?"

She offered him a tired smile. "Yes, but productive." Turning back to the grave, she lifted the left leg, and it separated from the knee in her hand. "Damn."

"It's been happening all day. Most of these at the bottom don't even have connective tissue."

"I shouldn't have picked it up that way. Just tired at this point." She wiped her forehead on her sleeve, grateful for the easing of the afternoon heat. A breeze had wafted through the valley earlier, but that had long disappeared.

"To be expected. I'll get the rest of this." Bruce motioned to the big rocks. "Sit and take a break."

Jade dropped her head back and stared at the blue sky. It had to be close to six o'clock. She closed her eyes for a long moment and took several deep breaths, hoping for a second wind.

Opening them again, she watched as Bruce carefully retrieved each tarsal and metatarsal lying loose on the ground. *Almost there.*

God, she couldn't wait to leave the site. She stared down the path toward the trailers. Another fifteen, maybe twenty minutes, and they would be on their way.

"There, that should do it."

She gently laid the tiny bones in the body bag and zipped it closed.

"Come look at this." Bruce frowned at her. "I know you're tired. Lord knows, so am I. Only … I'm not sure this is the last one." Bruce bent over the grave site, slightly to the left of where they'd plucked the last skeleton.

"Another one?" She knew it made sense for another one to be exposed, considering how many could be in here, and she knew they couldn't leave it that way.

"I think so. Only it's a layer down."

An odd silence filled the air. She studied the frozen look on his face. "Bruce? What's the matter?"

"We'll see in a minute." He stood and took a smooth stride—one she resented after the way her body was reacting—and snatched up a shovel. He gently dug into the ground near the foot. He didn't attempt to remove any dirt; instead he wobbled the tool back and forth several times and gently lifted dirt from around the foot.

The small rocks and gravel on top fell away. The bone shifted slightly to one side in the rotted too-large sandal. She leaned closer to get a better look and realized she was blocking the light. She climbed around to the other side, taking a wide path to avoid disturbing the shifting ground. "Would they have put a layer of dirt in *after* they'd put in so many bodies?"

Bruce didn't look up. "I don't know. The dirt could just as easily have fallen in on top from the sides, as the loader moved back and forth with each trip." Bruce put the shovel in a new spot and wiggled the dirt again. "There. Do you see what I see?"

Jade bent down and brushed the dirt away from the skeleton with her gloved hand—her fourth or fifth pair of gloves today.

Bruce knelt across from her and carefully removed the dirt from his side of the foot.

She did the same on her side. She gasped, leaning closer. "What," she whispered, "is that?"

"I'll remove a bit more, and then we'll see for sure."

She waited and watched. Her stomach churned. She worried her bottom lip, hating the silence that had fallen. The breeze had whistled over and around the hill for most of the day. And when the wind had calmed, birds or small animals rustled in the undergrowth. She stood to stretch out the kinks and glanced around. The place was deserted.

Silence had fallen on the valley, a silence that only highlighted the sound of gentle scrapes of spade on rock.

The shadows lengthened around them. Jade swallowed hard, grateful she was here with Bruce and not Meg. Something about a strong male presence made her feel better. Not that she was a wimp. However, right now, tired and worn out, she felt that way. "And?"

"Almost." He eased away some more dirt and shifted around slightly to attack the mound from the other side.

She stepped out of his way. "Where did everyone else go?"

A laugh escaped him; he stared at her, his big grin splitting his dusty face.

She couldn't believe he hadn't shaved off his thick red beard. That had to be hot as hell.

"They've probably gone back to the hotel to grab all the hot water before us."

She groaned comically, happy to have an excuse to ease the tension twisting inside. "They would too, wouldn't they?"

"Hell yeah." His boisterous laugh rolled across the rocks. "Hold on. Almost done. ... And I'm sure the hotel is equipped with enough hot water for us."

"I'm not so sure. If you're wrong, you're sacrificing your shower for me."

He grinned. "Like hell—" His voice cut off in shock.

She heard a weird jangle and dropped to one knee beside him to peer at the mix of bone, cloth, and ... Her breath caught. Her mind rebelled. She whispered—barely loud enough to be heard—"*Dear God.* What is that?"

"Look for yourself." He pointed where the tibia widened at the end. A few ligaments still connected to the foot were now slightly askew inside the shoe. Bits of cloth clung to the ankle and footwear.

Oh God. Her stomach heaved uncontrollably. Jade lurched off to one side, where her lunch made a hasty exit. After a long moment, when she was sure no more was to come, she spun around to face Bruce.

He waited for her, a worried look on his face. "Are you okay?"

She glanced back at the leg bone. She didn't know how to answer.

A chain lay twisted around the lower leg of the female skeleton.

Securely attached at the ankle was a rusted iron … manacle.

Chapter 6

THE DINNER CONVERSATION rippled on around Jade, as if she were a mere rock in a swiftly flowing river. That suited her. Mental exhaustion and stress had added to her physical deterioration during the day. Numbness had settled in.

"Hey, Jade, tough day? You look like you're ready for bed."

With a wan smile in Susan's direction, Jade couldn't help but agree. "That's where I'm going after this."

Dr. Mike studied her face in concern. "Don't overdo it out there. You're more valuable in the lab than doing grunt work."

Keeping an eye on the staff was part of his job, so Jade didn't take his comments too close to heart. He was a compassionate man, all too willing to help out himself, if need be. "I hear you. We've reached the point where I'll be in the lab from now on."

"See that you are."

Meg gave her a curious smile. Jade didn't know whether she should mention what she and Bruce had found or not. She shot a questioning look at Bruce.

He shrugged, then began to explain. "Part of the reason for her fatigue is the emotional stress caused by the last victim we found—after everyone else had left."

Bruce directed his comments to Dr. Mike. "We left the last set of bones we found, in the ground, covered with dirt and rock. We needed to consider the situation before proceeding. I believe this is an adult female. The shoe is still there on the foot. We don't know about other clothing. We only uncovered a foot and ankle." He put down his fork and took a long drink of water.

Watching him closely, Jade empathized when he swallowed heavily.

At the site, the horror and implications of what they'd discovered had quickly overtaken them both. They'd covered what they'd found and had then left—silently. They'd not spoken of it on their way back and had separated at the hotel entrance to get showered and ready for dinner.

Jade glanced around, noticed that the room reserved for their meals had a door that could be closed. Hopping up, she walked over. She realized no one was close enough to hear them, yet felt compelled to shut it anyway.

Bruce waited until she'd retaken her seat. He gave her a nod of thanks and elaborated. "This discussion stays with us. It's possible we'll have to bring the authorities into the mix, but they may also not have the manpower nor the interest in pursuing our findings."

"Like what?" Susan leaned forward. "Tell us. The suspense is killing me."

"The woman we found had a manacle and chain attached to her ankle."

Jade had to clarify. "She'd most likely been a prisoner at the time of her death."

"What?"

"Good Lord."

Everyone sat back and stared, their gazes going from

Jade to Bruce. Both nodded.

"Now you understand the problem. We need to figure out our next step," Bruce said, before taking another drink.

"Are we thinking she was murdered?" Meg's gaze stared at Bruce.

Bruce shook his head. "We can't say that—at least at this point. And, although Dr. Mike is qualified to make that determination back home, we have no authority here."

"Besides, she could have been killed by the earthquake or an infection, like any of the others. She might have been a prisoner. That doesn't mean the person responsible …" Jade added an afterthought, "… killed her. She could have been chained in a basement or shed and died in the earthquake—the same as everyone else buried here."

"Is it really possible that no one noticed the chain when she was thrown in?"

"Definitely—and there could be several legitimate reasons for that, including the time of day she was placed in the grave, where she was found, and even who found her. She might have been wrapped tight, concealing the chain." Bruce lifted his coffee cup and took a long sip. "Or no one cared. Think about it. If you have a woman chained somewhere, and she dies in a natural disaster, what will you do? You still have to dispose of the body. You still have to do it quickly, and, for all we know, this person lost other people too—ones he cared about. There was essentially no law at the time, no one to care what you did."

"God what a horrible thought." Meg shuddered. "Remember that serial killer, John Gacy? Didn't he bury a mess of boys in his basement and around the yard? What if this guy was a serial killer? What if her 'owner' was killed in the earthquake too? Anyone finding her wouldn't have understood or known what to do. They'd have been all too happy to dispose of her body, where no one would ask questions," she added, with relish.

Jade winced. "What better place than a mass grave where everyone is more concerned about expediting the burial of the rotting bodies and where no one is checking to see what killed them?"

Dr. Mike held up a hand. "Whoa. That's letting your imagination go way too far. All we know is that this woman was buried with a chain around her ankle. Now Haiti has some pretty disturbing rituals and beliefs when compared to Western ways, and we can't just jump in here and assume foul play. Maybe by burying her with a chain, someone was hoping to keep her soul chained here."

"Not that that is a great improvement, but I take your meaning. We can't assume anything at this time." After that, Jade stayed quiet and listened as the conversation rose and fell. The various hypotheses and suggestions kept them all busy.

They might not have the facts; still, Jade didn't need anyone telling her that this was bad news. She already knew it was.

Whoever that woman was, she hadn't had an easy ending to her difficult life.

SEVERAL DAYS LATER Dane drove up to the lab trailers and parked. He waved at Bruce, who stood outside the reefer truck, then walked over to see him.

"Hey, Dane. Good to see you. I wanted to thank you. Using your heavy equipment definitely lightened our load and improved the process."

Dane smiled at Bruce—an amiable caring person doing a very difficult job. So far, Bruce had done well keeping the lid on this project. Dane had heard only minimal grumbling about this place among his workers. Dane had stopped by to see how the team was progressing. And maybe check on Jade.

He asked, "How are you guys getting along with the language?" His own French was only passable and his Creole—a gibberish mixture of Spanish, French, Portuguese, and English—was just about as bad. If it weren't for his English-speaking foreman, he'd be hiring translators. Thankfully enough English was spoken here that Dane could get by.

Bruce grinned. "I'm amazed at how easy it is to understand the locals with a little bit of this and a little bit of that. I would have said I was only fluent in English, except I did take French and Spanish in high school. Who'd have thought I'd remember any of it?"

"Wish mine were better. Any trouble with the locals over the grave?"

"Everything is quiet—just the way we like it. We're hoping our free medical clinic in town will appease some of their worries. Plus we are willing to help out the locals with identification and burial of these people in any way we can. The DNA testing will take some time though, especially without DNA donors from surviving family members." Bruce shrugged. "Since when did anything like this go quickly?"

"I can't imagine the cost myself."

"No, but, if I had the money, and one of my family were buried there, I'd understand spending it this way. I lost my sister to leukemia years ago, and it gave my mother unending comfort to go to her grave to visit with her. She still makes the weekly trip, even though we lost my sister a dozen years ago."

Dane walked over and sat down on the boulder beside Bruce. "Understandable."

"Absolutely. We've pulled out over fifteen so far and are processing as fast as we can. Hopefully families will step forward and help us identify these people and give us direction for reburial. Otherwise, the remains will be reburied here." Bruce waved his hand toward the grave. "Maybe they'll erect a more formal monument, although I don't know. ... The people here live simply and don't need the same trappings that Americans tend to feel are necessary."

Dane studied the view in front of him. Peppe, Tasha's father, lived in the original Jacinte homestead just on the other side of the large clump of trees on the left. Dane couldn't help but wonder what the old guy thought about Bruce and his team's quest or if Peppe even understood what was happening.

Dane nodded. "Haitians have strong beliefs, though life here is basic. More about survival than anything else. I'm a little more sensitive to this issue as my sister-in-law is beyond distressed about this whole thing. Because she's pregnant, no one wants to upset her."

Both men shared a commiserating glance.

"Yeah, don't have any kids myself," Bruce replied. "However, some women go through pregnancy just fine, and then a few seem to change personalities over the nine months. Easy to see something like this tipping the balance."

"Right now," Dane explained, "my concern is more for my brother's sake than hers. Maybe that's not fair, and I'm sorry if that comes across as harsh. Tasha's personality shift in the last week or two makes it hard to be sympathetic." Dane grimaced. Talk about an understatement. "That sounds cold, and I don't mean it to be. My brother, John, he's being incredibly patient. Still, I don't know how long he can handle the tension. I would have said something way before this. Guess that's why I'm not married."

Bruce chuckled. "Yeah, me too."

Not knowing how to broach the subject, but really wanting to know the answer to the question that plagued him, Dane asked, "So … are other members of the team married? Can't be too easy to do this job and to leave a family behind." He bent his head to study his shoes. And waited.

"No one is married, though having a committed relationship is a big help for individual members when it comes to dealing with this type of work. I believe the easiest way to deal with death on a regular basis is to have a way to affirm life."

Bruce studied Dane's face, his grin widening. "Just for your information, all three women are single, and, although Meg, the tall brunette, appears to have a long-term relationship, she jumped at the chance to come here."

Dane smiled slightly.

Bruce continued, his voice light and tinged with humor. "Now Jade, the short blonde, appears to have a solemn attitude toward life, and I don't believe she is in a long-term relationship. … And then there is Susan—our bubbly black-haired technician. She's also single."

Dane almost winced. Damn, Bruce appeared to be really enjoying this. "Well-put about Jade. Life appears to be a serious business to her."

"Yes, she's quiet, yet focused and dedicated, and I love workers like that. She's determined to do right by everyone in that grave and to find each of them their home."

"*Hmm.*"

"She could do with a bit of cheering too. So if you want to stop by her trailer and say 'hi,' feel free. Isolation isn't good for her. She tends to be a loner most of the time anyway. Hard to break her out of her shell."

Trying for a noncommittal shrug of his shoulders, and knowing he'd failed, Dane gave it up. Pretense wasn't his style anyway. Besides, he really wanted to get to know Jade better. He stood. "Good. I'll stop by there after I'm loaded."

Dane walked away, aware Bruce watched him. Bruce was just looking out for his team. Was protective of them. That was fine. Dane could handle a little scrutiny. He had nothing to hide.

THE SOUND OF heavy machinery broke her concentration. Jade lifted her head from her workbench and frowned. Was Dane here?

She paused to straighten, wincing as her back crackled and popped. She needed to change the height of her worktable, or she'd resemble a hunchback by the end of this job.

At the open door, she watched Dane maneuver the big machine onto a trailer he kept parked here. He made it look easy, as he handled the equipment. As he hopped out, she gave him a small wave.

"Hey," he said in greeting. "Didn't expect to see you here." He walked toward her, that long loose-limbed stride eating the distance in seconds.

She watched appreciatively. "This is where you'll find me most of the time. The others will come and go from the hotel and the site. I'm likely to be a permanent fixture here."

"How are you making out?" He peered around the corner of the door. "Dark in here."

She stepped out of the way, so he could get a better view. "I have lights, only they're not very bright."

He shook his head. "You'll go blind in here over the long term."

A small laugh escaped. "Good thing three months isn't that long. I was actually hoping to move some of my work outside if I could, only that's not practical. There's no standing room, let alone a large enough deck or tables out here."

He backed up several feet, then walked around outside, looking at the simple plywood steps leading to the doorway. "*Hmm.*"

Jade walked down the steps and joined him, facing the trailer, trying to see what he saw. "*Hmm?* What does that mean?"

"I have a small portable porch with steps that attaches to my work trailers—for when we're on-site. It's not pretty, and it's really only meant to provide a bit of extra space, but it's handy. I could exchange your steps for that set." He walked closer, then glanced at her. "With a sheet of plywood on top of the railing you'd have a workspace. Not pretty but …"

Waving her arms around the area, she pointed out, "Do you see anything pretty here? The conditions are rough, but our equipment is top-notch."

His face lit with understanding. "That's all that counts. The job isn't nice to begin with, so get in, get it done, and then get out, right?"

She smiled. "Right."

His gaze stayed on her face longer than necessary.

She flushed at the naked appreciation revealed in his

gaze. It had been a long time since she'd seen that kind of look in a man's eyes. She kinda liked it. Actually, she liked it a lot. A shy smile slipped out.

His gaze deepened, warmed. After a long moment, he cleared his throat. "You should get out for a walk every day too. Being inside with poor light like that, well ..." He frowned at the dim light showing from the doorway of the trailer.

"Thanks, *Dad*."

Her teasing tone wiped the frown off his face. He laughed. "Ouch. I guess I deserved that, didn't I?"

"Maybe." She enjoyed the bantering. "Well, maybe not. You are closer to my brother in age."

"Well, thanks for small blessings." He studied her face. "I tell you what. I'll forgive you if you let me buy you a coffee."

She felt her face warm. Inside she was delighted at both the invitation and the idea of a fresh brewed java. "Coffee? Is there a place to get a decent cup?" Maybe staying here for three months wouldn't be such a hardship after all. Her smile brightened.

"Ah, there is, if you know where to find it. It would be my pleasure to introduce you to the pleasures of Jacmel."

She laughed. "I can't wait."

Chapter 7

JADE WATCHED AS the truck and trailer, loaded with his machinery, pulled slowly out of the clearing. With the lab trailers parked as close against the rocks as possible, she figured Dane had almost enough room to make the turn in one go. Again his smooth exit showed his exceptional handling skills.

She hated to see him leave. At the same time, he confused her, stirred feelings she hadn't expected to feel, … at least not here. Not now. The competent air he projected was seductive. That wasn't unusual; power in all forms attracted her.

A year ago she'd lost her own power. She was determined to make this trip work. To regain her power. To regain herself. To regain her soul.

Dane seemed understated, simple, exuded quiet control—a man to have in a tight corner. A man who wouldn't walk out and leave someone hurting.

The opposite of her fiancé.

Ex-fiancé. She doubted Dane would have trouble making simple decisions in life. Like what to have on a pizza or where to go for a special meal. Her ex would whine for hours when she brought him in on the little decisions. However, when she dared to have an opinion on more important things, like the type of vehicle she'd like to buy—watch out.

He'd thrown a hissy fit over that and had stomped her choice into the ground. She'd shelved her decision on vehicles. Good thing, ... considering.

She knew her brother hadn't been impressed with her choice of a partner, and thankfully Duncan hadn't dared to comment when that same partner bolted.

Her mental state wouldn't have withstood the criticism from outside herself.

How had so much changed in a week? She now sat out in the countryside of Haiti—a place she'd sworn she'd never return to—was active in a job she also thought she'd never have accepted, and had actually studied the muscular butt of one of the most attractive men she'd come across in weeks, make that months. On top of all that, she realized she hadn't cried since leaving home.

It was hard to admit, but she'd been so ensconced in her private prison, she hadn't realized that her prison had been a safety net to stop her from stepping back into the real world. She had needed that time ... in the beginning. But she'd been more than capable of moving on months ago. Instead she'd chosen to stay a prisoner in her own shell, rather than face the real world. How long would she have stayed there, if not for Duncan and this job?

She returned inside to continue her work with the adult male currently on her table. Meg had taken DNA samples earlier, while Jade did dental impressions. The body had been checked and charted, photos taken. This skeleton was complete. The victim had been wearing socks, heavy in nylon, encased in runners of some synthetic material that had helped hold the feet together. This male was young, maybe nineteen or twenty. He'd suffered a break to his right arm a long time ago.

Jade recorded everything she could see to identify him. A few personal effects found near the remains would go down on his chart but would also be entered into a main database in case they weren't his. The skeletons were so fragile that rings fell off fingers and the contents of any pockets could have fallen through to the body below, as the material holding them decomposed.

He'd had no wallet, watch, keys, or cell phone. Then again, most bodies had been stripped of anything useful. She'd seen that on her first visit. Pillaging had been rampant.

Straightening, she reached for her checklist and marked off the last few items. Everything would help family members, when trying to recall identifying marks and characteristics of loved ones.

As she slowly packed the remains back into the black body bag, she carefully checked the bones for other breaks or marks she might have missed the first time and added those to the chart. Once everything was back in the bag lying on the cart, she rolled it over to the door for safekeeping, until someone else came to help move it to the reefer.

In this way, she could operate on her own for a long time.

She had a second bag ready and waiting on the other side of her table. After opening the bag wide, she pulled the ends of it down over the stretcher's sides and started laying out the bones of a small girl on her table. She grabbed a new numbered checklist and wrote that same number in white permanent marker at the top of the body bag.

And started anew.

It wasn't just a slow job. She would also call it a careful one, particularly when she could be looking at one of the three people destined to return to Seattle. A child's skeleton lay in front of her, the bones clean and bare.

She quickly determined the child was female, and the skeleton was relatively complete. She'd been wearing a sundress in a red to orange color. Jade grabbed a magnifying glass and used it to identify stars on the material. She made a notation of it, added a quick sketch to her page, before beginning the slow job of cataloging the details of the child. Her left leg was broken, most likely as a result of the earthquake, and her skull showed a small fracture on the left side.

Jade spent the next hour learning every detail she could from the small skeleton. She found a piece of plastic between the largest toes on the right foot and not on the other. Her best deduction, based on the bright blue color of the plastic, was that the child had been wearing flip-flops at the time of her death. Testing for these details wasn't an issue on this job. No money. No time. No need.

Footsteps approaching the open door were followed by Meg's cheerful voice. "Hey, how's the work going?"

Jade smiled at her. "It's moving. Not too quickly. I'm trying to be really thorough, so I won't have to do this twice."

"I hear you there. The smell isn't too bad in here." Meg dropped her purse over by Jade's on the corner of the counter. Her light sweater was dumped on top. "Have you done the dental impression?"

"Nope." Jade looked down at the body on her table. "That's next."

Scooping up gloves on her way, Meg walked toward her, her work boots clumping on the thin floor. "Right. Then I'll work on the DNA, while you do that. Is the rest done on this one?"

"No." Jade reached for the silicone, then walked over and made the dental impression. "I'm not sure why we're doing dental. How many of the kids here would have been to dentists?"

"Lots of them. Especially our girl. She had X-rays done when she visited her grandpa last time. They'll be used to confirm identity."

"Makes sense." The two women worked together silently, until each finished the job at hand.

Jade grabbed her checklist for the little girl and marked off the completed steps. "Okay, she's done too." Writing out a toe tag, she attached it with an elastic band around the bottom of the small tibia and zipped the bag closed. She'd deliberately placed the bones at the top end of the bag and rolled the excess plastic up at the bottom.

Working with bags was different than with boxes. When she could, she laid out the remains properly and folded under the spare plastic. It felt better to her. More respectful. Plus this allowed for immediate visual confirmation of a child.

Not everyone's system ... but this worked for her.

Grabbing the cart, Jade pushed the stretcher toward the door. Meg walked behind her. "Let's move her first."

Lifting gently, they transferred the two sets of processed remains to the reefer truck. Inside the truck, they shifted the little girl first. Jade had added a simple system to let them know, without opening bags or searching for charts, that this was a female child. They would try to keep females on one side and males on the other, with children separated off as much as they could—given they didn't know how the population would break down into each demographic until they were done. Lifting the second body bag, they placed it on the male side of the refrigerator truck.

Like everything here, their system had to be flexible. The conditions were rough, and they didn't have the amenities they'd like to have. As Jade checked her marking system to ensure it conformed, she asked Meg, "How are the men doing?"

"Dr. Mike is ranting that he needs to get into the labs, but he's been busy securing more equipment for us. Bruce and Susan have been in town all day at the clinic, and Stephen and Wilson were at the site, shoveling to remove more of the top layer."

"Good. Stephen's doing the database too, isn't he?"

Meg nodded.

Jade was quite good with databases. In fact, she half expected those skills to be called into service soon.

Meg frowned, brushing a hand through her curls. She rearranged the body bags, until she was happy with them. "Are you ready? We can take one back now, if you want."

Jade looked at her watch. "When, what, and how are we getting lunch today?"

"I think bagged lunches were supposed to be here. If not, I can bring something back for you. I have to run the morning's samples to the refrigerator Bruce had delivered to the hotel."

They checked but couldn't find anything edible on-site. Once Jade realized it would be at least an hour before she could eat, she suggested, "Let's move another body bag into the lab. I'll keep working until you come back to feed me." She patted her tummy, a big grin on her face.

Meg shook her head. "You and your stomach."

Jade flashed her coworker a big grin again. "Hey, I lost a ton of weight when I was here last time. I can't afford to lose any more."

"I'll say. You're too thin now. Are you sure you don't have worms?"

The discussion degenerated from there, as they laughed and teased each other. But they transferred another bag onto Jade's table, using the portable stretchers. Right now, it looked like the reefer truck system might work out fine.

Stephen and Wilson had taken over looking after the reefer trucks—with a maintenance guy at the end of the phone, should they have trouble. They had a backup generator large enough to handle any issues, should a problem arise. On top of their temperature concerns, condensation was becoming a problem.

At that thought, Jade checked the temperature gauge outside the reefer truck. It was normal. Good thing, considering the daytime temperatures of Haiti. She frowned. "Have to keep an eye on the temperature."

Meg stepped over. "True, but it's fine now."

They returned to the lab. "If you want to grab those samples and go, I'll get to work on the next one."

"What you mean is, I should go grab *you* lunch. The samples could stay here a little longer for all you care." Meg shook her head. "As if I don't get your ploy."

"I imagine Stephen and Wilson must be starving too."

"Not likely. You're the only one starving around here." She looked toward the grave site. "I suppose I should check with them." She shook her head. "Ten years of postsecondary, another eight years of valuable experience, and I'm doing lunch runs."

Jade laughed. "And just think of the wage you're pulling in to do them."

"Good point." Meg strode down the path, her tall slim

frame disappearing quickly out of sight.

Jade turned back to her lab, wishing they had the data-bases set up already. Database work was Stephen's domain. Still, Jade had to handwrite, then enter each chart, and she found she missed her email access out here. The computers with internet were at the hotel. She'd seriously considered upgrading her electronics before leaving Seattle but then decided that the reception could be hit-or-miss on location, so had decided not to bother.

Frowning, she stood at the door to the lab and surveyed the long narrow room. The room would do fine for now. Just as her return to Haiti was working out fine.

Surprisingly.

She'd been busy enough that she hadn't had to worry about depression or grief overwhelming her. The team had been overwhelmingly accepting. Jade no longer worried about her placement here. She belonged. This had been the right decision. If she'd realized a change in focus would allow her to heal, she might not have wasted the last six months of her life.

Jade grinned. She missed Duncan. She'd make time to send him a long email tonight. He had to be worrying about her. She'd come a long way toward recovery. Sure there'd been some back-and-forth with her emotions. They could flare at the oddest times, but she was fine right now.

He deserved to know that.

EMILE HAD CALLED in sick for work today to check out the grave site and damn near shit his pants when Dane pulled in here. Damn good thing Emile had hidden behind the trees close to his father's cabin. This end of the property was heavier in vegetation than the rest, being part of the original plantation. He'd planned on just checking out the mass grave, seeing what they were doing.

He'd spied two men working on the burial ground with shovels. He shuddered. No way he could do that job.

Then he'd seen the tall brunette drive off, leaving the little blonde to work all alone in a small trailer with only one door.

Alone. In Haiti—where the normal trappings of civilization had been stripped clean, where animal instincts were laid bare by the destruction. Sure, some of those trappings had been quickly replaced but only by some. Others had reacted wildly to the chaos—like during wartimes—raping the women they could and killing others over food. Life had gone animalistic in those first few weeks. They'd calmed down some—actually a lot. But that didn't mean any of the men had forgotten that feeling of being what they truly were. *Predators.*

Leaving young, pretty white women alone and unprotected? Now that was asking for those predatory instincts to go on a rampage all over again.

From what he'd seen, it looked like Dane had his eyes on the little one. Emile had watched the two of them when they were talking outside the trailer. The little one was skittish, but Dane was making all the right moves, moving slowly, staking his claim.

He could appreciate that. Besides, Dane *was* the boss. He should have first pick.

That left the tall one for him.

He couldn't help himself; he licked his lips and watched, as she walked along the path and clambered over the rocks to where the two men were shoveling. Both greeted her as he'd hoped. Just casually friendly. *Good.* No sign of proprietary ownership. *Idiots.* They worked beside two single women and hadn't he seen a third the other day? He cast his mind back, pretty sure he'd seen a darker-haired woman with them too. Although he didn't know that any were single. Not that it mattered for his purposes.

Honestly, if a man couldn't protect what was his, then he deserved to lose it.

And the woman? Well, according to his father, she didn't get a say in the matter.

Chapter 8

THE NEXT MORNING Jade decided there was no use putting it off any longer. She needed to work on their *prisoner girl.* The authorities had come, had had a long talk with Dr. Mike, taken a few notes and pictures, and then left.

At that point, the woman had been removed from the grave as carefully as glass slivers from skin. Jade had documented every step, taken photos at each stage. It was only right that she continue the job. She knew how to follow procedures, but she wasn't a forensic anthropologist like Dr. Mike. Someone told her that he'd also worked for a dozen years as Chief Medical Examiner in Dallas. She doubted there was much he hadn't seen in his career.

Taking a deep breath, she pulled the cart to her worktable and gently unzipped the body bag. The remains had been wrapped in something at one time—a sheet maybe. Almost nothing was left now.

Using her brush, she cleaned off the top of the body and was struck by the feminine bits and pieces of material that emerged. Bits of pink ruffles, pink pleats in the skirt—stiffened and dried—its original prettiness now a macabre imitation. Jade grabbed her camera and started taking pictures, while the body still remain in the bag. She'd taken several at the grave site, unable to throw off the concern that this was a crime scene—maybe not a killing site but definitely a dumping site.

She worked steadily for several hours.

"Hey." Meg walked into the room, a brown bag in her hand, and a tall take-out cup in the other. "Wow, it's warm in here. I brought food."

Jade fired a wide grin at her. "Great. I'm starved."

With an eye roll, Meg said, "See? I didn't even make you ask today. Besides, Dr. Mike and Bruce are looking at the grave site. They'll be here over lunch too."

"Oh, good. I have our poor prisoner girl on the table. I'm hoping for a few more answers when I consult with Dr. Mike."

"Interesting." Meg stepped over to stare at the skeleton. "She looks young." Pulling on gloves, Meg bent over, then gently opened the girl's mouth to check her teeth. "Full dentition with the wisdom just crowning in the back. She could be anywhere from twelve to eighteen for that matter. How is the fusing of the bones?" She took a magnifying glass to the radius. "Not fused at the bone plate yet." Checking the cranium next, she straightened and frowned. "Cranial sutures are still evident."

Meg glanced over at Jade. "I'm thinking a female, a teenager, approximately fifteen to seventeen years of age. Pretty rough sutures at that."

Jade pursed her lips. "That matches my guess."

"Interesting age."

"Especially here. Girls are often married by then."

Studying the bones, Meg asked, "Is she complete?"

"Yes. Appears to be." Jade tossed her gloves in the garbage. She pulled a Sani-Wipe from the dispenser and cleaned her hands thoroughly. Then, opening her brown bag lunch, she pulled out a container with rice, beans, and vegetables.

She dug in. It was food, hot and tasty. They'd been offered sandwiches for lunch, but the team preferred to eat local fare. Turning back to Meg, Jade pointed out the remnants of the clothing she'd removed from the skeleton.

Meg let out a long whistle. "Pleats. Wow. I'm guessing it's the multiple layers of synthetic clothing that kept those from deteriorating."

Jade shrugged. "Possibly. I can't analyze the material properly here. However, it looks that way. No jewelry on the body."

"Interesting." She bent over the head area, then reached out a finger and checked the collarbone.

"Broken and healed."

"Agreed."

Jade munched happily. When her food was gone, she reached into the bag and pulled out a banana that she finished in six bites. She peered into the bag again, hoping for something else.

"I guess we need to get you a double-size lunch from now on." Laughter filled Meg's voice.

Catching her humorous look, Jade smirked. "Good idea." She tucked the container back in the bag and put it by the door.

Meg shook her head. "I'll work on getting the DNA samples and might as well take the dental impression too—unless you want to?"

"Go for it. I'm still charting."

"Right. We're hoping to take over the extra dining room at the back of the hotel for a communication room."

"Yeah, that side of the work is backing up." Jade motioned to her laptop, open and running, beside her. "I just emptied my flashcard, so I can take more pictures. I'll need hours to go through the ones I've already taken."

Meg studied the small workspace Jade was bent over. "Maybe we should have one person working in the lab in the morning, while the other does the computer work, and then switch?"

Jade walked around the small space, as she considered the options. There weren't many. "The thing is, I'm not sure anyone should be left alone out here for long periods. I'm not worried about being alone, but it's just common sense to stay together. And, if we're in pairs, we need to make them useful working pairs."

Meg cast a glance through the open door. "I'm not sure we should ever work alone. Sometimes it's like I'm being watched. It's a weird feeling."

Jade glanced up at her, then at the open door. She shrugged. "It could be the locals watching what we're doing."

"True enough." Meg reached for her tools.

The afternoon passed quickly, as they figured out a rhythm to sharing this space.

Working on prisoner girl took longer, as they used tweezers, brushes, and magnifying glasses most of the time. They needed to collect all the evidence there was. Once completed, they replaced her carefully in the same bag—after they'd upended it, just in case they'd missed anything. The bag had been empty, and Jade made a note of that on the chart. The two women then moved her to the reefer trailer.

Jade stood and studied the layout. It was anyone's guess if they had enough space for the contents of the mass grave.

At the sound of an engine, they both walked outside. "Looks like Dane's here again. What's he got in the back?"

Dane, driving a full-size black pickup, backed toward the

lab trailer, kicking dust everywhere.

The women retreated slightly. Jade coughed once, then took a drink from her water bottle. "Oh my gosh. He mentioned something about exchanging our small steps for a big deck he had at another site. We were discussing the lack of natural light in the trailer and how nice it would be to do some of the work outside. Fresh air and all that." She tried to make sense of the jumble of wood in the truck's bed.

Meg dropped her gloves on the stretcher. "And it looks like he's a man of his word. Got to love that."

"And he's not alone."

The two women waited until the truck stopped, before walking over to see who'd come with him. Dane hopped out, looking devastating in jeans and his snug T-shirt, rippling across his chest. He smiled. "As you can see, I didn't forget."

"Thank you. I'd forgotten about it." Jade smiled at the silent Haitian by his side. He was smaller than Dane, dustier, with dark skin. "Hi."

He inclined his head but stayed silent. His black eyes watched her closely. She walked over to Dane.

Dane shot her a look. "I hadn't." He walked around to the back of the truck and dropped the tailgate. "They're in several interlocking pieces." He studied the set currently on her lab trailer. "Emile, give me a hand moving these out of the way."

The women stepped back to stand in the doorway while the two men lifted the old set of steps and moved it off to one side. Unloading the largest piece of the new set first, they butted it up against the trailer. They then grabbed the second half and lowered it into position. Large squares of decking were laid down on top.

And just like that she had a small porch. Jade bounced

on her toes. "Is it safe to stand on?"

"Absolutely."

DANE WATCHED JADE run up and down the steps, like a kid at a new playground. And all because of such a simple thing. Her lab coat bounced as she moved. She had to be dying in the heat with jeans and a T-shirt underneath. But then, in her place, he would also want an extra layer or two between him and the skeletons she worked on every day.

She laughed.

He grinned. Good. She was way too serious. If something like this gave her a kick, then he was all for it. Meg followed Jade to stand on the little deck. It appeared bigger with the two women on it.

"Will that work for you?" Dane asked.

Jade smiled, and her eyes gleamed. "Thank you. This will work nicely. If I do nothing more than stand here and grab fresh air and sunshine for five minutes at a time, it's a help."

"Good." Motioning to Emile, they lifted the small set of steps and loaded it into the back of the truck. Dane walked to the front of the cab and opened the door to retrieve something. He turned around, a big grin on his face, his hands full.

"And speaking of coffee …" He held out two large take-out cups. Steam rose from the small opening in the top of the lid.

"*Ohhhh.*" Delight lit up their faces.

He grinned as the women almost danced in place. "See? I keep my promises."

"And that makes you a very special soul." Jade accepted a

cup and sniffed the small vent. "Wow. What is this?"

"It's a Haitian version of a cappuccino."

Jade inhaled again. "Really? Where did you find it?"

Dane grinned. "I told you I would show you the hidden gems of this area."

"Hidden is right." She took a tiny sip and sighed happily. "Thank you. It's lovely."

Dane held out the second cup to Meg. "Are you also a coffee fanatic?"

She accepted the cup gracefully. "I enjoy it, but I'm not crazy like she is. And I only eat a quarter of what she does."

"I'm not that bad." Jade smiled at Dane. "Don't let her scare you."

Dane walked back to his truck. "It would take more than a hungry female to scare me off."

Stephen and Wilson came around the corner of the rocks, dust covering their weary faces. They waved cheerfully. When Stephen spied Emile, his smile became more formal. He walked over and held out his hand.

"Hi, I'm Stephen."

Emile reached out and shook his hand. "Emile."

"Hey, you're Dane's brother-in-law, right?"

Emile frowned and glanced over at Dane.

Grinning, Dane answered, "He means you are related to my brother's family. The answer is yes, Emile is Tasha's brother."

"Ah." But Emile didn't smile with understanding.

Stephen stepped back, as Wilson walked over with a bottle of water in his hand.

Dane watched as each person spoke. Emile, like his sister, Tasha, was quiet—reticent with strangers. Still, he handled himself well in this context. He didn't exactly smile;

he did, however, gradually lose his stiffness.

Dane turned his attention to Stephen. "Is Bruce around?"

Stephen shook his head. "Bruce has gone to the authorities to update them on the progress here and to let them know about our clinic opening in town, giving free doctor's visits and hoping to get people to agree to giving a DNA sample, so we can match some of the victims."

"Clinic?" Emile struggled with his English, so Stephen explained. A strange look stretched across Emile's face that had Dane wondering, ... but Emile was a simple soul, so Dane let it go.

Though apparently Emile wasn't as simple as Emile's father, Peppe, whose mental health had deteriorated rapidly over the last few years. The necessary level of care was not available here for someone like him, and, according to John, Tasha wouldn't let Peppe go to a home anyway. Emile was supposed to take care of his father now. However, according to John, that wasn't happening.

Dane hated it, but it wasn't his place to interfere. He'd made his opinion of the situation clear. To no avail. He'd rather eat a bullet than sit in his own shit though.

Another reason to go home soon. It wasn't in his nature to let an injustice like that go on and on.

Neither had it been in John's nature years ago. What had the ensuing years done to him?

SITTING IN THE truck on the way back, Emile cast a wary glance at Dane, his boss. Questions burned in his mind. Only he didn't want to cross that invisible line between boss and employee. "Now those are good-looking women."

Dane tossed him a grin. "They are, aren't they?"

"Smart to help out. I would too." Emile twisted in his seat to stare out the back window. The women were gone from view. He turned around as the truck approached his home.

"Nothing stopping you. You live right around the corner from the site. Although I guess they aren't always there. And you work elsewhere." Dane nodded and turned a sharp corner.

"Exactly. You're the boss. You can come during working hours. Emile has to come after work, when women are long gone." He grinned. "Maybe Emile needs to stay home sick."

Dane laughed. "Well, at least I'd know where to find you to haul your ass back to the job." He shifted gears and made a right turn to John's house. "Those women are hard to ignore."

"Me, I like brunettes. Tall brunettes." Emile grinned.

"Me, I like blondes. Short, tiny blondes."

Emile laughed, a hoarse roughness to his voice. "Then again, I like all women."

As Dane pulled the truck to a stop in front of the main house, he smirked. "What's not to like?"

Emile hopped out and headed inside for dinner. He knew what there was *not* to like.

Women who didn't know their place.

Chapter 9

UNLOCKING THE LAB door, Jade accidentally swung her laptop bag against the side table as she entered and jarred the microscope. "Shit."

She'd woken late, barely made it for breakfast, and still hadn't gotten on track for the morning. She'd also been shortchanged on her coffee, and that was bad news. For everyone.

The air inside was stifling, so she opened the door wide. Sighing, she dumped her bags down on the floor and walked over to turn on the lights.

She frowned and looked around the lab. *What was different?*

Meg had been the last to leave and had closed the lab yesterday. It didn't feel like the same lab at the moment. *How odd was that?* The tools weren't arranged as Jade would have laid them out. Neither did her chair sit where it normally sat.

Was it because she hadn't been the last one here yesterday?

Must be. The door had been locked. She walked over to check the door mechanism. It didn't appear to have been touched or tampered with in any way. The windows had been left open though. Normally they closed and locked them when they left. The equipment inside was expensive and could be hocked for some serious money, if someone knew where to sell it.

They'd been tight with security on the first couple days. Then, when problems hadn't developed, they'd grown lax.

That needed to change.

A proverbial list maker herself, Jade booted up her laptop, then opened a new document to create a checklist for opening and closing the lab at the end of the day. She couldn't print it off here. That would have to wait until she returned to the hotel.

Dr. Mike showed up an hour later, coffee in his hand. But only one. "You dare bring java in here and not bring enough for everyone!" She shook her head in disgust.

Solemnly he held the cup out to her. "Actually, it's for you."

Shamefaced, she accepted the treat. "See? That's what happens when I'm deprived in the morning. I turn into a real bitch. I am sorry."

"*Nah*. Figured you'd run late this morning. Besides, I'm here to go over our prisoner girl. Can you point her out for me? I'll have Wilson give me hand bringing her over. Also," he said, looking around, "is there a space in here for me to work?"

"I'm just finishing this boy, and I need to enter the information into the computer, so this table will be clear in a couple minutes."

"Perfect." He nodded. "I'll grab the others to give us a hand when you're done."

Jade quickly cleaned off the table and brought out the prisoner girl's chart. They really should have some name for the poor woman. Jade pondered that for a second, remembering the plants flourishing around the grave site. She smiled and gave the prisoner girl the moniker of Rose and wrote it on the chart.

Stephen and Wilson entered, carrying Rose.

Grabbing her laptop, Jade headed to the far end of the trailer and tried to focus on her own work. It was hard to ignore what Dr. Mike was doing though. Not that there could be much to say about the condition of a body after an earthquake.

An hour went by.

Finally she couldn't wait any longer. She wandered over to his end of the lab on the pretext of grabbing her forgotten water bottle. In the silence, every move she made sounded extra loud. She waited impatiently, hoping he'd notice her presence. No such luck. She had to ask, "So did you find anything?"

"*Hmm.*"

She stared at his bent head, then leaned in for a closer look at what he was studying. "What's that?"

"Good question. The chains weren't put on after her death, as someone suggested. In fact, I'll say she'd been wearing them for a while."

Jade's stomach dropped. *Uh-oh.* She waited impatiently, until she couldn't stay silent any longer. "Anything else?"

"Lots. But not necessarily conclusive. See here?" He pointed to the neck area. "Her neck was broken."

"Which could have happened during the earthquake."

Dr. Mike bent for a closer look. "True enough but the hyoid bone has been crushed, and that's usually caused by strangulation."

Jade swallowed. Hard. "What about other injuries?"

"I'm working on it."

"Right."

Stephen blasted through the doorway, wide-eyed and gasping for breath, his emotions ravaged by … something.

Jade shook her head, as she went to his side. "Stephen, talk to me."

He took a deep breath, as Dr. Mike joined her.

Stephen struggled to breathe normally. "You need to see this."

Dr. Mike raised his brows. "All right. Let's go."

They exited the small trailer and headed toward the path.

"Hey, where are you all going?" Wilson called out from the reefer truck. He slammed the door closed, turning to face them.

Pointing to the grave site, Jade said, "Stephen found something he wants us to look at."

"I'm coming too." Wilson jumped down the steps, then raced to catch up.

The grave site looked the same as always when they approached. In fact, she'd half-expected to see natives, lodging a protest over their arrival or something, given Stephen's reaction.

"It's over here. I wasn't sure when I first started. Now there can be no doubt."

Frowning, they gathered around the spot in question. A path had been dug through the pile, almost to the other side. Enough to be sure that no other bodies were in the heap of rock. After opening the grave in the middle, the plan had been to dig out the lower part of the pile on the left, until they'd found everything to be found, then move to the right side.

Remains lay exposed.

"What am I looking at?" Jade asked in confusion.

"Exactly the question I was hoping you'd answer for me," Stephen demanded, explaining further. "I found more skeletons. But cleaner, older, deeper in the ground than the others we've found to date. These appear to have been covered by a thick layer of dirt and rocks. As if they were in a layer below the mass grave."

Dr. Mike shrugged his shoulders. "Some of the dirt would have slid down on top of the first bodies when they were dumping in more. This was done in a hurry by people without the skills to do it right. Hell, they might have done that deliberately, if there were a break between loads of bodies. That would actually be practical. They would have to keep the predators out somehow."

"True," Stephen agreed. "But why would these victims dumped in here be so clean and be buried with chains?"

Chains?

The color bleached from Dr. Mike's face. He could bare-ly get the words out. "More? Are you saying that you've found *more* people with chains on them? This doesn't make sense."

"It does if you don't look at this simply as a pile of earthquake victims. Sorry, but what we have here is no longer so simple."

Jade bent down to take a closer look. Stephen had opened a six-foot square. The remains and dirt had long married together into a brown sandy mess. Only the white of bones showed.

Coiling away from several of the bones were rusty-linked rings, ending in thick manacles.

Jade stared as Dr. Mike pointed out at least two sets of links crumpled in and over the top of each other. "We'll need to treat this site carefully."

Dr. Mike nodded. "Still, chains are not definitive proof. Again we can't let our imaginations run away from us here. There are possibilities other than foul play." He sighed heavily. "However, I'm really struggling to find a good one. … I think this should wait until Bruce returns. We'll need to treat this as a potential crime scene—just in case."

Jade cringed inside. She wished there was another way. "And how about an expert on Haitian culture? Surely we can ask someone about this."

Stephen snorted. "Be serious, Jade. What can *we* ask? This isn't exactly the type of question that you ask to start a conversation. *So …*" He mimicked a heavy Texan drawl, as if he were asking the authorities, "*Do you keep your whole family in chains—or just the women?*"

Jade winced at the images that refused to stop prodding the back of her mind. "I had worse thoughts going through my head." She took a deep breath. "I was thinking of the sex market. What if someone kidnapped young women for the slave trade in Asia or Malaysia?"

All the men stopped and stared at her.

"Now that's not a nice concept." Wilson ran one hand through his dust-covered hair and stared at her. "Why would you even think of something so nasty?"

"Because it's a huge problem. We all want to bury our heads but, just because we can't see it, doesn't mean it isn't happening all around us. After a disaster like what happened in Haiti, children were snatched off the streets, and, as always, young women are the prime victims."

"And this is as good a place as any to stop." Dr. Mike stepped in as the voice of reason. "No way to know exactly what we have here, not until we remove everything and analyze it."

"Just in case, we need to photograph this site and all the stages of our work here, until we have these bodies out and safely inside." Jade faced Dr. Mike. "Speaking of safe, has anyone considered security on the site, while we're working here?"

Stephen said, "Bruce requested more money be budgeted for security. I don't know what the end result is. Why?"

Looking around, Jade shrugged self-consciously. "I don't know if there is foul play involved here or not, but if people hear about what we've found ..."

Dr. Mike clambered over several rocks. "You think that the person responsible might find out? That's highly unlikely, isn't it? Not everyone knows what we're doing."

"Sure," said Stephen. "About as likely as finding a bunch of chained women in a grave intended for victims of an earthquake disaster."

Jade stood up. She glanced back toward the trailers, barely visible through the rocks. "Bruce said he'd be here around noon today." She took a long drink. "He was hoping you'd have information on Rose, that first woman with the chains."

"Right. That's why I'll go work on her right now." Dr. Mike rotated his shoulders.

Closing the lid on her water bottle, Jade nodded. "And I'll photograph what we have so far here. Then, when Bruce arrives, we'll proceed."

Relief lit Dr. Mike's face. "Good plan."

Jade walked down with him and retrieved her camera. As soon as she returned to the grave site, she adjusted her camera for the light and started with close-up pictures from all sides.

Stephen watched her for a few minutes. "Fine. I'll grab a

bottle of water then. The dust here fills my lungs and dries my throat."

"Grab me one while you're there, please." Jade focused and shot, changed her position and did it all over again. She tried not to think about the poor people in front of her. But her mind twisted through the endless possibilities. How did they end up in chains?

The stillness around her settled in. Jade felt as if she were being watched. She glanced around, wondering how long Stephen had been gone.

Weird. She continued to photograph their findings. Then, because she couldn't get the feeling out of her mind, she refocused her camera and started taking pictures of the surrounding woods. Just a nice series of shots showing that no one was there. By the time she turned back around again, Stephen stood beside her, grinning.

"And you are doing what?"

She smiled. "Sightseeing."

JADE STUDIED THEIR new communications room at the hotel and immediately laid claim to a small portable table, where she set about creating a workspace beside the window that overlooked the gardens. This space was a hell of an improvement. It was twice as large as the space they had before, boasted big bay windows that let in lots of natural light, and came with several large tables. Bruce had decided that they needed a more secure area at the hotel for work. This had been the perfect solution. Nice.

Now if only there was an answer to the on-site security issue.

Knowing she needed as much computer time as possible,

she focused on her charts, as the others moved around her.

"Couldn't find yourself any better spot to be in the way, huh?" Bruce grinned at her, pointing to the empty bookshelf along the wall behind her.

"Nope. Figured this offered optimal irritation."

"You're probably right." Stephen came over and dumped on the floor a large box of binders, destined for the bookcase behind her. "When you get a chance, you can put these on those." He patted her gently on the shoulder, before disappearing again.

She shook her head and entered the information Dr. Mike had added to Rose's file. Holding the chart in her hand, she puzzled over the handwritten notes. Dr. Mike's writing was damn near impossible to read. He also didn't do computers well. But, according to all accounts, he was a hell of a doctor.

"Hello, Jade. How are you?"

Surprised by the strange voice calling out to her, Jade glanced around and frowned. *Accountant Tony.* She should have expected to see him at some point. Still, his arrival on their moving day was a surprise—just not a good one. Though their relationship had been civil so far, she hadn't been at her best during their first meeting, and he hadn't been enthusiastic about her joining the team. He'd been desperate to complete the hiring quickly and, with Duncan's urging, had finally agreed to give her the position—with a warning he'd be keeping an eye on how she handled the job.

Still, she was here. And that made him her boss. "Hello, Tony. I didn't know you were coming."

"I'll be in and out several times over the next few months."

She smiled politely. That made sense. A lot of money

was being piped into this recovery. "To be expected."

"How are you handling your job?"

Was there something off in his voice? She studied his face, looking for anything other than general interest. "I'm doing well, thank you. The job is interesting, and, once we get properly set up, I can see we'll make a lot of headway."

"Are you finding it difficult to be here?"

Raising one eyebrow, Jade shook her head slightly. "Not at all. Haiti has moved forward—plus the job is *very* different—not many similarities between the two experiences at all." She shrugged her shoulders. "Things are good."

He appeared to be about to speak, then thought better of it, and left. She stared at the empty doorway for a long time.

Had he told anyone about their first meeting? Maybe not all of it, but someone must know to keep an eye on her.

She would appreciate it if her problems stayed private. But then Tony had a job to do too. Did he consider her a liability? Or was he just checking in on his investment?

Retrieving the chart again, she held it under the light to try and decipher Dr. Mike's notes.

It took almost as long to do the charts as to process each body. But when *didn't* paperwork take longer? She searched through her downloaded picture folder to locate the ones for Rose's case file. Jade attached over forty, wanting to be thorough, in case the police followed up. She finally turned to the last file.

Where had everyone gone?

"Are you done yet?"

Dressed in a long brightly colored cotton dress, Meg looked so relaxed, so beautiful, Jade sighed. She wished she could wear dresses like that. But she was so short, and the longer dresses only made her look shorter.

Then her eye caught sight of the wonderful ice cream and banana concoction in Meg's hands. Jade straightened, her stomach growling. "Is that for me?"

"Hell no." Meg laughed and took another bite. "Go get your own."

"Where? Are you guys eating without letting me know? I've been working hard in here."

"It was lunchtime a good half hour ago. Your stomach always lets you know."

Jade checked her computer. "Shit. I almost missed it." She bolted to the dining room, followed by the sound of Meg's laughter. Jade heaped her plate with something that looked like fish again. The rest of the team sat, eating and talking around tables. No one had made a new place for Tony, so he'd picked Jade's chair. *Of course.*

Shrugging it off, Jade took the only spare chair, Meg's spot, and focused on the food in front of her.

"Hungry?" Tony asked curiously, watching her eat.

She couldn't be eating that much more than everyone else surely? It only looked bad because she was the only one with food on her plate. She nodded and ate several more bites. She had taken rather a lot.

"Jade has a healthy appetite." Bruce smirked. "I think she eats more than me. And where she puts it, I don't know."

That started off a major joking fest—with Jade being the brunt of it. She took it good-naturedly. As it was, even with all she'd been eating, she could swear she was losing more weight, or her shorts had stretched. Not good. The weight loss might be because of the high temperatures here. She didn't know.

As long as she didn't get sick, she didn't really care.

"I think she has worms."

Shocked, fork halfway to her mouth, Jade stared at Stephen in astonishment.

"What? That would be the first thing I'd have checked." He grinned at her. Then forked a large bite into his mouth.

She gasped mockingly, "Are you implying I'm a bitch?"

"Well …"

Snatching up her napkin, she crumpled it into a ball and threw it at him. "Be nice."

He held out his hands. "Mercy. I wouldn't think such a thing, honest."

Jade rolled her eyes at him and finished the food on her plate. Replete, she pushed back the empty plate and sighed happily. Then she finally clued in on the conversation around her. Bruce had stopped in to speak to the authorities. "What did they say?" Jade asked.

"In short, they don't want to hear about supposition. If we have any proof of a crime, then we're to contact them, but otherwise don't bother them. I'm not surprised actually. They're swamped with more pressing problems."

Dr. Mike interjected, "I think their resources are stretched to the max. They have their hands full, dealing with current crimes instead of possible crimes from a year ago—if not longer."

Bruce agreed. "Exactly. They did say that chains are not part of any Haitian burial tradition—to their knowledge."

Surprise lit Susan's face. "Here I was so sure it was an after-death ritual."

"Apparently not."

"Do we proceed as if this is a crime scene?" Stephen asked, a frown creasing his forehead.

Studying him, Jade realized she'd enjoyed Stephen's

company these past weeks. He was her age, and, unlike Bruce and Dr. Mike, who were her superiors, Stephen was easy to talk to. She could see a nice friendship developing here.

"Why is one way different than another way?" Tony asked, not at all happy with the situation. "We're not here to solve crimes. We're here to find the remains of this man's family members and take them home. Quick and simple."

Jade had been on the verge of saying something but closed her mouth. She didn't want to rock the boat. Tony was right. CSI personnel they weren't—and he paid the bills. She winced. True, they couldn't justify spending more time on the manacled bodies than on the others, but, if they didn't, who would?

"Someone needs to consider these people." Wilson lounged back in his chair, his face a study of exasperation and anger. He glared at Tony. "We understand that you and your clients are footing the bills for this job, but, from the first, our understanding was that we'd do what we could for the others in the grave as well. Surely, being as meticulous as possible isn't beyond the scope of our job? Reporting a crime scene and possible victims shouldn't be either." A small tic played at the corner of his mouth.

Jade held her breath, waiting.

"As long as they are given the same consideration as everyone else and not costing additional monies to process, then there is no problem," Tony said stiffly.

"And if a little more money is required to properly process these people, then what?" Wilson challenged.

Jade winced at the aggression but agreed with her team member.

"I can't okay any expenses that aren't within the parameters we first set out," Tony responded primly. "Bruce knows exactly what those are. I expect him to enforce those limits."

Bruce grimaced. "Thanks for passing the buck."

Tony stood. "I have no intention of doing that. Just make sure you don't either. You are all here to do a job for my client. That is all. Nothing more and nothing less. The other people in that grave are to be processed, entered into a database, and reburied in the same grave, if no one claims them. Discussion finished."

He strode out of the room, leaving the rest of them to stare uncomfortably at each other.

Wilson snorted. "That went well, didn't it?"

Dr. Mike shook his head. "Or not."

NO LIGHTS. NO guards. No brains. So much gear and equipment left for the taking. Emile knew many men who would have cleaned out the trailers in no time. Although, if Emile told them about the dead bodies, he wasn't sure anyone would touch a thing. His people had respect for the dead.

The hills cast long shadows, though the moon offered him lots of light for walking the clearing. Not that he needed it. He'd spent his life here. The darkness held no secrets from him.

Avoiding the big reefer truck, he wandered to the lab trailer, quickly picking the lock as he had the night before. The women fascinated him. He'd never had a white woman. Their skin was so silvery and looked so soft. In the sun, they almost glowed. At first he'd checked out the little blonde more closely but decided to back off—figured one woman for the boss and one for him was good enough.

Besides the bigger one would offer more fight. She was older, more experienced, and a little less likely to be controlled, … and that was fine with him. He wasn't his old man.

As his boss didn't like fighting, the quiet one would suit him. He always walked away when Tasha and John got into it. Tasha would not let a day go by without letting everyone around her know exactly how she felt. She'd always been like that. Easy and fast on opinions and bossy to boot—only she was family. There was only so much Emile could do to change her attitude.

He wandered around the inside of the trailer, intrigued and repelled at the same time. How could they do what they did? They didn't see it as wrong—he understood that. But to stand here day after day and touch dead people? No, that just wasn't right. He walked over to the entrance to stand on the small porch.

He couldn't understand the women working in here.

Tasha would never touch a corpse. Then she did only what she wanted to anyway. Their father had tried to rein her in a long time ago, but, with the death of their mother, Tasha had gained the upper hand, and look at his father now. Christ, Emile would rather jump off a cliff than finish life like his old man. Speaking of which, … he stared off in the direction of Peppe's cabin. Chances were the old man hadn't had anything to eat all day. Damn Tasha for passing that job to him.

Emile hated dealing with his father. Sure Tasha was pregnant, but women had been having babies since time began, and other women managed to get their work done too. Why couldn't she?

Because she refused.

Well, he straightened—enlightened. Then so would he refuse. Damn weakling John could do it. He never refused Tasha anything. He could take care of Peppe too.

Grimacing, Emile remembered Peppe from last night. The old man had been sitting in soiled clothes. Emile had thrown down his food and had walked out. He wouldn't clean the old man's ass again. Once had been too much for him.

Damn women's work.

Well, he wouldn't do it anymore. And, if Tasha or John wouldn't take care of it, ... Emile's gaze glowed with inspiration, as he stared at the mass grave. Then he'd find someone who would.

Chapter 10

W HEN JADE ARRIVED the next morning, Dane's dusty black truck sat in front of the lab trailer. He leaned against the truck bed, waiting. Her heart smiled. She was such an idiot. Yet she couldn't deny that he made her feel like a woman again.

Good thing. Her self-absorption and self-enforced seclusion had shut down her hormones, as she'd allowed anger and hurt to dominate. No longer.

"About time you got here." His big grin warmed her heart. Dane opened the door of his truck, and reached in. "What do you think you're on, Haitian time or something?"

She laughed. "*Nah*, boss checked in yesterday. Meetings with him put us behind schedule."

With a regal dip of his head, he pulled out two cups of coffee. "And, as a boss, I understand the benefits of keeping workers happy. So one is for you." He presented her with a cup.

"*Woo-hoo*. You are a definite keeper. Thank you." She shuffled her bags, so she could take it.

His eyes darkened. "Glad you're so easily pleased."

She grinned. "Often the simplest things in life ..." She dropped her bags at the door and brought out her keys. She inserted the key into the lock but realized—when she turned the key—she'd actually locked it. The door had been unlocked. She frowned and pushed it open.

"Problem?"

"The door wasn't locked. It should have been," she declared, her gaze sweeping the interior. The equipment was all here, at least what she saw at first glance. Nothing appeared disturbed—other than what could be attributed to Meg or Dr. Mike, who had worked here the afternoon before.

"Someone forget to lock up?" Dane stayed on the porch, poking his head inside. "It looks the same."

"I don't know. The equipment is set out slightly different. I didn't close yesterday, so can't say if the others moved things or not." She wandered to the back and then down the far side. She shrugged her shoulder. "I can't see anything missing. It just feels off again."

"Again?" His voice sharpened. "This has happened before?"

She gazed back at him over her shoulder. "Yes. This is the second time. I can't pinpoint what's wrong. It's more a sense of things not being quite right." She shrugged and walked back out to the small porch. She took a sip of coffee.

"I thought they would bring in security guards?"

Blowing the steam off her cup, she nodded. "I did too. Might have something to do with our moneyman-slash-boss who's here now. I don't think he likes the added expense."

"Then maybe he should be told about this to get approval for the security funding."

She gave him a sideways look. "I'm not sure that would make a difference."

Dane's cheeks hollowed out, his jaw jutting forward. "It damn well should. You shouldn't be out here alone."

He was worried about her. She smiled. It had been a long time since anyone other than Duncan had given a damn about her safety. "I'm not normally. One of the others will be here in an hour or so."

"That's not good enough. It's not that this part of the country has a higher crime rate than the rest, but you've opened a controversy with this mass grave, and you're foreigners, and you have expensive equipment and facilities. That makes you and these trailers a target."

She grimaced. "I know. I'll talk to them."

His jaw squared, he planted his legs slightly apart. "To-day."

She glared at him, liking the power of his personality, just not so much when it was turned her way. "Fine. Can we leave it for now? Thanks."

Studying her face, he gave one decisive nod. "Sure, I have to go to work anyway. Unless you want me to stick around until someone else arrives?"

"No. I'll be fine."

He smiled and turned to leave.

"Thanks for bringing the coffee," she called out, as he descended the steps and got into his truck.

With a wave, he drove off.

Her good mood restored, Jade headed inside. After making sure nothing was missing, she went to the reefer to double-check the chart numbers. She left the reefer door open to allow for more light, as she wandered the rows of dead. So far the numbering system appeared to be working.

"Jade? Are you in here?"

Startled, Jade bolted upright from her bent-over position and spun around. "Jesus, Stephen, you scared me."

"What are you doing?" He peered around the door and grinned at her, as she walked toward him. "There you are."

"Hey. I was cross-checking the numbers on the bags."

Jade hopped out of the reefer truck and waited, while Stephen closed and locked the door.

"Wilson went to town with Dr. Mike instead, leaving me free to get back to work. I'm going up to the grave site." Stephen patted the metal handle. "Bruce is heading this way in a few minutes."

She smiled. "I'll go back to the lab and wait for him."

Stephen took off, whistling, and Jade busied herself around the lab for the few minutes she had alone. Before she had time to puzzle through the feeling she'd had in the trailer earlier, she heard the sound of yet another vehicle. This one an SUV.

Bruce.

He waved as he drove closer to the lab trailer. Jade walked to the railing to greet him. "Hey."

Hopping out, he climbed the steps and walked around the new porch. "I like the new addition. From Dane, I understand?"

She wandered around the small space, appreciating the simple two-by-four construction. "Yes, a simple switch for a few weeks."

"It looks good."

"Any word on overnight security for this place?"

"Tony has vetoed the idea for now. Why?"

Oh, shit. She explained about the unlocked door and the weird feeling. "Did he give a reason?"

"*Not in the budget.*" Bruce gave her a mocking look. "We'll need to follow protocol, as we shut down every night. To know that we've locked up properly."

"Why is everything all of a sudden about money?" She watched as Bruce walked the tiny porch, still grinning his approval regarding this upgrade.

"Because our moneyman is here on the spot. It's easier to deal with them when they are a long way away. But, when they are here, they're all about control, power, … and saving money."

"And because they pay our salaries, we are all about compliance?" She frowned. "Part of the reason I was interested in coming was the good we'd be doing. It's hard to see that come down to number-crunching."

He studied her face. "I understand how you feel, and I think this is only temporary. Once Tony goes back home, that negativity will ease back, as everything returns to normal." He entered the lab and dropped his bag on the counter. "I'm going up to the grave site. Are you coming?"

"Absolutely." The walk only took ten minutes, taking them from the large clearing, down a path, to an opening that showed the valley. It was gorgeous country. Add in the sunshine and the easy-to-tolerate temperatures, and it was no wonder Haiti was a popular tourist destination. At least it had been. The earthquake had made a dent in that.

Stephen met them at the spot where he'd found the newest remains in chains. He'd taken the tarps off the exposed area and had moved some more of the rocks that surrounded the bones. They stood and studied the big job in front of them.

"Is Tony coming here? This morning? He should see this himself," Stephen suggested.

Yet Jade doubted anyone was ready to bring Tony in on this issue.

Bruce laughed. "Not likely. Not willingly." He looked from them to the grave and back again. "He won't know the difference between these or any other set of bones. I suggest we excavate very carefully—and tell the authorities if our suspicions are confirmed. If and only if we have forensic evidence of foul play, it will be our duty to bring someone official in on this."

Stephen nodded. "I don't see how we can't. I can't just ignore this. If what we see here is what we think it is, I will tell someone. Then, if the authorities need help dealing with these bones, they'll have my free labor."

Jade had to agree with that. "We'll process this as we would any of the bodies. That won't take any more time or money than the others. Once processed, the information is there to turn over to the police, if necessary." As Bruce went to open his mouth, she added, "Or I will process them on my own time in the evening. I'll volunteer my labor, just like Stephen suggested."

"Okay, before we go a little nuts on this, why don't we start the processing and see how long it takes us to do these few bodies? We'll measure that against the time it takes to do the same number of the other bodies," Bruce suggested. "If this takes longer, we'll all stay one night and work together to make up the time."

Stephen and Jade looked at each other. Jade smiled and added, "Works for me."

"Good, then let's get started."

Jade ran to the lab to retrieve her camera, while Bruce grabbed the closest shovel. Two bodies. At least that's all they'd found today. Tomorrow, unfortunately, could be a whole different story.

When lunch arrived, in the form of Meg and brown bags, Jade was more than happy to head back to the hotel and handle her paperwork for the rest of the afternoon.

JADE CALLED HER brother later that night and dumped the story on him. Jade sat in their new office space with the windows open. A cool breeze wafted in, circling around and blowing back out again.

His stunned silence sat heavy on the phone line. "Shit. This was supposed to take your mind off your own problems."

She laughed. "Well, it did that."

"Sure. As much as I'd love to see you find justice for these victims, remember that they are dead, and you are not. Don't do anything that will put you in danger."

"I won't." But she wasn't so sure she could follow through. There were too many unanswered questions. Who knew where this would lead?

"What's the matter? What's happened? Are you in danger now?" His sharp voice snapped through the phone line, pulling her back to their conversation.

She rushed to reassure him. Her poor brother had done enough worrying over her lately. "No. Of course not. No. I'm fine. Everything here is fine. Honest. Don't worry about me."

A doubtful silence filled the lines. "I held off coming to Haiti to give you some time. I'm thinking it might be time to come over …"

"Now, don't you go off on in panic," Jade said. "Come for a visit if you want, just not because of this. I'm okay."

"And you damn well better stay that way."

She grinned. "I will. I love you too."

"Good. That's the first time you've said that since you were in Haiti last time."

She went quiet inside. How sad. Just another example of how self-absorbed she'd been. Damn her selfish soul. After a moment, she said softly, "I'm sorry. I've given you a lot of grief and worry recently, haven't I?"

His voice warmed. "No. Don't ever think that. You have been through a lot. You're entitled."

And she had been. But that time was over. This Haiti trip *had* been good for her. She hadn't expected these results. Certainly not the sense of things being back to normal. Not this fast. She knew there would be relapses, particularly when she returned home, but this trip had forced a paradigm shift, and she'd grown with it.

His joyous laugh came through so clear and sharp, she leaned back and closed her eyes. She missed this. Missed him. Her brother had been such a mainstay in her life, a stalwart support. She was blessed. And had so forgotten to see and to appreciate the good in her life because she had been locked in her self-imposed prison of pain and misery.

Instead of walking away, he'd been shining at her side for so long and so consistently that she'd become accustomed to it. She'd forgotten to appreciate his presence.

Not anymore.

"You are the best brother anyone could have, and I am so grateful that you don't belong to anyone else but me." Tears collected in the corners of her eyes, and, despite her best attempts, she sniffled.

"Jesus, Jade. You're killing me here."

Smiling through her tears, she said, "Sorry, I know you don't like emotionalism, but I just needed to say that."

"And needed to say it at a time that I can't wrap you in my arms and hug you." His voice deepened with emotion. "I love you, kitten. I don't know what's going on over there. If anything happens to you, I'll be heartbroken. You know that, right?"

"Yeah, I do." She sniffled harder. "I didn't mean to get into this right now, but all those dead women …"

"I know." He sighed heavily. "Wish I could help. I'd do anything to stop you from ever being traumatized again."

"I would too. And we don't know for sure that our theories are correct. *Yet.* We need to find out the truth—or what we can, while working here. That's on the table for tomorrow."

"Then you call me tomorrow. When you get back to the hotel, give me a quick call. Just a 'Hi, Duncan, had a great day, love ya' kind of call. So I know you're okay."

"I'll be fine," she insisted. She stood and wandered to the window, loving the cool night air and the sultry darkness that was so distinctive to this part of the world. If the phone cord reached, she'd have sat out on the patio, surrounded by the gardens. She'd been truly blessed to have the chance to come back here. Maybe she could think more charitably of Tony for granting her this opportunity.

"Good. Glad to hear that. But I won't be. Not unless you call."

"You're an idiot." She smiled, then chuckled. "But I will do as you ask."

"Good, and remember that this idiot loves you." His voice changed, became more teasing. "Speaking of love, any men over there making your hormones sing?"

She gasped, caught by surprise at the sudden topic change. Even though he couldn't see her, she shook her head. "No one. Don't be an idiot." *Okay, so there was Dane. Did he count?*

"I'm not convinced. Your voice says something different. Someone has caught your attention. And I, for one, couldn't be happier."

Sighing, she added, "No, there isn't, but believe what you will."

"I will. Don't worry. I will."

She could see his grin in her mind. "Idiot," she repeated affectionately. "I'm ready for bed now. Have a good tomorrow."

"I will, just promise to call me. I'll be waiting."

"Got it. Now, goodbye."

They rang off, leaving her sitting now, with a silly smile on her face.

She really did miss that big teddy bear of a brother. He was a good man.

"Now that is a lovely smile on your face." Bruce and Stephen walked into the office. "What are you doing working at this hour?"

She held up the hotel phone. "I'm not working. Just calling my brother." She grinned. "Or you could say, I'm doing as he requested and checking in with my brother."

Bruce sat down in the chair beside her. "Oh, he's protective, is he? That's probably a wise thing."

"There's just the two of us, so protective comes naturally to him." And she missed him.

"What does he do?" Stephen sat down at the computer next to her.

She stretched her back and rotated her neck. Something about bending over the tables in the lab had kinked her spine. The table was probably at the wrong height. "He's a counselor for kids at risk."

Stephen turned to look at her. "Wow. Good for him. That can't be an easy job."

"No, it isn't. Still, he's very good at it."

Bruce added in, "That's no surprise. You're also very

good at what you do."

The compliment, out of the blue, surprised her. "Thanks," she said, a squeak of shock in her voice.

He looked taken aback. "You're welcome. It's true. And what I expect from every team member here." He lifted a sheaf of papers and walked out, after saying good night.

Stephen rolled his eyes as Bruce left. "Yeah, we're all just one big happy family."

Chapter 11

HEAD DOWN, JADE shifted the camera lens, as she detailed the story of the next set of bones on her lab table. She had no idea how many pictures she'd taken so far.

Dr. Mike had been working at the second table all morning. Something was wrong. He'd been muttering for hours, as he pored over his work. That couldn't be good.

Dr. Mike's face had gone stiff and cold within minutes of starting on the first of the manacled bodies. Jade had been too concerned to bother him. He'd tell her soon enough. Ten minutes ago, the two of them had returned one set of remains to the reefer and brought the next one out. He never said a word, except to ask for her help to make the switch.

Bending lower, she snapped several more photos of the small breastbone, all but pulverized. She moved around, taking as many pictures as necessary, enjoying the calm silence of the room, despite the job she had to do.

She moved to the far side of the body bag and put down her camera. Time to move on to the next step. She charted the injuries, as she found them, and took out her measuring tape. She didn't think this boy could have been more than five or six years old. His bones had a stick-thin look to them.

Her heart ached for him. At least he would have died quickly. Not like the last one she'd processed.

The day's work hadn't been too bad; still they had a long

road ahead of them. Susan was helping Bruce at the team's free clinic two mornings a week. So far only one person had shown up, looking for their loved ones. Matching families to bodies would take time.

Dr. Mike sighed heavily.

Jade straightened, and stretched her arms over her head. "Problems?" she asked him gently. She glanced yet again at the open windows. Without a breeze the air hung heavy and hot.

He glanced at her and nodded. "Oh, I think maybe."

She walked to his table to see what he was working on. "What is it?"

"She was in the ground longer than the earthquake victims. Much longer. Possibly even as long as a decade." He pointed to the skeleton in front of him. "She died from blunt force trauma to the head."

"Meaning?"

"I don't know. Everyone that we've found in that mass grave had something in common. Especially their estimated time of death. All died within a short window, and, of course, we're using the earthquake to help determine that time. Then come these other remains." He shrugged. "All we can do is record the differences. Maybe there was an earlier grave under the mass grave. The countryside is full of small cemeteries. It could be a coincidence—not out of the realm of possibility.

"So one possibility is that these victims were from an earlier calamity, and it was easier to just bury more on top. We'd been told a cave had collapsed, creating a natural depression. That cave-in could have been an old grave site splitting open instead."

He groaned slightly, as he shifted his position. "Another

possibility is the earthquake could have opened another grave somewhere else, and the responders used the mass grave as a place to dispose of bodies that needed a new home. Again, not something that is necessarily a crime."

"And, if it's all guesswork, then we still don't have any evidence to bring to the authorities, do we?"

"I can only compile the information and present it to them. Will they care?" He raised his shoulders in a tired shrug. "I highly doubt it."

"Have you examined all the women? Did they all have the same cause of death?"

Dr. Mike stretched his arms. "These two died of blunt force trauma to the head." He stood and walked around, shaking out his arms. "But the first one we found was strangled."

"The first one we found died more recently than the others, right?" Jade frowned, beyond confused. "So the chain around their ankles is similar, yet the cause of death is different? Over a ten-year period? I wonder why? Different killers?"

Jade paced the small trailer, trying to find a reasonable explanation, but the pieces weren't adding up to anything other than criminal activity. "Of all the things that I keep coming back to, it was the absolute chaos and panic I saw when I was here right after the big earthquake. People were left to die, slowly and painfully. The dead were sometimes cut up in order to move them out of the way. In other cases, it was easier to kill trapped victims quickly than watch them die slowly. Chaos ruled. People were also being killed to gain food and blankets. Brother killed brother—out of compassion and for sheer survival."

Dr. Mike stroked his chin in a movement she'd come to

equate with slow, thoughtful thinking. "Except in this case, there were no missing limbs."

Jade agreed. "I've found enough crushed limbs to confirm plenty are in the mix."

"So, for a moment, we have a mystery. Not a crime, but a mystery." He took off his gloves and put them into the garbage can. "I need a drink of water and some fresh air. There is a little too much death in here for the moment."

"Are you done? Do you want to move the body back over to the reefer?"

"No, I'm not quite finished." He motioned toward her stretcher. "If yours is, can you process this one while I take a break?"

"I'll need another half hour at least to finish this one." Jade stopped, looked at her watch, and frowned. "I think Meg will be arriving soon with our lunch. Normally we switch at this time. However, if you'd like, I can stay and process yours this afternoon."

"If you wouldn't mind, I'd appreciate it. Although, if Tony finds out …"

Uh-oh. "I thought he left this morning?"

"He and Bruce were going over personnel files."

Jade grimaced. *Great.* She wasn't sure Tony was happy with his decision to have her here. She understood his reluctance. … Initially she might have agreed with his decision. Not now. Now she had a vested interest in finishing this job. They'd been here almost three weeks. They could see the end of the job within three months. She wanted to see it through.

Oddly enough, the more involved in these deaths she became, the more accepting she was of the loss of her own child.

At least she felt she was. Time did wonders for healing the pain. And closure here could bring her more closure once she returned home.

DANE HAD TAPPED every idea he could come up with and still did not have a decent excuse for going home at noon. So then he drove right past John and Tasha's driveway. He left a trail of dust floating toward John's small house. Dust. Another thing that was sure to be pissing off Tasha. Not that Dane could blame her. For years there'd been minimal traffic on this road. Now there were several vehicles a day.

Coming here to the mass grave was stupid because Jade had probably left already. She'd said something about switching off with Meg in the afternoons now. He parked, surprised to see two SUVs here. He checked his watch—after 2:00 p.m.

She'd be gone.

He strode over to poke his head into the lab.

"Hey, Dane," Meg called out cheerfully. "Haven't seen you in a few days. How have you been?"

"I'm doing all right. Just stopping in to see how things are going here. To see if you need the heavy equipment back again." He hoped not; it was off doing a job on the other side of town and wouldn't get back here anytime soon. Peering into the back, he was surprised to see as many people as there were. Tight quarters.

Meg turned to the back. "Hey, Dr. Mike. Dane's here. Any idea if you need the loader back today or tomorrow?"

Dane walked up the steps and went inside, surprised to see Jade working at the far end. "Hi, Jade. Didn't expect to see you here."

She lifted her head from whatever she'd been working on so intently and smiled. "Don't suppose you brought coffee, did you?"

He laughed. With her hair back in a clip, she looked like a teenager. "Sorry. If I'd known you'd be here, then I'd have stopped and picked up some. I thought you'd be at the hotel, sipping your own brew by now."

"Should be," she said cheerfully. "Dr. Mike asked me to stay and help out."

"Good for me." Dane smiled broadly.

She flushed charmingly and laughed. "That's nice of you."

Another of their SUVs drove up. "Looks like Bruce has arrived," Dane noted.

Dr. Mike came over to join them at the door. "Oh, no, Tony is with him." He glanced back at the body Jade had been working on. With his voice lowered almost to a whisper, he asked, "Are you finished with that one?"

She shook her head. "Not really. Could use another half hour, maybe even an hour." She waffled as she considered the work left. "Do you want me to pack it up unfinished or finish it while Bruce and Tony go to the grave site?"

He brightened.

Meg suggested, "Let's process it together quickly."

They didn't waste any more time but raced back to the end of the trailer and started work.

Dane pursed his lips and watched with interest. He caught Dr. Mike's look.

Dr. Mike grinned and said, "He's the boss, the big moneyman. Thinks things should be going faster and not cost so much."

"Right. That sounds familiar." And it did. Dane knew

many clients who were constantly watching that bottom line—even to the detriment of a project. He turned to watch the men get out of the SUV.

Bruce had a weary patience surrounding him, as if he'd heard everything more times than he wanted to and still didn't like the end result.

"Hi, Bruce." Dane walked over to greet the men. He figured the women needed some extra time to finish off whatever they were working on. He smiled at Bruce. "Don't you look a little on the tired side. … Heat getting to you?"

"Just a little. How are things with you, Dane? Business good?"

"Business will always be good here." With a casual friendliness, he added, "Just lacking the funding to do what needs to be done right."

Bruce rolled his eyes. "I hear you on that one."

Tony walked around the SUV to stand beside Bruce. He held a thick folder, clipboard, and pen in his hands. *The moneyman.* Talk about a cliché. Dane could have picked him out of a crowd. He smiled politely. "Hello, welcome to Haiti."

Bruce introduced them. "This is Tony. Tony, this is Dane Carver. He helped us in the beginning with the loader."

Tony's face thinned. "Right. Pretty expensive day rates too."

So *not.* Dane was in business here. He'd pulled the equipment off another job to give them a head start. He wouldn't listen to this crap. Dane smiled grimly. "Feel free to find someone else. If you can. Equipment is scarce right now."

Bruce interrupted hurriedly. "Sorry, Dane. We certainly

appreciated your help. Tony doesn't understand some of the costs related to this business."

Tony's glare was hot and lethal. "I've been doing this job for a long time, thank you," he said stiffly. "Now maybe we could start with a look at the grave site itself. If I could put that into perspective, I'd understand the need for machinery in the first place."

"That's a good idea," Dane agreed. Honestly Bruce should have taken him there on the first day. If Tony had no idea of the size of this grave that they were talking about, then of course he didn't understand the need for heavy equipment. "I'll walk up with you. I want to check on the progress."

Bruce led the way. Dane looked back once to see Dr. Mike still standing in the open doorway. Dane lifted a hand. Dr. Mike grinned and waved happily. Someone else was happy to see them leaving.

Turning the corner to fully see the mass grave, Dane stepped up to walk beside Bruce—in time to hear Tony catch his breath.

"A little different than you expected?" Dane asked, as he studied Tony's face intently. Shock, horror even—and maybe an understanding of the enormity of the problem.

"This is full of bodies?" Tony gulped. "It's huge." He lifted a shaky hand and rubbed a handkerchief across his forehead. "Good God, how many bodies are we talking here?"

"We're not sure exactly," Bruce replied. "We've brought out close to forty already but could be one hundred more … or only ten." He turned to face Tony. "Now you see why we need a storage solution. Either more refrigerator trucks or another location in town and a truck to haul things back and forth."

Tony stood and stared. He wiped his forehead again. "I had no idea." He brought out a camera from his pocket and quickly snapped off a couple pictures. "This will be something to show my client at least. The first set of photos didn't capture the scope of this site."

"Is he having second thoughts about the cost?" asked Bruce curiously.

Dane turned his attention from the grave site, where the two young men were working, to the conversation at his side.

Tony shook his head vehemently. "No. He's growing impatient. Everything is underway, yet he still doesn't have his family home. We've found several possibilities but have to wait for the DNA results to confirm."

With his hands on his hips, Bruce studied Tony's face. "We did say it would take months for us to get the bodies tested and confirmed."

"He knows that." Tony stuffed his camera away in his bag and brought out his clipboard. "Obviously heavy equipment was necessary to get started, and I can see that might be required again—even if only to refill this space. Okay, so that's no problem. I guess I'd better see the labs as well."

A much brighter-looking Bruce led Tony back down the path. He winked at Dane as he walked past.

Stephen walked over. "Now that they are leaving, it's safe to come over and say hi."

Dane motioned to the retreating men. "No one likes him, huh?"

Stephen snickered. "Nah. Tony's probably all right, just caught in the middle."

"True enough." Dane watched the others navigate the rocky path down to the lab trailers. "Speaking of which, did Bruce get security in for overnight?"

"*Nah.* Tony vetoed it."

Dane said goodbye hurriedly and raced back down the slopes. Security was mandatory.

They were too open here, too alone. Someone had to keep an eye on the place—and on Jade, when Dane couldn't.

JADE FOCUSED ON getting these poor women finished and out of the way. The light in the trailer was poor at the best of times. Urgency made her fingers thick and her actions awkward. She swore several times under her breath.

Meg wasn't faring any better.

Finally Jade stopped and stared at her. "Is she done?"

"Even if she isn't, I'd say let's get her back to the reefer and now."

Of like minds, they raced through the last steps, and, this time, Jade took off the paper sheet that she'd placed under the skeleton, while Meg processed it, just in case any evidence had dropped off. She started to fold it carefully, then realized they'd missed a hair. Pointing it out to Meg, she used tweezers to retrieve it and to bag it. For the moment, the little bag was tucked inside the body bag, which was zipped closed.

Both of them breathed a sigh of relief when the woman was secure again—from prying eyes and from Tony, whose voice they heard coming their way.

"Let's get her moved over." Meg shifted the bag slightly to sit better on their portable stretcher. "Out of sight and all that." Throwing her chart and white marker on top, Jade grabbed the other end and headed for the door.

Dr. Mike glanced from them to the bag and to the end of the room. Relief bloomed across his face. "Thanks," he whispered.

Bruce's voice boomed outside the trailer. "This is the lab trailer. In here we're processing the remains." There was a slight pause, then the sounds of heavy boots climbing the steps.

"Damn it," Jade whispered. They'd almost made it out. Still could actually. "Watch out. We're coming through with a stretcher," she called out loudly.

"Thanks for the warning," Bruce called back, and the men backed down from the small porch, as Jade came around the corner.

In a simple maneuver that they'd perfected with practice, Jade made it onto the porch, with Meg bringing up the rear. Smiling politely at the three men standing and waiting, Jade said, "Thanks, gentlemen." They walked over to the reefer truck. She rested her end of the stretcher on the steps and moved to open the door.

Dane raced over. "Let me grab the door."

She grinned. "We've done this many times, so it's not as if we can't, but a helping hand is always welcome." Jade picked up her end of the stretcher again and waited for Dane to open the door and then to move out of the way.

"Thanks, Dane." Meg smiled, as she walked up the stairs behind Jade.

Once inside, they moved the skeleton to the far end of the room and put her crosswise on the shelf. "Whew." Jade looked back to the door, where Dane peered in at them. "Glad we made it this far."

"As much as I'd love to hide away in here"—Meg handed her the white marker and the chart—"I'd better go speak with the bosses. Do your magic, then join us."

"Yeah, I'm *thrilled*." Jade watched Meg walk out and stop to speak with Dane. Then she disappeared around the corner of the trailer. Popping the top off the marker, Jade marked the bag as per her system and added a small series of interconnecting loops. *Chains.*

She straightened. No need to take another skeleton over. Dr. Mike probably had enough to work on this afternoon. Jade walked to the open door and closed it, checking the temperature as she did so.

"Everything all right in there?" asked Dane curiously. "You were a long time."

"I had to mark the bag with her chart ID." She smiled at him. "Are you taking the afternoon off? We don't get to see you often at this hour."

He snorted. "I wish. I'm on the way to the site right now. I had hoped that maybe I could convince you to go out for dinner with me this weekend."

Her eyebrows shot up. It was all she could do to stop her jaw from dropping. She stopped halfway down the stairs and stared at him.

His laughter rolled out easily. "Sorry, I've caught you off guard. So does that mean *no?*"

She shook her head, laughing self-consciously. "My reaction is not a reflection on you. It's a reflection on me. It's been a long time since I've been asked out."

"Then it's not a *no?*" He tilted his head and studied her.

She flushed. "No, it's not a *no*. It's a *yes*." *Crap.* She was handling this badly. She tried again. "Thank you, Dane. I'd love to go out for dinner with you." She smirked. "Is that better? I'm a little rusty."

He grinned. "Much better, thanks. So Saturday or Friday? Don't know what your schedule is like."

"*Hmm.* My personal life is just so full now. *Not.* Either works, but maybe Friday is better. There's talk of a team hike on Saturday, and I have no idea when we'd make it back to the hotel." She winced comically. "Or what shape I might be in afterward."

"Any idea where you're going?"

"No. Dr. Mike mentioned a couple ideas he wanted to check out further. I personally would love to spend some time out on the water."

"I know a couple tour operators who work out of Port-au-Prince. However, I'd have to ask around for local ones." As they walked toward the lab trailer, Dane added, "We'll figure it out. We'll be here for a few months so there's time to work in a few trips."

"I might also stay a little longer after this job is done. Several other team members have mentioned doing the same."

Dane's phone beeped. He pulled it from his pocket, checked the text, and sighed. "Back to work I go. Friday at seven, if that works for you?"

"Sounds good. Thanks." She watched him stride to the truck, hop in, and take off. Dane left a cloud of dust in his wake. Wafting her hand in front of her face, she walked to the lab trailer.

"We're not sightseeing on the job, are we?" Tony stood on the lab porch, watching her. "I'd hate to have to remind anyone that you are all here to work and not just to set up your social life."

She rounded on him. "I highly doubt anyone on this team is under any misunderstanding as to why we're here."

She wanted to say something cutting, but Bruce's worried face, just behind Tony, stopped her.

Tony loved power and control. She had no ax to grind with him. He'd given her the chance to come back and to face her demons. Although they weren't exactly gone, she was triumphing over them.

She owed him. She'd never cheated a boss before, and she wasn't about to start now. "Bruce, if you're done in there, I'll pack up the charts and head back to the office to start on the paperwork."

He nodded. "That's fine. I know you stayed late here to finish up, so thanks."

She shrugged it off. "Not a problem. Whatever works to get the job done, right?" She brushed past the two men, wishing the small deck were four times larger. Too many people were here now. She packed up her stuff and grabbed the charts, before saying goodbye to Meg and Dr. Mike.

Outside, she hopped into the SUV she'd driven to work and left, without saying another word.

As she pulled away, she noticed Tony was writing notes on his chart. *Brownie points or demerit points?* She hadn't been joking. Whatever worked for the team and the job worked for her. Still, she wanted to see this job through to the end, and, if he wanted to, Tony had the ability to prevent that.

She couldn't wait for the week to be over at this rate. *Friday.* That put a smile on her face. Wait until she told Duncan. He'd be worried and delighted. A real date. Wow.

THE GREASY CABIN window wouldn't let any light in again. Old Peppe had used his sleeve on the glass yesterday to try and wipe it, so he could see outside. He looked around for the binoculars that he knew were here somewhere.

He saw movement through the trees—barely. So many people on-site today. *Why? What had they found?* Surely nothing too important. He'd watched as they'd thrown body after body into that grave originally. Nasty business that. He'd wanted to help, but, not being as strong any longer, especially with his mind wandering the way it did, no one trusted him with anything. In fact, no one even came and talked to him anymore.

He was a prisoner in his own home. Dependent on his son for food. And his daughter? … *Well,* he hadn't even seen her hardly since the quake.

He missed his old life. The brief glimpses of better days. His wife's death had devastated him. He didn't even remember how long ago that had been. Tasha had been a teenager then, Emile not much older. Peppe couldn't function on his own for a long time after she died. His kids had suffered, and he was sorry for that. He loved them. He didn't understand why they hated him so much now.

He sighed and rubbed his beard. He hated the damn thing, and, when he could, he took scissors to it. Speaking of cutting it, he grabbed the dinner knife beside him and started sawing away. He threw the chunks of hair on the floor. His daughter should be coming to clean soon. At least he thought she would be. He couldn't remember the last time he'd seen her sweep the floor, but, in the back of his mind, he saw her with a broom. So she must have. She needed to come soon.

Damn useless child.

He'd taught her better than that. *Hadn't he?* Surely he had. He'd give her *what for* the next time he saw her. And that damn useless son of his. How about he come and swing a broom?

Then again, Peppe himself had never been lazy. He could manage a damn broom himself.

He stood and walked to the doorway, where the broom should be, and opened the door. He couldn't find a broom. At least he didn't see one. Damn kids. What had they done with it?

He shuffled outside and sniffed the air. Something strong assailed his nose, so he turned back to the house. *That smell was coming from inside?* Horrible. He'd really have to say something when someone showed up. Damn, he was hungry.

He left the door open and wandered back into the small kitchen to check for what there was to eat. Stale and crusty pasta and peanut butter. At least that's what he thought it was. Opening the jar he sniffed the contents and almost heaved. He tossed the jar in the garbage, watching as it hit the closed garbage can lid and bounced to the floor. The garbage was too full. It needed to go out.

He headed back to the front door, frustrated by his life. He needed them to come. *And now.* There was his cane, leaning against the front door. He'd been looking for it for a while now.

Figured one of them had taken it.

"Hey, Dad."

Finally. Someone. He stared at the face so familiar and yet so strange. "Do I know you?"

"Yes, I'm your son, Emile."

The overly exaggerated patience in his voice pissed off Peppe. "Says who? I wasn't born yesterday. How do I know you're my son?" He tottered forward. "Why does this place stink so bad? It's worse than the dump."

"This place has turned into a dump. Dad. You need to go change your pants."

"What's wrong with them? My wife got these for me. Who do you think you are?"

The young man rubbed a weary hand over his face. "I can't do this anymore. You don't even know us. So you won't miss us, will you?" He looked around at the mess on the floor and in the tiny kitchen. "We'll have to burn this place after you're gone."

"I'm not going anywhere. If you can't keep this place clean, then go get one of those women and have her do it." He muttered to himself. "Your mother would die if she saw this mess."

"She's dead, remember? From cancer. Made Tasha and I promise to look after you."

"Well, you haven't, have you? Look at this place. Where's Tasha? She should be here, taking care of me. The least you could do is bring me a damn broom so I can sweep, if you're too lazy to do it."

"Right. Tasha is in a bad way. She can't come. As for your request for a broom, you are leaning on it right now. So that doesn't make a whole lot of sense."

"I am not. Don't you try to make out like I'm crazy," he screamed. "I will not tolerate that kind of disrespect in my own home. Do you hear me?"

"Absolutely. So you don't want this rice and chicken then, *huh*? 'Cause, if you're starting your screaming fits again, I won't leave this food. In fact, I'll just walk away and hope you're not breathing by the time I check back in. Got it?"

The two men glared at each other, fury and stubbornness etched on matching faces.

And just like that, the storm blew over.

His face wreathed in smiles, Peppe said, "I love chicken. Thanks. What's in the jar?"

Emile groaned and held them out. "Your favorite—peanut butter."

Chapter 12

BEFORE TONY LEFT, he pulled Jade aside in the hotel lobby. The heat from outside penetrated through the large double doors.

"If you are having trouble handling this project or staying focused on the job, I will pull you off. This isn't a holiday, no matter what you think with your sightseeing tours and dates. We have a job to do, and I want it done right. I'm not a fool. Just because I can't be here all the time, realize that someone is keeping an eye on you. I need to ensure you're handling yourself here."

He walked away, leaving Jade in shock, staring at his retreating back. "What the hell was that all about?"

"What?" Bruce walked in the other door. "Did you say something?"

"I'm not sure what just happened." She motioned in the direction Tony disappeared. "Let me ask you something. Have I ever given you the impression that this job was too much for me mentally? Or that my social life is stopping me from doing my job?" At the astonished look on his face, some of the panic calmed, and she added, shaking her head, "Anything at all that made you consider I don't belong here?"

"No, of course not. Not a thing. Why?" An understanding settled into his eyes, and he glanced out the empty door.

"Was that Tony by any chance? Warning you? I am sorry. He's a bit of an overkill kind of guy."

"Ya think?" She studied his face. Would Bruce be honest? "He didn't ask you to keep an eye on my mental state?"

Bruce shook his head. "Absolutely not. I don't understand where he would have gotten that idea in the first place." Bruce frowned, scratching his chin.

"I do unfortunately, and you would have had to been there at the time to understand fully but …" She gave him a quick rundown on how she and Tony had met and the possible reasons behind his trepidation now. "The thing is, I've been here for over three weeks, and I hardly think I've let anyone down."

He patted her shoulder. "No, you haven't. Tony is nothing if not thorough. But I wouldn't let that worry you. There is always a team member assigned to keep an eye on the team—physically, emotionally, and mentally. So let them, and just be your normal happy self. Don't let Tony upset you."

"Will you be as happy to see him leave as the rest of us will be?" She shouldn't have asked. Bruce was the team leader. It wasn't fair to put him on the spot like that.

Bruce laughed. "Have to remember that people like Tony make the money flow. Either to us or away from us. We need them, and they need us. The partnership usually works." He grinned, more relaxed than she'd seen him in days. "It's still nice to see the boss leave for a while. Everyone will relax again and can work that much better."

"Unless we find another bunch of skeletons whose deaths appear a little suspicious."

"But he doesn't know about those, so it doesn't matter." He raised an eyebrow at her. "Right?"

"I don't know about what?" Tony stood in the doorway, his suitcases in his hand. "Are you talking about me?"

"No," said Jade, a calm smile on her face. "We were talking about Dane and the fact that he doesn't know any charters or tour guides in this town."

Tony's face lightened. "Good. Well then, I'm off. Should be back in a few weeks to a month, depending on problems and progress." He gave a perfunctory smile. "Goodbye and good luck." Then he disappeared.

Jade stared at Bruce, who stared back. Afraid Tony might still be around the corner, he mouthed back, *Thank you.*

"You're welcome."

They watched from the lobby as Stephen drove to the front of the hotel in a company SUV. Tony got in. While they watched, Tony was driven away.

"Thank God for that," she said.

"Amen."

WHEN DANE FINALLY made it back to his brother's house the next day, he asked himself once again if it might be time to leave Haiti. The sense of finality had been growing steadily. The hospital wing he was working on wasn't complete, yet it wasn't that far off. The interior finishing always took longer than expected. Much of the stuff they needed had to be ordered in. Dane's Seattle office was handling most of that. Dane had a good foreman here. He might go home and fly back and forth until the job was done. He'd originally hoped to remain long enough to see his niece or nephew born. Now he didn't think he'd make it that long.

He wouldn't mind being gone from this family scene. As much as he enjoyed rustic living, he would appreciate running water again. He'd been told the property used to be a lively and profitable farm, until the soil had been over-worked and the creek running through the property had dried up. He didn't think the property had provided Peppe's family a living in a long time. He'd learned that Peppe had been employed as a builder at one time, and, unlike many other natives, his kids had gone to school—at least for a while.

John didn't go into too much detail as to how he'd met Tasha or what they lived on. Tasha had worked in one of the bed-and-breakfasts in town, and Dane suspected that had been the extent of their income. Except for stuff she made and sold to tourists. And since the earthquake a year ago, John's business had failed.

As much as Dane loved his brother, John didn't appear to be bringing in much—if anything. And that was yet another area John wouldn't discuss. His brother took on mostly small jobs now to pay the bills—not that he'd seen John go to work much.

At this point, Dane figured that the money he paid them to stay in the cabin at the back of the property was what the entire family was living on.

His brother seemed happy enough, at least on the sur-face—only Dane didn't know how John could be. Was it the pregnancy that had turned his sister-in-law into a crazy shrew or something else—like this damn grave thing? Dane didn't know. At this point, he made a habit of staying late at work and leaving again early in the morning. And ate out often and showered at the hospital. He'd made arrangements to shower there, to avoid going home. Money bought almost anything here. Dane would have spent a lot more to minimize the time he spent listening to her berate his brother.

Tasha's appearance had started to slip as well. Her hair was unkempt instead of contained in the long braid she'd worn when he had first arrived. Her face was unwashed, more often than not. And her clothes? ... Had she changed them in the last week?

He immediately felt guilty for not being more understanding. He'd heard pregnancy could do things to families and that pregnancies could be incredibly stressful. Dane just didn't understand this change in Tasha because, according to John, she'd been fine for the first three and even four months. These days it was as if whatever control she'd had over herself had come loose. He felt sorry for her. But even sorrier for his brother.

Dane shook his head, as he walked to the kitchen door. She was at it again. Their argument carried easily on the air.

"Damn it, John. Emile says he can't look after Peppe. I need you to go give him his food. Emile did it yesterday."

"And why can't Emile give him his meal today? Peppe's his father."

"I'm sure he has a reason. What's your reason for not wanting to help out? I do all the cooking here, as it is. You don't work anymore. ... You could start doing that again too. When was the last time you cooked a meal?"

John's long-suffering sigh didn't go unnoticed.

She started in on him again. "Oh, don't start that again. I hardly ask you to do anything around here, and, the minute I do, you start complaining. Well, stop. Emile isn't home, and Peppe needs food."

Dane opened the door, wondering when Tasha was due. Another six to eight weeks? Dane shook his head, as he studied the beaten look on his brother's face through the open door. "I'll tell you what, Tasha. I'll go with you, and you can introduce me to your father," Dane offered, stepping through the doorway.

Horror flicked across her face. "What? No. No. I can't. I mean, I'm not feeling well." She dropped the food tray onto the table beside John and fled.

Dane stared, open-mouthed, then turned to face his brother, who looked equally surprised. "Well, that didn't go as expected."

John stood. "That's the story of my life right now. Nothing I say is received the way I expect it to." He glared down at the tray. "This Peppe-Emile thing is driving me nuts. Emile is Peppe's son. He should be the one to do this."

Dane didn't have an argument for that. He didn't know how bad the situation really was. He'd only seen Peppe a couple times since he'd been here, and the old man appeared more or less normal each time. Apparently things had deteriorated. "True enough. Still something is going on here if neither child wants to help the parent."

"I want him in a home. I haven't found a place, and Tasha fights the idea, but neither will she deal with him." John ran a weary hand down his face. "You even suggest that she should go see her father, and she bursts into tears."

"Perhaps she can't stand to see how badly he's deteriorating?"

"I don't know what the problem is. She won't tell me." His hands fisted, then relaxed on his hips.

Dane looked around the small kitchen. Pots sat on the table. He didn't know if food was in them or not. He was glad he was taking Jade out tonight.

He glanced down at the plate prepared for Peppe. It

looked like rice and beans. Looking around the kitchen, Dane realized how old and faded everything was. Definitely in need of a new coat of paint and new flooring. Another sign their financial troubles might be bigger than he'd initially believed. There'd been money here at one time. Not for a while though. Probably not since the death of Tasha's mother. They weren't at the level of poverty he saw rampant all over the rest of the country, but things hadn't been good here in a long time.

How had John made a living here before? As much as Dane would love to help, how could he? He had given his brother money when he'd first arrived to help him rebuild his business and to help out when the baby came. He gave them money for room and board—and yet didn't eat here.

So, if things were that tight, there'd be no money for Peppe's care either. "How expensive would it be to hire a local to care for him? Surely that would be a minor cost, given the economy right now?"

John's mouth twisted. He walked over to stare out the window. "I don't know. I mentioned something about hiring a woman to come and help out, only Tasha just got a weird look on her face and said, *No women.* Now I've seen for myself that Peppe can be in tough shape from one day to the next, and I know that Emile has lost his temper more than a couple times when he found his father had soiled himself. Apparently his father hadn't even noticed. Some furniture had to be thrown out one time."

Dane tried hard but couldn't quite contain the wrinkle of disgust. It wasn't Peppe's fault. He needed help and shouldn't be living alone. Usually in a case like this, the job fell to the family members, but, if they wouldn't or couldn't, then someone had to be hired to do the job.

"I don't think you have much choice. You can't leave him like that. If Emile and Tasha won't do it, then hire a man. Let him go there once a day and clean Peppe—give him a shave and a hot meal. I don't know what all else he needs. Surely, with so many out of work, you could find a brawny man with the right disposition to help out?"

John turned to face him.

Dane hated his brother's whipped-puppy look and the glimmer of hope sliding into the back of his eyes. Dane understood the situation John faced, but sometimes hard decisions had to be made. John would be a father soon. He needed to step forward and to be a man.

Dane couldn't resist pushing the point home. Not that John would listen. "John, if Peppe's children aren't capable of making a decision, then you have to step in and make it for them."

Straightening his back, John sighed. "I know that. Really. It's just not that simple. I need the pregnancy to be over and to have my Tasha back. I don't know what's eating away at her. It's most likely just hormones, but she's so volatile right now."

"Be that as it may, you can't leave Peppe like this. If it were your father, how would you feel?"

John snorted. "That old soldier boy would have walked off a bridge before ending up like Peppe."

"I highly doubt any of us would choose to live Peppe's not-so-golden years. I do know that we all deserve respect and to keep our dignity at times like this—and Peppe, if he really knew and understood, would be horrified."

John stared down at the tray and then back at his brother. "Do you want to come with me? Let's take a look and see how bad it really is."

"Hell no, I don't want to—but I will." Dane grinned at the dark look shooting his way. "Come on. Let's go face the Devil himself."

SUSAN CORNERED JADE in the computer room in the late afternoon. Jade had barely managed to get back to her charts, after the relief she felt at Tony's departure. Still, the work had to be done, and, now that she didn't have anyone watching over her—at least no one sitting here in the room watching over her—she wanted to plow through the charts.

"Hey. How is the paperwork going?" Susan dropped her bag on her computer station and took a tissue from her pocket.

It seemed she'd brought dozens of small tissue packets with her. "Are you getting sick?"

"I'd better not be. Tony asked me the same question." Susan grimaced, as Jade twisted her face. "Yeah, he made a good impression on all of us, *huh*? Anyway, he reminded me that no sick days were negotiated into the contract, and, if I wasn't capable of working because of an illness, he'd be forced to replace me."

Jade gasped. "What an asshole." She slapped the chart down on the desk beside her and turned to face Susan. "Did he just come here to upset everyone? 'Cause he succeeded. I am so glad he's gone."

"I second that. What did he do to you?" Susan asked curiously, pulling back her chair and sitting down heavily.

"He made a similar comment about my mental health, afraid that all these deaths would send me off the deep end … or some such bullshit."

Susan snorted. "Isn't this a fine time to worry about

that?"

"I know. We're almost a month into this. If I was going to lose it, I'd have done it when we first found those bones and chains."

Susan shivered and then sneezed. After a moment, she added, "Maybe I should go lie down. I'd hate to have this get any worse."

"Yes, you should. It's Friday. We've put in lots of overtime already. Go. Rest and come back on Monday, happy and healthy."

With a watery grin, the woman picked up her bag again. "Okay, you've convinced me. Besides, it's not as if we haven't worked every weekend so far."

"True enough. And this weekend won't be any different." Jade watched as Susan made a hasty exit, sneezing several times on the way. She returned to her workload.

Meg walked in five minutes later. "So are you excited?"

"*Hmm?*" Jade stared at her. "What did you say?"

"I asked if you were excited. About tonight? Your hot date with Dane?"

Jade flushed. She'd been trying to keep the date out of her mind all day. She found it a little hard to function with the butterflies rolling around inside. She didn't know what to expect, and her clothing choices were beyond limited. But then she didn't want to get hung up on that either. "I'm happy to be going out. Just not so secure in the whole *date* thing."

"Aha. If you haven't been dating for a while, I can see how that might be a little daunting. Still, you must get a lot of male attention. You're gorgeous."

Jade stared at her. Then laughed. "Aren't you a comic?"

Meg walked over and sat down beside her. "You, my

dear, need to work on your self-esteem. What happened to knock that down?"

The question caught Jade sideways. She leaned back to look at the woman she'd come to view as a friend. "I'm not so sure that it's been knocked down as much as knocked back a pace or two. I had a bad breakup close to one year ago and haven't ventured into that realm since."

Tilting her head sideways, Meg smiled compassionately. "That's a decent amount of time. You don't appear to be too upset over it now."

Was she? Not heartbroken, at least not now. In fact, Jade could honestly say that she'd had a lucky escape—at least from him. Other things that happened at the same time were more painful.

"No. I was angry for a long time, but that's dissipated." She shrugged. "I'm saddened at the way everything ended."

"And now Dane is in your life."

Jade grinned. "Right. At least for tonight."

"Hey, he lives in Seattle, where you live too, and he packs a load of sex appeal into that lean rangy body, doesn't he?"

"Yeah, he does that." She'd had a hell of a time falling asleep last night because of it. Damn, he looked good. That just brought back another worry. "Sex isn't an issue on a first date, is it?"

Meg raised her eyebrows. "Sex should never be an issue. It happens on some first dates, if everything is hot-hot and hotter. If that's the case, then go for it. Otherwise, it shouldn't even come up." She grinned. "Although it's a good sign if it does."

Jade smirked, as she shook her head. "It's been a few years since my last relationship started. I'd forgotten the initial heat of attraction."

"That should have been a bad sign about your previous relationship if the heat didn't last long. So Dane has got your juices flowing, has he?"

"Hell, he's probably had every female in Haiti paying attention to him." Jade said it with humor but didn't know how she felt about that.

"Hot males don't make bad mates. They are often very loyal. My partner and I have been together for a decade now. I still love him, and he's still the best-looking guy I've ever seen." Meg's smile saddened. "That's the only thing about this job. I hate being away from home."

"No wish to settle down and to start a family?"

"We've discussed it, but it's never the right time."

Meg slouched back in her chair, seemingly unaware of her own natural beauty. Then that was probably one of the reasons Jade had clicked with her so fast. She was natural, without pretention.

Jade shook her head again. "Don't think there is any one right time. If you have a strong foundation, you may want to think on it. You're what? … Thirty-three or thirty-four?"

"Thirty-seven and turning thirty-eight in a few months. I know the clock's ticking, but that's not the best determining factor. I'd rather know that gallivanting off on these jaunts is out of my system, so I'm content to stay home as a mom. I want to look forward to that stage of my journey, instead of feeling tied down by it."

"That's reasonable. At least then you'll be ready inside." Jade looked down at the stacks of charts in front of her. She might have to work all weekend to get caught up at this rate.

"*Hmm.* What about you? No desire to have kids? Although you have more time than I do." Meg smiled.

Inside, Jade winced. "Yes, I still have time. I've thought about it a lot. I was engaged, looking forward to starting a family. It's amazing how much your perspective changes after a breakup."

"Breakups are always tough. If you didn't make it to the married part, chances are you're much better off without him."

Jade agreed. She *was* so much better off. "I know that now, but that's the thing. When you're in a relationship, it's hard to see what you really do have. You're too close, so to speak."

"True enough. Just don't take that kind of baggage on your date tonight. Dane looks like he's the kind of guy who gets out and enjoys life a little. Sounds like you could use the extra attention."

Jade nodded. "I'm looking forward to that."

THE TREK TO Peppe's cabin took only a few minutes. They walked past a clump of spindly trees, their steps sounding loudly on the hard-packed dirt path. Dane stopped and turned around. "I thought he was a lot farther away. Although that's a good thing." He grinned. "I actually have plans for tonight."

John stared at him in astonishment. "Really? Who is she?"

Dane shook his head. "Not sure I want to say. I haven't let a lady get close like this in a long time. I'm taking her out tonight."

"Really? Wow!" He might have been planning to say more, but they'd reached the cabin door. No sounds came from within. John climbed the first and then the second step, before turning back to his brother. "All joking aside, … Peppe isn't quite right. I know I haven't said too much about him. It's complicated. He has good days and bad days, but his good days are often hard to distinguish from the others now." John turned to Dane quickly, uneasily. "I don't know what shape he'll be in.

Dane looked at the cabin door from behind his brother. The porch out front was wide, but the cabin had to be decades old. If it was sound, then age was no problem, but this building could also use some help. *Damn.* He needed to have a serious talk with his brother. "My question is, why is this such an issue?" He strode in front of his brother, opened the door, and reeled backward. "Oh, for Christ's sake."

His arm came up to protect his nose. He stumbled backward and down the steps, coughing. After a moment, he bent over his knees and took several deep breaths. "What is that smell? Jesus, John. Please tell me the old man isn't living in that."

"The place has been cleaned several times, but that damn smell never goes away." John winced. He stood with his back to the door, staring back the way they'd come. "That's why I can't do this. I'm standing here now because I can't force myself to go inside. How sad is that?"

Dane took several deep breaths, trying to clear his head. "Damn it, John. Leaving someone to live in that sewer is criminal. If you won't do something about this, then I will." He fisted his hands on his hips. "But you won't like my methods. I'll call in the authorities over this."

John snorted. "Like they'll give a shit. This isn't the States, Dane. We don't have the same regulatory bodies here as are back home." He grunted. "Besides, Tasha would never forgive you. Or me. They look after their own here."

Home? That's the first he'd heard his brother refer to the US as home. Did his brother want to return to Seattle? Take his family with him? Dane would have to give that some thought. In the meantime, this mess had to be dealt with. "That's fine, *if* they do look after their own. Living in this cabin can't be good for anyone. Damn it, John, stand up and be a man."

John shuddered, releasing a deep breath. His shoulders sagged, and he closed his eyes briefly. "Fine. I will look for someone tomorrow, and I just won't tell her."

"You'll have to hire more than one person, or you won't keep the first one. This place needs to be burned. It's unbelievable."

John turned to face the open door and frowned. "I wonder why Peppe hasn't come out. He never misses a good fight."

"Then go in and see. For all you know, the old man died from the rot in there."

Shooting his brother a dark look, John took a deep breath and raced inside. He came out several minutes later, gasping for air. "He's not here. I wonder if he's taken off again?"

Dane snorted. "Hell, I wouldn't stay in there either. Does he go out much?" Dane spun around, wondering where the hell the old man could have disappeared to. If he carried the aroma of this cabin, they should smell him miles away.

"He's been on his own for a long time, so I have no idea. I've avoided coming here for months. But, from what Emile and Tasha have said, he used to take off for weeks on end."

Dane hopped up, took a deep breath, pinched his nose, and walked into the small cabin. There was no sign of the old man. His bed was empty, the one chair in the place … empty. Nothing but dirt, trash, waste. He shuddered. Unable to hold his breath any longer, he bolted outside. "Whew. That is beyond rank, John."

"Tasha said Emile had been shaving and washing the old man." John turned back to stare inside the small cabin. "I wonder if Tasha knows Emile hasn't been looking after him?"

"He's her brother. She has to know what he's like." Dane stepped several steps farther away, gasping for clean air. "Hell, I know what Emile's like, and I can tell you that he does the minimum at every turn. If he can get out of a job, he will, and, if he can get away with a half-assed job, then consider that done too."

John shuddered. "I wonder if he's even been feeding him?"

"I'd say, chances are, he started out with good intentions a few months ago, whenever Tasha quit looking after Peppe, and then Emile's done less and less each trip back here. That's probably why Peppe's taken off."

John's face twisted.

"What?" Dane puzzled why John wouldn't meet his gaze.

"Tasha quit looking after her father a long time ago. She's using her pregnancy as an excuse to get out of coming to help with her father for right now, but she had a broken leg before that, remember? Anyway, I don't think she's cared for him for close to a year, not since the big quake, I think."

Staring at the woods around them, Dane shook his head. "Why? I don't understand. I'm trying, John, but your new family is a little weird."

"I know. The thing is, you don't realize just how weird

until something happens. It's like the earthquake changed things. She wasn't like this a couple years ago. I loved her so much then."

"*Then?*" Dane jumped on that one word. It went along with John's earlier comment about *back home.*

John ran his right hand over his short dark hair. "I didn't mean that. It's just that she was more loveable back then. I feel like I live in a war zone. Each day I have to work hard at being tolerant and patient. Sometimes I'm not sure I'll make it to the end of the pregnancy."

"As it is, I didn't think you had it in you to be this patient. I don't think I could be." Dane meant it. He thought he'd been a very patient man, until he'd seen his brother's tolerance. His brother was a bloody saint.

"I have to find a way to make this all work. I can't lose it all *again.*"

It was that one word—*again*—that broke Dane's heart. "Damn it, John. You have to stop letting the past haunt you. You won't lose Tasha. Just because you lost Elise in a car accident, that doesn't mean you'll lose every woman you love. You don't have to lose anything or anyone. If this isn't working out, you need to take another look and figure out how to make it work."

"I know. ... I know," John cried out. "Why do you think I've been paralyzed with inactivity on the Peppe issue? And it's the same for my company. I'm bankrupt. My marriage is on the rocks, and I don't know how to save it. My child is due to be born in a month, and I don't know how to make that a good thing. I can't stand my li—"

John's voice cut out, as if sliced by a knife. He stared at Dane, horrified. "Oh God. I didn't say that, did I?"

Dane's heart broke. "Yes, you did." He pursed his lips

and thought about what John had really said. "How much of your problem is because you don't know what you really want?" John appeared to not want anything he currently had—but had he figured that out yet? Some truths had to be reached on their own. God help John, if he decided that to be true.

John lifted a trembling hand. "Probably everything. I should never have started my own company. I'm not cut out for it. I need a job that pays decent and lets me go home to my family every day. I can't keep doing this." John plunked down on the bottom step of Peppe's cabin. "I haven't told Tasha that no money's left. No business is left."

"That's why you've been so patient and let her walk all over you?"

He nodded. "I feel like I'm coming apart at the seams. I've been waiting for the right time to discuss it, but it never comes."

"Jesus, John, there is no right time for bad news. You have to tell her." Dane groaned and stared at the festering cabin in front of him. "That's why you haven't done anything about Peppe. You don't have the money, do you? What about the chunk I gave you?"

Gazing at his brother with a defeated look, John shook his head. "No. It's all gone."

Chapter 13

MIKE STARED AT the bones, the poor light in the lab trailer derailing his progress. He hadn't left with the others, even though it was the end of work on a Friday afternoon—their time for beer out on the garden patio. And beer would be good right now. Not to mention he'd planned on talking to them about the hike he had in mind. Only he hadn't had a chance to check the options yet.

This mess with the manacles and bones sitting on his table had to be sorted out first.

He didn't know what to do with the information he had. The authorities didn't care. The local people didn't appear to care. So few people had shown up for DNA tests that he was beginning to suspect all their processing would be for naught. They could have just created a second grave site right beside the first one and moved over the bodies that didn't fit the parameters of the ones they were looking for. Would have cut the work in half.

Damn it. He knew these manacled women had been murdered. He'd bet his thirty-year reputation on it. And no one cared. *That's what hurt the most. All these women mistreated, captive for who knows how long? ... And then they'd been murdered. And no one cared.*

And the details his team unearthed weren't required or welcome because, as far as the police were concerned, this wasn't something they would follow up on.

In the US, there would have been teams of specialists digging out this site to determine the type of dirt above and around, collecting the bugs, etc. Here, there was only him—and his team. And he didn't have the necessary equipment to collect all the evidence and to record all the details.

Tony had been adamant. Pass over the information to the authorities and get off the case. He'd said, *There's no joy in being the bearer of the bad news here. They won't thank us, not with the thousands of people unaccounted for here. Let it go. Process and move on.*

Speaking to the empty trailer, Mike said, "Right. And what about justice for these women?"

He walked over to the front of the trailer and stuck his head out. When he looked around, he heard something rustling in the woods, only he couldn't see anyone.

"Hey, Doc."

Mike squinted. John's brother-in-law walked toward him. *Emile.* Dressed for the heat in a tank top and blue jeans—the uniform of choice the world over—he strolled toward the lab trailer.

"Hi. Are you looking for Dane?"

"*Nah*, I know where he is. We're all looking for my father, who's gone wandering. He's not quite right in the head and gets lost easily." Emile's gaze shifted from the lab trailer to the rocks surrounding the clearing.

"Oh, dear. I haven't seen him around. Sorry." Mike couldn't help but glance around the clearing at the same time.

Emile shoved his hands into his pockets. "No problem. I figured you were here, so I asked."

Mike hesitated. He hated to ask the young man, but a

few minutes of his help would be huge. He needed to get the remains stored away. "Hey, while you're here, would you mind giving me a hand moving a few things over to the other trailer?"

Emile's face twisted. "As long as it's not bodies. I don't hold on touching the dead."

"It is bones, only you won't have to touch them. I already have them in sealed bags on the stretchers." His words rushed out to reassure Emile. "I just need you to grab an end and help me move them to the other trailer."

Emile looked like he wanted to refuse but couldn't figure out how. Mike pressed his advantage. "Honest. A five-minute job—not even that. I can't leave them here over the weekend. They need to be locked in the reefer truck."

Emile's face scrunched in horror.

Mike spoke faster, before Emile could run as far and as fast as he could in the opposite direction. "I promise. You won't even see them. They are packed up. They're so small I can even put them both on the same stretcher." He stared hopefully at Emile. "Please."

Emile stared around, as if hoping someone else would show.

"There's no one else. It has to be you."

Emile's shoulders sagged. "One trip—and I don't touch anything but the stretcher handles."

"Done." Mike brightened. "Let's do it right now. It'll be over in five minutes."

Emile, once the decision was made, followed along willingly enough. He grabbed the one end of the stretcher and waited while Mike shifted the bags and laid them on top of each other. Mike grabbed his end of the stretcher. "Okay, here we go."

He'd been right. The trip took about two minutes. And Emile, true to his word, refused to help open doors or touch the bags. Mike shook his head, trying hard to understand. Not everyone could handle his profession. Death freaked out so many people.

Too bad. Everyone came to the same end, regardless of how hard they tried to avoid it.

"Thanks, Emile. I can take it from here."

Emile backed away from the freezer trailer as if afraid he'd be bagged and laid next to the others. Mike watched him almost hyperventilate with relief.

"Hey, are you all right?" He walked down to check on him.

Emile glanced back. "Yeah. I'm okay. Just don't want to be in there." He motioned toward the trailer. "Have these ones been identified now?"

"Not yet." Mike looked back down the long interior. "We have lots to do."

"What about the ones we just brought over. Are they done?"

"They've been processed, just not identified." Mike walked out the rest of the way and slammed the heavy door shut. He slid across the bolt closure and snapped on the big lock.

"Most are on one side. We put those on the opposite side," Emile pressed.

"Yeah." Mike gave him a weary smile. "Those ones are special."

Emile's gaze narrowed. "Why? Are they not all special?"

With a long look at the grave site and the bodies that still waited to be uncovered, Mike couldn't help but agree with him. "That is so true. Yet even in a large grave like that, some are different." Mike headed back to the lab. "Thank you for the help."

Emile followed him back to the lab trailer and glanced around the small room. "Lots of equipment. Not much space."

"Yeah. That should be our new logo." Mike glanced up at him with a smile—in time to see horror scrunch Emile's face. "What is it? What's wrong?"

Emile pointed to the floor, where they'd moved the stretcher. "What's that?"

Bending down, Mike found two chain links that must have fallen out from one of the women's body bags. The rusty iron clanged as he placed the links into a clear bag. "Damn. I missed these. I wonder which bag they came from."

Emile's face paled. He straightened and raced outside.

"Thanks again for your help, Emile," Mike called after him.

He never responded. Mike walked outside, sealing the chain in a small plastic bag. Emile was bent over a bush off to one side. *Uh-oh.*

As Mike watched, Emile coughed and spewed again. Mike stepped back to give him some privacy. *Damn.* He hadn't meant to upset him. Some people just didn't handle this stuff well. He set about putting the piece of chain away properly.

He walked out to check on him a few minutes later, but Emile had left.

Mike hoped he'd find his father. This wasn't a good place to go missing. Then again, this grave was right next to the old man's property, and he'd lived here for decades. He probably knew every rock and tree in the area. Positioned in the rocks and hills as their camp was, the sun had long disappeared behind the greenery, throwing lengthening shadows and weird fingers of light through the area.

Straightening, Mike stretched out his sore back and shoulders. Lord, he was tired. Long day. Long week actually. He double-checked the temperature and the lock on the reefer, before heading over to lock the lab trailer.

Time to leave.

EMILE SLIPPED AROUND the rocks, watching as the old man left the smaller trailer. Emile's mouth still smarted from the sour retchings of his stomach. How could people work in there? Touching the dead, violating their bodies, their souls. He shuddered.

How wrong could life get? He'd thought things had been bad after that big earthquake. He'd seen things that still gave him nightmares. He'd watched things people had done to each other in the name of survival.

Survival also had little to do with some of what he'd witnessed. Predators had preyed on the dead, the living, and those caught in between. He'd seen thieves empty pockets, steal shoes, grab anything that could be removed, and run to the next body, alive or dead. It hadn't mattered.

The things Emile had seen in town had been unbelievably difficult. And none of it touched on the horror of what he'd found later. Something so awful, so terrible, he couldn't stop thinking about it since. He'd had to clean up the mess, and doing something to protect another had seemed right at the time—until he'd been seen.

His stomach dry heaved with the painful memories.

He hadn't been the same since.

Then the horror had turned to fascination, and that scared him even more. The very idea had settled into his psyche and had rooted, then had sprouted into another horrible concept, only this time he was a part of it.

He shuddered.

He couldn't do that to a woman.

He shouldn't do that to a woman.

But he would—if he got the chance.

With one last look at the empty lab trailers, and the place he'd find two unprotected women, he refocused on finding his old man.

Damn him, anyway.

THE BEAUTIFUL EVENING and cool breeze blowing over Jade's heated skin made warmth blossom inside her. She sighed happily. Her hotel room held a lightness that she enjoyed, and it certainly beat the afternoon mugginess that had settled in today.

She'd spent all week in a state of nervous anticipation. Now that the time for her date had arrived, she was listening for vehicles, checking out every unusual sound, and doing lots of heavy sighing. Much to Meg's amusement.

For tonight, Jade had chosen her one decent sundress and a light sweater, just in case a wind came up. Sandals and a little light makeup too. Why she'd brought makeup when she almost never wore it, she didn't know. She'd been thinking ahead obviously. Plus she thought it was a good sign that she wanted to look special for Dane, … and that made her smile.

She missed the closeness, the specialness that came when she was part of a loving twosome. Even if it had been a long time ago. Even if it hadn't stood the test of time and trauma.

At the same time, trust and confidence were now bigger considerations for Jade before entering a new relationship.

Dane made her heart warm; she'd be happy to see where this went. Actually she'd be more than happy to help it along. He did make her hormones pay attention. She'd always enjoyed sex. She hadn't missed it because she'd been so busy being mad and hurt. Now, however, a part of her was raring to make up for lost time. How contrary could she be?

Still, the butterflies in her stomach wouldn't calm down, and honestly, she was starving again. She hoped he'd planned for a decent meal. She took a deep breath and walked downstairs to the lobby.

Dane walked in the front door as she reached the front desk. The sight of him stopped Jade in her tracks. *Damn.* He looked beyond good. Black jeans and a white cotton shirt with a stand-up collar. Only it wasn't the clothes that caused her breath to hitch. It was the way he wore them.

She sighed. All that casual muscle and grace. Like a lion roaming his territory. He knew how he looked, was proud of it, and didn't need to show off to be appreciated.

"Hi." Dane stopped in front of her, a warm welcome on his face. His eyes ran appreciatively over her.

Yeah, he was good for her self-confidence. "Hi. You didn't tell me what we were doing or where we're going, and I only have a limited wardrobe with me, so—"

"You look great. Come on. Let's get out of here." He put an arm over her shoulders and walked her out to his truck. "We're heading to a place my brother told me about."

"Perfect. I haven't been anywhere here, so it will be new and different."

"Good. I like an adventurous spirit." He opened the truck door and helped her up to the passenger seat. After walking around to the other side, he hopped in and started the engine.

She buckled her seat belt and settled in for the drive. "Adventure is nice. Life has been a little depressing lately."

"We can fix that. That's one thing I learned in my time here. Every day is a gift. Haiti has been through so much that sometimes we all need to work a little harder to find the good in the bad."

Jade glanced at him. He drove the same as he did everything else. Capably and with restrained power. *Sexy.* She sighed. Lord, she had it bad. When she'd decided to move on with her life, she'd done so with a vengeance.

"Problems?" He frowned, glancing over at her quickly.

"No. I've been thinking the same thing about Haiti. Everyone here has been through so much. It makes our lives back home look easy in comparison. It's been good coming back here. I needed to see the progress."

"Coming back? Were you here before?" He turned the truck around the next corner and headed for one of the main roads.

"I was here in the aftermath of the big earthquake. Did a three-week stint with a mortuary team then. It was brutal. Emotionally and physically."

He whistled softly and gunned the truck forward. "Then let's show you some of the better sights of Haiti and replace those more painful memories with beautiful ones. Help you to put these old memories where they belong—in the past."

Chapter 14

T HE QUIET DIGNITY of the small restaurant surprised Jade. As if it were proud to be standing after all these years. Old, distinguished, and family run, the restaurant had the bulk of its seating area under the open sky on decks of different levels. Jade and Dane sat on an outside edge, surrounded by brightly colored hanging lanterns. Several other tables full of diners were discreetly placed throughout. Small screens offered privacy, while allowing almost everyone a view of the sleepy harbor. The tang of the salty ocean mixed with the heavenly smells coming from the kitchen.

Beaches were everywhere here—gorgeous blue water, smooth sand, with the locals working their boats from one side of the bay to the other. Not the typical resort beach but a working, living, breathing part-of-the-people beach.

Now that work had settled into a routine, Jade would like to take a day off every weekend and explore. Going out on a date, like tonight, was a wonderful way to start her new plan.

While they watched, the sky slipped through a rainbow of colors. The sunset shifted and changed so quickly, she couldn't take her eyes off it. "I've never seen anything so beautiful," she murmured. Warmth wrapped around her heart. She wasn't lying. Right now everything felt perfect. She smiled, turned her face up to the evening sky, and closed her eyes.

"Neither have I."

Startled, she turned to face him. "Sorry?"

"I haven't seen anything so beautiful either."

Only he was staring right at her. Heat swamped her cheeks, as she blushed like a schoolgirl. "Wow, thanks." She gave a light laugh. "I'm not used to flattery."

"And why is that?" His curious gaze studied her face. "You're seriously gorgeous, you know?"

Flustered from his sincerity, she answered with a soft smile, "Thank you again. I haven't been out much in the last year, and I've forgotten how to accept a compliment."

"Nursing a broken heart?"

Her fingers tapped a tempo on the table, as she tried to sort out the best thing to say. "Not quite. Started that way. Now it's a matter of not allowing my history to dictate my future. In other words, not to see my ex and his deficits in every man."

"Ouch." He winced.

A giggle escaped. She clapped a hand over her mouth, staring at him in astonishment. He gave a shout of laughter. When her merriment calmed, she said, "Sorry, I was trying to be honest, only maybe that was too honest. I'm not judging you, and, if I were, you've already got him beat by a mile. So let's change the subject. This evening is too nice to ruin."

Deep-blue eyes gazed into hers. He reached across the table and clasped her hand in his. "Nicely put. And you're right. It is too nice an evening for such conversation. However, I am sorry about the bad experiences."

"Everyone has them." She smiled down at their hands. His so rough and strong, working man's hands. Hers so soft and small—she lived in surgical gloves. Yet their hands fit together like interlocking puzzle pieces. She stroked the long line of his thumb, loving his instant response, as her hand was captured between both of his.

"I don't know," Dane replied. "My life hasn't been filled with drama or heartache."

His tone held no suggestion of anything dark in his history. No censorship either. She searched his gaze. "No bad breakups?"

Dane frowned and stared down at his fingers, clenching automatically.

Her fingers, of their own volition, squeezed back. She didn't want him to be alone with bad memories. As she had been. "Yeah. That's what I mean."

He looked at her in surprise. Then understanding lit the depths of his gaze. "Not me. My brother. He's the reason for whatever you were assuming. He's been through some seriously bad periods in his life. I thought he'd found better times."

"John?"

Dane nodded. "Just the two of us are left, so I tend to keep an eye on him, although he's obviously an adult." Dane shrugged self-consciously. "Family. You can't let them wallow."

Jade laughed, a warm smile blooming across her face. "Isn't that the truth? You sound just like my brother, Duncan. I'm here because of him. He convinced me to come back."

"It was *that* bad?" Dane searched her face. "John won't talk about it much."

"It's not easy. Duncan wanted me to spew everything too. Only talking about it actually made it all come alive again. I had to relive stuff I'd rather not see again."

Dane leaned back, though his index finger gently stroked the back of her hand. "I'm sorry. Sorry that so many people suffered. I never considered the impact on volunteers and rescuers." He stared off at the sunset.

From the look on his face, Jade didn't think he was enjoying Mother Nature's artwork.

"John has slipped back into someone I barely recognize. The things he's doing—or rather, not doing—" Dane shook his head. "It's hard to stand by and to let life happen to those you love."

"Duncan basically said the same thing to me." She studied their interlocking fingers. That felt right somehow. She hadn't expected to feel anything in Haiti, except pain and anguish. She'd been wrong, and Duncan had been right. She'd have to remember to tell him that. "I'll call my brother tomorrow and tell him that he's the best brother anyone could have."

Dane chuckled. "See? That's the difference between having a little sister versus a little brother. John would die before saying something like that."

"That's a guy thing. Duncan pushed and prodded me for months now. He deserves to know that I'm healing."

"Absolutely. What does he do?"

She gave him a quick rundown, turning the conversation to more generic issues. Several hours later, after they'd worked through many topics, dinner, and dessert, Dane looked at her and asked, "Do you want to go back to the hotel now or would you like to walk down by the water?" He pointed out a path that led to the beach via the side of the restaurant.

"Oh, perfect. I'd love to go for a walk. I'm in no hurry

to return."

She waited by the path, as he took care of the bill. When he walked over, he slipped an arm around her shoulders and led her to the water's edge.

Tonight was about magic. About possibilities. About the future.

They spent a sensual hour in the moonlight, with water lapping at the shore, as they walked close together, discussing anything that came up. By the time they came to a small wooden bench, Jade realized how much she'd learned about Dane and his character. The more she learned, the more she liked and respected the man. He reminded her of Duncan.

She sat down on the bench, tugging him down beside her. "I'm having a wonderful evening tonight. I know we have to leave soon, but this is truly special."

He grinned. "Glad you've enjoyed it. Maybe we can do it again."

"Absolutely." She'd love to repeat this evening—several times if possible.

"If you don't have any plans for tomorrow, maybe we can go for coffee or take a walk. Something simple."

She smiled. "That would be lovely."

PARKED OUTSIDE HER hotel twenty minutes later, Dane studied her fine-boned features, the delicate blush of color. She didn't have the same suntan that most of her other team members sported, probably because she worked in the lab so much. He loved the relaxed peacefulness he read on her face tonight.

Jade often looked like life was a serious business, … one that reaped few rewards. He wanted to show her how much fun life could be. How good relationships could be. How good the two of them could be. If she gave them, … *him*, a chance.

But he didn't want to scare her off.

Somewhere in all of this, he needed her to feel comfortable with him. For her to move at her own pace. For her to be in control.

He leaned back in the driver's seat, turned slightly to face her, and opened his arms, waiting to see what she would do.

When she smiled shyly, it made his heart melt.

She slid across the bench seat and snuggled close. She grasped both sides of his face, then stretched up slowly, oh-so-slowly, and put her lips against his. In a kiss so gentle, so special, it almost broke his heart. Gently stroking her arms with one hand, the other moved soothingly down and across her back and tucked her against his chest.

He felt a shiver slide down her back, so he drew her in closer, warming her slowly beneath his caressing hands. He wanted her. Had wanted her since he had first laid eyes on her. And a little cuddling in the truck was a great prelude, except he was no untried kid. He wanted so much more. And not in the truck, like two crazed teenagers. She deserved a soft bed and all the trappings that were possible for their first night together. And him? Well, he deserved time. Time to savor her, to explore, to enjoy. He moaned softly against her lips.

She pulled back slightly and smiled at him. "That's your goodnight kiss."

He smiled slowly, wickedly. "Fine, then here's *your* goodnight kiss," he whispered, caressing her lips with his breath. His warm hands slid up her back to comb through her silky hair, anchoring her in place. Then he lowered his head. He didn't ravish; he didn't take. He coaxed, soothed, and enticed. When she sagged against him, he pulled back slightly, dropping his forehead against hers. "If you're going in alone, you need to go now."

She smiled and nuzzled against his face and chin. "And if I don't?"

"Then you'll be going in with company. And I don't want to cheat either of us by rushing you at this stage. If you need time, I'm happy to move slowly—well, as slowly as we can go when we're short on time." He laughed self-consciously.

She laughed too, a soft joyous sound that enchanted even as he questioned it.

"What part was funny?"

"Slightly slow is good, but I'm finding I'm much less affected than I thought I was." She dropped a kiss on his chin.

His breath caught. *Damn.* Images ripped through his mind. He almost groaned aloud. "Meaning?"

"I might be okay with quick, but this voice of reason is telling me to slow down slightly." She retreated, a regretful smile on her face. "Have to say, I'm not comfortable with sex on the first date. No matter how tempting."

He kissed the tip of her nose, before she retreated out of reach. "Tempting? So how about dinner tomorrow? The next day? The day after?"

Her gaze widened.

He rushed in with words. "I want to spend as much time with you as I can. To find out what we have. So think about me. About there being an *us.* And, if a weekend away appeals, give me some dates that work, and I'll set it up."

She laughed. "So I get to decide?"

"Absolutely. I can get away any weekend. Your schedule is a little different. I'm serious about seeing you after we return to the States too, but I'd like to spend as much time as we can together here."

Dane's cell rang, interrupting the intimate moment. Jade slid back slightly to give him room. She'd been snuggled tightly against him, and he hated the immediate coolness that drifted into the space. He wanted to tug her back, but the moment was lost.

He pulled out his phone, wondered at the number on display, and answered it.

DANE TWISTED ON the front seat of his truck and clicked a button on his phone. "I've just put the call on Speaker. It's Bruce. Something's wrong."

Jade's eyes widened, and she cast a glance out her window toward the hotel. "Bruce, what's up?"

"Have you seen or heard from Dr. Mike?"

The anxiety level coming through the phone made Jade's stomach knot and her throat catch. "Not since lunchtime. I worked in the office here at the hotel all afternoon. I don't think he'd returned by the time I left tonight."

"Right. He's not answering his phone. He's got one of the SUVs, and we don't know where he is."

She swallowed and stared at Dane. Dr. Mike wasn't old, but anything could have happened. "Could he have gone out for dinner or into town for a little fun after a tough week? It is Friday night."

"Maybe." Bruce's doubtful voice didn't put any credence to her theory though. "He should be back, if he went for dinner."

"What time is it?"

"Almost midnight."

Dane pointed at his lit watch display to confirm the time. "Wow. I had no idea it was so late. What do you want me to do?"

"I don't know. I can hardly raise an alarm just because he didn't come back from the job site and isn't answering his phone. So I guess we wait." He sighed heavily. "But I don't like it."

"We're in the truck, almost at the hotel," she lied, rolling her eyes at the wicked grin that flashed on Dane's face. "We can take a run past the site, if you'd like us to check for him there. Just to ensure he's not still working. You know how he felt about processing those remains."

Bruce's voice brightened. "Hey, I never thought about that. Maybe that's what he's doing. But he should have answered his phone then."

"Not if his battery is dead. Besides, I don't think Dane will mind driving out there with me." She glanced over at Dane, who nodded in agreement. "Dr. Mike may also have stopped in at the authorities to talk to someone, … and that could take hours."

"You're right." Bruce paused. "He could be anywhere. I'm just paranoid."

"Better than uncaring. We'll take a drive to the lab to be sure." She disconnected the call and handed the phone back to Dane. "Sorry, I guess I should consider picking up a cell phone of my own while here."

He started the engine. "I gather Dr. Mike is missing?"

"I don't know that he's missing, but no one's seen him in hours, and he's not answering his phone."

Dane pulled the truck onto the main road. "I know it's none of my business, however, what's with the going-to-the-authorities business?"

"Dr. Mike found something—well, we all did actually—that raised a few questions." She smiled apologetically. "I'm not at liberty to say what, but Bruce stopped and spoke with the police yesterday. Said they weren't too bothered." She frowned. "They told him, if we came across definite proof, then we could come back and talk to them again."

Dane raised an eyebrow at her, before turning his attention to maneuver through the surprising amount of traffic for a Friday night. "*Hmm*. Drop a bomb like that, then don't fill in the details. Okay. I don't like it, but I can understand you not being able to speak freely." He thought for a moment. "I don't know how effective the police are here at this time. They are dealing with high-priority issues that affect their people *now*. If whatever you found is associated with the grave from a year ago, ... I don't think it'll be a priority."

"True enough." She shrugged. "It's easy to judge. From their perspective, we waltzed in here with fancy degrees and equipment and tore open a grave that everyone had been happy enough to leave alone. Now we want to make waves because of a few of the bodies."

"A few. So not an isolated case?" Dane frowned. "That's not great."

"Nope." The sky had taken on a dark-on-darker splotching look. Stars had all but disappeared behind clouds. She pointed it out. "I hate to say anything superstitious, but now the sky's almost angry looking."

He laughed. "Wait until you've been here a bit longer. I've never known such a people for their rituals and beliefs.

Tasha helps her cousins make and sell these little eerie dolls and totems to the tourists. The house is full of them in various stages. I honestly don't know why anyone would pay good money for them."

Jade shuddered and told him what Magrim had said to her that day she'd gone shopping. "What freaked me out the most was the weird look in her eyes when delivering the message."

"Did you believe her?" Dane raised an eyebrow, as he studied her face.

Shifting uncomfortably, Jade wished she hadn't brought it up. "I didn't *not* believe her. Her message was just so weird." Jade quoted, *"Danger stalks you. You see it, but you don't understand it. Careful. Or you will join those who have gone before."* She shuddered again. "If I'd gone to a séance or something else as ridiculous, then I'd have tossed it off as a marketing ploy. However, the hotel manager says Magrim is for real, and I'd better watch my back." She shivered in the slightly cooled air. Magrim, murder victims, and now a missing Dr. Mike. Not an uplifting series of events.

"Well, I wouldn't let her worry you. Just be careful. If anything suspicious is going on at the grave site, then you don't want the news to get out. Things are still pretty primitive here—the laws, minimal. People disappear all the time."

Horrified, she stared at him. Swallowing hard, she asked, "Like Dr. Mike?"

DANE DROVE FAST in the building darkness. He had bright headlights and great night vision, and he pushed the truck to eat through the miles. Though she was quiet, he could tell

Jade was beyond freaked out. He should not have said anything about disappearances. Still, if something had gone wrong, no point in sugarcoating it. Bruce hadn't brought in the necessary security, and there could already be one casualty.

He hoped he was wrong.

"Do you have to drive this fast?" Her timid voice penetrated his thoughts.

"Sorry." He eased back on the gas. "I'm used to it, and I know the roads."

"I thought you might have been angry at something," she said in a small voice.

Startled, he looked over at her. "In a way I am. But not at you. I texted my brother to see if they'd found his father-in-law earlier, and your conversation about Dr. Mike reminded of that conversation."

"What? Is he missing too?"

He kept his gaze focused on the road ahead, as he answered slowly, hesitantly. "Not really. He's walked away from home again, something he's done many times over the last few years. It's more worrisome now, as he's not himself mentally anymore. I spent time looking for him earlier, before I picked you up. Now the family doesn't want me involved. They don't like what I was saying."

"Saying?"

He felt the intensity of her gaze, rather than saw it. "Yeah. You know, like call in a search party, notify the authorities. Basics." Dane turned to watch the shock develop on her face. She was so open and expressive, she'd make a lousy poker player.

"And they didn't want to get help to find him? Why not?" she asked incredulously.

"Beats me. I expected more from John. That's what I meant earlier. He's changed—and not in a good way. Or maybe he's been this way for years, and I haven't seen it because we've not had much to do with each other over the last decade."

"Do you think he's influenced by his new family?"

"I suspect so. Tasha was muttering something at the kitchen table when I left. Looked like she was creating more of those damn dolls."

"Yuck." Jade explained what she'd learned about Vodou from Susan. "The ones I've seen were beyond freaky."

"The ones she was working on today were just papier-mâché, from the looks of it." He turned his attention back to navigating through the potholes on the road. "I didn't ask. I remember once, when I first arrived, I made a comment that she didn't like. Not sure if she took exception to what I said or to the way I said it. It was the first time I'd seen the temperamental side of her …"

"And you've seen plenty since?"

"Yeah, you could say that. John says the pregnancy isn't easy on her."

"Oh."

A weird silence filled the cab. *Uh-oh.* He glanced sideways at her. "What did I say?"

"Nothing."

Now that was a lie. He didn't need to see her face to know something was wrong. "Yes, I did. You're different. As if I said something offensive."

She avoided his gaze, staring out into the dark of night instead. "It's not you. It's me. I lost a baby a year ago, and sometimes I'm a little sensitive."

He sighed. "I am sorry. I didn't know."

"How could you? I didn't tell you."

Her voice was lighter, but still she wasn't saying something. "Was that related to the bad breakup?"

"Yeah. I can't say the breakup caused the miscarriage, as I was pretty broken up over everything going on in my life at that time—but my ex came to me in the hospital to let me know that he wasn't upset about the loss, as my mental state was questionable. And maybe I should seek help."

"Bastard." Soft and deadly, his voice hardened with fury. "There is no excuse for that kind of stuff. Why are people such assholes anyway?"

Her voice, when she answered, was soft, contemplative. "I'd like to think he was hurting from the loss of our child."

"Losing the baby would have been rough, but it wasn't your fault."

"Maybe it was." She shifted uncomfortably on the seat. "I hadn't been home from Haiti for very long, and I wasn't handling that experience well. It had been a terrible trip. I felt so guilty because I had a comfortable home, and the poor people here had no place to go." She stared out the window.

He had to lean closer to hear her next words.

"Worse, I wanted to stay home."

"Which is understandable." At the lack of a response, he added, "And you've stayed home since?"

She laughed. "Yeah. Until my brother forced me to face my fears, and you know what? I found out that it's much easier to let go than I thought."

He couldn't get his mind wrapped around what she'd been through already. But, as long as she was handling it and moving on, then he was good. Emotional women, as he was learning from Tasha, weren't the easiest to be around. He wouldn't expect caterwauling and screaming from Jade, but one never knew what existed underneath.

The rocks shone in the headlights as he pulled into the small clearing. "No SUV."

She frowned. "I see that. I'll check the doors, as I'm here anyway."

He drove to the small porch, his headlights shining on the front door. Jade hopped out and went to check the lock. Giving him a thumbs-up, she went to the refrigerator truck.

On her way back, she told him. "Both are locked tight. I want to walk to the grave site and confirm he isn't lying injured somewhere."

"If he was, his vehicle would be here."

"Not if it was stolen." She raised an eyebrow.

She was right. He turned off the truck, hopped out, and pocketed the keys. "Let's go."

There was enough moonlight to show them the way. He reached for her arm and tucked it against his anyway. He didn't want her falling and hurting herself. The path was uneven and rocky in good light, and, with poor light, this path could be an ankle breaker. In a few minutes they reached the grave site.

"I don't see anything." Then again he hadn't brought a flashlight.

Jade motioned to the rocks in front of them. "I'll climb up to make sure. At least that way, I can have a good look around."

Dane moved first. He stepped onto the first big boulder and then onto the second and the third. He held out his hand and helped her up beside him each time. The moonlight cast an eerie glow on the rocks and created squat blue shadows off others. "I don't see anyone here."

She stared around at the empty vastness surrounded by

dark trees and hills. "I guess you're right. It was a faint hope. I just thought that maybe …"

"It only took us a minute to be sure. Now we are. Are you good to go back to the hotel now?"

"I guess. What about you? Do you want to check in with your brother? See if they found the old man?"

"I'll text him."

Jade released his hand and made her way down to ground level. She walked around while he sent his brother a text. He waited for a moment, then sent a second one. "He's not answering."

She turned to stare at him. "Do you want to stop on the way back and check in?"

He stared at her. What he wanted was to spend the night with her, and that wouldn't happen, … not this weekend. Next weekend—who knew? He did not want to take her to John's house because she'd be party to any scene that developed there. Perhaps an ugly scene he didn't want to expose her to. Lately there'd been plenty of those. "No, I'll take you to the hotel first."

She shrugged and walked to the clearing and his truck. She stopped abruptly and pointed to something in the rocks, over by the property line. "What's that red spot in the rocks, just below the tree line?"

He frowned, barely making out what she was talking about. "Let's find out."

She led the way. The moon slunk behind the clouds, dimming their vision yet again. Dane hopped over several rocks and came down beside the crumpled figure in front of him. "Shit."

"What is it?" She reached his side, as he answered.

"It's not *what*, but *who*. … It's Emile."

Chapter 15

JADE WOULD LIKE to think that, in emergency situations, life in Haiti would move at top speed. Only they couldn't raise anyone on the phone when they tried to get help. She didn't understand it. Bruce's line immediately went to voice mail. John wasn't answering. And the cloud cover was building, dimming their natural light even further. "So now what?"

"I think he's coming around," Dane said, bending down. "Emile. It's Dane. Can you hear me?"

Emile groaned softly. Jade watched as Dane ran his hands over Emile, looking for injuries. "He's lying at an odd angle, but I can't find anything broken." He lifted his hand, rubbing his fingers together, peering more closely under the dim moonlight. "There's blood on the back of his head."

"Poor man. It's so damn dark here we can't see anything clearly anyway." She turned to the path. "I'll go grab a flashlight from the trailers." She stopped. "I don't have the trailer keys with me."

"I'm not sure that's an issue. He's waking up now."

She crouched in front of the two of them. "Did you check the back of his head? Perhaps he fell on the rocks and hit his head?"

"Yeah, blood is here and on the ground beneath him. Head injuries can really bleed." Dane glanced at her and nodded. "He was probably searching for his father and fell."

"Let's hope he's not too badly hurt." As she watched, Emile opened his eyes, his gaze widening as he took in his location. Took in them.

"I'm fine." Emile tried to lurch to his feet and fell sideways. Dane lunged to catch him before he fell again. "Hey, take it easy. You've hit your head on a rock."

"Is that why it feels like a watermelon about to explode?"

Dane grinned at Emile's truculent tone.

Jade didn't know how to compare him to what was normal. The few times she'd seen Emile, he'd been reserved and not terribly communicative—about the same as now.

"Sit and relax for a moment or two."

Jade watched as Dane forcibly pressed Emile onto the closest rock. "Do you know what happened?"

"*Huh*?" Emile peered up at Dane. "What happened?"

"That's what I'm asking you. Do you know what happened to you? What were you doing here?"

"I hit my head, you said."

Oh, dear. Emile wasn't connecting the dots. Jade peered into his eyes. Concussions were nothing to make light of, and neither were head wounds. "We should take him to the hospital."

"Hospital?" Emile reared upward, swaying slightly. "No hospital. Home. Emile go home."

"Okay. Home it is. Come on. Let's see if we can get you to my truck."

Jade watched as Dane half-lifted the much smaller man over the rough rocks to the path. She accepted the keys from Dane and ran ahead to unlock the doors.

Emile settled into the passenger side. Jade ran around and slid into the middle seat and buckled him in. Dane started the truck. Just hearing the engine turn over and seeing the headlights come on made her sigh with relief. Enough had gone wrong tonight, and her skin prickled with foreboding.

Taking the road slowly, Dane bounced the truck to John's gravel driveway and pulled in as close to the kitchen door as he could. Lights were on inside. "Wait, Emile. I'm coming around."

Emile didn't say much, and his breath was raspy and unsteady.

Jade whispered, "Dane, he doesn't look so good. We should take him straight to the hospital."

"I know." Grimly, Dane headed around the truck and instead of coming to the passenger door, he knocked hard and went into his brother's house. A cry, several shouts, followed by heavy footsteps could be heard as John, Tasha, and Dane raced back to the truck. Jade stayed quiet, while Tasha howled over her brother's condition.

John tried to comfort her. Dane tried to talk them into taking Emile to the hospital to get checked out, except, when the hospital was mentioned, Tasha started screaming at the top of her lungs.

Jade had never seen anything like it. Actually that wasn't true. She'd seen too much like it in the aftermath of the earthquake. "Dane?" He couldn't hear her.

It occurred to her that Bruce was a doctor. In fact several of the team were doctors. Surely one could come and take a look? Their professional opinion might sway this emotional, nonsensical reaction. Jade hopped out of the truck and walked over to Dane, standing still, staring at the sky in frustration. She tugged on his sleeve and pulled him aside slightly. "Call Bruce. He's a doctor. He won't mind helping out. You've helped us."

His face brightened. He pulled out his cell phone and made the call. Walking away a distance, Jade studied the very pregnant Tasha in front of her. She looked worse than her brother.

Her hair was mussed and hung lank—her eyes wild.

Jade couldn't quite see the whole picture, but she figured Meg would know what to do or suggest, *if Meg were here.* Jade ran to Dane. "Have him bring Meg, if she's there."

Dane frowned at her and repeated her request. After closing his phone, he asked, "Why Meg?"

"She's a doctor and a psychologist of some sort too. I can't remember exactly what her degrees are."

He stared at her, not comprehending.

With a quick glance in Tasha's direction, she lowered her voice. "Something's not right with Tasha."

His eyes widened, and he turned to study his sister-in-law. Grim lines settled in. "She really doesn't look very good, does she?"

"No."

"Let's hope someone can help. Things are deteriorating on all sides here." Even as he finished speaking, Emile slumped. "Hey, watch him!" He raced over to Emile's side and helped John, who was struggling to hold Emile upright beside the truck.

"I'm fine. Leave me alone." Emile staggered, tried to swat away their hands, and stumbled to the door.

The two men stayed close, managing to get Emile inside. Tasha stood outside and stared at the moon. As Jade approached warily, she heard Tasha muttering under her breath.

"Tasha, come inside. Let's go in and sit down. Get you

off your feet," Jade suggested gently.

But Tasha just turned her head, and her black eyes, wide and dark as obsidian, latched onto Jade. "It's too late."

"What's too late? Are you feeling okay?" Jade couldn't hide her concern now. Fear radiated around Tasha. From the size of Tasha's belly, Jade guessed she wasn't far off her due date, a month, … two at the most. Jade gently put an arm around Tasha's shoulders and urged Tasha into the house.

Tasha went meekly. Jade led her to the first chair they came across. The men had Emile reclining on the couch. A plaid blanket had been thrown over him.

Another brightly colored blanket lay over a second chair. Jade picked it up and draped it around Tasha's shoulders, then gave her a quick hug. She gently patted Tasha's distended belly.

There was no response. Lucky baby, it was getting to sleep through this nightmare.

Jade felt beyond useless, as she wandered the kitchen area, waiting. She noticed no teakettle here.

As she turned back to the two brothers, who argued in the middle of the living room, she stopped and felt her insides pinch. She looked and noticed the small three- or four-inch-high papier-mâché dolls hanging to dry on lengths of cord throughout the living room and eating area. Like the ones in the market. Tasha reached up and offered one to Jade. Not wanting to offend the woman, Jade accepted one and put it in her pocket. For the first time, Tasha smiled at her. Briefly. Then her face went blank again.

Creepy. … She remembered the old woman's warning in the market and felt a shiver across her back, when she felt the bulge in her pocket. She'd throw away the doll at the first chance she got, good or bad magic be damned.

Jade gulped loudly, her hand leaving her pocket to massage her tight neck. In the middle of the living room, under a doll hanging low enough to tease his hair, Dane argued violently with his brother.

His brother, shorter, chunkier, younger, was arguing back just as strongly. She didn't want to know what it was about but couldn't help overhearing because her choices were either to stay in the small house and watch or to go outside and to leave Tasha alone. A sidelong glance toward the silent woman showed no change.

"He needs to go to the hospital," Dane stated.

"He won't go," John replied.

"He's unconscious now. He doesn't have any say in the matter."

"He'll be pissed when he wakes up."

"That won't matter because he may not wake up if he doesn't go." Dane ran his fingers through his hair, and his elbow accidentally hit the doll hanging above him. He glanced and half ducked. "If it's the money that's bothering you, forget about it. I'll cover it, if I have to." He spun around throwing his hands up in the air in frustration. And stopped. "What the … ?" He gazed around the living room, as if seeing it for the first time. "Jesus, there are even more of them now."

"Yeah, I commented on them earlier, and she started screaming that it was all my fault," John said. "That everything bad that happens is because the grave had been opened." He stared at his now-almost-catatonic wife, a bitter look crossing his face. "I'm wondering if maybe *she's* to blame for everything instead."

Jade gasped softly.

Holding out his hands, John closed his eyes. "I'm sorry.

I don't mean that. But God, Dane, I don't know what to do anymore."

"Jesus. This is like a bad zombie movie."

John ran a weary hand down his face and dropped down on the arm of the couch at Emile's feet. "Yeah, only this isn't fiction. When Tasha found out about Peppe disappearing, she really went off the rails. I didn't understand half of what she was saying. Just something about me not understanding how bad it could get, if something came out of the grave. I figured she was talking about bad spirits, but I don't know if that's what concerns her about Peppe's disappearance or not. And, no, we still haven't found Peppe." He stared at Dane with bloodshot eyes. "I don't know what the hell is going on anymore. Things are so out of control."

"Ya think? Look at your wife, for Christ's sake."

"I know." John closed his eyes. Worry pleated his forehead. "She's fallen to pieces over Peppe and Emile."

"Then stay strong. Get someone over here to help her. What about her aunt, cousins? Isn't there someone, anyone?"

"I have tried to contact several people. So far I can't reach anyone." John turned and walked over to Tasha. He crouched down in front of her. "Tasha? Honey? Look at me."

Tasha raised her head and stared at John. Tears leaked down her cheeks. He pulled her into his arms. "Oh, honey. It'll be okay. Take it easy."

She tucked her head into his shoulder, as he rocked her gently back and forth.

Jade walked over to Dane. "Bruce should be here soon."

Dane slipped an arm around her shoulders and tucked her close. He dropped a kiss on the top of her head. "Sorry. Not a great end to the evening."

"Not your fault." Appreciating the warmth and comfort he offered, she relaxed against him.

Lights of an approaching vehicle flashed in the window. "Oh, thank God. That should be them." She almost ran outside, Dane at her heels.

Bruce hopped out of the SUV, and Jade groaned with relief to see Meg in the passenger side. "Hi, Jade. Did you find Dr. Mike? And how's Emile?"

"Unfortunately no. We didn't find Dr. Mike. We went to the grave in case he'd fallen on the rocks. Instead that's what must have happened to Emile, while he was looking for his father. Emile was talking and walking with assistance but refused to go to a hospital. We brought him here and called you. So you've heard nothing on Dr. Mike either?"

Bruce shook his head. "No, not yet. Where is Emile?"

"Inside." Dane led the way.

Jade stayed behind. "Thanks for coming, Meg. I'm sorry about Dr. Mike. This has been a terrible evening."

Reaching out and giving Jade a quick hug, Meg said, "I'm glad to help. I just don't understand why I'm needed."

"It's Tasha, John's pregnant wife. And I don't know what you can do for her." Jade shook her head. "Something is definitely not right there."

"Mentally or physically?"

"Both. Add in emotionally too." She led Meg toward the kitchen door. "There's a weird smell to her—I don't know. It's way beyond me." Taking in a deep breath, she added, "I'm afraid there's something wrong with the baby."

Meg's gaze sharpened. "Where is Tasha?"

"In the living room, with Emile. Also, as you walk in, take a close look at the inside of the house. Especially the ceiling." Jade shrugged. "I need you to see it for yourself."

Meg walked through the open door. "Whatever you say."

Jade followed behind. She watched Meg take several steps toward the living room … and falter. She came to a stop and studied the shadowed interior and the closed curtains, but especially the dolls. The house was small, cozy even, but gave off an eerie darkness, suggesting something was not right.

Jade whispered, "See?"

"Very interesting," Meg murmured.

Jade stepped around her and motioned toward Tasha. "Now look at the mom."

Meg directed her gaze at Tasha, who rocked in the big easy chair, a shuttered look closing her face down. Meg approached slowly.

"Tasha? My name is Meg." Crouching in front of the pregnant woman, she tried to study her face, but Tasha dropped her chin lower.

Jade stepped off to one side, where she could keep an eye on both patients. Bruce was bent over, checking Emile's eyes.

Dane stood guard, while John chewed his fingers. Dane's comments repeated in her mind, and now she understood his concern. John obviously wasn't stepping up to the plate with his wife's emotional breakdown. In fact, he appeared close to sliding into one himself.

She couldn't help but think back to Duncan and how he must have felt, watching her decline. Still, with his help, she'd pulled herself up, so there was hope John would too. Now, if only they could find Dr. Mike. She glanced out into the dark night. The thought of him lost was bad enough, but, after finding Emile tonight, she couldn't help worrying that Dr. Mike might be in a similar situation.

She sidled over to Tasha and Meg. Tasha still wasn't talking.

Jade crouched beside Meg and asked, "What do you think?"

"She needs help. Serious help." Meg studied the large belly, her hand pressed gently, lower down. "How far along is she?"

"I think seven, ... almost eight months. I can double-check with the baby's father, if you need to know exactly."

"She needs emergency medical care and fast." Meg stood and motioned toward John. "Is this man the baby's father?"

"Yes, come on." She led Meg to the men. "John, this is Meg," she said, with a bright smile. "She's another member of the team."

John's face scrunched. He attempted to step away in the small room but backed against a wall in the overly crowded space. "Hi. Thanks for coming by to help Emile."

Meg, her voice as gentle as a summer breeze, said, "I didn't come for Emile. I came to see your wife."

John's eyes widened. "Tasha? Why? What's wrong with my wife?"

Meg raised an eyebrow, as she glanced behind him to Dane.

Dane stepped around him, so he could face his brother. "John. You know something's wrong."

"You called this woman in?" John's voice sounded as if he didn't know whether he should be outraged or thankful.

"Theoretically, yes. I did, at Jade's request."

"Jade?" John frowned, as if he couldn't place who she was.

Jade grimaced and gave a small wave. "That's me, re-member? Your wife and your child need help, John. Now."

Fear visibly shivered over his body, and his eyes panicked. "Is she having the baby now?"

Meg reached out a gentle hand. "She isn't having the baby right now, although ..." Meg looked back at the woman rocking silently in the chair. "Well, she needs emergency medical attention."

"That's good then. She'll be much better once she has the baby. Everything will be back to normal then." He made a wide sweep with his arm, taking in Emile and Tasha. Eagerness lit his face, and Jade's heart broke. She didn't think it would be that easy to fix this.

"We need to call an ambulance or whatever service is available here. If it can't get here fast, we need to take her to the closest hospital." Meg spoke to John in a calm voice.

His eyes widened in skepticism. "No. No, she'd never allow that. You don't understand. She, *they*, don't trust in doctors—not like we do. She'll have the baby at home. She planned for it." He spun to his brother. "Dane, you know that. I explained that."

"No. You tried to explain, but I didn't understand. I *don't* understand. I see that they want their own spiritual leaders, and that's fine. Call them. See if there's anything they can do. We're telling you that you need to get medical help for Tasha and Emile—and *now*."

Meg added, "You don't want to hurt the baby, John. And Tasha needs help."

Before their eyes, they saw John crumble.

"No. It wasn't supposed to be like this. I don't know what to do," he cried out.

Bruce walked over. "How long to get an ambulance here?"

Dane shrugged. "Ten, twenty minutes? I don't really

know. Depends on how busy they are."

Bruce's face pinched. "Call them, please." He cast a scathing look at John. "You're no longer making the decisions here. Your brother-in-law is going to the hospital." He stopped and studied Tasha for a long moment. "Meg? One patient or two?"

"Two, actually three. The baby is in trouble too."

Both looked to Dane. He nodded and opened his cell phone to make the call. Bruce stood beside him, giving the medical details to the EMT service.

Jade wrapped her arm around John and moved him to the closest chair. "John, sit here for a bit."

"What?" Dazed and confused, John blinked several times.

Jade frowned and glanced around. Dane was just pocketing his phone. She walked over, calling to him softly. "Dane?"

He met her gaze, then followed the tilt of her head, his eyes lighting on his brother's features. Dane's face turned grim. "What's the matter now?"

"Your brother. Is it possible he could have drugs or something in his system?"

"Not drugs. At least I don't think so." He bent down and studied his brother. "Hey, John. Stay with me here. You don't look so good."

"I'm fine. A little shaken, that's all." He tried to smile but failed miserably. "I'm okay." This time his assertion was stronger. Not quite strong enough to be believable but he was pulling himself up. "And I don't do drugs." He glared at Jade, as if she were the cause of all his problems. "Neither does Tasha."

"Glad to hear it. Stay alert, please, or you'll be the next

patient."

"I'm fine." His temper shone through, strong and defiant.

Jade was satisfied with that reaction. Better fire than ice. She left the brothers to work things out, while she checked with Bruce on Emile. Emile's color had slid from white to dead white. "Shit. He does not look good."

"No. Not at all. Where the hell is that ambulance?" Bruce stood watch, a careful eye on Emile.

"It's only been ten minutes."

Bruce placed a hand on Emile's wrist again, checking the pulse, his frown deepening. "They'd better get here soon, or they won't have to rush on their way back."

Jade winced. "That close, *huh*?"

He gave her a sharp nod. Jade hastened over to Meg, who was attempting to wash Tasha's face. "How's she doing?"

"No change. She's almost catatonic."

"Will that affect the baby?"

Meg frowned and gently cleaned Tasha's cheek. Tasha didn't respond at all. "The baby is very calm. Too calm."

"Any idea what could cause this?"

Meg sighed and gave her a sad smile. "Unfortunately a lot of things. I don't know if there is something physical going on here, but even emotionally… Her father is missing, her brother injured …" Meg shrugged. "Some people just snap, others give up, and then there are those who go inside, where they can't feel the pain. It's way too early to make any kind of deduction."

Meg went to the kitchen sink and rinsed her cloth. She came back and finished cleaning Tasha's face, then did her hands. She turned Tasha's hands over and studied the chewed nails. In one spot they'd been gnawed so low she had dried blood in the corners.

Meg and Jade exchanged grim looks. Jade noticed a change in the room. Something was different. Too quiet. Emile's harsh, raspy breathing had become staggered, erratic. He was having trouble breathing. "Shit!"

Bruce returned to Emile's side, just as loud sirens filled the air. Meg's eyes opened wide. Jade raced to the kitchen door. "It's the ambulance." Doors slammed outside. "Thank God. They must have been close when they got the call."

The ambulance parked beside the SUV. Two men hopped out, one carried a large bag. Jade joined them. "Hurry, please. He's having trouble breathing."

The pair ran into the house.

Jade stayed outside, gulping in the clean, fresh night air. The house smelled terrible to her—of stale sweat and fear and something strongly herbal. Maybe it was from the doll-making materials?

While they worked on Emile, Jade walked around outside, praying and hoping for Emile's recovery. She didn't know what had happened to Tasha. She hoped she'd be okay. Her baby needed her. But was the baby okay?

The moon hid behind the clouds above, dimming Jade's view of the property. The darkness provided an appropriate background to the horrible events of the night.

"How are you doing?" Dane strode toward her, his arms open. "I'm in the way in there."

She ran into his embrace. "I'm fine. Wish things were different though."

He leaned back slightly, so he could see her face. "Yeah, same here." He sounded so sorrowful, so despondent, she squeezed him tightly. He held her close, dropping his chin to rest on her head, and they just stayed like that, in the darkness, for a long moment. "I'm glad you're here," he whispered.

Just then the kitchen door opened, and one of the men ran to the ambulance. He pulled out a stretcher, dropped the legs, locked them in place and raced to the house again.

"I always feel like I should do something in situations like this, but I never quite know what," Jade muttered.

"Me, too." They stared at the house and the sounds coming from within.

She added, "How sad that John has to take care of both of them."

"I know. He's almost a patient himself."

"I'm glad you can see that too." She shifted back. "What about his missing father-in-law?"

Dane ran his fingers through his hair. "Who knows? I'll try and talk to John when this calms down a little bit."

Jade watched in silence as the two patients were transferred to the ambulance in two separate trips. After Tasha was brought out, Meg walked over to Jade, a weary sadness on her face. Jade met her gaze with the burning question in her eyes. Meg shook her head once.

Jade gasped. She bit her lip and wrapped her arms tightly around her stomach.

Dane reached out to stroke her shoulder. Leaning down, he whispered, "What?"

She shook her head violently. "Not now," she whispered. John walked beside Bruce, but either he didn't understand Meg's motion or couldn't take much more.

Dane dropped his arm from Jade's shoulder and walked over to his brother. "John, do you want me to take you to the hospital?"

"I'm going in the ambulance." John gave Dane a tight smile. "Would you mind following?"

"I'm right behind you." Dane fished the keys from his pocket and watched with the rest of the group, as the ambulance flicked on its lights and sirens and took off into the night.

Dane turned to Meg and Bruce. "Thank you."

Bruce shook his head. "Sorry the prognosis isn't better."

"I didn't hear. … Is Emile that bad?"

Bruce sighed. "He might pull through, if they can stop the bleeding fast enough. He's young and strong."

Dane winced. "I guess that was quite the blow to the head."

"Not at all. Even a light fall can cause this kind of trauma." He rotated his neck. "I'm thinking Emile will recover. Tasha now? … I don't know."

Dane's eyes widened. "What? I don't understand."

Meg sighed. "I don't know how she's doing mentally. As for her baby? Well, … we couldn't find a heartbeat."

PEPPE DUCKED BELOW the old dead mango tree close to Tasha's house. Wide enough to hide him, close enough to see the flashing lights and the crowd of strangers moving in and out of his daughter's house. Darkness had long descended. He'd forgotten how long before. He crouched lower. His stomach growled. He couldn't remember when he'd eaten last. Surely his kids would bring him a meal soon.

Not Emile. Something was wrong with Emile. Peppe squeezed his eyes shut. What happened? Yelling, fighting, ropes. Running. He opened his eyes again, moisture collecting in the corners. Why couldn't he remember anything?

As he asked the questions, visions of Emile's anger and more yelling swept through his mind. They'd both been so angry. He thought his son had done something wrong. Again. But he was a good kid, just always getting into scrapes. Fighting over nothing.

Peppe didn't know what the fight had been about this time. But Emile didn't deserve whatever had happened to him. As Peppe watched the activity at Tasha's house, the moisture in his eyes dripping down his cheek, the stretcher was loaded into the ambulance.

Emile didn't deserve this. He was a good boy.

The stretcher came back out and went into the house. He straightened—fear sending icicles down his back. He hated doctors. All of them. They'd taken his money and had let his beloved wife die. They'd smiled and said they'd help. … Instead he'd gone broke, trying to keep her alive. In the end, she'd still died, and the bills had continued to come.

He huddled deeper in the darkness. The flashing lights hurt his eyes. Made his head ache. Made him confused.

It was hard to keep watching the house. Small groups of people clustered around. He glanced around the property. It was still his place. But he didn't know who everyone was. What were they doing here?

They didn't belong here.

Neither did all the vehicles.

He squinted. The stretcher came back out.

Tasha. He perked up. The baby was coming. He would be a grandpa.

His enthusiasm fell. His wife hadn't gone to any hospital. She'd delivered their two children just fine at home.

So why was Tasha on the stretcher?

That bastard who'd married his daughter stood beside

the ambulance. John. He was to blame for all of this. Things had been good before he'd come. Now look at this mess. Even worse had been John's brother, ... and all those strangers digging their noses in where they didn't belong.

Shivers racked his thin frame.

Maybe they were all to blame.

Chapter 16

JADE FELT THE sun shining on her face and tried to open her eyes. Grit and dried tears had mingled to damn-near seal them shut. She yawned and burrowed deeper into the blankets. Thank God it was Saturday. She didn't want to go anywhere.

Her body felt like wax that had poured itself into bed, then hardened overnight.

Memories slammed into her heart, as she opened her eyes and stared across the empty room. Last night …

Emile. Tasha and the baby.

Her eyes burned. No tears were left. She'd cried herself to sleep, asking herself and God why it had happened this way. *Why the baby?* She could deal with Emile and his sister and their father, if the news turned out to be bad. But the baby? The unborn baby. Just like hers. Only worse because Tasha had been seven or eight months along. To lose a baby at that stage?

Had Tasha known? Would that, along with her father's disappearance and then Emile's injury, have ensured her mental slide downward? Even a healthy mind would break under far less.

God knows Jade had struggled over the loss of her baby.

A light knock sounded on her door.

"Hello? … Jade, it's Meg. May I come in?"

Jade groaned softly, as she forced her aching limbs to action, grabbed her robe, and walked to the door. She unlocked and opened it.

Meg smiled at her, looking marginally better than Jade felt. "Hey. Tough night, *huh?*"

"That's an understatement." Realizing she hadn't opened the door fully, Jade motioned her coworker inside. "Sorry. I only woke up a few minutes ago."

"Good for you. I woke up at six, as usual."

Closing the door behind her, Jade added, "I normally would have but …"

"Yeah." Meg looked around the small room. "This room is the twin to mine."

"Is it? Makes sense, I suppose." Jade could sense Meg had a purpose to her visit. Jade walked back to her bed and crawled under the covers, waiting for Meg to get around to the main topic.

"I have an update." Meg took a deep breath. "Tasha's baby is dead. Usually when a fetus dies, the body aborts it. In some rare cases, the body continues to ignore the fact, until it can't be ignored any longer."

Poor Tasha. Blinking several times to hold back her hot tears, Jade tilted her head back and thought about Meg's news. Regaining control, she looked her colleague in the eye. "So you're saying the baby has been dead for a while?"

Meg winced. "Yes. In the US, an autopsy would likely be done to find the cause. Here, I don't know what happens." Rotating her neck as if to ease some stiffness, she continued. "Emile is alive. They think they've stopped the bleeding. It's still touch-and-go for him though."

Swallowing hard, Jade couldn't do much more than nod to acknowledge Meg's words. She didn't trust herself to speak.

"Tasha …" Meg stopped. "Tasha goes into surgery this morning and will undergo a psych evaluation when she's healthier. The bottom line is, there's been no change. She's not talking, eating, or acknowledging the world around her in any way."

Jade couldn't help wincing. "Poor John."

"Yes." Sitting in the single chair, Meg rested her feet on the corner of the bed. "I've also spoken to Dane. I wanted to know if there was anything I could do for his family."

"And? Is there?" Jade leaned forward.

Meg slumped back. "No. John's a mess. Dane said he'd call you or stop by here later, if he can. He's sticking close to his brother."

"He was worried about John's mental state before this."

"It's out of our hands." The two women sat in depressed silence.

Then Jade remembered. "Any idea if their father has been found?"

The two women stared at each other, frowning. Meg shook her head slowly. "I forgot to ask."

"I ask because of Tasha. Dane said Peppe isn't right in the head. Makes me wonder if Tasha has a heredity issue here." Jade considered Tasha's life. "Not that what she's been through isn't enough to make anyone retreat inside."

"Any idea how old Peppe is or how long he's been like this?" Meg asked.

"No. You'll have to get Dane to ask John." As much as she wanted to laze around the hotel today, Jade couldn't stand the thought of the old man out there, wandering around lost. "We should also sort out if he's in need of finding or if he's home and fine."

"Yes. Do you want to call Dane, or should I?"

"I will." Jade threw back the covers. "As soon as I have my shower and get dressed. We might as well meet in the dining room and figure out what's next."

"I'll see you there." Meg tossed her cell phone on the bed for Jade to use, before walking to the door.

"Hey, Meg. Where was Dr. Mike last night? Did anyone ask him?"

A funny look crossed her face. "I haven't spoken to him. Haven't heard anything."

"He's back though—isn't he?" Dread edged Jade's words.

"I don't know. Things got a bit crazy last night. I'll find out." Meg rushed out, leaving Jade standing in the middle of the room, shocked.

DANE STRETCHED OUT his long legs on the stone patio to his cabin, tilting his face to the morning sun. Sleep had been hard to come by when he had finally collapsed on his bed in the wee hours of the morning. The few hours he'd managed hadn't helped much; he still felt worn out. Not the ending he'd hoped for.

His cell phone rang. He checked the number before answering. Meg's—therefore, hopefully Jade.

"Hi, Dane."

Jade's warm voice flooded his senses. Damn, it was good to hear her voice. "Good morning. How are you today?"

"Better than most of the people involved in last night's emergencies. I have several reasons for calling. First, how is John? Second, did anyone ever find Peppe?"

Peppe? Shit, Dane hadn't given that crazy old man a second thought. Not after last night's chaos. "Peppe might have come back overnight. We're just up, so I'll walk over and check in a few minutes. John is okay, but not good—still, he's holding on."

"Not a good night for any of us."

"Yes. The doctors didn't say much." Dane checked his watch. "Tasha should be out of surgery by now. We might know more soon."

The kitchen door slammed shut. He spun around to see John walking down the garden path, head bent in the morning sunlight, hands in his pockets. "I'll call you back."

Dane disconnected the call and tucked his phone back into his jeans pocket and hurried to catch up with his brother.

JADE WALKED BACK to the hotel patio table, where Meg sat waiting. Bruce came out to join them. "Dane says he'll walk over and check on Peppe and will call us back."

Bruce scrunched his face, as he pulled a chair back to sit. "What a mess."

"That's one way to put it." Jade lifted her cup of coffee, letting the steam waft upward to bathe her eyes. The shower had helped but not enough. She still ached inside, as if she were a faded version of herself. In direct contrast the thick bushes beside her were many shades of vibrant green, their branches lively in the breeze. Typical of so much of the vegetation here, it took her breath away.

"Dr. Mike's still missing," Bruce said. "I've contacted the authorities and will be heading there shortly to give them Dr. Mike's photo. He has to be missing for twenty-four hours before they'll do anything official. However, because of the work we've been doing and the missing SUV involved, they'll look into it earlier." He grimaced. "I've also contacted Tony—to give him the heads-up."

"Oh, joy," Jade muttered. "Will Tony return?"

Settling back into his chair, Bruce took a sip of his coffee, before answering in a grim voice. "No. Not at this point. He does want to know, as soon as possible, whether he needs to find a replacement."

"What!" Meg stared at him in shock. "A replacement? For Dr. Mike? Are you serious? Surely that's jumping the gun?"

"Tony is thinking of the project and his client. If Dr. Mike is injured or missing or … anything else, then Tony needs to find a replacement." Bruce's gaze went from Meg to Jade. "It's not unreasonable, given the schedule. But we aren't going there yet."

Jade shuddered and walked off a ways. She could see both sides regarding Tony's concern, but that didn't mean she wanted to contemplate anything nasty. Last night had been enough drama for a long time. "Let's hope he went on a bender and is sleeping it off in the SUV somewhere."

"Dr. Mike doesn't drink."

Jade spun around, raising her hands in the air. "Then maybe he found a lady friend or something. Let's remain positive, please."

"Right. I'm heading out now. I don't know what you two are planning to do today, but, if it involves searching for Peppe and Dr. Mike, please wake our two party animals and get them involved. Leave Susan alone. She needs to rest. Maybe she can throw the flu that's plaguing her."

Jade shook her head, a small grin on her face. "Is that what Stephen and Wilson were doing? Partying? We were so busy last night that I never gave them a thought."

"Me neither. Which is why we dropped the ball on Dr. Mike," Meg said tiredly.

Bruce leaned over slightly, so he could meet Meg's gaze. "Don't think that. We didn't drop the ball. Priorities shifted, due to emergencies. I'll go to the authorities right now. We'll find him."

Meg stood, as he walked back inside the hotel. She motioned to Jade. "Why don't you bring your coffee and join me in the conference room? If I stay out here, this morning sun will put me back to sleep."

Talking quietly, they walked inside to their desks and turned on their computers. Meg's phone rang. She checked the number and handed it over to Jade. "Dane. You might as well answer it."

Jade's heart lightened. "Hello, Dane."

"Hey. Too bad you don't have your own cell phone. I wouldn't have to keep bothering Meg this way."

She heard the smile in his voice that said he wasn't too bothered by the inconvenience. Still, he had a point. If she wanted privacy, she'd have to get a phone for the duration of her time here.

"Anyway, Peppe is not in his cabin. The door is open now, and it wasn't left that way yesterday. John believes Peppe came home last night and was probably confused and scared off by the sirens. We'll keep an eye out for him."

"Oh, that sounds reasonable." In fact, that was excellent news. They could focus on Dr. Mike now. "How is John holding up?"

Dane's voice flattened. "He's coping somewhat. He opened up a little, admitted that he and Tasha had been having problems for a bit. At the time he figured that was because she was upset that he allowed you to work on the grave."

Jade wrinkled her nose. "Yeah, I can see that. Relationships being what they are." Meg looked at her, an eyebrow raised. Jade continued. "Let us know if there are any developments with Peppe. We'll turn our attention to finding Dr. Mike."

"What? Dr. Mike didn't come home?" he asked, his voice rising.

Jade had forgotten what they'd been doing when they'd found Emile. "No. There's no sign of him or the SUV. Bruce left a few minutes ago to speak with the police."

"*Hmm.* While I look for Peppe, I'll keep an eye out for him too. Let me know if there is anything we can do to help *you.*"

"I'll get back to you on that," Jade promised, then hung up. She quickly filled Meg in on the latest developments.

Meg brightened. "If Peppe had seen the ambulance take his kids away, then he'll be confused and upset. I can see him going into hiding. That doesn't mean he's not in need of care though." She thought for a moment. "Any idea what happened to Tasha and Emile's mother?"

"No. I never thought to ask." Jade stared down at the phone, wondering if she should call Dane back. Some family history would be good to know.

"Not to worry. It's not our problem."

She stared at Meg. "You're right. Yet somehow it seems like it is."

Chapter 17

THE TEAM DISCUSSED the previous night's events over lunch, when Bruce returned.

Susan walked in slowly, just behind him. She fielded all the questions with a smile. "I'm feeling a little better. Thanks, everyone. Apparently I missed lots of excitement last night."

Jade shook her head. "And you were the lucky one there."

Pulling out her chair, Susan sat down next to Stephen. She frowned. "Not really. I think someone tried to break into my room last night."

"What?" A chorus of cries erupted from the table.

"Really?" Meg stared at her in horror. "What happened?"

"I'm not exactly sure. I took some decongestants to try and throw this cold. Those things always knock me out." She sighed, reached for her coffee cup, and took a sip. "I woke up in the night, everything was dark. But I heard movement in my room."

"Jesus." Jade so didn't want to think about what could have happened. "Did he just leave? On his own?"

Susan nodded. "I coughed a couple times, sat up to clear my throat, and this shadow detached from the wall. Then the door opened, and this person went out. Had a hard time getting back to sleep after that. The front desk sent someone up to check the lock for me."

Stephen growled. "That had better not happen again. We've got enough problems, without worrying about intruders while we sleep."

Susan gave him a wan smile. "I did get up and lock my door. Figured I must have forgotten to before climbing into bed.

At that, Bruce highlighted something they all knew but found easy to forget. "Remember, people. This area is incredibly poor. Lock up your belongings. The hotel has a safe, if you want to make use of it. And be sure to check that you've locked your room doors at all times."

Everyone had something to say. Jade sat back and listened. She couldn't believe the shitty luck the team had been having lately.

Bruce gave everyone another moment, then held up his hand. "Now on to my news. We're in luck. There's a tracking device on the SUV. The police called the rental company. Apparently, with the unrest in Haiti in the last year, thefts were up, along with every other crime imaginable. In order to keep their rental fleet insured, they'd been forced to boost their security measures." He pulled out a chair and sat. "I handed over all the paperwork on the leases, and they're doing their thing as we speak."

"Oh, wow. That is great news." Jade sat up straight. She'd never considered a tracking device.

Bruce's phone rang. He answered, gesturing for silence. The room fell quiet. He put the phone on Speaker. "Hi, did you find him?"

"We found the SUV. However there's no sign of your missing person."

Worry lined Bruce's face. "He's not there? Could he be anywhere nearby? A hotel or restaurant, something?"

"The SUV isn't far from where you're staying. There is no sign of damage or forced entry to the SUV. It was unlocked but still full of equipment. It looks as if the driver just got up and walked away. It is near a popular hiking spot. Would he have gone for a hike on the spur of the moment and not told anyone?"

Silence.

Stephen spoke first. "He's a hiker, but I can't imagine him going without letting any of us know what he was doing. He'd found a couple trails that the team would discuss, then pick one to do this weekend, but that's after we'd planned and prepared for it."

"Right. Can you please meet us at the vehicle, so we can confirm nothing has been stolen?"

Jade scratched down the location, as it came rattling through the phone.

"We'll be there in fifteen minutes." Bruce disconnected and tucked his cell back into his pants pocket.

"I want to go with you," Jade said quietly. She really didn't want to go, but she wanted to be a second pair of eyes, making sure that no one missed anything. Dr. Mike was a good man. She'd do what she could for him.

"So do I." Meg stood up.

Susan started to cough. Everyone stopped to look at her in concern. When she could, she said, "I *want* to go, but ..."

Stephen pointed a finger at her. "Bed. That's the only place you're going. And lock the door behind you this time."

"I think we all want to go." Stephen raised an eyebrow at Wilson, who nodded. "Good, that's settled. We're all going." Everyone stood and headed for the vehicles. As Meg walked past Bruce, she nudged him in the arm. "We're all in this together. If Dr. Mike is in trouble, we all want to help. Accept it."

Bruce smiled and fell into step beside her. "It's good to know that the team has bonded so well in such a short time."

"Isn't it though? Susan hasn't been as involved as much, but she seems happy to be with us."

Stephen interrupted them, as he came up behind them. "Any update on the patients?"

Meg filled him in.

Stephen winced. "That's tough on everyone."

When they reached the SUV, all of them clambered in ahead of Bruce. He shook his head. "Eager or what?"

"Anxious," corrected Jade. "Dr. Mike is family. We're all family."

Bruce stopped, studied her serious face for a moment, and then smiled. "Thanks. That's the nicest thing anyone has said to me in a long time."

He hopped in and started the engine.

"It's the truth," Jade added to the thoughtful silence in the car. "We may not have been here together for long, yet bonds have started. It's up to us how we want them to continue." With those profound words, she sat back, quiet again.

Meg reached out and gave her a hug. "Thanks, sis."

Jade chuckled.

"Hey, pass the hugs around. No keeping them just up front," Stephen protested from the back row.

The jovial atmosphere kept the darkness at bay. At least until they pulled into the location they'd been given and saw the SUV parked in a small gravel lot at the foot of a large hill. Boulders piled high at the base of it, and there was no sign of Dr. Mike.

The laughter shut off like a faucet, replaced by grim silence.

"Shit." Stephen's word echoed loudly through the small space, as Bruce stopped the engine.

"I don't get it." Jade opened the sliding door and hopped out. The others stepped out behind her. They were in a small parking lot, off the main road. They saw one police car and two officers standing at the SUV, waiting. She couldn't help the horrible sinking feeling in her stomach. The SUV doors were closed, and the SUV looked deserted. She walked toward it slowly. The closer she got, the worse she felt.

Bruce walked over to speak with the officers, and the rest of them trooped over to check the SUV. One officer left Bruce and walked over to talk with the others.

"Was the door open when you found it?" Stephen asked.

"All doors were unlocked. Lucky everything didn't get stolen." The officer stood off to one side, watching the group.

"Weird," Wilson piped up, checking out the front passenger side.

"Not weird. *Bad*. Dr. Mike was particularly careful about his equipment." Meg was adamant.

Jade had to agree. "He might have gone hiking. He might be out there injured." She pivoted around, looking for any sign of him.

"He'd have said something, invited one of us along," Stephen protested. "I don't see him going out hiking anyway, at least not alone, and not late in the afternoon. And he has a cell, if he needed help." He opened the driver's side and looked inside.

"No, not hiking, but it makes total sense to come and check out a hike before suggesting it for everyone this weekend." Wilson shrugged. "That's what I'd do."

Jade frowned. "The only way he'd leave the doors unlocked and go on foot from here is if he thought someone needed him—or if someone forced him to."

"There goes that wild imagination of yours." Stephen's voice didn't hold any humor. If anything, it sounded like he was searching for another answer—any other answer. He hopped in the SUV to check the contents in the back. A moment later, he popped his head out. "I can't see anything missing or different about the SUV. Anyone else?" He jumped out the back door and stood with his hands on his hips and studied the SUV's exterior. "Meg, do you want to take a look?"

Meg obliged. Jade stood at the open rear doors and studied the stacks of boxes in the back of the SUV. A small stain looked suspiciously like blood on the corner of one box.

She shook her head. There went her imagination again. She had no reason to assume something bad just because of a tiny brown spot. "Is this blood?" Jade asked.

Meg moved in for a closer look. "What if someone found him injured? They'd take him to the hospital, right? It's not like they'd just leave him here."

Meg poked her head around the stack of boxes. "It is blood, but it's not enough to indicate anything. Still, that's not a bad idea. We spent so much time in the hospital last night, yet I never thought to check if Dr. Mike had been brought in.

Wilson called over, "Hey, Bruce, did you contact the hospital?"

Bruce shook his head. "I checked last night. I haven't yet

this morning."

The younger officer beside him pulled out his cell and moved off a few paces. "I'll do that right now."

Everyone stood quietly, waiting, hoping. The officer returned within a few minutes. "No one has been admitted in the last twenty-four hours fitting that description."

"Okay, if he's not at the hospital and he's not in the SUV, what are our options for finding him?" Bruce asked.

Meg stood, hands on her hips, frowning at the vehicle. "A search party to start from here?"

Wilson rubbed his hands eagerly. "I volunteer."

"Except that he may have been mugged, and the vehicle just dumped here. Although that doesn't make any sense, as this area is facing incredible poverty. The SUV would have been stripped," Jade pointed out.

Wilson walked closer to the path to check it out, while Stephen turned to the officer. "Will the rental company's tracking system tell us where the SUV has been? So we can see where Dr. Mike may have driven?"

Bruce frowned. "They'd have told us if they had, wouldn't they?"

Stephen shrugged. "Depends on the system they're using. Tracking isn't the same as built-in GPS, I don't think. But then I don't know."

"It's just another phone call." The cop added, "I'll have someone at the station make that one. If there is any information, we'll get it."

Stephen nodded his head, then asked the cop, "Can we take the SUV back? It's full of our gear."

"We've processed it already. Lifted a couple fingerprints that we'll run. No confirmed blood or anything else suspicious." He shrugged. "We don't have a crime at the moment.

We *might* have a missing person."

Meg frowned.

Jade could understand. No one knew what to do or where to start.

Wilson spoke up. He stood slightly apart from the group, staring at the woods to the far side. "Let's think about this. We're at the base of a popular hiking spot. Dr. Mike had several hikes in mind for this weekend. On top of that, we're not far from the grave site, are we?"

Jade gazed in the direction he pointed. All she saw was a small mountain with boulders at the bottom and a path twisting its way up the side to where it disappeared in the brush and small bushes. "I wouldn't know. I'm horrible with that kind of stuff."

Bruce walked over to study the same patch of hills and woods. "We can't be that far. I've driven around this area a little bit." He turned back to the others. "Anyone have a map?"

"Why does it matter where the grave site is?" Jade asked.

Wilson replied, "Because Dr. Mike could have walked over that hill to the lab."

"Why?" Meg asked, joining them. "When the SUV is here? Besides, Jade and Dane checked the mass grave last night." The first officer came back with an open map in his hands. Stephen and Bruce clustered around him.

"So I stop here, park, and then hike over that small mountain to the grave site when it'll be dark soon—for fun? Does that make any sense to you?" Jade asked, as she stared at the men in astonishment.

Meg shook her head violently. "Walk away from a working SUV to a spot you *think* is on the other side, ... a decent climb from the grave site? With no wheels and without letting anyone know? No way. Not in this lifetime."

"I'd so do that," Wilson stated, a grim smile on his face. "Honestly I *have* done things like that. Except either I would return to the SUV or I'd call for a ride, once I made it to the other side—if not before—to let someone know where to bring the cold beer."

The grin on Stephen's face said he agreed with Wilson.

Jade shook her head. "So … we'll have to hike over there, if only to ensure he didn't do just that and get stuck somewhere along the way?"

Stephen laughed, while nodding.

The two women stared at each other. "Men."

"I hear you." Jade couldn't think of one woman in her life who would do what Wilson described. Not in a million years.

Bruce walked over with the one officer to speak with the other one. He returned a few minutes later. "It appears to be about a two- or maybe three-hour hike over the top."

The five team members turned to stare at the sparsely treed hillside. Shaking his head, Bruce said, "So, I suggest Wilson and I do the hike. Stephen, why don't you meet us on the other side in a couple hours? We've got water and phones."

Jade jutted out her chin. "Two of you aren't enough. Wilson can go with you too, and Meg and I can meet you at the grave site afterward." She turned to the two officers. "What about organizing a search party?"

Both officers simply shook their heads and stepped back.

"They don't have the manpower, and, even if they did, they don't have enough evidence to prove that Dr. Mike is even missing," Bruce explained. "So Jade and Meg can each drive an SUV back to the hotel. They can leave Dr. Mike's parked there, then meet us at the grave site."

Leaving the rest of the words unspoken, Wilson walked over to the first SUV and pulled out his backpack. He hefted it over one shoulder and turned toward the hillside. "Come on. Let's go. We've only got an estimate of how long this will take. It could take us twice that."

"Good thing it's a nice day for a hike." A grinning Stephen walked past, his camera in hand.

Jade and Meg watched until the men disappeared from sight. Meg had the foresight to speak to the police before they took off; she got their contact information, in case the three men didn't show up as planned. After they were left alone, Jade hopped into Dr. Mike's SUV. Meg fired up the other SUV and led the way back.

Maybe this day would turn out to have a happy ending after all.

DANE WATCHED HIS brother pace from the living room into the kitchen and back again. He let him do it a couple more times before deciding that maybe he'd worked off enough energy to talk. "What's going through your head?"

John spun around and looked at him, his face flushed with temper.

Good, he'd get this out, one way or another, and, if they had to resort to fists, like old times, well, then that's what they would do. Dane stood and shifted his weight to the balls of his feet.

"What's going through my head? What's *not* going through my head? My child is dead, for starters. My wife is out of her mind. My brother-in-law is in a coma, and my crazy father-in-law is missing. Other than that, not much."

In a sarcastic tone, he added, "What the fuck do you think?"

"That's about what I figured."

John gave him a look of absolute disgust, before storming out the kitchen door. Dane stayed behind but kept an eye on him. John's life had been flushed down the toilet and not much either one of them could do about it. Still, he didn't want John to do anything stupid.

Dane decided he'd check on Peppe's cabin again. Maybe he could get John to walk that way too. "Let's see if Peppe came back."

John raised his hands in surrender. "Fine, let's go check on the crazy bastard. Then I want to go back to the hospital. See how Tasha is."

Dane nodded. He didn't think there'd be any change but didn't want to mention that. Temper was better than depression. Some seriously hard questions would need to be addressed soon though.

Together they strode over to Peppe's cabin. The door was closed.

John pushed open the door. Dane stayed well back, until the interior had freshened slightly with the open door.

"Peppe? Are you in here?"

There was no answer.

John called out as he entered, "It's empty. Doesn't look like he's been here recently either."

Dane stood by the entrance. "Can you tell if anything is missing? Like could he have come home for supplies and then taken off again?"

"What supplies? The guy doesn't have much."

"Not having much usually means that the little bit you do have is important."

John shook his head and walked back out, pushing Dane

outside ahead of him. He closed the door behind them and stood staring out across the land. "Dane, what the hell have I done so wrong in my life that this is happening to me?"

Dane's heart ached. "I don't think you did anything. Your wife has a delicate mind, and recent events may have been too much."

John bowed his head. "I guess that's the easiest way to put it."

They wandered the acreage. Dane didn't want to say the wrong thing but wanted John to talk or he would button up again. John spoke before Dane had to push the issue.

"She's been so weird since her pregnancy, and then that damn grave business started. She'd been her normal sunny self before that. Sure, she had bad days and was grouchy a couple times, but nothing like this. She didn't like gaining weight and blowing up like a balloon, but she adored the baby. She acted as I would have expected. But you've seen her yourself this last month. There was something really wrong there."

"I figured it was the pregnancy and the grave business."

John sighed. "So did I. For a while I wondered if her superstitious beliefs were right—about opening the grave being an omen of bad things to come. Only I'm not superstitious. She is. She asked her priestess for help several times. And when the team arrived, and she knew that everything was going ahead, that's when she started going downhill. Faster."

Dane shook his head at the word *priestess*. Instead of speaking, he stomped on his prejudice. John needed Dane's support, not his questions.

John stood silent, thinking. "I'm afraid she might have done something that accidentally caused the death of the baby." He spun around to face his brother, obviously upset. "I don't *want* to think that, but I can't help but wonder."

"Whoa. Stop right there. You just said she loved the baby." He reached out and shook his brother's shoulders. "Right?"

Relief lit up John's face. "Yes. She was happy, … was looking forward to the baby's arrival."

"Here's what I'm thinking. She knew that something was wrong inside. She couldn't handle it and probably started blaming everything on the mortuary team opening the grave."

John asked hopefully, "Do you think that could be it?"

Gently Dane said, "Makes sense to me."

John blinked several times. "Thanks. I hope you're right."

Chapter 18

JADE AND MEG didn't waste any time at the hotel. More worried than she wanted to be, Jade changed into jeans and the light work boots she used at the grave site. She scrounged up stuff to take with her for a longer wait, stuffing her pockets with snacks. Filling a couple water bottles finished the job.

She grabbed her laptop. Who knew how long they might need to wait? She might as well make good use of the time.

At the site, Meg went to check on the reefer truck, while Jade walked over to the lab trailer, unlocked it and went in. Half expecting to see something wrong, she searched the trailer carefully, then shrugged. All appeared normal. Same as it had last night before she left.

Meg joined her a few minutes later. "Dane just drove in."

Jade blinked. A slow smile spread across her face. "Nice."

Meg grinned. "Really?" She snickered, as she started to leave. "Don't be too long primping."

Shaking her head, Jade walked outside. Dane was the perfect distraction for the long wait ahead of them. He walked toward her, his stride strong and effortless. But fatigue worried away at his face, and, instead of his normal confident smile, his mouth had a grim set that looked like it had taken root. John wasn't the only one suffering. Jade's heart went out to Dane.

"Hey. Don't you look like shit?" Meg never did hold back.

He grimaced, yet never slowed his forward motion. "Tough times."

Jade walked down the steps and watched as his face warmed. Especially nice was the smile that chased away most of the worry lines.

Opening his arms, he waited for her to get within grabbing distance, then snagged her close and hugged her tightly. "I need this," he murmured against her ear.

She squeezed him back too. "So do I."

He pulled away slightly. "No news on Dr. Mike?"

She shook her head, mortified to find tears threatening. She sniffled and turned to Meg to have the taller woman speak for her. "Meg?" she asked, her voice thick.

"We found the SUV, unlocked, yet still full of all the equipment—at a bluff on the other side of this." Meg wafted her hand in the direction of the hills behind them. "Three of our team have started to walk through from the point where the SUV was found. They're hiking toward us right now."

Dane's frown came lightning quick. "Why would he walk this way if the SUV was there and fully functional?"

"Yeah. That's one of those questions we don't have answers for. He could have fallen and hurt himself. Broken bones, head wound, … all are possible reasons why he didn't return to the vehicle. The guys didn't want to sit and do nothing, and we know head wounds are tricky. If Dr. Mike tried to start the SUV and couldn't, he might have figured he was stranded, and this was the fastest way home." She shrugged. "We don't know much but couldn't leave this option unexplored. The police are checking with the leasing company to retrace the SUV's route. Maybe that will shine a little light on the mystery."

Dane nodded. "Let's hope so."

The three studied the hill. "Stephen seems to think it was perfectly normal for Dr. Mike to have done the hike to see how difficult it might be, in consideration of the rest of us."

"Is he a hiker or something?"

"A GPS buff, outdoorsman, hiker, mountain climber. Yeah, he's very active."

Dane pursed his lips. "When did they leave and how long are they expecting to be?"

Checking her watch, Meg said, "They left over an hour ago, and we're hoping to see or hear from them in another hour or two."

Jade walked around the two of them and studied the hillside. "No sign of them yet."

Dane added, "They'll be lucky to make it in that time frame. John and I have both been over that rise—a couple times, in fact."

Jade spun to look at him. "Really?"

He nodded. "There are several big caves where an injured person could hole up overnight."

"Is it a tough hike?" Jade felt immeasurably lighter, now that she knew there was shelter of a sort. "Maybe we should check those out ourselves. The guys don't know about them."

Walking around, Dane pointed to a small rise. "That path comes out just behind the grave site—and Peppe's cabin, for that matter. Long ago, it was a common path from town to town, and, when there was heavy flooding, people took the hill paths."

Meg wondered, "What are the chances that Peppe and Dr. Mike are in the same place? If Dr. Mike found an injured Peppe …"

"Why don't we go see?" Jade studied the path in front of them. "We can go up to the top and still keep an eye open for the men. The caves need to be checked out, and the men don't know to look for them."

The two waited, as Jade locked up the lab, before they walked up to the grave site together. Dane took them along the tree line, pointing out Peppe's cabin in the trees.

Jade shaded her eyes from the sun, as she studied the area. "It's nice to see the trees here. I hadn't realized, but Haiti's got a huge issue in that area."

"When Peppe was growing up, this was a flourishing farm. Full of fruit trees, and they even grew coffee for a while. They were one of the first in this area to have running water and electricity. Now the property is past its prime."

"Why are there so few trees in Haiti?" Meg asked.

"So many were cut down for firewood. It's actually a huge issue. Many groups are involved in tree planting here."

"Firewood for cooking. Right. That's another issue here, along with the lack of electricity and running water in most areas."

"Exactly. John says there hadn't been any money to sink into the property for a long time—but they tried different things. Peppe's wife worked, and that kept them floating. They put in the electricity when the hospital went in. Once she was gone, … well, it really fell down."

Dane kept to the left of the rock pile, and they suddenly arrived at a path that wound its way up the hill. "Here it is. If they find the path and come this way, they shouldn't run into any trouble." Dane took the lead. "I wonder if Peppe is up there. He's at home in this terrain. He wouldn't think twice before going over that hill."

A horrible thought slipped into Jade's mind. "Dane, I hate to ask this, … but is Peppe dangerous? Like, if he came upon Dr. Mike, would he hurt him?"

Meg's soft gasp told Jade that she'd just followed her train of thought. Dane on the other hand stared at her in confusion. "I don't think so, but I don't really know."

Jade swallowed. "I know it's probably just my crazy imagination again, but we also found out that Susan, the other female team member, had an intruder in her hotel room last night. While we were out, I think."

Dane's brows pulled together. "Did she recognize him?"

"No," Meg piped up. "She could barely make him out in the shadows. She did have the lock checked, and there was no sign of a break-in."

He pulled out his cell phone. "I can't say I'm surprised. This economy has been struggling to recover. Crime is up. That you haven't had any other problems before now is what's surprising. I'll tell John what we're doing."

Jade continued up the hill, Meg right behind her. Dane caught up before they'd gone any distance. "John says he'll give us five hours to locate Dr. Mike, and then we're to call him back. Otherwise he'll call the same officers you spoke with." He grinned at the two women. "At least I get a chance to take you sightseeing. Maybe another time we can do another outing for fun?"

Meg smiled. "Sounds great. We haven't done anything like this since arriving."

"We went shopping," protested Jade.

"Sure we did—once. Since then you won't go back. Not after Magrim scared you. You believe her now, don't you?

There's been nothing except bad things happening since she spoke to us."

"Too many." Jade shivered. "Thanks for that reminder."

"True. Maybe we should talk to her again. She might foresee a better future for you now."

Jade made a face, saying, "It would be hard to make it any worse."

They'd been walking the whole time they'd been talking and now started up the incline. Dry needles crunched under their boots. They moved at a steady pace. The dust rose with each step, and the bushes on either side of the path gave off an odd aroma when disturbed.

It wasn't a steep incline. Just enough that Jade needed to focus on her pace and her breathing. She hadn't done anything remotely exerting in the last year, and she didn't want to slow the others down or be left to drag up the rear. She took a sip of water and kept an ear to the conversation.

Meg and Dane were discussing Seattle, of all things.

"Any idea how long you'll be here?" he asked Jade.

"I think about six more weeks." Jade shrugged. "Maybe longer."

Meg piped up. "What about you, Dane? How long are you staying here?"

"A week ago, I would have said a couple more months. Now with the mess of John's family situation, I don't know."

That sobered the conversation.

"Any news about Tasha?" Meg asked.

After slugging back a hefty drink of water, Dane shook his head. "John's tormenting himself over this. He knows she'd been bothered by something for a while. He put it down to the reopening of the grave. She increased her production of those little dolls and the tourist stuff she makes and sells. He thought she was trying to keep her mind off what we were doing and to make extra money before the baby arrived."

He wiped his brow before continuing. "John says he can't remember when he last felt the baby move. Tasha hasn't been sleeping well. So John moved to the couch. Before then, he used to sleep with his hands wrapped around her belly and could feel the baby turning around, like it was doing yoga."

"Is he blaming himself?" Jade wouldn't fault him if he did. She'd probably feel the same way, if she were in his position.

"Oh, yeah. He's worried that he missed something. Something that—if he'd seen it in time—would have saved them both."

"That's normal. He'll move past it eventually, and, when he does, he'll start the healing process." Meg's tone was gentle, yet professional.

The group continued to climb as they talked. Jade listened mostly. It was easier to climb that way.

Meg continued. "John's healing may take a bit. There's no change in Tasha's condition, and Emile has slipped again. I don't know that he'll survive. If Tasha does recover, they won't tell her about the baby right away, for fear she won't handle the news well and could retreat inside herself again."

Dane strode forward confidently, unaffected by the strenuous climb. "Honestly, I don't know how John is handling this. It's got to be tough. I know it would be tough on me."

Meg nodded, sadness and compassion blending in her features.

Jade didn't know how Meg could deal with people's

problems, not to this extent, not all the time. Jade couldn't do it. "She'll get over losing the baby. I know that sounds harsh, and it's way worse in that she was so far along in her pregnancy. However, in time, women do recover."

At least she had. And now, seeing Tasha lose her baby, Jade realized time had helped her. It's not as if she'd ever forget, but the pain had receded, softened. She'd moved on. "They have to grieve though. If they don't, it's harder to recover."

Meg suggested, "That's often the problem. They don't go through the grieving process. Life stops for them."

Jade agreed. She knew all about that. "I wonder how much of Tasha's condition is genetic, considering her father."

"It's too early to know. First the doctors have to get her physically healthy. Hopefully her mental and emotional states will start to stabilize and strengthen, as her body starts to heal."

Dane turned and asked, "And if it doesn't? What's there for her?"

"If she remains in a catatonic state," Meg explained, "they'll try different treatments, as they attempt to bring her around. If nothing works, she'll have to be institutionalized."

Jade shook her head. *Not nice.* John would go from being a proud papa-to-be, with a beautiful young wife, surrounded by family, to being the only one left alive and sane. Not good. Hadn't Dane said something about John struggling after losing his wife years ago? Tough to go through that again.

Jade wiped her forehead on her T-shirt. It was another gorgeous day in paradise, and that meant the sun was intense right now. She hoped it would ease, as they crested the next hill. She wished for more shaded spots to take a break from the direct sunlight.

Meg seemed oblivious to the scenery. "I'm sorry for John. There's no easy answer. It's a waiting game."

"And, with everyone gone," Dane explained, "John doesn't feel like it's his home anymore. It was Tasha's and Emile's home. They grew up in that house. Without them there, John says he feels like an interloper."

They came upon a series of rocks, obviously walked on over the ages to the point that they were almost stairs cut into the hillside. Dane led, Meg came next, and Jade walked the last of the line. She turned to look back. "Hey. You can see the grave site from here."

Meg joined her and stared over the open expanse of valley. With the blue sky, sunshine, and a gentle breeze, it was almost perfect. "It's beautiful, not such a bad place to be buried."

"From the sounds of it, most of the bodies will be going back in there too. Susan said that they had so few people coming to look for remains of lost loved ones that she didn't know why they were running the clinic."

Jade didn't know how she felt about that.

"I imagine most people know their loved ones are here and are happy to leave them." Meg smiled. "It's a beautiful resting spot."

"*Hmm.*"

They carried on for another twenty minutes and stopped for another breather and to enjoy the view. Jade couldn't get enough of the valley scenery. It was truly beautiful. The air was cleaner, fresher, the higher they climbed. She took several deep breaths, enjoying the easing of the tension on her shoulders as she did. "Shouldn't we have found them by now?"

"Not yet. Another hour maybe?"

"Why don't we call them? Maybe they're right around the corner," Jade suggested.

Meg pulled out her cell phone from her pocket and called Bruce. The three of them stopped and waited. "It's ringing, but he's not answering."

"Then send a text," Jade suggested. "That often works if you can't get through. Could be the hill interfering with the signal too."

With a shake of her head, Meg quickly tapped out a message. They kept walking upward. "Dane, where are the caves?"

"We should see the first one in ten or fifteen minutes. A couple of them are quite big."

"I suppose travelers would have been glad to have them too." Jade didn't think much of the idea though. All she could think of was that predators hid out in scary dark places.

They rounded a corner and came to a stop. Dane pointed off to the right. "Look partway up that hill. Do you see the cave?"

Meg nodded.

"Is this the first one?" Jade studied the black crevasse in the wall, slightly off to the left. "It's a little hard to see, unless you already know it's there."

"Approaching from this side, it is. There are more just ahead."

Meg and Jade looked at each other, then over at the cave.

"I'll check this one out. Just in case." True to his word, he climbed to the opening in a few easy steps. He stared into it for a moment, before disappearing into the yawning mouth. He reappeared within minutes to half step and slide his way back down to them. "Nothing in there. It's small and empty."

"Good. Let's check the next one."

Five minutes later, they approached the gaping black mouth of the second cave.

Jade couldn't say why they all fell quiet. But they did.

DANE STUDIED THE large opening in the side of the hill. John had shown him the caves because they wanted to see if they'd sustained damage in the quake. To rule out that anyone had sought shelter in them. There'd been nothing unusual in any of them back then.

The path appeared well traveled. Any number of locals could come through here. Just because Emile and Tasha considered this their backyard didn't mean it was.

With a glance toward the two women, Dane started toward the second cave. They stayed behind. Maybe it was due to their nervousness, but he approached warily. Large boulders sat piled high off to one side of the dark entrance, as if from a cave-in. The opening was smaller than it looked. Bending over slightly, he peered in, until his eyes adjusted to the darkness, then he navigated to a spot farther in.

Inside, he straightened slightly and surveyed the small open space that narrowed almost to a point at the back. The cave appeared empty. Large boulders dotted the floor, and the light was dim, but there was enough that he could see, as he walked all the way to the back, to ensure it was empty. He understood that the women were looking for Dr. Mike, but Dane hadn't forgotten that Peppe could have taken up residence anywhere here or been injured and lying wounded or dead inside. However, with Dr. Mike, Dane assumed the doctor would be closer to the entrance, if he were here, in the event help came along.

Not so in the case of the missing Peppe. Dane had the utmost respect for the medical profession, yet, when it came to mental instability, they often didn't have any answers. Look at Tasha. He gave the inside one more cursory glance.

"Dane? Is anything in there?"

He headed back to the sunlight. "No, it's empty."

"Nothing in the back?" Meg asked, frowning.

"Not that I saw. And, yes, I walked right to the back."

Jade stepped forward carefully. "I think I'd like to check it out. I've never really been in a cave like this."

Dane stepped aside, as Jade bent down and walked past him. He followed.

She glanced around and walked to the far back. "It really goes deep, doesn't it?" She peered into the darkness. "Did you say there was a third cave? We've checked two. Might as well take a look at the last one."

"Sure, it's only a minute or so away. Come on."

He led the way back out to where Meg was enjoying the sunshine.

"Jade wants to see the last cave. It's actually the biggest."

Meg brightened. "I'd like to see it too. This is a great hike."

Jade smiled slightly. "It would be, except, *where are the guys?*"

Meg glanced down at her watch. "Trust a little more. I'm sure they'll be here soon."

Jade sighed. "Let's hope so."

Dane, who had continued along the path, turned back. "Ladies? Will we check out the last one or not?"

The two women raced to catch up.

Chapter 19

JADE STARED AT the massive black hole and shuddered. That cave might look good to some people. Not to her. Nothing was comforting about it. In fact, the shivers going down her back told her the opposite. "I so don't like the look of this place."

She felt Dane's curious gaze. He reached out and grabbed her hand. She stared down at their entwined fingers and smiled weakly. "Thanks. Let's go in, then come back outside. I think I've had enough."

"Done," he said easily. "You don't have to come in with me, if you don't want to."

"No, I don't, but I will. Then I'll know there isn't anything to be afraid of inside."

Dane smiled and tugged her closer. She didn't mind. It was nice to have a strong protective male around. For that matter Meg was walking pretty darn close to them both.

At the entrance, they paused for a long moment, allowing their eyes to adjust, then walked around the stack of boulders protecting the entrance. Inside, the cave showed signs of heavy use over the ages—not so much recent activity. A fire pit was close to the mouth of the cave, only no wood or coals were in the area. There were ledges and large flat rocks though. Jade pictured people spending hours here, talking.

At the back of the cave, where the blackness was so thick you couldn't see two feet in front of you, were more boulders. Dropping Dane's hand, Jade headed to the back, toward all the boulders. No reason for anyone to be back here. She just needed to make sure.

She wandered around, stubbing her toes on rocks in the dark and scraping her hands, as she clambered over the bigger ones in her search. She'd just about given up, when she heard the faintest of sounds. "Did you guys hear anything?"

Meg called from the entrance, "No. Nothing."

"Dane? Did you?"

"I'm not sure." He navigated toward her.

Jade thought the sound had come from her left. She climbed carefully, so as to not twist an ankle in the treacherous debris lying up against the walls. A soft moan sounded. She gasped with excitement. "I think I hear someone. Dane, come here."

She moved carefully, struggling to make out what she'd heard. The noise had definitely come from somewhere off to the left and in a little farther. The walls slanted sharply and were heaped with rocks along the bottom. The darkness was cloying. She scrambled over a boulder and came to a halt.

"Dr. Mike!"

"WHAT?" SHOCKED JOY lit Meg's voice.

Dane reached Jade first; Meg came tearing back to join them. "Is it him? Really?"

"I think so. It's hard to see."

"Hang on. Let me move some of this." Dane bent and cleared a space so he could crouch down. Meg and Jade kneeled down beside Dr. Mike, who lay in a crumpled ball. Dane ran through his mental checklist of first aid training, even as Meg checked the unconscious man's head. Dane leaned across the prone man, tracing down his arms to his hands that were tucked behind his back. He came to a stop. Please not. "Shit."

"What?' He felt both women stare at him. About all he could see were the whites of their eyes.

"Christ." His mind raced, even as he reached for his old Swiss army knife.

"Dane, you're scaring us."

"And you need to be scared. He's been tied up."

Shocked silence, then gasps of horror were followed by tears. "Tied up, as in someone brought him here and left him to die?"

"We don't know that. Someone obviously left him here, but they might be coming back." He opened the knife and hesitated. "I wish we'd thought to bring a bigger flashlight. I can't see what I'm cutting by this phone one."

"Let's move him out into the sun and then cut him loose."

He studied the path ahead of them. "I need to clear a few of these rocks. Then we should pick him up and carry him out."

"We'll help you." Meg and Jade started moving more rocks to clear a path. Five minutes later, Dane scooped up the injured man, wincing at the unconscious man's groans, and carried him out into the sun.

JADE HOVERED LIKE a mother hen with a long-lost chick, as Dane gently laid Dr. Mike on the ground. More rocks than dirt and so little shade as not to count, but the sunlight would be warm and welcome to the injured man. Dane cut the bonds around Dr. Mike's wrists. Dr. Mike's arms fell apart as if boneless, and a soft pained groan erupted from the man. Meg grabbed one of his arms and rubbed with short hard strokes. Jade snatched up the second arm, and together they massaged life back into them. Dane worked on Dr. Mike's legs. She didn't know how long he'd been lying in there, but getting the circulation running properly through those limbs had to hurt.

Meg checked Dr. Mike over thoroughly. She found dried blood at the back and side of his head, but not very much. She pointed it out; both Jade and Dane peered at it and shrugged. It didn't look that bad. Meg continued to check Dr. Mike over. "Right ankle is puffy, and he has just the one head injury that I can see. The rest of him appears to be fine. Unless he has internal injuries."

With those words, Dr. Mike blinked several times and tried to open his eyes in the bright sunlight. "Hi," he said in a raspy voice.

That prompted Jade to reach for her water bottle, and, with Dane's help, they hefted Dr. Mike up slightly. Jade held his head steady in the crook of her arm. "Dr. Mike, try to drink some water." She poured the water gently into Dr. Mike's mouth. Just a little to begin with, moistening the inside of his mouth first. Then she poured in a little more.

He swallowed greedily. Taking in more, sip by sip, until he could drink fully.

"That's better," Jade said.

Dr. Mike sighed, then smiled gently. "So glad you found me."

"So are we."

He made an effort to raise his head, then gave up. "I don't feel so good. It seems like forever that I was in there."

"Overnight most likely. The thing is, you're off the beaten track a fair bit." Meg continued, hoping to get him to answer some questions. "We found the SUV and had no idea where you'd gotten to. Or how. Can you tell us what happened?"

He winced, took a deep breath, and lunged to a sitting position. A surprised look washed over his face. The color drained from his cheeks, his eyes rolled into the back of his head. With a weird squeak he crumpled back to the ground.

Jade cried out.

Meg leaned over Dr. Mike. "His pulse is slow and steady. We need to get him home." Meg stood and spun around suddenly. "Did you hear something?"

Jade turned to look at her. She searched the surrounding rocks and shrubs. "No. What did you hear?"

"Voices."

Dane took several steps toward the main path. "I'll check it out."

Staying on her knees beside Dr. Mike, Jade called out, "Be careful. Don't forget, Dr. Mike didn't tie himself up."

Dane nodded and loped off.

The two women waited several long minutes. Dr. Mike moaned again.

Jade turned to scan the area for Dane. "Still no sign of him. We'll give him a couple more minutes."

Meg glanced at her, a wry look on her face. "Yeah, and then what?"

"Give him another few minutes?" Jade shrugged, shifting to stretch her legs out. "I don't know. I can't say I'm comfortable up here alone like this. Who the hell broke into

Susan's room? Could it have been the same person who did this to Dr. Mike?" She glanced down at the injured man. "We have to get Dr. Mike down the mountain somehow. He's our first priority. Will your phone work up here?"

"Oh." Meg pulled it out and called Dane's number. "Dane? Where are you?"

He laughed, his voice easily loud enough for Jade to hear. "I'm coming around the side now."

Meg ended the call and turned to look up at the rocks, where Dane just appeared. She laughed. "There he is and look who's with him."

Hope leaped in her heart. Jade spun around. She stood so she could see better. It was true. "Oh, thank God." Jade waved exuberantly. Dane headed in their direction, with Stephen, Wilson, and Bruce walking beside him.

All four men waved back.

When they reached the women, Stephen gave Jade a hearty hug. "Hi. What a surprise to see you here. And, thank God, you found Dr. Mike. Dane told us all about it."

Jade laughed happily, as the three men gathered around Dr. Mike, pelting Meg with questions. Bruce dropped to the ground beside Dr. Mike, checking him over. Jade joined Dane a little way off to the side and watched the reunion. "Thanks. Where did you find them?"

A grin split his face. "They were walking toward us on the path. I couldn't help running into them."

"Well, I'm grateful everyone is here. We need to get Dr. Mike to the hospital—and now." She looked around uneasily.

"You're really not comfortable up here, are you?"

Jade couldn't help the shiver that slid down her spine. "Back home I did a lot of day trips. Here—with all the weird stuff going on—not so much. Besides, whoever tied him up could come back."

Despite her worry, she smiled at the laughing group in front of them. They really hadn't expected to find Dr. Mike on this adventure. She felt the relief in their overexuberance. But it wasn't over yet. "Any ideas how to get Dr. Mike down?"

"We could call for help, except we're a little short on clearings for a chopper to land. No stretcher here, and it could be hard to make something like that out of the little bit of materials we have available. So …"

"Oh. I just might have an answer." Stephen plunked down his backpack and pulled out a roll stretcher. "Can we make this work?"

Jade stared. "Why would you carry that in your backpack?"

His boyish grin burst out. "The handle broke, so I took it to the hotel to fix in the evenings. The thing is, this one doesn't have a spine board. If he's severely injured, we might cause more damage this way."

Meg studied it. "Have you fixed the handle?"

He grinned. "More or less."

"We already moved him once. … I suggest we try it. Our options aren't great otherwise."

Silently, working in unison and using their years of experience, they stabilized Dr. Mike's head and neck and shifted him onto the modified stretcher.

Bruce motioned to Dane. Both men took up their positions at either end of the stretcher and picked it up carefully. Dane called back over his shoulder to the women, "So are you coming, or will we wait for you back home?"

Jade shook her head, grabbed the empty water bottles

lying around, and ran to catch up. Together with Meg, they slipped past the three men to take the front position. Stephen and Wilson stepped in behind. Close enough to talk and far enough away to not be in each other's way, they managed the path for close to an hour—at which point they stopped for a short break.

They rested a bit, as shadows lengthened. After a few minutes Bruce called for an ambulance to meet them at the lab. Bruce stood. "Ready? Let's go."

Stephen and Wilson protested that it was their turn to help carry Dr. Mike. Dane and Bruce vetoed the switch, citing the differences in height between the other men as a reason to continue as they began.

They started off slower this time. Jade led the way, with Meg following. Jade's heart lightened when the grave site came into view below. She didn't know how the men were holding up. The two carrying Dr. Mike were doing at least twice the work of everyone else, but they refused the many offers to switch off. At least, Jade thought, going down was easier than hiking up the incline.

Finally they made it to the grave site.

She stopped and wiped her brow. Dr. Mike still hadn't regained consciousness. "Thank God, that might have been a bad trip for him, if he were awake," she said to Meg. "Am I glad this day is almost done."

After that, things moved quickly. The ambulance was waiting at the lab trailers. Dr. Mike was taken away. The others piled into the SUVs and drove out in a procession. Dane turned off at John's house, while the others took a direct route to the hospital.

Dr. Mike was quickly admitted into the ER, but they were told it might be some time before they received news of his condition.

While waiting, Jade decided to wander over to see Tasha. She didn't really want to see her, yet felt compelled to check on her and Emile. She couldn't find their rooms. Heading to the nurses' station, she stopped to ask about Tasha. A friendly young nurse sat at the computer, her smile a gentle welcome.

"She's been moved to a different ward for assessment."

Jade's face froze. She expected that would happen, only she hadn't thought such a move would be made for another week or so. "Right. Is it possible to get an update on her brother, Emile? I was part of the team that brought them both in."

The young nurse's face brightened. She flashed her a white smile. "Oh. Now I know who you are." Then her face fell; she lowered her voice. "Emile didn't make it. He passed away late this morning."

Jade bowed her head, as her heart ached for the family. Poor Dane. Poor John. And then she began to worry about Dr. Mike. Emile hadn't looked that bad when they found him, but he got worse fast, and now he was dead. Could nothing go right for them? "Damn. I'd hoped he'd pull through."

"I think everyone did. I went to school with him, way back when. And we were optimistic here. He started to pull out of it, but, like any of these head wounds, you can't count on that." The nurse smiled sadly, her eyes huge wells of emotion. "Once he started to slip, he fell all the way down."

Jade shuddered. "I am so sorry. Has Tasha been told?"

The nurse took one look around and lowered her head. "It wouldn't do any good. She's not aware of anything. Can't talk and isn't responding to treatment at this point."

Pain filled Jade's mind. "Poor John. He lost his child, his brother-in-law, and his wife. … Hopefully time will help, and Tasha will come home someday."

The nurse shook her head. "Miracles do happen, but I can't say that I've seen one this bad pull out of it."

"What's her husband to do then?" Jade couldn't help herself from asking, even though she knew there was no answer.

The nurse lifted her face and stared, her gaze somber, wise—and directed right into Jade's eyes. "There's only one thing he can do—start over. This family is gone."

DANE STOOD IN front of the kitchen door to John and Tasha's house. He really didn't want to go inside. Physical exhaustion pulled at him, the kind he hadn't experienced since his football-playing days. Carrying Dr. Mike down the hill had been hard work.

Now he had to deal with John.

He poked his head into the kitchen. "John? I'm back. I'll wash up. See you in a few minutes." Closing the door, he headed to his small cabin for a quick wash and clean clothes. His shoulders ached.

Damn.

He wanted to go home. He needed to stay—but he didn't want to be here anymore.

Except for Jade. If she stayed, then he wanted to stay for a little while longer, for her. It could take that long to settle his affairs here anyway. And then he wanted to return to his old life—in Seattle. His house, his comforts. His home.

But he didn't want to return to it empty. Again his thoughts jumped to Jade. He was determined to explore a relationship with her. And if it worked out …

He was almost done here. He was only here for his brother. He knew it; his brother knew it, and neither one voiced it. He'd stay as long as John needed him. An idea flitted around in his head. Maybe he could convince John to return to Seattle with him? At this point in time, he couldn't see John leaving Tasha. However, if there was no improvement over the next month, then maybe …

John had some hard decisions ahead. Dane frowned. How would this play out? John couldn't make the easy decisions. How could he make the really difficult ones?

And had anyone seen Peppe? Or was he still missing? *What the hell will we do about that if he is?*

And what had happened to Dr. Mike? Dane hoped he'd be fine, hoped he'd regain consciousness soon. The injuries hadn't looked too severe. Then look at Emile's; that hadn't looked bad either. That one really bothered him.

As did the thought of someone breaking into the hotel rooms. Who and why would someone want to tie up Dr. Mike, then abandon him in a cave? Was someone targeting the team? Or was some *crazy* out there, wandering around and attacking people, and the hotel break-in was an isolated incident? Given the poverty here, that was most likely.

That the attack on Dr. Mike could have been done by Emile or Peppe hadn't passed Dane by. That Emile had been injured and in the hospital looked bad, pointed to his guilt, because no one came back for Dr. Mike. Maybe his attacker had been Emile. That certainly reinforced that he was likely the culprit. Dane just couldn't imagine why Emile would do something like this though, and Dane didn't know how to broach that possibility with John either.

Something had shifted. Dane didn't get it. His life had

been calm and quiet before the mortuary team arrived. Now it was almost as if the grave being opened had poisoned everything and everyone. But surely that wasn't possible—was it?

Chapter 20

HUNGRY, TIRED, AND now showered, all team members arrived for dinner on time. Except Bruce, who'd stayed at the hospital with Dr. Mike.

Jade walked in, as the first plates came out of the kitchen. Her stomach growled as the smells of delicious food reached her nose. She groaned and grabbed her chair. "Oh, Lord, thank you for this food. I am so hungry."

"When are you *not* hungry?" Stephen grinned and passed her the first bowl. "Everyone has taken some of this dish, so help yourself."

She grabbed the bowl. *Fish.* She took several large pieces and motioned for the next dish to be passed her way. Finally, with much joking, all of them ended up with full plates.

"By the way, I sent an email to Tony, updating him on Dr. Mike's rescue and current condition." Meg chuckled at the horrified looks shot her way. "Maybe now we won't have to worry about training Dr. Mike's replacement."

Everyone groaned. "That's not funny."

Meg piped up. "Speaking of which, Tony wants us to increase our productivity."

Outrage rippled through the room.

"Increase?" Stephen barely managed to get the word out through his stuffed mouth.

Forking up another bite, Meg said, "He's hoping we can reduce our time here by a week or two."

"Really?" Jade didn't think that would be possible, … unless the right DNA results came back soon.

Susan, looking better after a long nap, asked, "What's the rush?"

Meg shrugged. "I don't know. He didn't say."

Just then Bruce walked in. A chorus of questions filled the air. Holding up his hand, he ticked off on his fingers, as he shared information. "Dr. Mike is fine. Has a sprained ankle. They're keeping him overnight for observation. They aren't expecting any problems. He did regain consciousness but was asleep again by the time I was allowed in to speak to him. … So, no, we don't know what happened to him. He did say Emile's and Peppe's names."

Jade stared at him. "I don't know what possible motive either of them would have to hurt Dr. Mike, and, now that Emile's dead, we might never know. Depends if we can get any answers from his father."

Bruce filled his plate, then answered further questions as he ate. He pushed his empty plate off to one side and faced the group. "And there is one other thing we need to discuss."

Jade knew what it was. She'd been waiting for it. She refilled her plate, stuck her tongue out at Stephen for laughing at her, and waited for Bruce to speak.

"I stopped in at the police station to update them on Dr. Mike. They weren't thrilled obviously. However, the authorities have agreed to look into the skeletons with the chains …"

"Yeah!" Cheers erupted around the table.

Jade waited. This still didn't feel like a cheering moment. She studied Bruce's face. "But?"

"Only if we do the processing and turn everything over to them."

She put down her fork. "We already agreed that we'd

help out in our own free time to be certain that happened." She frowned and looked at Meg and Stephen for affirmation. "Or was I wrong?"

"No, that's correct."

She turned back to Bruce, "So what's the problem?"

"The problem is that Tony doesn't want us doing the work, doesn't want the company name associated in any way with this mess. He also doesn't want any of the remains to be handed over to them, not until we have found the remains we're looking for and have removed them."

"You mean, he's afraid that, if a crime has been committed, then it would reflect badly on the company or interfere with our ability to complete the job?" Jade picked up her fork again and continued to eat. *How typical.*

Bruce sighed. "He's worried that, even if we do locate our target family members, the authorities here won't release the remains we want to ship to the States. That's a possibility. And I can't fault Tony for his logic. We've gotten slightly off on a tangent, and he's just trying to rein us back in."

"Except we had no idea what we'd find in that grave."

Bruce picked up his coffee cup. "No, of course not. Our loyalty has to remain with Tony. Yet I can't walk away from those other victims either."

"There's only so much we can do." Meg sipped her coffee. "We've taken loads of pictures, and we've dug up the remains and processed them to the extent we're able."

Stephen nodded. "So then there is no big deal. We can turn over our findings, and the remains in question, to the authorities and carry on."

A strange look crossed Bruce's face.

Jade caught it and wondered. Then the missing piece clicked. "You mean, that might work, unless one of those women with the chains, like the most recent one, happens to be the adult female we're looking for?"

DANE PUSHED OPEN the kitchen door and wandered inside. "John? You in here?" He walked through the kitchen and into the living room, in case his brother left him a note. He kept his gaze off the creepy dolls. Why the hell hadn't his brother taken that shit down?

"John?" He poked his head inside the only bedroom in the tiny house.

What the hell? The bedroom was a mess. Incense bowls filled the top of the dresser and more little creepy dolls covered the nightstand. He didn't know what had gone through Tasha's mind these last few days and weeks, but it looked as if the slide had been in progress for a while.

John worried him now. How could all this have gone unnoticed, and why didn't he do something about this? Then he remembered his brother's inability to make decisions …

Where the hell was he? Dane pulled out his phone and called him yet again. Was this the fifth time? Maybe John had gone into town to see Tasha? Then why the hell wasn't he answering the phone?

"Hello."

Dane ran a tired hand over his damp hair at the weary sound of his brother's voice. "John! I've been looking for you. Trying to reach you."

Sounding like he'd hit the last of his reserves, John said, "Emile didn't make it."

Dane closed his eyes briefly. *Shit.* "I heard. I'm sorry. I'd hoped he'd pull through."

"Yeah, … well, he died this morning, before noon. I

came down as soon as I got the message." A yawn, came through the phone. "Ah, hell, Dane. Life pretty much sucks right now."

Dane agreed, yet stayed quiet, not wanting to depress his brother any further. Wincing against the answer to come, Dane asked hesitantly, "And Tasha? Any change there?"

"No improvement. They've moved her to the psych ward."

"What? Already? Surely she hasn't improved physically enough for that move, has she?"

"I don't know. Something about needing round-the-clock care and no beds. The psych ward isn't all that thrilled to have her either. I don't know where she belongs. I want her home with me, only she doesn't see me, hear me. … She doesn't seem to know I'm even there."

"Aw, hell." Dane couldn't think of anything else to say. "I'm sorry, man."

"Yeah. Me too. The thing is, no one can tell me if she's improving, will improve, or could take a long slide down. She's my wife. For better or for worse. And never did I consider this could happen." He sighed. "And I didn't mean that in a bad way. She's my wife. I love her. I want her home, where she belongs. I know she lost the baby, and that'll be hard on her, … on us, but we can make more babies." His voice caught on a sob. "I can't live without her. I don't want to."

"You can if you have to. I know this is hard. There has been enough hurt and suffering. I don't want to lose you too."

"I'm not dying. Nor am I suicidal. I do wonder why God hates me so much though."

Dane winced and let his brother ramble. "I don't think He hates you."

"He sure as hell doesn't love me."

In an effort to change the subject, Dane asked, "When are you coming home?"

"Soon. I'm just driving around. I had to get out for a bit."

"Understood. Give yourself time."

"So why is it that I don't feel as I have any time?" Bitterness slipped across the phone line.

Dane frowned. He didn't like the way this was going. "Have you heard or seen anything of Peppe?"

"No. I don't know where the old bugger has gone. Don't care much at this point either." Then moments of silence filled the phone.

What could Dane say?

"I know I'm being a bit of a bastard, yet I can't help it," John continued. "I'll pick up something for dinner and come home. Will you be there?"

"Yeah, I'm beat. Been hiking all day, looking for one of Jade's coworkers. Make it dinner for three. I'm starved."

"On my way."

Dane hung up and smiled. "Now that sounds better." He stood in the middle of the living room, talking to himself, uncertain what to do. Tasha's stuff filled the house. He couldn't begin to get inside Tasha's head; even worse, he now understood her mind had broken. His brother would be back in about fifteen minutes. What could he do to help John? The poor guy had been sleeping on the couch for months now. Not that they'd spoken about it. Should he clean out the bedroom for his brother? Maybe through that process he'd find a clue to help them understand her behavior.

Not bloody likely.

The smelly bedroom made his skin crawl.

He turned on the overhead light and winced. The darkness had hidden the extent of the mess. There wasn't a spot on the floor to be seen. He couldn't believe she owned that many clothes. She'd only worn a couple outfits.

He returned to the kitchen and grabbed several garbage bags. Then he walked out to his truck and put on his work gloves. Taking a deep breath, he started bagging the mess on the floor. There was no easy way to do it, so he just picked them up and shoved it all into the first bag, until it was full. Then grabbed a second one. The third one he stuffed with bedding. He hauled the bags to the patio. Returning to the room, he grabbed a broom, opened a window and finished cleaning. He hadn't found anything but filth.

He stopped beside the first of two small tables on either side of the bed—each had a drawer. Dane was tempted to open it. But this was his brother's bedroom. He shouldn't be poking his nose anywhere here. He tried but couldn't turn away.

Shit. Shit. Okay. Just one quick look. The first table was almost empty. On top were a small clock and a lamp. Nothing else. The other one had to be Tasha's, and it was different. The drawer was full of small bags of herbs, maybe potions of some sort. Or drugs? He winced. That might explain her behavior. Not that he was an expert. It wouldn't explain the loss of the baby, but then, like the doctor had said, sometimes losses like that just happened.

Did John need to know the details? The whys? Would it be easier? Help him with his recovery?

Headlights shone through the living room window. John was home.

Great. Would he appreciate what Dane had done or be devastated by the intrusion? Only time would tell.

He walked outside to meet his brother.

HE STOOD IN his son's cabin—originally built decades ago for the foreman on the farm, then for guests as a way to make extra money, before his son grew into a man. Emile had moved in when Tasha had gotten herself married.

And Emile wasn't here. He hadn't come home.

The ambulance had taken him, and the night had swallowed him.

Peppe ran a shaky hand through his thinning hair. His world consisted of slices of memories that, even when pieced together, made no sense. He'd been in the main house several times since the ambulance had taken away his kids. There'd been no sign of them since. No sign of Tasha. No sign of Emile.

Instead the interloper had moved in. John's brother. He'd cleaned out Tasha's stuff—bags full left on the patio, like garbage. Her things weren't garbage. His little girl wasn't garbage—not like some women.

Someone would pay for this. And soon.

He didn't see John being responsible. He'd always been good to Tasha. To Emile. To him. Not that he'd seen John much. Still, he'd been here for a while now.

John's brother on the other hand … and that group he hung around with? Peppe shook his head. At the mass grave, he'd seen Dane sniffing around that little blonde who worked at the trailers.

Someone had to pay for this intrusion into their lives and their homes. This was his place. He wanted his son and daughter back. Maybe he could force them to bring the kids home? *Hmm.* The brother? The grave team? He smiled grimly. Or one of the women who were connected to both?

Perfect.

Chapter 21

MORNING CAME TOO early. Jade groaned and rolled over to bury her face in the pillow. She did not want to be awake this early on a Sunday. Weekends were supposed to be for fun and rest. … Still, they'd found Dr. Mike, and the word was, his condition was improving.

She smiled into the pillow. Today was a whole new day. Sitting up, she grinned at the sunshine peeking through her curtains. Good, another nice day. A day to stay home, kick around, and take it easy. Maybe hit the beach, like she'd promised herself. She'd had enough drama for a lifetime.

Her hotel phone rang. She picked it up. Her brother, Duncan, calling. A happy sigh wafted through her. It was so nice to hear from him. "Hey. What's happening?"

"That's why I called. How are things over there?"

She filled him on the last few days and wasn't surprised at his exclamations.

"Holy crap. Are you nuts! You were supposed to go over there to recover, … to get back to normal. Not to experience more stress."

She kicked back her covers and leaned against her headboard. "You're right, and I'd be happy to have missed this. But today, after finding Dr. Mike last night, things are looking much better."

"Well, is everything else okay now?"

She told him about Tony's visit and the progress on the site, then remembered to ask him about his life back in Seattle. After they said their goodbyes, Jade got up and took a shower.

Breakfast was a quiet and calm affair, in that she was alone in the dining room. She ordered a big meal and took it to the outside patio to sit in the sunshine. It was still early, and the sun already had enough heat that she chose to sit by the palm trees in a shaded spot. She took her time and relaxed. She was going nowhere today.

A sleepy Meg stumbled out onto the patio to join her.

"I didn't expect to see you here so early." Jade smirked at the disgruntled look on Meg's face.

Meg yawned widely. "I don't want to be here either. I want to be in bed, sleeping. As that's apparently not an option, here I am." Meg carefully put her cup on the table. "If there were any justice, we'd recoup all those lost hours of worrying by sleeping late." Meg pulled a chair over and sat down. "My face feels like sandpaper was scraped over it while I slept."

"I have some nice cream in my room, if you'd like to try some." Jade reached for her last piece of toast and spread jam over it. "Have you ordered your breakfast yet?"

"Yes. I'm just having French toast." She crossed her arms on the table and rested her head on them. With her eyes closed she looked ready to drop back off to sleep.

Jade brightened. "I forgot about that option. I could use some too."

Meg lifted her head and snorted. "Are you nuts? You just ate."

Jade shrugged. "I burned a lot of calories yesterday. Can't afford to lose any more weight."

Cindy, the one waitress who worked on weekends, refilled their coffee cups. Jade ordered another round of French toast, while Meg snickered, perking up enough to butter her toast, then poured on the syrup. Coffee and food seemed to revive her.

By the time Jade's second breakfast arrived, Stephen and Wilson had joined them. Everyone looked tired and worn out, but they smiled broadly, and bright eyes abounded. Yesterday had turned out for the best for their team. In the bright sunshine of the morning, it was easy to see the world in a more positive light.

When Dr. Mike hobbled in, bright but a little worn around the edges, with Bruce behind him, everyone cheered. Jade jumped up and held out a chair for the doctor. She snagged his crutches and leaned them against the palm tree behind her. "How are you?"

He smiled and hopped the last step to the table. "I'm fine. I'm so happy to be back here."

Bruce dropped onto a chair too. "After a great night, the doctors were happy to release him early this morning. We even snuck in a quick stop to update the police. Wait until you all hear his story." He stared at Jade's plate. "I hope you left some for others."

With a cheeky grin in his direction, Jade forked up a large piece of French toast and popped it in her mouth. "I did. Cindy will be happy to bring you a plate too."

"So what happened? Who tied you up and left you there?" Wilson picked up his coffee and took a sip.

Even Jade put down her fork and turned to watch the mixed emotions pass across Dr. Mike's face. "What?" she prompted.

Dr. Mike rubbed his temple. "I just feel a little foolish,

that's all. I had locked up the lab, and, on the spur of the moment, I decided to check out this trail. It was right around the corner, nice and close. What could go wrong? I wasn't planning on climbing it. I just wanted to see if it was something we could all do." He sighed, took a sip of tea, then put his cup down and continued. "I parked, got out, locked the SUV, and went to the base of the path. ... The next thing I know, I'm on the ground, my hands tied up, and this old guy is trying to wake me up."

Gasps lit up the room.

He winced. "Now I know it was Peppe. He had a wild look in his eyes, and he smelled something terrible. At the time, I tried to reason with him, then tried to offer him something, anything to let me go. He hardly talked. That guy, for all his lack of size, was on a mission."

He glanced around the room, a wry look on his face. "I know. How could a small crazy old man go up against me? I've got fifty pounds on him, am younger and stronger." He stared down at his teacup, remnants of memories chasing across his face. "Yeah, I'm feeling pretty stupid today."

Silence hit the table.

Bruce smacked him on the shoulder lightly. "Don't be. You might be younger and stronger. However, you aren't insane, and you were out for a hike. You weren't looking for an ambush."

Dr. Mike gave him a half smile. "I tried to fight him, and he whacked me over the head again." He shrugged. "I decided to wait for a better chance. He forced me to walk up the mountain. When it got dark, he still knew where and how to walk. I didn't. Just after we'd topped the rise, I made it a little farther, then fell on the rocks."

He motioned to his crutches. "I couldn't walk anymore.

He actually helped me get up and into the cave." Dr. Mike shifted uncomfortably. "I heard voices and hobbled forward enough to see Emile and Peppe having an all-out argument. Emile saw me and my tied hands. I thought he'd help me. Instead he took off down the mountain, screaming at his father something fierce." He shook his head. "Peppe took off after him. Not sure what that was all about."

"We found Emile on the rocks by the grave site. He appeared to have fallen and hit his head. He died in the hospital yesterday."

"Oh, Lord," Dr. Mike whispered, shock rippling across his face. "I'd hoped he'd gone to get help."

"He might have been coming for help when he fell." Meg smiled gently at him.

Jade, speaking in a hushed voice, had another suggestion. "Or Peppe might have caught up to him and attacked him."

Silence filled the room once again.

Everyone sat back.

"Unbelievable. If we hadn't found you …" Stephen left the rest unsaid.

Dr. Mike grimaced. "Thanks for pointing that out."

Jade reached over and kissed the older man on the cheek. "Except we did find you, so all is good."

Stephen raised his eyebrows. "Except for Peppe. He's still out there, loose. What possible reason could he have had to kidnap Dr. Mike?"

Putting down his cup of fresh coffee, Dr. Mike said, "He kept mumbling about a doctor. As if he or someone he knew needed a doctor. I don't know for sure, but I wonder if he thought I could help Tasha?"

"Oh, wow." And Jade could almost believe that. Especially for someone in Peppe's mental state. "That almost makes sense."

"It would mean he knew that Tasha was in trouble." Everyone turned to stare at Dr. Mike, then at each other.

Stephen snorted. "Anyone would know that. You only needed to look at her to know something was wrong. Jesus, I almost admire him if that's why he did it. At least he was trying to do something for his daughter."

That brought murmurs of agreement from the others.

"Anyone know if there'll be a funeral for Emile?" Meg asked.

Jade shook her head, before answering, "No idea. I doubt Dane and John have it all figured out yet either."

"Yeah, you're not kidding. Is the chaos over?" Bruce asked. "Obviously we'll have to be careful, as long as Peppe is still wandering around. But now that the police are looking for him, we might soon have an end to that problem too. I'll call Dane, after I get a bite to eat. We should be the ones to tell him what happened. He can decide the best way to tell John."

Jade winced. That wouldn't be much fun. Dane wouldn't be impressed with the idea of Peppe being responsible for Dr. Mike's disappearance. He'd feel guilty. He shouldn't because he'd wanted the authorities called in to help find the old man in the first place.

Bruce changed the subject. "We should be getting the next lot of DNA results back soon too. Seems like we've spent a lot of time here, and yet we're still just getting started. I don't feel that we're even close to halfway. What's it been? … A month now?"

The discussion turned to the job in progress.

Jade settled back, content to listen to everyone else work

things out. There was a sense of calm in her heart. She knew John had to be going through a bad time right now, and she felt sorry about his family. Still, she was beyond relieved to have things approaching normal in her world.

Now if they could just stay out of trouble for the rest of their Haitian work term …

MONDAY DAWNED BRIGHT and clear. Everyone showed up in good spirits, ready to make major inroads on their work—as if the long Friday night and draining Saturday had never happened. Of course a relaxing Sunday had helped to revive everyone's energy levels.

Dr. Mike had chosen to work in the lab trailer. His ankle rested on a second stool, and he worked on charts, while Jade worked on the skeletons. Stephen and Wilson worked up at the grave site. Both men sported decent tans after weeks of outdoor work.

Susan, in good health again, had gone into town with Bruce to attend the clinic. There'd been a lot of discussion about closing it, if no one showed.

The end result was to give it a couple more weeks and then reassess. So far they'd only had a half-dozen people turn up. None of those wanted or could afford to have their relatives buried elsewhere. They just wanted to locate their family members, to find closure as to where and what had happened to them—nothing more. Even though Tony had contacted the media outlets throughout Haiti, to broadcast the offer, the response from the local families had been disappointing.

Jade bustled around her two new cases. She had an adolescent male and a young adult female on her morning docket. With Dr. Mike doing the charts, they could proceed that much faster.

Before long, they were finished. "I'll go grab Stephen. We'll switch these two for two more."

Dr. Mike nodded, but his focus remained fixed on the screens in front of him.

Jade smiled at his intensity, then headed out. While walking up the path, she heard the men's shovels banging away on the rocks. She wished Dane would drive up, even though it was Monday, and she knew he had his own business to take care of.

He'd been at the back of her mind all morning. How was he holding up?

They'd talked several times on Sunday but hadn't managed to squeeze in more than a few minutes of togetherness. Again she wished she had her own cell phone here. She could send him a text to just say hi and to let him know she was thinking of him. She'd put buying a phone at the top of her list of things to do.

"Hey." She smiled at the two dust-covered men. "Can I get one of you to come help move bags for me? I'm done with the first two and could use two more."

"That was fast." Stephen put down his shovel. "I'll help."

"I might as well too." Wilson joined them. "We'll do the switch for you. How's Dr. Mike holding up?"

"He appears to be fine. Having him help out in the lab is speeding things up."

The men quickly exchanged the bags, leaving Jade and Dr. Mike alone again.

"Jade? Any updates on Peppe from Dane?"

"Haven't heard anything." Jade picked up her camera

again. "Then I haven't spoken to Dane today."

"I'm sure the authorities would let us know if they found Peppe anyway."

"Good thing." She replaced the camera on her table and picked up her pen and clipboard and wrote down a few notes. She removed a solid gold band from a finger barely holding together. She checked for an inscription, then laid it on a white board and picked up her camera again. "I wonder how John is holding up," she added, as an afterthought.

Dr. Mike pointed out another consideration. "And I'm wondering if Peppe understood the significance of the ambulance taking away both of his kids, with only John and Dane there since. Who knows how much he saw or understood? If he realizes the truth, no way to know how he'll react now. He could blame us. He could blame John or even Dane. They are on his property. And his family is gone. Or he might not even comprehend what's happened."

A heavy silence filled the small room, as they worked.

"Any idea when his wife passed away?" Dr. Mike asked.

"I don't think I ever heard. He's probably done a slow decline since then." Jade looked at him.

"*Hmm.*"

"What are you thinking?"

"Someone mentioned his wife dying about ten years ago. Just looking to confirm. That's within my time estimate of how long the two oldest skeletons have been in the grave. Eight to twelve years is my informed guess at this point."

Jade straightened, a dawning understanding filtering in. "The timeframe puts Peppe as a potential suspect, doesn't it? If his wife died anywhere around then, it could have set him on that path?"

He studied the chart in his hand. "I will admit my

thinking is colored by Peppe trying to drag me over the mountain, … but the proximity, the timing, the means? … It all fits. He could have caught any young woman and dragged her over that hill into his cabin and who would have known? Of course motive is still an issue."

Jade put down her camera slowly. It was either that or drop it. "Does anyone twisted enough to imprison women need a motive? Seriously. That's a horrible thought."

"Don't worry about it. Probably nothing to it. It was just the coincidence of being a prisoner myself for that short time period that brought it to mind." He pushed up his glasses. "Then again any one of these bodies could have been buried somewhere else, then brought here as a better hiding place. Mixed in with all the others, no one would know. Even the dirt layer could have been added in between. Enough to hide the new arrivals before the loader came back with the next load. It's not as if any security was here at the time of the big earthquake."

"And wrapped in sheets, the chains wouldn't have been visible anyway."

Dr. Mike sighed. "No one cared. This grave was the solution to their major problem. Imagine the chaos at the time. We've found bodies that had been wrapped in sheets, plastic, some taped shut, and others just tossed."

The image he'd painted turned her stomach. "So what you're really saying is that there is little means to find the truth." She spun around in the direction of the reefer truck. "Do you think the kidnapper was in the grave himself?"

"Could be."

She winced as she glanced down at the adult male on her table. "Or even here?"

He grinned. "Absolutely. The thing is, we may never

know. We can turn over the evidence to the authorities but—"

"It will be up to them to follow up on it."

Dr. Mike nodded. "I don't think a few more dead bodies in a mass grave will bother them much."

"These women were murdered, weren't they?"

"Yes. The first one we found could have been a captive at the time and killed by the earthquake. Or the kidnapper might have decided it was time to get rid of her."

"And had a perfect grave ready-made for him. Nice. *Not.*"

"And Peppe could also have walked across his property and thrown her in, between tractor trips."

They stared at each other.

"Just sayin'," said Dr. Mike.

So that's how he'd worked his way around to thinking John's Haitian family could be involved? Jade pondered the information. "Which also makes Emile a suspect, based on that thinking. Physically stronger, also in close proximity, also devastated by the loss of his mother? And with Emile dead and Peppe and Tasha off their rockers—chances are good we'll never know."

Straightening his back, Dr. Mike grimaced. "Exactly. The only thing we can do is our job. And hope that, even if the authorities here don't do anything, that a higher power will."

Jade hated that some creep could have been kidnapping and killing women, possibly for years, without paying the price for their crimes.

She slammed down her clipboard and glared at Dr. Mike. A higher power nothing; she wanted justice. "I'm hoping the bastard's already dead. And that it wasn't an easy death. Pinned down and dying without water and food, … for days in a deserted empty house. … Now that sounds about right."

"Exactly." Dr. Mike smiled. "I'm not all about sugar and spice, you know."

AT THE END of the day, Jade really wanted to stop in and to see Dane on the way home. She did not want to see John though. She'd stayed later at the lab, hoping Dane might show up—only he hadn't. On top of that, the trailer was hot, and she was tired. She sighed.

"Okay, what gives, Miss Lovelorn?" Meg's perky voice showed she was back to normal, after the difficult weekend.

Jade wiped her forehead, reaching again for her water bottle. "*Huh*? What? Oh, nothing."

"Nothing? That's like the fifth heavy sigh in the last ten minutes. Call the man, for heaven's sake."

"Call? *Nah*. He's busy." She took a long drink and re-capped her bottle, then stared out the open door. Dust swirled outside in the breeze. Too bad it wasn't swirling inside the trailer, exchanging the old air that sat in here from the weekend with fresh air.

"You're supposed to be working too, but apparently this isn't half as interesting as wondering what Dane's up to."

Jade turned back to Meg and gave a small laugh. "That obvious?"

"Hell yeah. Just be happy the men aren't around," Meg teased. "They'd be hassling you constantly."

She gave a mock shudder. "Nasty. Okay, I'll stop."

Meg straightened from the close-up examination of a leg. "Why don't you just call him? You're an adult, not a teenager."

"So why do I feel like a schoolgirl again?"

With a delighted grin, Meg walked over and nudged Jade's shoulder. "Be the one to make the first move. Call him."

Feeling like an idiot, yet unable to stop herself, she dialed Dane's number. It rang once, then twice.

"Dane, this is Jade." With a half smile at Meg, Jade walked out into the afternoon sun to speak more freely. "I'm just calling to say hi and to see how you're holding up. How's John doing?"

"I'm fine. And I'm glad you called." His heavy sigh came through the line. "John's adjusting. He's already concerned about Tasha and now with this Peppe business …" Dane groaned painfully. "I don't know what to do for him. His repair business closed after the last earthquake, just before you arrived, but apparently it had been failing for a while. He rented a storefront a few months ago in an effort to get more customers but never even got set up before the smaller more recent earthquake. I've been helping him along financially, but he's proud, and it's awkward. Now, with Emile's funeral and Tasha's long-term care issues, I just don't know."

The sun's rays beat down. The big rocks around the trailers seemed to soak up the heat and radiate it outward. Shadows of light and dark played over the burial ground. Jade wandered from one splotch of sunshine to another. It was a beautiful afternoon. "So what now?" she asked.

"Bury Emile. Wait for word on Tasha. And I don't know what John wants to do about the baby."

"Oh dear. I never thought of that. A child born alive is buried when they die. I don't know what would happen in this case." That decision might rest with the parents, but she didn't know. Also, in this case, the mother wasn't capable of making any decision. "John has to sort through that. It was his child."

"A daughter." Dane's voice thinned slightly. "The nurse at the front desk told me, in private."

Jade winced. That made it real. She'd never known her own child's sex. "Does John know that?"

"I imagine so. We've never spoken of it."

Jade wanted to cheer him up. "Dr. Mike is doing much better. He's back at work. This last weekend has changed the atmosphere. We like the idea of working harder and going home earlier."

He sighed heavily. "Yeah, I have to admit that going home is looking pretty-damn good from my perspective too. I just can't leave John like this."

"Is that place his?"

"No, it's Peppe's and then Emile's and Tasha's."

"Except, with Emile gone, it will be Tasha's, and, as long as she's incapacitated, it's still John's place. … Right? Meaning, he still has a home?"

"Oh, yes. Look. I'm just about ready to leave off work for the day. Are you at the hotel or at the lab?"

"I'm still at the lab. We're almost ready to go home now. Meg is locking up." Meg did just that and then walked over to the reefer and checked the thermostat. She turned to face Jade, the SUV keys dangling in her hand, waiting for the call to finish.

"Are we still on for dinner on Friday?" Dane asked. "And coffee anytime between now and then would be great."

"Sounds perfect." Smiling, she ended the call and hopped into the SUV, feeling like a schoolgirl again.

"Dinner is definite for Friday."

"About time."

PEPPE HAD KEPT watch all week. Waiting. He had a place outside his house where he could keep an eye on everyone's comings and goings. Right now he was more interested in the lab trailer.

He'd waited, but she hadn't been left alone. It's as if she knew. And maybe she did.

Instincts had been bred out of most people—unless they were hunters like him. Peppe huddled deeper into the hollow. He'd kept an eye on the two houses, waiting for his kids. They hadn't come home. He didn't know where they were. He didn't know how to find them.

John might tell him. ... And John might just laugh in his face and call him crazy.

Maybe he was crazy. Peppe couldn't remember anything, not in a straight line. The days were mixed up. His wife's face swam through his mind. He thought he'd seen her yesterday, but, when he'd spoken to her, she was gone again.

Maybe he was crazy.

But he had kids. *Emile and Tasha. Emile and Tasha.* He kept the mantra going over and over again. He had to believe they'd come home.

If they didn't, then what? This one was Tasha's house, but John and his brother lived there now. That wasn't right. It was still Peppe's house.

They'd taken over. John was even driving *his* truck. At least Peppe thought it was his truck. Except he didn't remember the last time he'd driven. He'd driven his wife to work sometimes. He remembered that. Then again, he remembered the farm full of healthy green trees and fruit pickers working the place too. Was that last year? He studied the dead trees, the cut-off stumps, and the dead grass.

Couldn't have been.

He wiped his hand over his face. So many memories. So much time gone. All he wanted was to join his wife, but he had something to do first.

John's truck—his truck—drove into the yard and parked outside the main house.

Right. Now he remembered.

He turned his attention back to the lab trailer.

Chapter 22

FRIDAY DAWNED BRIGHT and clear. Jade couldn't be happier. She'd been focused and dedicated to getting the job done. The week had passed quickly. She'd spoken with Dane several times, and he'd delivered coffee two mornings in a row. She'd come to love those little surprises. He kissed her when he saw her. He kissed her when he left her. She was coming to love those gestures too. She was coming to care for Dane—at least a little bit.

Okay, more than a little.

Emile had been buried in the family tomb on Wednesday. The team had been told on Thursday.

She hadn't had a chance to call Dane all day, as the pace had picked up, and, with Dr. Mike's help, they'd accomplished the workload of two days' worth just today. Now, walking into the lobby of the hotel with Meg at her side, Jade was looking forward to a hot shower and dressing up.

"In a hurry, I see." Meg grinned. "Finally, it's Friday!"

"Finally. We're going out on the water." Jade bounced, as she raced to the stairs.

"Oh, I am so jealous!" Meg's astonishment-turned-envy made Jade perk up.

"What do I wear sailing?" Mentally she ran through her minimal wardrobe. She'd done no shopping here, other than in that first week, and clothes for dating hadn't been on her list of priorities then.

"Good question." Meg stared at Jade. "Pants maybe? When is he coming?"

Jade smiled; that's what she'd been thinking. "Five-ish. So in an hour."

Meg glanced at her watch. "You mean, in fifteen minutes."

"Oh my God. No. That can't be." Jade grabbed Meg's watch and checked for herself. "Oh no. I'm so dead." She bolted up the remaining stairs to her room. Where had the last hour gone? She would have sworn she still had time. She glanced through her limited wardrobe. She really didn't have much choice. It would have to be layers. First she needed the fastest shower possible. Then she dressed in cotton pants, a T-shirt, with a sweater and sandals. It might be warm out now, but there could be a wind out on the water. She'd freeze within an hour, if she didn't have something to cover up with. Her sweater would have to do.

She grabbed her purse and raced to the hotel's front door. Even as she stood here and caught her breath, Dane drove up.

"Perfect. Hop in."

Jade opened the passenger door of the truck and waved goodbye to Bruce, driving up in the SUV. Dane honked as they left the drive and moved onto the main road.

She glanced at him. Damn he looked good. "Are you doing okay?"

He took his gaze off the road to send her a quizzical look. "Yes. I'm fine." He refocused on the road. After a moment he looked at her again. "Don't I look fine?"

She studied his profile. This man always looked good. In a light teasing voice, she said, "Fishing for compliments?"

"Hell no." He grinned. "I don't have to fish normally."

It was her turn to grin. "No, I bet you don't."

He reached across and caught her hand, squeezing gently. "Hey, I'm not a womanizer or anything like that."

"Good. I don't do those." She'd said it flippantly, then realized how he might take it. She stared out the side window, feeling the heat climb up her throat.

His gaze burned once and then twice. She refused to meet it. Damn her quick tongue.

"I'm really enjoying our time together. We've known each other what? … A month now? I'm serious about seeing you when we're back home."

She flushed, smiled brilliantly at him, yet responded shyly, "I'm serious too."

They drove in companionable silence for several miles. Jade sat up, realizing they were heading toward the water. "This town is so pretty. I never saw anything this nice when I was here last time. The architecture, the palm trees, the blue water …" She sighed happily, as they drove along the streets.

He pointed to a large marina she hadn't seen before. "Our boat is down here. I've booked a dinner tour. This sailing company was recommended by someone who works for me. This couple will take us out on the harbor and serve a full dinner, while we get to enjoy the scenery." He drove the truck into a small lot and parked.

She smiled with delight. "What a great idea."

Laughing and holding hands, they ran the length of the big dock. The yacht was huge. White with golden trim, The Painted Lady was proudly proclaimed on the bow. It gleamed chrome and steel and quietly stated money—and class. At the ramp, they were greeted by the owners, a native

Haitian husband-and-wife team, sporting big smiles and friendly faces. As soon as Dane and Jade boarded, they were offered a choice of wine or coffee. Jade suggested coffee first and wine a bit later.

Dane grinned. "She needs her caffeine fix."

Up on the top deck was a large couch in a brilliant white that almost blinded her in the sun. It was perfect. They had the space all to themselves, with their hosts staying below to give them privacy. Jade leaned back and sniffed the salty air. "Oh, wow. Now this is nice."

"Happy?" He wandered the small space looking at the activity going on around them, as they slowly motored into the bay.

"Oh, yeah. It's a great way to end the week." She slumped lower and tilted her face to let the warm sun and the cool breeze waft across her face. It had been a long week. "I can't believe how much I needed this."

"Now here's something to make it even better." Grace, the woman who'd initially greeted them, arrived with coffee, topped with whipping cream and cinnamon, in big Spanish mugs.

"Thank you." Jade almost swooned at the rich coffee aroma hitting her nose. "I could take this every day."

"Then we'll have to find time to repeat this."

She settled back to enjoy the ride. Jade didn't know anything about boats, and this one was huge. They had perfect service. Small sailboats sauntered by with their cheeky brightly colored sails. The odd powerboat bounced across the water. The coastline drifted by. Jade just drifted.

She asked Dane a ton of questions about Haiti and couldn't believe that he seemed to have most of the answers. When he couldn't answer a couple, he went and asked their hosts. Several times, Grace came up the stairs to ask if they wanted the tourist spiel for different attractions.

Both of them said yes and stood, while she pointed out the various highlights, as they cruised slowly through the water.

The magic continued with the delivery of the promised red wine, followed by a dinner of fresh fish. Jade had no idea what kind, but it was wrapped in large green leaves and baked on coals in a brazier. Bowls of rice and veggies went with it. The smells were heavenly, the taste divine. The longer they cruised, the lower the sun slipped. Deep oranges and pinks blanketed the evening in a peaceful, intimate cover. Replete, and caught up in the enchantment of the evening, Jade settled back onto the couch, with another glass of red wine, while Grace efficiently cleared their table.

Dane sat down beside her. He lifted one arm, and she slid over to cuddle closer. A wonderful meal, gorgeous scenery, company that made her heart lift—it was magical.

Hours later, the cruise returned to port. Not ready for the evening to end, they stood and watched the lights flash on the rippling water. "We'll do this again. I'm glad you enjoyed yourself."

"I more than enjoyed tonight. It was perfect."

Dane slung his arm over her shoulders. "It's only eleven. Bedtime? Or sit by the water?"

"Oh, let's sit by the water. I don't want the night to end."

"*Hmm.*" Dane, his arm still wrapped around her shoulders, tugged her in the direction of a large circular dock, with benches all around. They walked past many other couples. At the end, they sat on a small bench they had all to themselves.

"So much to be said for moonlight on the water." She smiled, laughing lightly at the waves smacking up against the docks all around them. The moonlight danced on the ripples. "There's no visible current, or not much of one, yet the water is so alive."

"Lots of activity going on here, just on a smaller scale than Port-au-Prince.'"

Her voice sobered. "Now that wasn't my favorite place."

He caught her hand in his, squeezing it gently. "I can imagine. We'll fix that one of these days."

"Is it obvious that my experiences there still haunt me?" She watched an expression flit across his face. It was hard to get a clear look in the dim light.

"No, not really," he said slowly. "However, I also know what I've seen and heard from John, and he barely speaks of it."

"I think everyone who was here was affected, changed by the experience. My ex-fiancé wanted the old me back, and she was gone." Said so simply, it was the first time Jade realized how true it was. Her life had changed at that point. "He wasn't able to handle it."

Dane lifted her hand to drop a kiss on the back of it. "I'm sorry for you. It must have been traumatizing. I still wish John would talk about his experiences. I think it would help him."

"And here I thought men didn't like to talk."

A wry smile slipped out. "Maybe. This is different. He's holding in so much, and I can't help but think that all that emotion needs an outlet. It's as if he's two different people— the one he keeps locked up and the one he lets the world see."

She could understand that. "I needed to be alone, yet, at the same time, I needed support. And it was tough for Duncan to recognize that fine line. It was all about balance." She gazed up at Dane, concerned by the darkness in his warm gaze. He cared about his brother so much. "Does John have friends, other family members who would understand? Has he bonded with any of Tasha's family?"

"No. He only tolerated Peppe and Emile."

"Too bad. He has to be feeling isolated, lonely even. He's lucky to have you." She studied the moonlight. "It's beautiful out, … an incredibly romantic setting, and we're discussing problems."

He laughed, caught her hand in his left hand, so he could drape his right arm around her shoulders. "So what would you like to talk about?"

She cuddled in closer and laughed lightly. "You. Tell me about the rest of your family. What's your life like in Seattle? How old are you? How come you're not married with the requisite two-and-a-half kids?"

Laughing, he filled in the details of his life. She listened, enthralled. Jade turned slightly to watch a small cruiser move smoothly through the water. Its cheerful lights shone and danced on its bow, reflected on the dark water. "This area is very beautiful."

"Not as beautiful as you."

Jade shivered unexpectedly. Was it from the evening air? The magic of the moment? Or his unexpected flattery and the obvious sincerity behind it? He really thought she was beautiful.

Dane hugged her tighter. Jade leaned her head against

his cotton shirt. She loved the ripple of muscles and the steady beat of his heart. Something was so very sexy about a man who could take control—and not abuse it. *Someone like Dane.*

She would like to see where this relationship would go.

Starting with tonight.

He'd said she could set the pace.

"Are you okay?"

Tilting her head back, she murmured, "Just thinking about how much I like being with you."

His arms tightened around her, and he cuddled her close. "Good. I'm very glad to hear that. I miss this."

Tilting her head so she could look up at him, she studied the warm look in his eyes. "The closeness? The hugs? Or the hopeful prelude to so much more?"

A rumble of laughter rolled through his chest. "All three?"

She giggled, her mind taking that next leap.

Was she ready? Did she still want to wait? She'd lost most of this last year. She hadn't expected her recuperation to take so long. But it had. She didn't want to lose any opportunity to regain a full and happy life. Now that she was back to the land of the living, she wanted to live. Before it was too late.

Look at Tasha and Emile. Both young, and both had lost everything. Look at John. He'd suffered so much.

And then there was Dane ...

She wanted to celebrate what was building between them. Revel in the fact that her body was reawakening, her heart reopening, her emotions rejoicing because these feelings coursed through her.

Dane gently grasped her chin between his fingers, tilting her head so he could see her face, a puzzled look on his face. "Heavy thoughts?"

"No," she murmured, "Light thoughts. Thoughts of joy, peace, satisfaction." She lifted her face to his, sighing against his lips. "Definitely of satisfaction."

His eyes suddenly widened in understanding. She felt a shudder ripple through his body. "What are you saying? Be very clear here." His eyes darkened to almost black. His lips brushed gently across her lips. Once. Twice. Waiting.

Jade smiled, held his head firmly, and kissed him. Heat seared between them, as she laid the hottest kiss she'd ever laid on a man. She burned through her own reserves and burned through his in a greedy all-consuming lust-filled kiss that left them both gasping. "Sleep with me tonight?" she murmured against his lips.

He groaned, his lips feathering across her cheek to whisper against her ear. Shivers raced down her spine, as his husky voice said, "I'll stay, … but … we won't sleep."

He turned his head and sealed his promise with his lips.

THERE WAS A sense of urgency now. Dane grabbed her hand, and they ran, laughing, all the way to the truck. She'd jumped into the passenger side, but Dane dragged her across the seat to sit snugged up against him. She could damn-near drive the truck herself, she sat so close. And it was perfect.

She cuddled closer, her hand on his thigh.

He covered her hand with his much bigger one. "Happy?"

She heard the tinge of worry that had crept into his

voice. "Very."

Her hand was squeezed tight, then he relaxed. "Good. 'Cause it would be better if you back out now—not later …"

In the darkness of the truck, with only the headlights for illumination, the air had a sultry mysteriousness to it. Jade was loving this. The last thing on her mind was to retreat. "I'm not backing out. I'm wishing you'd drive a little faster."

He gave a shout of laughter and hit the gas.

The trip back to the hotel was fast and furious, steeped in sensuality and promise that Jade swore she'd never felt before. She wanted Dane something fierce.

They arrived in the hotel parking lot ten minutes later. Most of the lights were off—given the hour, almost everyone should have gone to bed. Jade didn't want to meet anyone on their way up to her room, not because the relationship was a secret; she just didn't want the intrusion. She was selfish. There was magic in the air. She wanted to keep it to herself—and Dane.

At her hotel room, she unlocked the door and walked over to close the curtains. Twisting back, she dropped her key and purse on the small dresser and turned to face him. It suddenly struck her how unbelievably far she'd come this past month. With much of that distance due to this man. Oh, she would agree that returning to Haiti had been the best thing she could have done for herself, but mostly because it had brought Dane into her life.

He stood in the middle of the room, studying her, a slight frown furrowing his forehead. Waiting. She smiled, slowly, sensually. "I won't change my mind."

That wicked grin of his flashed, and he opened his arms.

She walked into them. They closed tightly around her.

"Thank you," she said, tilting her head back, so she could see him.

Surprise lit his heated gaze, his eyes dark and intense, … waiting.

She loved that about him. Loved the patience. Loved the control. As much as she might not think she was ready to love, she understood she was already at least halfway there. "Thank you for showing me there can be a bright future. For showing me that not all men are the same. For showing me that being in a relationship again is possible."

He dropped a light kiss on her forehead. Patient. Caring. Understanding. "And are you sure you're ready?"

"I wasn't—until I met you." Her hands stroked his chest, reveling in the smooth expanse of muscles rippling under her touch. She slipped her hands down his arms and around his back as she rejoiced in the sense of rightness. She really wanted this time together.

He seemed more concerned about making sure she was okay with tonight.

Leaning back slightly, she whispered, "I'm pretty sure, when you promised we wouldn't sleep tonight, talking wasn't what you had in mind." That wicked grin flashed again, and he laughed. She tugged his face down and kissed him. Hard.

He groaned. His arms tightened, and then he stole the kiss away. Trailing his lips across her cheeks, he nuzzled her ear, his hot breath sending tingles down her spine, warming her insides. His words, though, lit them on fire. "Oh, we'll talk. Later."

Then, full of powerful and possessive lust, he kissed her.

And she stopped thinking altogether.

Heat flashed between them. Dane's kisses lit her senses. Nothing else was in this moment but him, this passion, this heat that threatened to consume her. His hands were everywhere, stroking, caressing, soothing, as they explored her back, her belly, and slowly, ever-so-slowly, they inched higher. He teased her, stroking below her bra strap, sliding along the top of the lace edge covering her breasts. She twisted, caught in a mindless haze of passion, desperate to have his hands where she needed them.

Finally he stroked upward, cupping her breasts. She moaned as her insides melted and her breasts swelled in joy. Shudders rippled down her spine.

For a moment he paused, pulled back slightly. Sliding his hands under her shirt, he lifted it up and over her head. Her world tilted slightly as he swooped her up and over to the bed, laying her down on the covers. She kicked off her sandals, unhooked her bra. *Whoosh*. ... Her cotton pants hit the floor.

She bounced to her knees, wearing only her panties. She reached for the bottom of his shirt, trying to pull it up his chest and over his head. He took the job from her, tossing his shirt to the floor. She barely noticed, her fingers were so busy with the snap on his jeans. She couldn't undo it. Frantic, she slipped her fingers eagerly inside.

He groaned a half laugh, tugging her fingers free. "Just a minute." He kicked off his shoes, then stripped off the rest of his clothes in what seemed like one motion. Such a wonderful expanse of sun-kissed skin and muscle was before her that she didn't know where to start. Her fingers spread across his chest, exploring, learning, loving him.

She followed the triangle of chest hair down to his navel,

where his erection prodded her hands. Unable to resist touching him, she stroked him, her fingers circling and sliding down the long length of him. Then back up. He moaned. She bent her head on impulse and kissed the very tip. He gasped and flipped her onto her back.

"There's only so much of that I can take right now," he whispered. Holding her gaze, he captured her wrists and tugged them above her head in a gentle grip.

Her gaze widened. He lowered his head. He stroked and caressed and nuzzled the smooth skin on the side of her neck, the delicate undersides of her plump, swollen breasts. She ached with wanting—twisted and moaned with need. It had been so long since she'd been held. So long since she'd been loved like this.

No. It had *never* been like this.

Tugging her hands free, she caressed his shoulders and back, loving the small catches of breath she heard from the back of his throat. He raised his head and dropped a deep, drugging kiss on her lips, their tongues dancing deliciously. He trailed his mouth downward, leaving a pathway of heated kisses to her breasts.

Mindless, she arched her back, and he obliged, taking first one nipple, then the other, deep inside. His hand slid across her belly and down to the juncture of her thighs to explore her dewy curls. She parted her thighs for him, opening for his touch. Wanting him. His wicked fingers stroked and caressed, teased and tormented, until she surged wildly against him, twisting, searching for satisfaction and surcease.

"Dane," she whispered, reveling in her body's response, in the heat coursing through her. "Please."

His magical fingers found her sensitive bud, and her hips bucked. She cried out, "Dane, now."

Moving up and over her, he bent and shifted her thighs slightly wider, settling himself closer. Resting on one arm, that hand buried in her hair, his other arm slid under her hips to hold her still. He sat at the center of her. Waiting.

Reaching up, she pulled him down to her, raining fiery kisses wherever her lips could reach. He tightened his grip on her hair, tugging her toward him, and sealed their lips in a kiss that promised and delivered … everything. And plunged deep into the heart of her.

She cried out. Her legs wrapped tighter around him. It wasn't enough. She needed more.

He settled on top, his kiss gentle, waiting for her to adjust to the invasion, to his size. "Are you okay?" he whispered against her lips, the strain of holding back obvious in the corded tendons on his neck and face.

Wiggling her hips, she purred against his lips, "Better than okay."

He dropped his forehead to rest on hers, staring deep into her eyes, and he started to move. Slowly, at first, almost experimentally. Then he picked up speed, plunging harder and deeper than ever before, driving them closer to the edge. She cried out with each thrust, wanting, striving, needing more. Dropping one hand between them, he touched the tiny nub in her curls, and that did it, just that one stroke of his finger and she soared free, crying out as the explosion overwhelmed her.

She barely heard his shout of release, and her body flew apart a second time, as he emptied himself into her.

Exhausted, he collapsed, rolled quickly to one side, and

tucked her up close against him.

She curled into him, happier than she could ever remember. Sated, feeling a peacefulness she hadn't expected, she dozed off to sleep.

Chapter 23

THE NEXT DAY Jade sat out on the garden patio, a coffee in hand. She loved the brilliant green of the palms. Dane had left a couple hours earlier. She couldn't stop smiling. He hadn't quite kept his promise but came damn close. They'd napped, made love, talked and laughed and made love again … and again.

She should be exhausted. Instead she felt invigorated, full of energy—and very content. She smirked. Maybe *very satisfied* was a better way to describe it.

"Wow. So what has put that look on your face?" Meg and Bruce walked over to join her.

"What?" Jade tried to rearrange her features, but thoughts of Dane filled her heart to bursting. Keeping those feelings inside just didn't work so well. And no way she'd hide their relationship for long. She grinned. "Dane is hot, isn't he?"

Meg giggled.

Bruce rolled his eyes. "Shall I go away? Leave you two together for this girl talk?"

Jade laughed. "No need. Nothing to discuss."

"That's not what it looks like from here." Meg sat down in the chair next to Jade.

"True enough." Bruce ordered coffee.

As they sat in the sunshine, Dane's truck drove into the

parking lot. Jade's heart lightened. It was hard to know how to greet him in front of the others. Part of her wanted to race over and kiss him, and another part of her wanted to flatten him on the ground and have her way with him right here and now—again.

Then he came into view, but Dane wasn't alone. A very unhappy-looking John was at his heels.

Standing, she pulled over a couple chairs and ordered two more coffees.

Bruce rose and shook John's hand. "Good to see you. Sorry you've had such a bad couple weeks. Any news on Peppe's whereabouts?"

John grimaced and sat down. "Thanks. It's been rough. No news. I've checked his place a couple times. I'm sure he's returned and left again, but he's sly, coming and going in the night. He left a box full of papers open on the kitchen table. Papers I'd never seen before."

Dane gazed at Jade, gave her an intimate smile, then winked at her. She gave him a quick wink back, hiding her grin from the others, while her insides melted. Now, at least, her nerves could settle down. She tuned into the conversation.

John continued. "A family tree was atop the papers. Peppe and his wife, Anne, were first cousins. I don't know if that even makes a difference, but I passed the information on to Tasha's doctors."

That bombshell took a bit to settle in.

"So then Tasha's mental instability could be a direct result of faulty genetics?" Jade shook her head slightly. Why don't people consider the results of their actions? "What about Emile? Was he fine?"

"As far as I could see," John replied. "We'll never know

how he might have developed over time."

Dr. Mike frowned. "In Tasha's case, it could be a contributing factor. That's something for the doctors to determine."

Staring almost bitterly at each person in the group, one by one, John nodded. "I guess so."

Jade winced. "I just hate that it's turning out this way."

Bruce leaned back. "We all do." He picked up his coffee and had a sip. "Sometimes things happen, and we can do nothing but accept and move on."

"Some things we won't ever know or understand." John stood, leaving his coffee untouched. "It was nice to see you all again. I'll be at the hospital." He turned to Dane. "Are you coming with me?"

Dane stood too, smiled goodbye at everyone, and turned to leave—stopping beside Jade. He bent and gave her a quick hug, dropping a brief kiss on her lips. "I'll stop by a little later."

Her cheeks warmed. Not trusting herself to speak, she smiled her goodbye.

The rest of the group had knowing smiles on their faces but stayed quiet—thankfully.

JADE TOOK THE rest of the day off. She relaxed, did laundry, did her hair. In short, she just lazed around and did nothing work related. She couldn't remember the last day she'd taken for herself. She called Duncan, but her brother wasn't home. Restless, she realized she had a whole Saturday afternoon stretching ahead of her. … She'd start with a stroll.

She walked out the front door of the hotel and took a deep breath of the humid air outside.

Keeping to one direction, enjoying the flavors of Jacmel, she found herself in a small center, where vendors hawked their wares. She avoided the crowds surrounding one noisy vendor, selling food Jade didn't recognize. As she went around that, she almost walked into another person. Flustered, she apologized and tried to get out of the way.

Her arm was grabbed.

She jerked back instinctively, spinning to see who had grabbed her.

Magrim.

Dressed in a loose multicolored blouse, with dozens of equally colorful beaded necklaces wrapped around her neck, Magrim jingled loudly, as she tightened her grip on Jade's arm. Her black eyes stared up at Jade. "What you believe is wrong. Only the truth can set you free. You are in great danger, until you find the truth."

Jerking free, Jade swallowed hard. She closed her eyes briefly and fought the urge to run all the way back to the hotel. But, if Magrim knew something about what was going on, then Jade wanted to know it too. "Magrim, what is the truth?"

"Evil spirits dwell in those close to you. Save yourself, before it is too late." Magrim sat on a vendor's chair, going quiet and still.

Jade stepped away, cast another look Magrim's way, then bolted for the hotel. Her panic gave her feet extra speed, as she dodged the crowds, ran across the roads, not daring to slow down or to look behind. She only wanted the safety of her hotel room. And Dane. She wanted Dane.

She entered the hotel, sweat running down her back, gasping for breath. She ran into the team's office and found Meg. "Oh, thank God." She slapped her purse down on her desk, collapsed into the closest chair, and spilled out the sorry mess.

Meg gasped, then said, "That's nuts. Danger still? Evil spirits in those closest to you? Surely all that bad stuff is over?" Meg could only stare at her, shaking her head. "I know there's no science to it. I know that, and yet I'm still freaked by what she told you."

"I hear you. Why can't she tell me stuff like, *You'll meet a tall, dark, and handsome man?*" Jade frowned. "Isn't that what they're supposed to say?"

"Yeah, except Dane isn't dark." Meg smiled broadly and shook her head.

"True enough." Jade ran her fingers through her hair. "Christ, she scared me."

"Can you ignore what she said?" Meg suggested, a frown forming, as she studied Jade's face.

"I'd love to," Jade muttered. "But, since I told you what she said, aren't you already considering the handful of people we've met since being here?"

"Considering what? Wondering if they're evil? What is evil anyway?" Meg exclaimed, raising her hands in the air.

"I don't know. I don't want to know." Shuddering, Jade sank lower in her chair.

Reaching out a gentle hand, Meg patted Jade's arm. "I'm sorry. I agree the trip has been fraught with weird accidents and happenings. However, don't let our imaginations take the place of common sense."

Jade released a big sigh. "Right. Got that. Ignore Magrim."

"Jade ..."

She spun around, startled at the unexpected voice. "Dane. Hi." Standing up, she headed toward him. When he opened his arms, she ran right into them.

A grin lit up his face. Then he became more serious and stepped back to study her. "Nice welcome, but what's wrong? You look like you just ran a marathon."

"I'm fine." She shook her head. "Just a little weirded out. That's all."

At his puzzled look, she explained about the woman and her prophecy. When she finished, the *nasty* bubbling up in her eased back down again. Anything to do with Magrim set her nerves on edge.

He frowned. "Let's go find her, ask for more information."

Jade stepped back, shaking her head violently. "No. No way. You can go. I'm staying here. I don't want anything to do with her."

Dane glanced over at Meg. "Are you game?"

With a raised eyebrow, Meg stood, a pensive smile on her face. "Actually I would kinda like to go."

Jade gave a mock shudder. "You two are nuts. Feel free. Not me. No way. I'll sit right here and have a coffee." She nodded, liking that idea better and better. "Where it's safe."

Meg studied her curiously. "Have you forgotten? She said the evil is close to you."

"Gee, thanks." Jade turned around, hating the clarification. "So maybe, according to her, I'm not so safe, ... but I feel safe, and that has to count for something."

Meg gave her a quick hug. "That it does. Dane and I'll walk over, talk to her, and walk back. We'll be maybe twenty minutes. You okay for that long? Which direction?"

"Oh yes. I'm just fine. Shoo, ... run along." She used hand motions to push them out the door. "I went that way." She pointed to the street across from the hotel. "No turns and about five minutes straight forward. … That's where I found the vendors. Go. Get this foolishness over with, and come back safe and sound." She waved them away. "Hurry up. Go."

Meg and Dane laughed in astonishment. "Are you sure you won't come with us? Maybe you should. See her for what she really is?"

"Nope. I'm good right here. I'll go sit outside in that chair right there." She pointed to a deep cushioned lounge chair in the shade out on the patio. "That's where I'll be when you come back. Sitting there, enjoying my coffee and my day." To prove her point, Jade picked up her purse and walked out with them. She headed to the chair and plonked down, waving goodbye with a big smile.

Dane shook his head, then followed Meg through the small gate. Jade sat and watched them leave. Dane turned back to look at her, before heading off.

She smiled. God, he looked devastating, close up or in the distance. She sighed happily, but waved him on when he hesitated. He'd be back soon enough, and they could spend time together then.

With a wave, he turned and hurried to catch up to Meg.

As soon as they disappeared, Jade dropped her smile. Her face hurt from trying to put on a good show. She wasn't smiling inside. In fact, Magrim had terrified Jade this time. She hated to be so susceptible to the crone's words, but some scary shit was going on. She knew the others thought she was foolish. She didn't care what they thought—she was too busy being scared.

"Is she always like this?" Dane asked Meg, as he caught up

with her. Meg could move. Those long legs of hers easily matched his stride. He preferred walking with Jade though, and he missed her already. He'd stopped in at the hotel, hoping to spirit her to the beach for the afternoon.

Then she'd told him about Magrim. Best to get to the bottom of this business and ease her mind. Truthfully he found Jade's behavior kind of cute. She was such a contradiction of science and belief. Look at the difficult job she did identifying dead bodies and how efficiently she did that. Yet she was also freaked out by an old woman's words. Surely her scientific background would allow her to throw off such words as nonsense? Anyway, the fact it didn't made Jade even more interesting and appealing … and brought out his *knight in shining armor* instincts to rescue and to protect.

Meg's voice pulled him out of his reverie. "To a certain extent. Jade is blessed with a strong imagination. Anytime we have a scenario to puzzle through, she comes up with the more morbid conclusions. Take the first earthquake victim—that was a little different. Jade is sure that person was living as a captive, was a sex slave or something along those lines, … and that she was murdered. Jade might be right. … Then again she might not be."

Odd. Dane didn't understand how Jade had come up with that hypothesis in the first place. "I'm sure lots of people suffered major injuries from this disaster. Why would she think anything of that particular victim?"

Meg leaned closer, dropping her voice to a whisper. "That would be because of the chains around the woman's ankle. Something we're trying to keep quiet."

Dane came to a halt. "Chains? Around the ankle of a skeleton? In the mass grave? Are you serious? That's enough to spark anyone's imagination."

"I know, right?" Meg halted beside him. They'd almost reached the busy street corner. A park stretched across one side, while vendors fought for customers and space on the other.

Dane shook his head. *Chains.* "Did anyone ask John about them?"

"No, but we've spoken to the authorities. They want more evidence before they worry about another body in a mass grave. They're short-staffed and have too many other problems right now. Actually I think they'd like to see us walk away from this, just disappear for good. I know the medical problems they're dealing with are brutal, what with cholera and tetanus … and more. Plus the crime rate has spiked too. They don't want to deal with old unsolved crimes right now. For all anyone knows these women *liked* to wear steel anklets."

Her tone made Dane look over at her sharper. "Did you say, *women*? How many?"

"Three, so far."

Dane whistled. "Jesus. No wonder Jade is freaked out. I can ask John if he knows anything about it. He helped move the bodies. If he saw something, I'm sure he'd tell me." Dane couldn't let go of that idea, as he followed Meg through the crowd. He phoned John. "Hey. I'm talking with one the team members, and they found something odd in the grave. They found a body with chains on the ankles. Did you see anything like that when you buried these people?"

Meg dodged around several groups of people, standing and talking. Dane tried to keep her bright blue skirt in sight, as she moved ahead of him. "What was that? Sorry I'm on the street corner, and I can hardly hear you for the vendors hawking their wares. What?"

"Not likely," John yelled.

Dane laughed. "I didn't think so. That's not something you'd forget."

He picked up the pace to catch up and saw Meg stop and talk to an old woman. *Magrim.* "Okay, I'll talk to you later. I'm meeting Jade at the hotel in ten or fifteen minutes, I'm hoping to spirit her away to play with me this afternoon. Don't know when I'll be home." He put away his phone and hurried to hear Meg's conversation.

"She's not talking. Doesn't even respond. I don't know if she's asleep or what." Meg stared down at the old woman in confusion. "I don't want to disturb her."

"Did you call her name?" At the sound of Dane's voice, Magrim reacted violently. She surged to her feet, her necklaces rattling with the sudden movement, her eyes blind. "Danger. You must be careful. It's all around you."

"What the … ?" Dane stared down at her. No wonder Jade had freaked out. This was beyond his experience too, only he was long past the point of letting a pathetic old woman scare the crap out of him.

"Specifics please, Magrim. You scared a friend of mine today. I'd like to know what danger you see around me."

"Little blonde. She's in trouble. Death reaches for her even now."

Shivers slid down his spine. "*What?* Why are you saying this?" His voice rose, hardened.

A small restraining hand squeezed his forearm. "Easy," Meg whispered.

Dane glared down at the old woman. "She terrorized Jade with her warnings. Why and for what? If there's a specific danger, then she needs to say what it is."

"Chains. More chains. So many chains. To bind, to

hold, to keep forever." Magrim cackled, like the nutty witch she was.

Dane threw off Meg's hand. "Let's go. She's nuts."

"Tasha, Emile, and Peppe. Tasha, Emile, and Peppe." Magrim continued to parrot the names in a singsong voice.

"Do you know them?"

Magrim dipped her head, setting the necklaces rattling. "Family. Family."

"Oh, *great*. You're related? You're all nuts."

"Careful, Dane." Meg turned back to Magrim. "Is Peppe okay?"

Magrim turned her blind eyes in her direction. "Peppe is dead. Peppe is dead. Emile is dead. Emile is dead."

Dane sucked in his breath. Meg pressed the point. "And Tasha?"

"Tasha is dead. Tasha is dead."

"What?" Meg gasped in horror.

"Don't listen to her. That's what she wants. Just forget about her." He glared at the gathering crowd.

"Dane, that's a horrible thing to say." Meg glared at him.

He raised his hands at that. "Fine. Whatever. However, Tasha isn't dead. We visited her this morning, for Christ's sake."

Chapter 24

D ANE AND MEG hashed the issue over all the way back to the hotel. Meg suggested, "Magrim might be picking up on Tasha's withdrawal from the world."

Dane snorted. "All she's doing is repeating herself. She's a fraud."

They stopped to let the traffic go by before crossing the road. Meg hopped up onto the curb on the other side. They walked at a fast clip back to the hotel. "I don't know how you can be so sure. She did mention chains, and that was just freaky."

"Coincidence. She hasn't said anything helpful. If she'd given names, places, times—then maybe. Instead there's nothing except conjecture and fearmongering. She lives off scaring people. Like Jade."

"The locals believe in her. At least according to the hotel manager, Magrim's held in high regard." Meg related the conversation they'd had around the dinner table with the manager, after Jade's first encounter with Magrim.

"That's good marketing." Something he understood and could appreciate.

"What's good about it?"

"It's a business to her. And her strategy works. You paid her, didn't you?" Dane opened the small gate at the side entrance and waited for Meg to walk through. "I saw you slip her some money. If you believe she can tell you something that no one else can, then you'll pay her for more."

"I have to admit that she kind of shook me up."

"See? That makes for a good business. Magrim just gets to repeat the same information over and over again." What she'd just said proved his point, didn't it?

Meg tried a different tack to get him to at least consider the possibility of Magrim's prophecy. "I'm a doctor and a scientist, but even I can't deny the possibility of Magrim's abilities. The more we learn about our brains and our bodies, the more we realize we don't know everything. We don't have scientific answers for all aspects of our knowledge or experience."

Dane wasn't having any of it. Bruce overheard them and came out to see what all the ruckus was about. They told him about Jade and then their visit with Magrim.

Bruce shook his head. "I don't play around with that stuff. I'm a scientist and shouldn't have any problem shooting it down—but, because I don't understand it, I like to leave the topic well enough alone." Lively intelligence gleamed in his eyes as he spoke, reminding Dane how much brainpower the team had tapped.

The three arrived at the patio, still wrangling.

"Jade's got quite the imagination, so I can see how Magrim might freak her out a little." Bruce pulled up a chair and sat down. "Speaking of which, where is she? What did she do, go get another cup of coffee? Or another breakfast?" They laughed.

Jade's lounge chair was there—she wasn't. Dane turned slowly, looking for Jade. Meg pulled up a chair and sat down.

Dane frowned and looked around, then sat down on the

edge of a chair. "We left her right here, when we went to talk to Magrim. Jade said she'd stay here and wait for us."

"I haven't seen her. I was in the office working for the last couple hours. She never came in there."

Meg stood hurriedly. "This was twenty minutes ago. I'll go check her room." She bolted.

Dane watched her go.

"You don't appear to put much stock in the witch woman's words." Bruce propped one leg on his knee and studied Dane.

With a heavy sigh, Dane rubbed the back of his neck, continuing to scan for Jade. "Hard to when there's nothing concrete. I hate to give credence to nebulous warnings." He sighed heavily, finally acknowledging that inside he was starting to wonder. "I'd feel better if Jade were standing in front of me right now."

"That's the scientist's perspective. Give me something to prove, and, if I can go prove it, then I'll consider it. For the strong of faith, they believe that, if your faith is strong, you don't need any proof. For them, asking for proof is doubting your faith."

"Convenient," Dane said, shaking his head.

Bruce grinned. "Isn't it?"

Meg came running out the side door. "She's not there. I asked Susan. She hasn't seen her in the last half hour either."

"Damn." Dane shifted in his seat, and his foot caught on the table leg and then kicked something. Looking underneath, his heart froze. He snagged a small black leather bag and tossed it on the table. "Please tell me that isn't Jade's."

JADE ROLLED OVER, a slight moan escaping. A rumble under

her ear irritated her. It sounded so close and yet so far away. She groaned and tried to curl up into a ball and go back to sleep. Yet she didn't think she'd really been asleep. More like adrift on floating clouds. Except she wasn't floating in a sunny space. Everything was gray. Gray light, gray clouds. She would have shaken her head in dismay, only the thought of doing that stopped her.

It would hurt.

She knew that … somehow.

She couldn't seem to reason out an explanation of how or why.

She noted a mustiness to the air—oils, metals? She almost moaned but caught it before it slipped out. It was important not to make a sound.

But she didn't know why.

Tired, confused, and sore, she slipped deeper into the clouds and slept.

MEG STARED AT the bag, shock, worry, and horror mingling to twist her features. "That is hers." She bent to look under the table, as if thinking she'd find Jade huddled under there.

"And it's been here since we sat down." Dane stared at it, a sense of unease growing in the pit of his stomach. "Shit."

"What?" Bruce studied their faces. "So she left her purse out here. What's the big deal about that?"

"Maybe nothing—maybe everything." Meg and Dane stared at each other. "Except it doesn't feel like nothing, … does it, Dane?"

He shook his head, his mind racing. "If she's not here, not in the hotel, where would she be?"

"Nowhere without her purse." Meg was adamant on that point. "She never goes anywhere without it."

Bruce pursed his lips and considered the issue. "You're thinking something's happened to her?"

"She promised to sit and wait here for us. We weren't gone twenty minutes." Meg glanced over at Dane for confirmation. "And all this on the heels of Magrim's warnings."

Dane tilted his head and nodded. "Yeah, maybe I can see why you believe we should be a little worried. There have been enough strange things going on." He couldn't help the fear knotting his stomach. Where the hell was she?

"If she's gone, did she go willingly?" Bruce questioned. "Or did trouble come her way?"

Meg nudged the purse. "She wouldn't have gone anywhere without her purse. She takes it out in the field, for God's sake. Something is wrong."

Bruce whistled softly. "Seriously? Are we thinking she's been kidnapped?" He shook his head. "Do we call the authorities *again*?"

"Let's search first," Dane stated. "Start with the hotel. Ask everyone if they've seen her in the last half hour and if they saw anyone else around, other than your team, staff, and the other guests. Are there any other guests in the hotel right now?" Dane asked, standing up, his unease twisting into panic.

"There aren't. The last group cleared out earlier today." Bruce stood too. "I'll start with the kitchen staff and then the manager. Too bad no security cameras are in this place."

"I'll walk through the front door and see if anyone is there or in the offices. I'll find the guys too. See if any of them know where Jade is." Meg hurried inside.

Dane looked around and spoke to the empty patio. "And I'll walk around here and see if I can find anything else." He headed to the parking lot first. If Jade had been snatched, her kidnapper would have had a vehicle. Would anyone just drive in here and snatch her—and that fast—without someone noticing? Could they have walked right up to her on the patio and forced her into a vehicle?

He spun around to study where he'd last seen her. If she'd been taken from under the palm tree, tucked away in the shade like that, it was quite possible that no one noticed. And then he remembered Magrim's words to Jade. Something about *Evil spirits dwell in those close to you. Save yourself before it is too late.*

He spun around and came to a dead stop. The team had gathered inside. He could see them standing and talking. All of them were here and accounted for. Except for Jade. Had one of them convinced Jade to go to their rooms and knocked her unconscious? Not likely, and why would they? They worked with her day in and day out. There'd been better times to snatch her. Like when she worked alone at the lab. Money for security had been approved but only just. They still had to hire someone.

He realized they were standing in a group, staring at him. He walked inside to join them. "Did you find her?"

Meg shook her head. "No." Grim understanding showed on her face. "I guess you didn't either?"

"No." His heart raced inside. He could hardly think straight. Panic built, as he was no longer able to ignore what his mind and heart had been screaming at him for the last ten minutes.

"She's gone."

JADE WOKE SLOWLY, as if from a deep, dark sleep. She yawned and tried to slip back under but the surface was hard. And she was cold. Pulling into a tighter ball, she willed herself back to sleep. But couldn't get there. She shifted onto her back, wincing at the aches and pains of lying too long in one position. Her head pounded, like a steady sledgehammer going off inside.

Her eyes popped open. A basement ceiling stared back at her. A dirty basement ceiling. More like a root cellar ceiling. She frowned, yet even that movement made her head hurt. She groaned softly, even as other aches and pains slowly entered her awareness. Hell, most of her hurt—and what didn't had gone numb. She struggled to sit up, then looked around. She was sitting on a concrete floor.

That explained some of her aches and pains. There were no windows. No lights. Just an all-encompassing gloominess. She could see, just not very far or very clearly.

Reaching up, she rubbed her temples and tried to swallow. Her fingers came away sticky, with a little blood.

Her throat felt like cotton had been stuffed inside and had sucked all the moisture out, making it impossible to swallow. She tried anyway, wishing for water. It took several minutes in the dim light for her eyes to adjust. There was nothing—no cupboards, no furniture, What the hell? An odd noise sounded in the distance. With her head too woozy to think, she lay down on the floor, trying to let the bits of information roll around, hoping to come up with answers.

Ten minutes later, all she had was a headache.

She sat up again and rolled onto her hands and knees, then stood slowly, anticipating the rush of blood—and pain—to her head. Once standing, she closed her eyes and breathed deeply for several long minutes, before she stood steady. The same odd noises popped in and out of her consciousness. As did cold and chills. Her feet were almost numb, as were her legs. She couldn't sort everything out.

"I don't know what happened, but something's sapped all my energy and strength. ... Just standing is a major accomplishment," she murmured out loud.

Feeling comforted by the sound of her own voice, she took one faltering step. Then another. She had to stop and breathe deeply before trying a third. "Hello? Is anyone there?"

She stepped forward again and came up short. The same odd sound had grown louder. Her leg couldn't move any farther. She turned around. The odd sound fell into place. So did the odd chill on her ankle.

Lifting her leg, she pulled up her jeans. She couldn't think; her mind was blank with shock. Then understanding slapped her up the side of her brain. Wrapped around her ankle was a manacle. A chain extended from that to the concrete wall behind her.

A chain, so similar—too similar—to the ones she'd seen on the dead women from the grave.

Like them, Jade had become a prisoner.

WHILE BRUCE CALLED the same officers who had helped during Dr. Mike's disappearance, the team assembled in the office to compare information. Dane sat back and closed his eyes. His throat closed.

Damn it.

Impatience and the need for action seized his gut. His instincts said to find her before it was too late. What the hell could have happened? The hotel was a public area, but they'd had few guests this past week. Still, any stranger could have walked in and out without attracting too much attention. But not with Jade, … unless she knew him and went willingly. "Could her disappearance be related to the grave site?" he asked the group.

Everyone stopped and stared at him. "What do you mean?" asked Stephen.

"Have you had anyone angry or complaining about the grave being opened?"

Meg glanced at her team, then back at Dane. "To be honest, the lack of any reaction from the locals is what surprised us. I know everyone is still reeling from the earthquake, the flooding, the cholera, the tetanus, … but instead of concern about the work we're doing at the mass grave, there's almost an air of apathy. Like they can't deal with much more."

Dr. Mike spoke up. "Their lack of interest and caring suggests we should only remove the remains if they meet our search criteria and should leave the others be. Not test the others at all. So few family members have come forward at our free clinic. … And, with the pressure from Tony too, putting all our efforts focused in the lab trailers, we'd be done that much faster."

"Have you turned anyone away? Anyone approach you about disturbing the spirits? Anyone give you any kind of suspicious or unsettling reaction? What about more break-ins?"

Dr. Mike glanced from one face to the next, then turned to stare at Dane. "There's been one minor one at the clinic, but nothing was taken. There's been no more here at the hotel that we know of. And, as much as I hate to say it, the only one particularly bothered by our work here was Tasha, your sister-in-law."

"*Great.* Well, she's not capable of kidnapping Jade." He pulled out his phone. "As far as I know, she is safe and sound at the hospital."

"Did you ever check with John to see if anything new was heard about Tasha?" Meg asked. "I'm thinking about what Magrim said."

He grimaced. "Right. She said Tasha was dead."

"What?" Stephen leaned forward. "Did she die?"

"I don't believe so." Dane let Meg tell the others about Magrim's prophecy, while he dialed John. "John? What's the matter? You don't sound very good."

"I just called the hospital. Tasha passed away during her nap, just after you and I left her. I've been wandering around town in a daze ever since."

Dane closed his eyes and slumped against the wall. His brother just couldn't catch a break. "Shit. I am sorry, John. I didn't see that one coming."

"Neither did I. Now I have no reason to stay, do I? Except for Peppe, my entire Haitian family has been wiped out," he said bitterly. Dane walked away from the others. "I'm sorry, John. I know how much you were looking forward to the baby and having Tasha back to normal."

John's unsteady voice was hard to decipher. "Instead I have another funeral to arrange. I wonder if the baby can go in the coffin with her. I think she'd like that."

Dane's heart broke. "I'm sure that can be arranged."

Silence filled the phone.

"What did you call about?"

Dane straightened. "We're looking for one of the team members—Jade, the tiny blonde. I wondered if you'd seen her?"

"Seen her? No. Why would you think I had?" John's voice was devoid of curiosity. Devoid of anything for that matter.

Dane winced. "Sorry for bothering you. When I called, I knew it was a long shot, but I'm desperate to find her. I left her for a few minutes, and, when I came back, she was gone."

"I don't know why you'd be calling me. It's not as if I know her."

Dane clenched the phone tighter at the petulant sound in his brother's voice. "I'm calling everyone. Keep an eye out for her, will you please? By the way, did you ever find Peppe?"

"No. No idea where he is. He might be dead too. Lord knows everyone else is," John said, his voice gloomy and without energy.

Damn. His brother had been through so much. "I'm not. I've been here for you all along. I can't bring them back. I wish I could, but that's just not possible."

"Yeah. I know. But I would like to know why your life is so easy and clean … and why mine is just plain fucked-up."

The phone went *click*.

Dane stared down at his cell and groaned softly. He didn't know how to get John through this. It had been hard last time. This would be much worse.

"Dane?"

He spun around to find the group staring at him. "Hey. Sorry. Tasha passed away earlier today, right after John and I visited her."

Meg gasped, her hand going to her throat. "So Magrim was right? At least about Tasha. Although we don't know about Peppe. … Is he still missing?"

"Apparently." He stared down at his phone. "John's in a bad way."

"Of course he is." Wilson stared at him. "He lost his wife and unborn child."

"That would be tough on anyone." Bruce winced, exchanging glances with Dr. Mike.

"And worse when it happens twice." Dane sighed. "He lost his first wife in a car accident. John didn't know she was pregnant, until the doctor told him afterward."

Shocked silence filled the room.

Dane frowned. He studied the uncomfortable look on Dr. Mike's face. Bruce cleared his throat, before adding, "Twice? That's an awful coincidence."

"What do you mean?" Dane asked.

"The chances of that happening twice in one man's life are pretty slim."

Stephen and Wilson slid sideways glances to the other two scientists. "Right, Dr. Mike?" Stephen asked.

Dr. Mike and Bruce were having a silent conversation. As if coming to an agreement, Dr. Mike nodded. "It's not impossible. Some people seem to be plagued by bad luck. If there had been a police investigation in the first incident, the second would definitely warrant a closer look. Particularly if anything else were in John's history. However, both deaths were unrelated and came about by different methods, so it *could* be very bad luck."

It took a moment for Dane to digest what he was really saying. "No. Oh no." He shook his head violently. "Don't even think that. *There. Is. No. Way.*"

Silence filled the room.

Dane added, "Besides, maybe Tasha caused her own death, accidentally or intentionally." Filled with anger, he stood with his hands on his hips, his phone still in his hand.

Meg spoke up. "I don't see Tasha having done something. She's been catatonic since she went into the hospital. Did John say how she died?"

Dane stared at her, trying to sort out how everything had suddenly twisted upside down. Finally he said, "I didn't ask. John didn't volunteer."

The others exchanged sober looks.

Dane could feel an insidious doubt twisting in the back of his mind. No. It wasn't possible. Not John. "Better you consider the missing Peppe. I don't know when I last saw him, but, in his mental condition, he could have killed Tasha too. *Not John.* John wanted his family. He lived for them. Besides, we're jumping to conclusions here. For all we know, Tasha died from complications of the surgery." He pulled out his cell phone. "We can call and find out for sure."

Bruce interjected, "They won't have definitive results from an autopsy yet."

"Easy, Dane," Dr. Mike added. "We're not accusing John of anything. Honestly the prime issue is to find Jade."

Meg cleared her throat. The others turned to stare at her. "I know this won't be popular, but honestly we don't have too many people to consider. So we have to look at everyone, including ourselves." She took a deep breath. "Plus John. Is there any reason that John may have wanted to talk to Jade? Would he have taken her for coffee? Anything?"

Anger twisted inside Dane. Meg was actually suggesting his brother might have had something to do with Jade's disappearance. Red filled his mind. "There is no way. Don't take the suspicion from one bad scenario and make it fit another. John didn't kill either of his wives. Nor did he 'take' Jade anywhere. He hasn't seen her. I just asked him." He stood up, barely holding back the anger threatening to explode. "I will start looking farther afield."

"Didn't Magrim also say Peppe was dead?" Meg repeated.

"I don't give a rat's ass what that old bitch said." Bitter, angry, confused, and—dare he admit it?—slightly afraid, he headed toward the parking lot.

"Dane," Meg called out.

He stopped short and turned back. "What?"

"Be careful."

He shot them all a look of disbelief and walked away.

JADE HAD SCRUNCHED up to keep warm. Her mind raced from idea to idea … and always slammed into the same blank wall. Her ankle was truly locked in a manacle, and the chain was truly bolted to the wall. She wasn't going anywhere, and she didn't know where she was. Except that she figured it was a basement, with no windows or doors and just the one set of stairs. The mustiness seemed to be growing stronger. … Maybe something dead was down here.

The reality of her situation added to the chill in the place and sent shivers down her small frame. Cold and hungry, she waited for her captor. Surely he'd come back soon?

Her mind kept returning to the poor victims from the grave. She had no doubt she was in their shoes right now. She just didn't understand why.

Or how?

She had no recollection of being snatched or the journey to this place. The only clue was the dried blood in her hair and that damn booming headache. Her eyes focused farther into the dim space. … Something was in the far corner, hidden by the dark, and didn't move. Some lumber leaned against the wall; something else was stacked on the floor. Once again she regretted not having a cell phone.

Why her? Had someone looked for her specifically? Or had it been a crime of opportunity? Was her imprisonment related to the excavation of the grave site? Her stomach heaved. She might never get out. She might end up in a nameless grave, like the other women. Unmarked and unknown. Duncan would go mad. He'd blame himself for talking her into coming to Haiti for the second time.

She buried her head in her arms.

She didn't want to die.

She'd just returned to the land of the living.

Chapter 25

MEG SAID, "I'M presuming that's not the way to gain Dane's cooperation."

"Do we really think that John may have killed Tasha?" Stephen shook his head. "That's crazy."

"Better ask Dr. Mike that question." Meg turned to look at Dr. Mike.

"It's a possibility. A probability? Who can say?" Dr. Mike cleared his throat. "We don't know the details on his first wife and know almost nothing about Tasha's death yet."

Bruce joined in. "I will say that the only time I've come across something like this, it was exactly that. Two pregnant wives unexpectedly dying. I agree. It sounds suspicious but without further details …"

"Even if John did do something to his wife," Stephen's voice rose slightly, "what does that have to do with Jade? Isn't that an entirely different issue?"

Dr. Mike spoke again. "Maybe. Maybe not. Dane appears reliable. Responsible. What's going on with John? I can't say I like the little bit that I saw, but that's just my opinion."

Meg stepped in. "Yes. Jade said something about him having had a bad time of it before these deaths. That he struggled in his relationship with his wife … and that his business was failing."

Dr. Mike glanced over at Bruce. "That just reinforces the profile. Failed business, failed marriage. Rather than look at himself, it's easier to blame the wife. Blame leads to the solution. Get rid of the wife. Get rid of the problem."

Stephen leaned back. "That's cold, man."

Dr. Mike's face twisted. "Murder usually is. And I've seen way too much of it."

"Why would he get rid of the baby too? It's his child. Are there no parental feelings?" Meg gave a delicate shudder.

Dr. Mike shook his head. "Again, not if the baby has been pinpointed as the cause of a problem."

Wilson jumped in. "And what if he had nothing to do with the baby's death but blamed Tasha for the death of his baby?"

"Even if he did, what does that have to do with Jade? Let's focus on her and leave the dead for later." Meg stood and paced the area nervously. "We have to find her."

"Do we want to try talking to John? Call in the authorities?" Wilson asked. "You said, wait until we searched. Well, we have. Now what?"

"Not to mention, this is only sheer conjecture," Stephen said, groaning. "I think Jade's imagination is getting to all of us."

"Well, she came up that damn hill to find me. I can't go to bed tonight until we find her." Dr. Mike glared at his crutches. "However, I am a little handicapped. I can stay here and run command central, or I can be a passenger, as we drive around looking. Two pairs of eyes are better than one."

"Was she so unnerved at that old lady's words that she might go for a walk? Go to the beach maybe? If so, someone should drive around that area, check out her familiar haunts, her places to walk … on the off chance of finding her. Do we know if a vehicle is missing? Oh, right. Bruce, you checked that, didn't you?"

Bruce agreed. "They're all here."

"Magrim said Jade should not trust those close to her …"

Wilson snorted. "So what? We're supposed to look at each other with suspicion?"

Meg shook her head. "No. That's not what I meant. I'm wondering if we can trust Dane? And does John count as someone close to her—because of his connection to Dane?"

"How about this? We assume they're both psychotic killers." Wilson stood. "I can't just sit here. I'll walk toward Magrim's booth and the little park. Otherwise, everyone stay together and keep in contact. Enough people have gone missing."

Susan stood next to Meg. "We're coming too."

Bruce pushed back his chair. "I'll loop back through the hotel again. Talk to the staff. Maybe she's showed up since we checked with them." He disappeared into the main building, leaving the other two men alone.

ALONE IN HIS truck, Dane pounded the steering wheel. No way John would survive an accusation like this. He'd been through enough already. It would destroy him. Like it had last time.

Last time?

"Dear God." From the back of his mind, came one old memory he'd forgotten about. With good reason. John's high-school girlfriend, Melia. She'd gone missing years ago. Was it important? Or would it just throw unnecessary suspicion in the wrong direction? Dane needed Jade back, not wasting time doing a useless search in the wrong direction.

His stomach clenched with bubbling acid. Did the story of Melia's disappearance have any bearing on today's? John's teenage sweetheart had run away several times during high school. So, when she took off for good, no one thought anything of it. Dane didn't know where or when … *or if* … she'd ever surfaced. She might have. He hadn't kept in touch with anyone from back then. No one he could call and ask.

If he could find out she was fine, then he could forget about any connection to John's wives. And clearing that away would help John's case, letting Dane focus on Jade's disappearance, without John distracting him.

Then again, Dane just might know someone who could give him the answer he needed. *His foreman back in Seattle.* He pulled off to the side of the road, took a look around, hoping to see Jade walking toward him, as he dialed the Seattle number. He waited impatiently for the call to get picked up.

"Thomas? Hey, yeah, it's Dane. I have an odd non-work-related question. Do you remember Mark Coombes? From high school? Do you remember if his kid sister ever surfaced? Remember? She ran away again just before graduation?"

Thomas, his curiosity leaching through the phone lines, asked, "What's that about Mark's sister? Why are you asking me? I don't know. Ask your brother, John. He was closest to her."

"Was he? I couldn't remember." Except he did remember that much. Dane leaned his head back and closed his eyes. He swallowed hard. "I missed a lot of that year. I was in my second year of college back then."

"Yeah, we both were. Her brother, Mark, had a hard time back then. Melia was forever saying how she hated her life. So, when she went missing that last time, everyone took it as normal behavior. Only she didn't come home. I was pretty hot for her back then. Unfortunately she only had eyes for John."

Thomas spoke in reminiscent tones, without any understanding of the turmoil twisting through Dane. He cleared his throat. "I thought they'd broken up before then?"

"They broke up and got together again constantly. It's hard to remember anymore. Like I said, talk to John. He was the last one to see her before she disappeared."

Dane's gut clenched. "Okay, I will. Everything there all right?" Christ he hoped so. His life here had just drained to the sewer level.

"Yeah, everything's fine. I need you to go over that bid for the Stortex job. Any chance you'll get that done today?"

Hell no. "I'll see what I can do. I might be coming home sooner than I'd planned."

Thomas cheered. "That's great news. We need you here. I know long distance is fine for a while, but I'm not you, buddy."

And Dane knew he needed to go home, not just for his company but for himself. But not until he'd found Jade and had helped his brother get his life together. "I hear you. I'll call in a couple days."

"Do that. Don't forget to put that bid together."

"Will do." Dane rang off. He dropped his head back and closed his eyes again, letting Thomas's words repeat in his mind. His stomach wanted to heave, as he considered a possibility he could no longer ignore. *Oh, God.*

Had John done something to the women he'd loved?

Even worse, could he have done something to Jade—the woman Dane loved?

"I DON'T WANT to just sit here, waiting until the authorities arrive. What can we do?" Dr. Mike studied the area where Jade had been sitting.

Stephen nodded. "If she were sitting here, she would have been taken out the back way." He pointed behind him. "That's the most direct route. With the road right there, someone could easily have snatched her and stuffed her in a vehicle."

Stephen got up and walked around while Dr. Mike watched. A short hedge separated the hotel's property from the side street, but it was easy to step over. "It would have been too damn easy. Especially if he was already parked here."

Stephen stood where the vehicle could have parked and in ten steps reached where Jade had sat. He made a motion with his arm, demonstrating a simple choke hold, bent down, tossed an imaginary Jade over his shoulder and hopped over the hedge. "Simple."

With a decisive nod, Dr. Mike said, "Less than one minute. Walk up behind her, pick her up, and walk out. Done."

Frowning, Stephen added, "And no one would have seen her abduction, unless they were sitting right here."

"No windows face this direction, no glass doors, nothing."

The two men smiled grimly. "That's what happened. I can just see it," Dr. Mike stated.

Stephen added, "Particularly if he'd watched Meg and

Dane walk away. He'd have known he had that window of time."

"I'm sorry to say that I agree. So much strange shit is going on with John and his family that John comes to mind automatically. But he wouldn't have known Jade was here. Or that she was alone. It could just as easily have been an abduction by a stranger. And those are the worst to solve."

Casting a narrow eye around the road and parking lot, Stephen grimaced. "Maybe Peppe is behind this? He's conveniently gone missing."

Shifting his crutches to the other side, Dr. Mike hobbled to his feet. "We only have to look at what Peppe did to me to realize what he's capable of. He could have snatched Jade. He could also have snatched those manacled women we found in the grave. Hell, maybe Emile was even in on it."

"Now that's stretching it." Stephen stared at Dr. Mike, doubt clouding his voice.

Anger colored Dr. Mike's voice. "Is it? Some asshole kept those women chained up. Who had opportunity? Look at where they live. No one would ever hear a woman scream out there."

Stephen stared at him. "That's ugly."

"True, but that doesn't mean it's wrong."

DANE HAD ALREADY checked all the side streets close by when he pulled up right in front of the hotel. His heart was heavy. This time everyone raced to meet him before he'd even hopped out. He slammed the door and hurried in their direction. From the looks on their faces, they hadn't found her.

"Dane? Did you find her?"

He shook his head, as he joined them.

"The others have just returned after looking everywhere for her." Dr. Mike pointed toward the three team members racing toward them from the other side of the hotel. "Any luck?" he called out.

"No. Nothing." The three arrived, gasping for breath. "Do you have any news? Please tell us you have news," Meg asked, worry creasing her face.

Bruce walked out from the hotel. As everyone turned to him, he shook his head.

Hope died from everyone's faces.

Dane opened his mouth again, then closed it for a second to gather his thoughts. "Except, … well, I don't know if this has anything to do with what's going on. I wanted to confirm something that happened a long time ago, so I phoned a friend of mine. Now this isn't for sure, but …"

"Spit it out, Dane. We don't have time." Bruce frowned at Dane.

"I've been considering what you said about John. When he was in high school, he had this girlfriend, who ran away from her home several times. She always came back. The last time was six weeks before her high school graduation. As far as I can determine, she's never been seen since."

Meg gasped, the color leeching from her face. Susan reached out and grabbed her hand, then asked, "She's still missing?"

"Yes. I just talked to my foreman in Seattle. He was a friend of the family. It may be that John had nothing to do with her disappearance but …"

"He had motive and opportunity." Bruce pondered the information. "What did the police say?"

"The police put her down as a missing person. Apparently John was the last person to see her alive."

Dr. Mike leaned forward. "Don't tell me. They'd had a fight, and she ran away without him, breaking his heart."

Dane stared at him. "Something like that, yeah."

Bruce stood. "Let's go."

"Go where?" Dane looked over at the others in confusion. What did they know that he didn't?"

"To John's place."

Whoa. "What?" Dane asked. "On the basis of Melia having gone missing years ago? There's a chance this is all a coincidence." But even he had trouble believing that now.

Wilson's angry voice sliced through Dane's protestations. "You said his other wife died too. ... Maybe he's killing Jade right now."

The color bleached from Dane's face.

Meg gasped.

Bruce walked to the parking lot. "Let's not go overboard. However, if I can consider this guy killed a girlfriend and then his two wives—I have to consider he's gone after Jade too."

Stephen, impatiently jingling the keys to one of the SUVs, stood by the closest vehicle, waiting. He asked, "Maybe, but why target Jade?"

Dane's face turned from white to red as a growing fear burned the shock away. "*If* he's done this, and it's a fucking big *if*, then he's lost everything. He might, in his anger, and considering his mental state, want to strike out at me. He said something that surprised me earlier. Essentially he wanted to know why his life was shit and mine so charmed."

The others stared at him.

"Typical siblings," suggested Meg hopefully.

"Stepsiblings," he corrected. "My mother married John's

father, and he came along as part of the package deal."

Dr. Mike and Bruce exchanged grim looks. "Greed and envy could be motive for snatching Jade. Not well-thought-out though, if that's what he's doing."

Stephen opened up the SUV doors. "He's not thinking. He's reacting—to his anger and fear. He'll lash out in the same way he has in the past."

Meg groaned. "I feel for him, after what's happened to his life. I can understand the anger, but to do something like this to his brother … and Jade?"

Bruce hopped into the front passenger seat. "And we need to find her before he has a chance to release some of his anger … on her."

THE TRIP TO John's house was completed in silence. Meg sat in the passenger seat, as Dane drove there. The SUV full of team members followed Dane's truck.

Dane's mind churned with the mess in his head. It was hard enough to consider the girlfriend-wife thing, but to take that one step further and to contemplate John abducting Jade was another thing altogether.

He didn't want to believe any of it. This was his little brother. The kid brother he'd adored, had helped, and had been there for all these years. And now Dane was wondering if this same man could have done what these professionals suggested. And, if John had done these things, how well had Dane known him? Really known him? Dane understood anger—any man did. He didn't understand lashing out and hurting others while in a temper. There were other ways to let off steam than hurting the people you loved.

Yet John had changed. Had become someone Dane had

trouble understanding.

The property looked deserted, as they drove into the yard. There was no sign of John's truck. Maybe he was still in town. But, if he were in town, that meant he could have been at their hotel when Jade went missing. He swore under his breath and closed his eyes briefly.

"Did you say something?" Meg turned to face him.

"No. Just hoping this mess turns out better than it's looking like it will at the moment."

"Right. Dane, I have to ask. Who said Peppe was not in his right mind?"

He glanced over at her in surprise. "I don't know. I didn't need to be told. I could see it for myself. Why?"

"I'm just trying to sort out the behavior, that's all. And what about Tasha?"

"When I first met her, she was fairly happy and seemed like any other eager mother-to-be. At the end? No. She wasn't normal at the end. And no way you can blame that on my brother."

"I'm not trying to," she said gently. "I'm trying to understand, to sort through the possibilities."

He parked and turned off the engine. Stephen parked beside them.

Dane gave her a hard look. "This is my brother. Remember that when you look at those possibilities."

Chapter 26

DANE WALKED PAST the small picket fence he'd once considered cute. Not any longer. Now it looked run down and unloved. Everything in his life had taken on a dark tinge. He headed to the kitchen door and didn't wait for the others to follow. They would.

He could already hear Meg running behind him, and the vehicle doors opening and closing as the others hopped out to catch up.

He strode through the kitchen. No sign of John. He headed for the master bedroom and found it undisturbed from the day he'd cleaned it out. John hadn't moved back in. Frowning, he made a quick loop through the rest of the house. "He's not here."

The others stood in the middle of the kitchen, faces blank.

Dane shrugged. "He could be anywhere. Let's check the other cabins. There are three of them. I'll check mine first." He bolted out the door and ran to his place.

Flinging open the door, he strode into the small cabin. Nothing had been disturbed. At least at first glance, that appeared to be the case. He walked through the space and headed back out to the front.

Everyone stood on the small porch or just inside the door, waiting for his verdict.

"Empty."

He led the way to Emile's cabin. They passed several outbuildings. Old sheds, storage rooms, and working buildings from years past, when this place had been a thriving farm. They checked every one.

No sign of John. Nothing.

Lots of rusted equipment and wooden boxes filled the spaces, but mostly they were full of junk.

Arriving at a clearing, Dane pointed out Emile's cabin. "I don't know if anyone's been in here since Emile died."

"Not likely, considering only John and Peppe were left." Bruce strode beside him. "He had enough on his plate without worrying about minor things like that."

Dane shot him a sideways look. "Still think he could have done what you think he might have done?"

Bruce was quick to answer. "Yes."

"Kidnapping doesn't fit John's pattern. Jade wasn't his girlfriend. She's mine. She's not pregnant, as far as I know."

Trying to maintain the pace as Dane's long legs ate up the distance, Bruce explained, "I wasn't thinking of that pattern as much as it could possibly be his way to get rid of a problem in his life. Once something starts to go wrong, he's faced with failure. Rather than accepting that a relationship or a business has come to an end, it sounds like he's getting rid of the cause of his failure—blaming something or someone else, so to speak. And by removing it from his life, he doesn't have to face it."

"Failure?" Dane shook his head. "That's a bit harsh."

"There's no way of knowing. Killers don't think like we do. Although most of the time these people have had a tough upbringing—child abuse, that sort of thing. According to you, you two were always close. You had a good childhood."

"More or less."

"So what could have gone wrong for John? What could have started him on this path?"

Dane looked at him in confusion, very conscious of the others listening in with interest. "Wrong?" He stopped and reared back slightly. "Nothing was wrong. Unless you mean our parents' deaths? My dad passed when I was an infant. John's mom died when he was in kindergarten. Our parents married several years later. We were all close, until they died on a European holiday in John's second-to-last year of high school."

Bruce was quiet for a moment. "Their deaths could have initially triggered his actions." Taking a deep breath, he added, "And it's quite possible that being forced to confront death on a large scale, like the mass grave here, may have triggered his behavior again. Made him reassess where he was in life and what he really wanted."

Dane shot him a look of disbelief, not wanting to consider the possibility. He turned and pointed to a cabin in the distance. "That's Emile's."

Their pace picked up. At the steps, the others stopped and waited for Dane. He unlatched the door, wrinkled up his nose, and flung the door wide open. "God, it's stale in here."

"Not being cleaned and aired out will do that."

"I suppose." Dane headed in. The cabin had an identical layout to his—was maybe a little larger. Clothes were tossed onto the backs of the furniture, shoes forgotten on the floor.

Dane shook his head and strode into the bedroom.

Empty. But then, what had they expected? It's not as if Jade would be sitting there, waiting for them.

"It's empty. Only Peppe's place is left." Dane pointed

toward the heaviest treed area of the property. "Let's check it fast, then, … hell, I don't know what we'll do after that."

"One thing at a time." Bruce turned to survey the treed acreage. "Talk about privacy. Dane, where *is* Peppe's place? I can't see anything."

He pointed. "Through those trees. Peppe's place is the original homestead. Peppe built the main house for his wife." Dane raced off in that direction, while still explaining, a sense of urgency dogging his heels.

The cabin was set among the trees. Older, more worn, the front door hung crooked … and stood open. "The cabin should be burned because of the state it's in." Bruce backed away, his hand wafting the air in front of his face. "God, that is rank."

"No kidding."

Dane glanced over to see Stephen and Wilson hold their noses as they tried to breathe. A quick glance at Meg showed a similar reaction. He climbed the few steps and entered. The others stayed well back.

The cabin looked the same as he remembered from his last visit. In fact, it looked exactly the same. The same clothes and brown stains on the floor. The smell could have been just the decomposing food though. He bent and peered closer at the stains on the floor. They were old. He kicked them with his boots. Very old.

He searched the small cabin, his mind wanting to panic. A part of him would be happy to accept all kinds of theories, if they led to finding Jade. Instead they'd hit a dead end. He rejoined the team. "It's empty too."

"Really? I thought for sure we'd find Jade here, somewhere." Meg peered into the room behind him.

Stephen shook his head. "Why here? She could be anywhere."

"I hope not. It'll be impossible to find her then." Bruce backed up several paces to stare around the side of the house, as if looking for an outbuilding.

Dane watched him, and finally something went *click*. "Goddamn it." Dane said suddenly. Something he should have thought of earlier fell into place. He hopped off the porch and headed around the corner of the house. The others followed. The old outhouse stood in the back, the door open.

"'What?" The others stared at him, following blindly, confusion on their faces. "Dane, what are you doing?"

"There should be a root cellar here someplace." He shook his head at his own stupidity, as he circled the small building. "John mentioned something about Peppe having done a lot of renovations to this old place. I remember asking to see it when I first arrived, but John said it wasn't his place. Said he was too busy fixing up his store. Another place he wouldn't show me."

"What's that about John's business?" Bruce asked loud enough that everyone trying to catch up could hear.

Dane spun around to explain. "He was working from home, then decided a storefront in town would be better. He leased a place before that recent small earthquake and lost everything. Then last week he told me that everything was gone. He was bankrupt and couldn't bear to tell Tasha." He looked around. The root cellar should be here somewhere. It's the only thing that made sense.

"Dane, is there a building left standing that was John's business?" Bruce called out, his sharp voice finally penetrating Dane's focus.

"Not much of one. I finally drove by there today, but I

couldn't see that he'd done anything. I kept asking to see it, offering to help. I'm in the construction business after all," Dane said in confusion. "Only he kept saying he was working on it, and that it wasn't ready to show me yet."

"As in, he kept giving you an excuse to keep you away?" Bruce's sharp voice made Dane stop and turn to face them.

"Yes, I guess so, … but why?"

"More failure?"

"Dane, where is this building? Might he have stashed Jade in it?"

"It's not structurally sound. Half of one side is cracked and caved in. I didn't stop to look beyond that. There's been so much going on."

"Is there a downstairs? Or a part of the structure that is safe? A place where he might keep her?"

Dane's face shut down. "I don't know." He stopped in front of a blue tarp. "This has to be what I want." He leaned down to pull back the tarp. "I figured there had to be an old root cellar down here." An old rusted padlock secured the large wooden doors.

"Someone give me a hand with this." He looked around for something to smash it with and spied a large rock.

Bruce leaned down and yanked on the lock. "This sucker isn't moving."

"Hell, yes it is. Move back." Dane crashed the heavy rock down on it.

The padlock held, but the old wood splintered in every direction.

JADE TRIED FOR the thousandth time to get her foot free of the manacle. Her blood ran warm down her bare foot. She just couldn't get her heel through the small hole. Desperate for escape, she considered breaking her bones if that would do the job—then discarded that idea. She studied the pin mechanism and the new lock that held the manacle closed. She'd studied the ones on the women's ankles in her lab but not to figure out how to open them. Neither did she have any tools or rocks available to do the job.

She collapsed on the ground. Tears once again welled up in her eyes. She wiped them away. She couldn't function if she let her fear take over. It took anger to beat the fear into the ground. And anger had been a little scarce recently.

Then she thought she heard something above.

Her heart stopped. *Friend or foe?* Then again, what friend of Jade's would know where to look? It had to be her captor.

Panic rose. She pounded it down again. *Think, damn it. You've got a brain. Use it.*

A heavy *thud* above her head had her studying the ceiling. Her muscles tensed. She could hardly breathe.

"Oh God, please. Someone help me," she whispered, as she heard noises at the back of the building. "Please let this be someone looking for me."

She closed her eyes and prayed.

MEG STEPPED BACK. "You guys can go look. I'm staying up here, in the sunshine, where the world doesn't look so dark and creepy."

"That works." Bruce pulled apart the wood fragments and tossed them out of the way to reveal old cement steps, going down into the cellar.

Dane led the way. "Jade, are you here?"

Silence. Stretching out a hand, he was amazed to find a light switch. The small room flooded with opaque light from a single bulb hanging from a cord in the middle of the room.

"Holy shit!"

The other men clambered down the steps behind him and gasped in shock.

Bruce, his voice grim and sad, said, "Well, I guess we know what happened to those manacled women now."

The small room had a bed with blankets, a small dresser with an old-fashioned pitcher and bowl for water. A few blankets and clothing of some kind were tossed on the bed. The other corner of the room had a bucket with a toilet seat resting on top. The structural support standing in the middle of the room was decorated with the one thing that made Dane's blood run cold.

Chains. Chains with manacles on the end, open and loose, hung down from the nails.

"Oh, my God. So it *was* Peppe who kidnapped the women? Holy shit," Stephen muttered.

Dane's stomach sank, and his mind roiled. "*This* is fucking nuts."

"I've been telling you that, man," Stephen said. "This is beyond crazy. We've got a crazy old man kidnapping, abusing, killing young women, and I'm scared to think of how many he took or how long he kept them. Then he tossed their bodies in the mass grave because … what? … It was convenient?"

Bruce, his voice haunted by what was in front of him, said, "Depending on how many women, he might have had several graves. Maybe the earthquake unearthed one? Maybe the mass grave was accidentally put on top? Or maybe he had to move the bodies from their original resting place because it opened with the earthquake, and the mass grave was a perfect opportunity. I don't think Peppe's health or strength is what it used to be. The quake and mass grave would have provided an easy answer. Particularly if he still had one prisoner locked in here at the time of the quake."

Bruce walked to the dresser and using a towel tossed on top, he opened the first drawer then the second. "We need to get the police out here. There are purses, pictures, clothing, even jewelry. Maybe these things can help identify his victims."

Stephen stood in the middle of the room, staring at the center support beam, careful to not touch anything, as he studied the chains. "These are covered in blood."

"No surprise there."

Dane walked over to the center support beam. His voice caught, before he rasped out, "There are names and dates scratched into this pole."

The other two men came to look and found even more than a dated tally. Pleas for help scratched into the wood made Dane turn away, his eyes closing in pain and disbelief.

Grimly Bruce said, "Good, this information will help us identify the victims and provide answers for their families."

"Yeah, except we don't know where this asshole is," Stephen added. "He's still on the loose, and here we are, so focused on John, that we've lost sight of Peppe. For all we know he planned to kidnap Jade from the beginning."

"Christ." Dane sighed, feeling as if he'd just been given a huge reprieve. "This just gets better and better. So my brother is innocent, and Peppe is a killer? Did Emile know? Did he help his father? Did Tasha? Is that why no one could bear to look after him? Why they didn't dare hire a local woman to look after him? In case he killed more women or in case someone found out what he'd done? As that would bring everything back onto them?"

Stephen snorted. "This place gives me the creeps."

Dane smiled, relief washing through him as he realized something major. "At least this proves my brother's innocence. We need to get the police out here right now."

Stephen, shaking his head, took one last look around the cellar. "I'll wait here for the authorities. You go check in with the others, and you might as well check out John's shop. Peppe could just as easily have stashed Jade there. Especially if it's close to the hotel."

Bruce turned to go. "Wilson is waiting outside with Meg. He started retching when he saw this room. We'll leave the three of you here to wait. I don't need to remind you not to touch anything. If you find anything else, contact Dr. Mike and Susan back at the hotel. Call and fill them in. Dane and I will go straight to the shop." Bruce had his phone out and was climbing the steps to call the police from outside.

"And, if you hear anything or see anything, call me on my cell." Dane wrote down his number on a receipt he found in his wallet and handed it over to Stephen. "We have no idea where Peppe is, so be careful. I don't know what the old man might have in his arsenal. He got these women here somehow."

Dane drove into town in a much more positive mental state than he'd left it. Surely his brother was innocent of all the suggested crimes.

And Dane desperately needed to find Jade. To know she was okay and to hold her again. There was so much ugliness here. He couldn't wait to go back to Seattle now.

When this was over, he'd convince his brother to come

home with him. That was the best answer. Put this all behind him and start again. Dane could give him a job, a place to live, help him get back on his feet.

Bruce called Dr. Mike with an update that had Dr. Mike gasping with outrage. He told Bruce there'd been no sign of John or of Jade. Fifteen minutes after Bruce had finished his call, Dane pulled into the back of the shop, which he'd only ever driven past before. It looked the same. He reached into the glove box of his truck and pulled out a small clipboard. He rifled through several sheets of paper to find the one he was looking for. "This is it—726 Main Road."

Bruce stared at the broken door numbers on the entrance. "Well, let's go check it out. I really don't want to find any more nasty horrors, like what we just found."

"I just want to find Jade—safe and sound."

The men approached carefully. It was late afternoon now, but still, people walked the sidewalks, and vehicles moved quickly along the street. An ordinary day.

But not for him. For Dane it was as if time had stopped. If Jade were here, it would devastate him. But even then, it didn't mean John was to blame. And, if Jade weren't here, he'd be even more upset and concerned for her. He needed to find her. Fast.

"This wall is cracked enough to enter." Dane shook his head. Why the hell hadn't he come here earlier and checked up on his brother? The back wall wasn't just cracked. It was half gone. Shrugging, Dane stepped through carefully and followed the dirty pathway to a small door. He opened it. Dirty footprints led down the stairs.

Bruce stepped up behind him. "What is it?" he whispered. Dane motioned to the tracks. Bruce grimaced. "Are we thinking he's down there?"

The two men exchanged looks. Dane knew that if some-one were still down there, they had the advantage. Then again, Dane didn't have an option. He slipped down the first couple risers as quietly as he could.

He bent down to peer around the corner.

"Oh my God."

JADE'S HEART CLOGGED her throat.

Even as she watched, a large square of light appeared, highlighting stairs in the far corner.

Her muscles tensed. She could hardly breathe. She didn't know whether she should try to make it look as if were sleeping or to sit casually and wait.

That she would finally find out who was behind her kidnapping almost scared her more than not knowing.

Her heart beat so hard that she could barely think. Work boots like Dane's appeared, followed by jean-clad legs. Long and lean. She gulped and shoved her fist into her mouth to stop the whimpers forming in the back of her throat. *It couldn't be. Please not.*

Then a familiar face came into view. Jade stared in disbelief and horror.

It was.

Chapter 27

DANE RACED TO her side. "Jesus, Jade. Thank God, we found you."

"Jade?" At the sight of Bruce's worried face, Jade burst into tears. Dane wrapped her in his arms. "I'm so sorry. It'll be fine now. I promise. It's over."

She couldn't stop crying. "Thank you for finding me. I can't get free." She kicked her leg out to show them the chain. "I've been so scared. I was afraid he'd come back. Then I was terrified he wouldn't come back, and I'd die here forgotten and alone."

"Never forgotten, sweetheart. We're here. You'll be fine now." Dane gave her a big hug, then stepped back. She reached for him again, scared he'd leave her alone. He grabbed her hands. "Bruce, come hold her. I need to find something to knock that manacle off."

Bruce stepped forward and wrapped his arms around her. He held her close. "I just called the authorities again. I expect they'll escort us all to the airport after this and wait until we get on the plane to confirm that we leave."

Dane shook his head. "I can't say I'd blame them. Now what the hell can I use to get that damn thing off her leg?"

She pointed to the far corner. "A mess of stuff is over there. You might find something to use."

Dane headed to the corner.

"Damn it, Jade. What the hell happened?" Bruce gave her a quick shake. "We were so worried about you."

She sniffled slightly, touching the side of her head, still tender but no longer bleeding. "I was sitting at the table, waiting for Dane and Meg to come back, when the lights went out. I woke up here. With this." She pointed to her foot again. "What *is* this place? Where are we?"

"We're still in town. It's been about five hours since you went missing. Oh, and you wouldn't believe what we found out."

She slid her arm through his, unable to let go of him. They both watched as Dane bent down to check something, then stood again. He returned quickly, with an odd assortment of tools in his hand.

"Dane, what's over there?"

He shot Bruce a hard look. "I'll work on this lock. Bruce, why don't you go see? Maybe you can identify it."

Curious, Jade watched as Bruce hurried to the far end, where he became lost in the shadows. She could barely see him, as he stopped and stared, before dropping to the floor. "What is it, Dane?"

He sighed and stopped fiddling with the lock to look up at her. "It's not what, as much as whom."

"Oh, God." Jade's stomach threatened to heave. *Was* a person over there? *Dead?* Dane hadn't said so, but she hadn't heard a word the whole time she'd been here.

"He'll need to add an ambulance to the fleet on its way." Dane shook his head. "I never thought to call. All I wanted was to get this damn manacle off you." He struggled to break the manacle while Jade watched, willing him to hurry.

The longer it took, the more she started to panic. They had to get away. Fast.

A hoarse, hard voice sliced through their concentration. "Well, well. Look who finally came to visit. Checking up on me, big brother?"

Dane froze. He closed his eyes briefly, his face contorting in disgust. And pain. Jade gasped and huddled in a ball in front of Dane, who was between her and her kidnapper. She couldn't believe it. She didn't want to believe it. Poor Dane. She tried to peer around Dane to be sure. "Dane? Is that *John*?"

Slowly opening his eyes to look into hers, he whispered, "Yeah. I'm so sorry. I'd hoped to get you safely away before your kidnapper returned. Looks like he found us first."

"Stand up, *step*brother."

Jade couldn't see John's face, but his voice conveyed no sign of the weak, ineffectual man she'd believed him to be.

Sighing, Dane dropped the tools and slowly stood. Turning to face John, he motioned at the gun in John's hand and casually said, "What's going on, John? I don't get it. Explanation, please?"

"You never did have the brains everyone gave you credit for. To the world, you were always the first, the best, the biggest. God, I hated that. You were always trying to steal the limelight. And here I find you, trying to steal my new girl."

Dane shook his head. "*Your* girl? You actually kidnapped Jade? Are you crazy?"

John smiled.

Jade peered around Dane. *Oh God.* That look on John's face. So empty, so lacking in anything recognizable. She reached for the tools Dane had dropped and worked frantically on the lock.

"No," John said softly. "I'm not crazy. I didn't figure

you'd find Jade so fast."

"I have to admit I had some help from friends."

"That damn team. They're the reason everything's wrong. Then again, they also offered the perfect avenue to bring about a much-needed change."

"Change? Is that what you call the destruction of your family?"

"I didn't touch Emile. Peppe fought with him and knocked him down. The two of them had a whopper of a fight about the doctor he was trying to bring in behind my back to look after Tasha. Peppe was just getting his own back. Emile had already washed his hands of the old man. His death just finished off Tasha, but that had nothing to do with me." He smirked. "Except for the pillow over her mouth and nose."

"What about your high school girlfriend, Melia? Did you do her in?" Dane's voice held a plea that Jade had trouble understanding.

Her gaze shifted from one brother to the other. *Who the hell was Melia?*

Shock sat heavy on John's face. "Wow, you have been doing your homework, haven't you?" He smiled, a gesture that shot ice rippling through Jade.

God, whoever Melia was, Jade was sure that the poor woman had died at John's hands.

"And your first wife, Elise? Did you kill her too?"

"That stupid bitch. She thought she could leave me. She asked for a divorce of all things. Then she didn't even tell me that she was pregnant. Doubt it was mine anyway. Besides, she deserved what she got."

Jade switched her gaze to Dane's face, watching myriad emotions wash over him. His fists clenched, then relaxed.

These people Dane mentioned had been people he'd known. People who had been part of his life too.

Anger and disbelief fired up Dane's voice. "And Tasha— had she wanted a divorce as well? Or did you think the baby wasn't yours? Is that what you do? Get rid of women when you don't want them anymore?"

"No. You should give me a medal for Tasha. Now that lady was a bitch. Especially toward the end. And I didn't kill the baby. She lost that all on her own. You can't lay that one on me."

Jade could listen no longer. "She lost it, or you helped her lose it?" Bitterness flowed from her voice. She didn't even try to hold back. This innocent-looking man had caused so much pain and suffering. She stared down at the chain in her hand. So much misery. "Did you kidnap and abuse those poor women under Tasha's nose too?"

Dane shook his head at her, but she didn't understand why.

John chuckled, a hard, nasty sound that made her shudder. "You're as stupid as Tasha was. I wasn't even here then. At least not for all of them." He relaxed slightly, rocking back on his heels. "I didn't kidnap those women. That was Peppe. I had no idea he could be so ingenious. No idea all that time I was stuck with Tasha that he was out scouting new victims. It still pisses me off that he thought of it first. That he'd been doing it for years."

He waved the gun around. "I only found out when I was burying those fucking bodies. Talk about a turning point in my life. Emile brought a woman over and threw her on top of the pile, thinking I wouldn't notice. I might not have, except for the goddamn manacle. They didn't even take the thing off her in death.

"Peppe has a mess of them, hanging in a busted-down shed. They are seriously old. We'll probably find his whole damn family were either slaves or slavers at one time themselves." He grinned a nasty smirk that made Jade wince. "I confronted Emile at the mass grave, and he told me about Peppe—that Peppe hadn't been strong enough to get rid of the body on his own, so he'd had to do it for him."

John laughed, a cold sound that sent shards of ice down Jade's back. "The women were Peppe's slaves. They looked after his every need. Emile wouldn't have anything to do with his father after that. Little wuss. And Tasha could never look him in the eye again. She lived in terror of him being found out."

"Emile even built a mess of crosses with inscriptions for the poor women. Said he didn't know how many his dad had killed, but it had to stop." John laughed again.

The sound crawled inside Jade's skin, like ants to an open wound. She'd bet anything Emile had been the one to write the inscription For All Those Who Have Gone Before.

In memory of his father's victims. How sad.

"Although, the way I see it, you owe me. I'm pretty sure Emile changed his mind about things. That he was looking to snatch one of the team members for himself." John sniggered. "Oh, he never said anything directly, but you could tell that something was bugging him. I bet the idea wouldn't leave him alone. It's not as if he had a wife." John continued, his voice brutally cold and confident. "I'd seen what Peppe had built too. Had a little talk with him myself. Scared the pants off him. He was pretty easy to control from then on, until the dementia really started. Who knew what he might have said."

John motioned behind him. "I don't have to worry anymore. That crazy Peppe was stalking Jade too. I took care of that." He shrugged. "He just cemented my decision to kidnap her. Now I have the perfect place to pick up where he left off."

"You mean, Peppe's little dungeon in the root cellar? Well, the police are there right now."

John's face mottled as rage filled him. "Fucking assholes. That's where I would take *her*. It's a perfect hidey-hole."

Jade gasped. That *had* been his intention. She refocused on the manacle's lock. She tried to keep one ear on the conversation, while she had one eye on that damn gun and the other eye on her ankle and lock. She couldn't see Bruce, but he had to know what was going on. What was he doing? And thank God that John hadn't noticed Bruce.

"The cellar's a crime scene now." Dane's hard voice left no doubts.

John's color receded, as he considered the problem. "I'll keep her here then. When they're done, I'll put it back in order." He shrugged. "No problem." He sneered and studied his older brother. "I'd planned on taking you out eventually, but I wanted you to suffer first. That's why I took Jade. I hadn't planned on it. But you were so happy. So delighted at the unexpected turn in your life.

"Yet mine was shit, and, once again, you were coming out with the gold. No point in you having all that money— or her—when it could all be mine. Poor timing though to kill you so soon after the other deaths." He brightened. "Unless I can make it look like you killed them."

Click. Jade stilled in shock. Dane shifted to stand in front of her, giving her more cover. She slipped her hand into Dane's and stood beside him, finally with the manacle unlocked but still in place.

Dane's hand latched onto hers. He tucked her farther behind him.

"*Aww*. Isn't that so cute?"

Jade cringed at the mockery in John's voice. She leaned her head against Dane's broad back. Her breath caught. They needed a distraction. ... Something to give Dane and Bruce an advantage. Dane couldn't outrun a bullet. But John would have a hard time fighting them both off.

"Shut up. Why did you have to pick on Jade anyway? Surely you knew I wouldn't rest until I found her?" He tensed. Jade recognized his change in stance, just not the reason for it. She peeked around his shoulder. He squeezed her hand tightly, then released it. She accepted the warning and took a second, more cautious look.

Bruce stood in the shadows, a large chunk of broken wood in his hand.

"And you'd have suffered for it every day." John grinned.

"You hate me so much? Why? I don't understand. I gave so much to you. Helped you out so many times. I was always there for you. Always." Jade stroked Dane's back, offering him that support at least. He sounded so disbelieving, so heartbroken. So hurt.

"And that's because, in your mind, I always needed your assistance. My big brother bailing me out again. Pathetic. I don't need you to *fix* me. Or to make my problems disappear."

Bruce approached, the block of wood ready.

"You're the one who asked me to stay here. To help you rebuild."

"Yeah, I needed more money. And time to figure a way out. Money buys anything here." He lifted the gun higher as an example. "Your life has been too damn easy. Besides, having you here made it so much easier for me to do what I needed to do. After all, that's the way I always am around you anyway. You're the big man. The good man. I'm the weak younger brother. And because of that, you made the perfect alibi too. Bet you told everyone, *My brother, John, would never hurt anyone. Life has been hard on him, but he's a good man.*"

Jade buried her face against Dane's shoulder. Oh God, Dane had said almost that exact same thing to her. She didn't want to see what was coming next.

Dane, his voice weary and sad, said, "You could have asked. I'd have given you what you needed."

"Yes, and I would have accepted and hated you even—"

A heavy *thump* cut off his words, as John bent over and gasped. "God damned son of a bitch."

Jade stuffed her fist to her mouth to stop the scream from escaping as Dane headed for his brother. John came up in a lunge and decked Bruce. Bruce's head snapped to one side, and he went down—hard. John spun around as if realizing the window he'd opened.

Too late.

Dane sprang across the last few feet, hitting his brother in the chest. They both went down in a flurry of arms and legs, as they fought for control. The gun skittered across the floor. Jade kicked free of the manacle and raced after the gun, keeping a wary eye on the two men.

She picked up the gun and pointed it at the men. Only Dane was sitting on his brother, one hand at his throat, the other, fisted, wailing into John's face.

Bruce groaned. Jade raced over and bent down to him. "Easy, Bruce. John hit you hard."

He opened his eyes, took a moment to register what had

happened, then came off the ground with fire in his eyes.

Jade turned to see Dane land one last blow to John's jaw. John slumped to the ground.

It was over.

"Damn it," Bruce bellowed. "I wanted to get a good one in."

Dane sat back on his heels, still straddling his brother, now gasping for air. "Sorry, I gave it to him for you. And Jade. And Tasha. And Elise. And Melia." He glared down at John, as he stood up. Taking a step away, he added, "So many lives lost. So many more ruined."

Dane turned to look at Jade. He opened his arms. She raced to bury her face against his chest and squeezed him tight. Dane held her close against his heart. Fearing it wasn't over, she peered around Dane's shoulder at John's crumpled body. John wasn't moving.

Sirens whistled from far away. Bruce bent down to check on John's pulse. "He's alive."

"Too bad. What an asshole." Jade reared back to look up into Dane's eyes. "I'm sorry, Dane. I'm not feeling very generous toward your brother at the moment."

He tucked her close against him. "Neither am I. Neither am I."

She turned to face Bruce. "Bruce, who or what is back there?"

He looked at her confusion. She pointed in the back corner. He dropped the wood to the floor, before running his fingers through his short hair. "I think it's Peppe."

The color drained from her face. "Oh, God!"

Bruce smiled sadly. "Looks like John was on a house-cleaning mission."

Jade shuddered and burrowed deeper into Dane's arms. "Thank God, it's over—before he got around to you."

Chapter 28

Three Weeks Later

AT THE SOUND of the truck arriving, Jade walked out of the lab trailer, a big smile on her face. *Dane.* She checked the time on her new cell phone, a gift from the team. *He's on time.* She laughed and waved.

"You two are almost too much, you know that?" Meg stood at Jade's shoulder, shaking her head.

Jade laughed, enjoying the great friendships she'd developed with the team. They'd become like a real family, with bonds that wouldn't break. "Great, isn't it?"

"I'm jealous," Meg admitted. "We've only got about two weeks left. And I miss my Pete. Maybe I should have him fly over for a hot weekend too."

Dane exited the truck, a grin on his face, as he walked toward them. "I heard that. Take him on a cruise. That's where we're headed, as soon as you guys are done here. I can't wait."

"You need the break," Jade murmured, walking into his arms. "How was the meeting?"

"Good and bad. I barely recognized John. These last three weeks haven't been easy on him." He sighed, the rumble rolling up from deep down. "The extradition process is going ahead." He dropped his head to rest against the top of Jade's. "I spoke to one lawyer who said the U.S. wants to try him for the murders of Melia and Elise. Plus they will go through John's history to see if there could be other victims."

Jade closed her eyes at the pain in his voice. What a mess the last few weeks had been. Dane had had it the hardest. She still had nightmares, only they were less disturbing. Dane had them too. Although she hadn't let him know that she'd watched him twist in torment while he slept. "I'm sorry," she said.

He tightened his arms, then released her, keeping one around her shoulders, as he smiled at Meg. "How's it going here?"

Meg smiled. "It's great. We've found the mother and daughter we've been looking for. The DNA results came in today for them. Just waiting for the father's DNA to match up. Then those three can go home, where they belong."

"Wow." Dane smiled down at Jade. "That's excellent. I guess that means you'll relax a little when Duncan gets here next week?"

She laughed. "Maybe."

When Duncan had heard the story of her kidnapping, he'd freaked on the phone and had wanted to come over right away. It had taken a lot to convince him to hold off. Now his visit would be a joy. She couldn't wait to see him.

Jade leaned away a little. "Also, the police have a tentative ID on two of the prisoner women from the grave. But, as in John's case, it's important to find all of Peppe's victims. To find them, identify them, and bring them home."

Tony had pitched a fit over identifying Peppe's victims, but he underestimated the wealthy business owner who had been horrified and had quickly offered financial support to see the job done right.

Thank heavens.

"Home and family is important. So is friendship. And love." Dane's smile turned intimate, Jade's insides now mush.

This trip had done so much for her. For all its horrors and violence, the job here had brought about many good things. She was being held by one of them. She'd survived. Not only survived but thrived.

In fact, by now, she was pretty sure she could get through anything.

That's what she called progress.

This concludes Book 1 of By Death: *Touched by Death*.
Read the first chapter of Haunted by Death: By Death, Book 2

By Death: Haunted by Death
(Book #2)

Meg Pearce is haunted by a death that may never be explained, … and so she can never truly be healed. During the summer before she started college, she and her boyfriend went on a camping trip that ended with one of their friends disappearing. In one fell swoop of destruction, she lost not only a friend but her own innocence, her future, her best friend and lover, her everything.

Seventeen years later, Meg's career as an anthropologist drives her to seek understanding about why things happen and the answers for human behavior. Those questions that torment her have her returning to the same campsite of the tragedy that defined her life. A part of her hopes to solve the mystery that has plagued her for most of her adult years. Ultimately she longs to find a way to deal with the loss. Instead of gaining closure though, she stumbles onto a gruesome discovery that has her reeling back to the darkest time in her existence.

Detective Chad Ingram has spent the last seventeen years

attempting to solve a stone-cold mystery—one that also stole his life and his true love.

Death seems supernaturally determined to shake up their lives for good or evil—only this time, Meg and Chad are both in the crossfire.

Find Book 2 here!

To find out more visit Dale Mayer's website.

https://geni.us/DMhaunted

By Death: Haunted by Death (Book #2)
Chapter 1

THE CLOUDS SWEPT across the sky, whipped by a blustery northern wind. The sun was high, shining brightly over the lake and shore. It was a perfect summer's day at the lake. Not far from the water's edge, where multiple brightly colored tents sprawled, Chad Ingram followed his buddies up the beach for a short hike. Bruce and Josh, his best friends, were in charge of today's adventure. The girls had elected to stay behind.

This was their last camping trip of the summer, before college started next week. The long-standing group of three young males and their three girlfriends had made the most of the summer weather to get out and to enjoy their time together. This weekend, Tim and Bruce's cousins—Anto and Pero, who'd moved to the US a couple years ago—had joined them.

Chad liked them both, and Pero was easy to get along with. However, his broody brother, Anto, was, by contrast, hard work. But so long as he was on his best behavior, he fit into the group just fine. Some of the group had worked full-time for the summer, others only part-time, and one of their number was doing summer school. Making time together had been a challenge.

And they all knew it was the end of an era. And that making time for each other was important. Next week, each would start on the pathway of whatever future they'd chosen. This weekend was a last chance to let loose before life intruded. Good thing too. Futures were serious business.

Josh had organized this day hike, which was intended to be a fun couple of hours, exploring this side of the lake. With only T-shirts, shorts, and runners, they weren't equipped to do more. Chad liked to do at least one hiking trip a day when they were out. Not going too far and not putting out too much effort, just a break from the beach and swimming and beer drinking. Well, maybe not that last one, as several of them usually carried an open can of beer with them.

This was their second trip to the popular northern area of Washington State. They'd camped at the other side of this same lake earlier in the summer, close to where several members of Bruce's extended-family had cabins. That trip had been such a blast that they all wanted to come back and check out the opposite side of the lake, the less popular side. Where they'd first camped out were hundreds of cabins up and down the lakeshore. That area was open and sunny, with lovely sandy beaches. All of which made it a big attraction for kids and families.

This time the group wanted a different experience. They wanted seclusion, isolation, privacy, and a chance to enjoy their last bit of freedom, without having to follow curfews and noise restrictions.

And, from the looks of the tightly grown forest and steep incline on parts of the hill behind them, they had it.

The group took off up the hill in good spirits. Chad

walked last in line, smiling at his friends' antics up ahead. Their laughter preceded them, filling the dense woods, even as the sun fought to reach into the old growth and the tightly grouped stick trees on the left. The air was filled with a heavy pine-scented atmosphere. Although the walk up the hill on the left side had started out easily, it hit the way-too-much-work-to-be-bothered-with category very quickly. Besides, they hadn't brought enough beer to fortify themselves for that much effort.

"Hey, Chadwickie, what's taking you so long?" Josh yelled back from up ahead. He'd been leading the group of males for the last ten minutes but had stopped to see what was holding up his friend.

"I gotta take a piss," Chad called out. "That beer is running right through me."

"Weakling! Jesus, you really can't hold your liquor, can you?" Raucous laughter filled the air.

"Ha, ha. I can hold it that way just fine. I wasn't the one slobbering all over the girls last night, like you and Bruce were."

Chad—or Chadwickie, as his buddies liked to call him to rile him—stepped farther into the dense woods and slightly off the path, then opened his fly. Immediately a bright stream hit the mossy ground and ferns in front of him. He tilted his head back and sighed with relief, enhanced by the mild buzz going on in his head. Life was good.

"Aren't you done already?" called back one of his friends, probably Bruce. "It's almost time to go back to the girls. You're taking so long."

"When you gotta go, you gotta go," Chad murmured quietly, with a contented sigh. He could hear his friends moving farther away, but they were still within hearing distance.

The stream went on and on. Finally he tucked himself back inside and zipped up his khaki shorts. He turned to look for his buddies. No one was in sight.

Shit.

"Hey, Josh? Bruce?" He spun around. "Where the hell are you guys? Anto? Tim?"

There was not a sound, not a whisper of laugher or a crackle of leaves. Nothing. Crap. Where were they?

"Pero?"

Just then, the sun went behind a cloud, and the air around him darkened, adding a sinister overtone to his growing fear. Crackling noises off to the left had him bolting to the right. "Hey, guys!"

Nothing.

Laughter from the way ahead wove through the air. He ran toward it. Tripping over roots and piling through bushes, Chad chased after his friends. They would hide from him for hours—or for as long as they were having fun—if he didn't find them first. They were all jokesters, him included.

But going for a two-hour hike as part of the group was one thing; getting left behind and lost was another thing altogether. *That* was not something Chad wanted. The group had been making hiking and camping trips for the last year. They had been a blast. But they'd all been on fields or beaches in open terrain, where it was easy to see the surrounding area, easy to pinpoint landmarks to avoid getting lost. Never had they been in woods like this, but, of course, that had been the attraction this time around.

Open spaces were fine; beaches were good—great even. This place was eerie in a good way. Kinda like ghost stories around a campfire, a creepy kind of good.

Besides, he knew his buddies, and he trusted them. This was all in fun. He'd take his hit now and dish out more to the others later.

Just to the guys though. The girls didn't prank like the guys did. And he should know. One was an ex-girlfriend and the other? She was the love of his life. There had been a little occasional camping with both his ex and his current girlfriend, but he hadn't gone out with Cia since last Halloween. He'd hooked up with Megan—or Megs as they often called her—in February. She was special. He'd had several girlfriends already, but she had been the first one to touch him inside and to make herself right at home with him. She belonged with him. He loved that connection, that specialness of knowing he'd found the right partner.

His friends thought he was nuts and were always pointing out other chicks and telling him to test drive a few more models before he made a decision. The thing was, he'd already done that. Cia had been one of the worst ones. And his friends just didn't get it about Megs. There was no decision to be made. It had been done for him. He couldn't explain this to someone who'd never experienced such a feeling, but Megs was his, and he was hers. End of discussion.

Chest heaving, he stopped his headlong rush and caught his breath, while he searched the hillside for his friends. Still no sign of the others. Shit. How far ahead could they be? The incline now looked to be a half-mile deep. He checked his watch. *Jesus*. They'd been gone forty-five minutes already. Given that they were close to the time of returning anyway, the others may have circled back toward the lake already.

And that was a damn good idea. They'd always said, if someone got separated from the rest, they were to return to base. Chad should have done that right off. They could be anywhere by now. He didn't want them to send out a search party looking for him. His friends would never let him live that one down. If it weren't for the steep incline, he'd be seriously worried, but the lake had to be down somewhere at the bottom, so how lost could he be?

Still, he'd go back to the girls, while he could still find his way and before he'd take the chance of getting really lost out here.

A flock of birds flew up in a cacophony of sound right behind him. He dashed around a huge tree trunk and slammed up against it, his heart racing in shock. Shit. Somehow a fun afternoon's exploration had stopped being fun. He took a deep breath, hating the nerve-induced adrenaline snaking through his system. A lot of country was out here.

And he was starting to freak himself out.

He'd never been lost or alone in the woods before. Didn't like it much either. Talk about feeling small and unimportant in the vast world of Mother Nature.

"Hey, Josh? Bruce? Very funny, guys. ... *Where* are you? Pero? Anto?"

No answer from any of them. Shit.

He hated this. He couldn't see anything but more brown trees and moss and green bushes in every direction. That wasn't good. His friends were good people, but they were assholes when they pranked each other. Yet Chad had been as guilty as they were.

A branch cracked off to the left. His heart jumped, and he hid behind a tree. He held his breath. *What the hell was that?*

The undergrowth crunched as if someone—

something—were walking heavily on it.

All other sounds had stopped.

He swallowed hard and slithered downward to the base of the tree. After a long moment, he peered around the edge of the tree trunk. He couldn't see anyone. Yet he heard a stealthy noise—barely. Branches rustled; leaves slid against each other, and the birds had gone silent, as if they saw something which he couldn't. The noise could have been from an animal. A bear? But he wasn't so sure. It hadn't been his friends. He knew that. They didn't have the skill to move so quietly. They were all elephants.

But hundreds of cabins were here—and likely thousands of people, counting homes, campgrounds, and the park. He waited, still peering from his hiding spot, but he couldn't hear anything else.

Then it hit him. The noise had come from the direction of the lake. From where they'd left the three girls alone.

Alone. … Oh, Megs.

For the first time he realized how stupid they'd been. His heart went into overdrive, and he could barely breathe. Oh shit. Oh shit. *Oh shit!*

Taking a deep breath, he plowed through the brush the way he'd come, around trees, ducking under branches, jumping over fallen logs, and dodging the bushes that reached out to slow his progress. He had to get back. Something was wrong. He knew it. He just didn't know what.

He crossed what seemed like dozens of miles. He wished he knew where his buddies were right now, but it was the thought of the girls that scared him. They should never have been left alone, never.

He broke through the tree line, gasping in pain, his body

trembling with panic, sweat coursing down his back and soaking his T-shirt. And, at last, he came to a dead stop.

Megs was there, with Stephanie. The two girls were in the lake, floating on air mattresses about twenty feet from shore, talking and paying no attention to anything but their conversation. Relief washed through him at the sight of Megs's long, lean body stretched out under the sun. He bent over, struggling to breathe.

She was fine.

Even as he watched, she was pointing out something in the sky to Stephanie. He doubted they even knew he was here. Those two had been close friends for years and could talk about nothing for hours. Confused, he straightened slowly and looked around.

The area was peaceful. Normal. And this normality made him feel like an idiot for overreacting.

But where was Cia? She wasn't emotionally close to the other two females. And she wasn't the type to share confidences with other girls. She was all about the guys. And that had made it a little hard with all the relationship-switching that had happened within the group. Cia had been the one to break up with Chad, and a good thing it had been too. It had saved him the job. For all her good points, Cia came with a couple really negative characteristics.

Normally she could always be found sitting to one side, reading one of her never-ending books. He spun around, looking for her, but found no sign of her.

Maybe she was napping, as she'd been tired, complaining of the heat when they'd left.

"Megs," he called out, "where's Cia?"

Megs twisted around, saw him, and gave him a warm smile. "She went to lie down. She has another headache."

Right. Of course she had. Cia got major migraines. He'd never known anyone else to have them before. It had been quite an education, as they completely crippled her at times. Feeling better, he walked to the water's edge and splashed cool water on his face. If anyone realized how completely he'd overreacted, they'd make fun of him for days.

As he straightened up, his face cooler and his heart no longer trying to escape his chest, he realized that the inner disquiet hadn't been fully calmed. Not able to let it go until he was sure, he walked over to Josh and Cia's tent. "Cia? Are you in here?"

He hated to wake her, but he had to know for sure.

The flap was down, so he lifted the corner and peered inside.

Empty.

He straightened up, cupped his hands around his mouth, and called across the water, "She's not here. The tent is empty."

Just then the rest of the guys thundered through the trees, half running, half crashing into each other, all laughing and joking. "There you are." Josh grinned at Chad, as he jogged over to him. "We got into a crazy game of hide-and-seek in the woods. We weren't sure if you were with us or not at that point."

Bruce and Tim approached, gasping for breath but still scrapping over who had arrived first and second.

"I wasn't," Chad snapped, hands on his hips, as he glared at his friends. "And no thanks to you guys. You could have waited for me."

The others grinned, totally digging him being pissed off. He couldn't blame them. If their positions had been reversed, he'd have done the same. No sign of the Novak brothers. Chad spun around to see them—Anto first, coming through the trees; then Pero, much farther down.

Damn. Chad faced the gathering crowd. "I can't find Cia. The girls said she went to lie down and have a nap, but she's not here."

The responses came from all of them at once.

Bruce brushed off the news with a shake of his head. "Stop worrying. She won't be far away."

"Probably grabbed her book and found a shady spot to read."

"Anyone check the outhouse?"

Chad was having none of it. A horrible certainty had filled him. This was seriously bad.

At his insistence and, with the other two girls now back on shore, they spread out to search … everywhere. Grim-faced and sober, they finally regrouped an hour later.

There had been no sign of Cia.

She was gone.

Find Book 2 here!

To find out more visit Dale Mayer's website.

https://geni.us/DMhaunted

Simon Says... HIDE: Kate Morgan (Book #1)

Welcome to a new thriller series from *USA Today* Best-Selling Author Dale Mayer. Set in Vancouver, BC, the team of Detective Kate Morgan and Simon St. Laurant, an unwilling psychic, marries all the elements of Dale's work that you've come to love, plus so much more.

Detective Kate Morgan, newly promoted to the Vancouver PD Homicide Department, stands for the victims in her world. She was once a victim herself, just as her mother had been a victim, and then her brother—an unsolved missing child's case—was yet another victim. She can't stand those who take advantage of others, and the worst ones are those who prey on the hopes of desperate people to line their own pockets.

So, when she finds a connection between a current case and more than a half-dozen cold cases, where a child's life hangs in the balance, Kate would make a deal with the devil himself to find the culprit and to save the child.

Simon St. Laurant's grandmother had the Sight and had

warned him that, once he used it, he could never walk away. Until now, her caution had made it easy to avoid that first step. But, when nightmares of his own past are triggered, Simon can't stand back and watch child after child be abused. Not without offering his help to those chasing the monsters.

Even if it means dealing with the cranky and critical Detective Kate Morgan …

Find Simon Says… Hide here!
To find out more visit Dale Mayer's website.
https://geni.us/DMSSHideUniversal

Simon Says… HIDE: Kate Morgan (Book #1)
Chapter 1

Vancouver, First Monday in June …

NEWLY MINTED HOMICIDE detective Kate Morgan sat on one of the many benches positioned in this child-friendly park, watching the kids play on the swings in downtown Vancouver. She'd passed her first three months in her new position amid the craziness of too many murder cases to count. Vancouver, BC, was like any big city around the world and had its share of criminal activity. The city had its issues—just being on the coast and blending many different nationalities—yet somehow it all worked. Plus it was home for her. Always had been.

Because of those life-and-death issues, Vancouver had three homicide units, usually with six or seven detectives in each unit. She chuckled. At one time, the two other units called themselves Team Canuck or Team Flames, showing how hockey crazy Canada got. She didn't know what her unit used to call themselves, as she was the odd-one-out still. New enough to know her place and not so new to misunderstand the team needed time to meld.

Her ever-assessing gaze watched two men on a bench on the far side of the park. One got up, tossed a bright yellow ball at the other and then, with a raised hand, turned and walked away.

Her focus flitted to the storm approaching in the distance, assessed its threat, and dismissed it. Rain was part of the reality when living on the coast. The more pressing threats in her world were the two-legged predators. She'd known the dangers ever since her younger brother had disappeared, even now, twenty-five years later with still no trace of him. She kept a copy of his file on her desk, as a reminder of the work she'd dedicated herself to. Timmy was always close to her heart. She could only hope to get closure, as she worked to give closure to others.

Sudden movement on her left had her watching a lean man of average height, walking into the park and staring at the kids on the swing. Something about his gaze set her nerves on edge. He was slightly turned away from her, only letting her see his jeans and well-worn jacket with the upturned collar. He perched on a nearby bench seat, seemingly fascinated by the boys' antics.

The single male on the far side stood suddenly and strode her way, tossing the yellow ball and catching it smoothly with every step. He gazed at the street beside her, unconcerned for the kids or other adults. His focus was internal. From the power suit he wore, business deals most likely.

As she turned back to the other man, he'd disappeared. Her gaze zipped to the boys at the swings. They were still there. Relaxing slightly, she studied the park exits. Both men had left at the same time. From opposite sides of the park.

It shouldn't have meant anything.

But it felt like it did.

Her phone rang just then. Rodney, one of her team.

"We found another one. Prepare yourself. It's a little boy."

Tuesday

SIMON ST. LAURANT had had a bad week. He twisted in bed, kicking off the blanket. His body shimmered with sweat. He drifted in and out of sleep. He'd been up until two in the morning in one of his friendlier gambling games and had crashed soon afterward. Now it was five in the morning, and the last thing he wanted was to be awake. He rolled over, pulled the sheet over his sweating body, and closed his eyes.

As he tried to fall asleep again, he drifted down the same godforsaken dark street, just a halo of light coming from the streetlamps across on the other side. A small man, holding the hand of a very young boy at his side, walked quietly down the street. The little boy asked, "When will we be there?"

"We'll be there soon," the older man promised.

Something was just so damn wrong about that picture that Simon kept telling the little boy to run, wanting to reach out and drag him to safety. But, even as Simon reached out a hand, he saw that it wasn't real, that he wasn't there, that he couldn't grab that little boy and escape. As the older man walked under the streetlamp, Simon caught the hungry look on the man's face. A predator's look. Yet not clear enough to identify him.

Simon woke immediately, sat up, and groaned in frustration. "Why that same goddamn freaking nightmare?" he cried out, before flopping to his back yet again.

He was exhausted, his mind overwhelmed, as he drifted once again into the deepness of sleep. This time he landed in a small room, with lots of toys on the bed and on the floor.

A bed that broke his heart because it had a plastic sheet for the little kids who might wet themselves. A blanket was atop the bed but was otherwise empty. Simon's mind knew that a light was on the side of the room and that Simon would see the child soon, but he didn't want to go there. He kicked himself out of the dream, sitting up again, shuddering in the dark. "Damn it," he muttered, rubbing his eyes. "What fresh hell is this?"

Almost as if by asking that question, his body stiffened. He fell backward again, and this time he was in a different room, and the bed was bigger. It had little pink roses around the base and unicorns across the headboard. A little girl sobbed her eyes out, curled up into a tiny ball, hugging a teddy bear. The problem was that fancy little bed was completely out of place, surrounded by bare concrete walls and old cracked floors. The lack of carpet or any other niceties suggested this would not be a nice little home for her.

Instead Simon saw the bloodstains on the mattress around her, the pain and the terror in her heart, and the loneliness in her soul. He wanted to hold her and to tell her that it would be okay. But the same words rippled through his mind: *Hide. He's coming.*

Then everything went dark …

When he woke again, he lay in his bed, staring at the ceiling, dry-eyed, but felt as if he'd bawled his entire life away. Every part of his body hurt, especially his soul. He sat up, felt like he was thirty years older than his thirty-seven years on this planet. Thirty-seven years of pain and fighting to get the upper hand, trying to ensure that he wouldn't be a victim in this world again.

Years ago he'd sworn to be a victor instead. He played

the game, but he didn't let others play him. That wasn't part of his new reality. Not anymore—not for a long time. He looked down at his bed, the bottom sheet literally pulled off the mattress and twisted beneath him, while the top sheet was crumpled on the floor beside him.

"Looks like I had a party—and not the fun kind," he muttered, as he slowly straightened. He stretched, turned to get the kinks out of his neck and his back. A bad night had the effect of turning his spine into a pretzel that he could spend hours trying to untwist. He needed a hot shower to complete the job. Yet every time he went under the water, he kept seeing images of the boy that he'd seen in the first nightmare this morning.

It made no sense, when he'd seen many other children throughout his lifetime of nightmares, but, for some reason, he identified with that one. That night terror always upset him because he didn't know that child. It wasn't Simon as a child, and he didn't understand the dialogue, didn't remember it from his own life. What he did know was that these nightmares had to stop.

If he had a friend who was a doctor, he might have talked to him or her, but unfortunately he didn't even have that. In truth, speaking out loud of this weakness, … in the wrong hands, that knowledge could crush Simon. As he walked naked to the shower, he knew something had to change; he couldn't keep going on this way. The nightmares had restarted suddenly, for no current reason, and they were getting stronger, clearer, and more traumatic to view.

He should get away for a few days. Book a gambling cruise to take his mind off this mess. Maybe see Yale there. Simon's gaze caught sight of the yellow child's ball that Yale had tossed to Simon, the two men out of the blue both at the park yesterday.

Simon often walked that corridor and had come upon his old friend, looking sad and depressed. It had been nice to see Yale unexpectedly. Normally they'd be in on the same poker games or cruises, but he hadn't seen his old college friend in over six months.

Much happier after their visit, Yale had laughed, as he'd tossed him the ball, and said, "For old times' sake."

With a shrug, Simon stepped under the rain showerhead and let the hot water slosh over his head and down his back to the tiles below.

As soon as he was dry and dressed in lightweight pants with a linen shirt, perfect for summers in Vancouver, he picked up his blazer, flipped it over his shoulder, and headed out. He needed coffee in a big way, but he also had to escape the solitude of his own thoughts, preferably out in public, where he could disappear into the crowds. He walked off the elevator, crossed the lobby, and headed toward the front door, held open by the doorman.

Once outside, he stopped for a long moment, lifted his head, and sniffed the early morning Vancouver air. The nearby harbor, with that scent of salt, plus the noise and the bustle of city life, all of it melded together beautifully. With a smile he turned and headed toward his favorite coffee shop.

Find Simon Says… Hide here!
To find out more visit Dale Mayer's website.
https://geni.us/DMSSHideUniversal

Author's Note

Thank you for reading Touched by Death! If you enjoyed my book, I'd appreciate it if you'd leave a review.

Dear reader,

I love to hear from readers, and you can contact me at my website: www.dalemayer.com or at my Facebook author page. To be informed of new releases and special offers, sign up for my newsletter or follow me on BookBub. And if you are interested in joining Dale Mayer's Reader Group, here is the Facebook sign up page.
http://geni.us/DaleMayerFBGroup

Cheers,
Dale Mayer

About the Author

Dale Mayer is a *USA Today* best-selling author, best known for her SEALs military romances, her Psychic Visions series, and her Lovely Lethal Garden cozy series. Her contemporary romances are raw and full of passion and emotion (Broken But … Mending, Hathaway House series). Her thrillers will keep you guessing (Kate Morgan, By Death series), and her romantic comedies will keep you giggling (*It's a Dog's Life*, a stand-alone novella; and the Broken Protocols series, starring Charming Marvin, the cat).

Dale honors the stories that come to her—and some of them are crazy, break all the rules and cross multiple genres!

To go with her fiction, she also writes nonfiction in many different fields, with books available on résumé writing, companion gardening, and the US mortgage system. All her books are available in print and ebook format.

Connect with Dale Mayer Online

Dale's Website – www.dalemayer.com
Twitter – @DaleMayer
Facebook Page – geni.us/DaleMayerFBFanPage
Facebook Group – geni.us/DaleMayerFBGroup
BookBub – geni.us/DaleMayerBookbub
Instagram – geni.us/DaleMayerInstagram
Goodreads – geni.us/DaleMayerGoodreads
Newsletter – geni.us/DaleNews

Also by Dale Mayer

Published Adult Books:

Shadow Recon

Magnus, Book 1

Bullard's Battle

Ryland's Reach, Book 1

Cain's Cross, Book 2

Eton's Escape, Book 3

Garret's Gambit, Book 4

Kano's Keep, Book 5

Fallon's Flaw, Book 6

Quinn's Quest, Book 7

Bullard's Beauty, Book 8

Bullard's Best, Book 9

Bullard's Battle, Books 1–2

Bullard's Battle, Books 3–4

Bullard's Battle, Books 5–6

Bullard's Battle, Books 7–8

Terkel's Team

Damon's Deal, Book 1

Wade's War, Book 2

Gage's Goal, Book 3

Calum's Contact, Book 4

Rick's Road, Book 5

Scott's Summit, Book 6

Brody's Beast, Book 7

Terkel's Twist, Book 8

Terkel's Triumph, Book 9

Terkel's Guardian

Radar, Book 1

Kate Morgan

Simon Says… Hide, Book 1

Simon Says… Jump, Book 2

Simon Says… Ride, Book 3

Simon Says… Scream, Book 4

Simon Says… Run, Book 5

Simon Says… Walk, Book 6

Hathaway House

Aaron, Book 1

Brock, Book 2

Cole, Book 3

Denton, Book 4

Elliot, Book 5

Finn, Book 6

Gregory, Book 7

Heath, Book 8

Iain, Book 9

Jaden, Book 10

Keith, Book 11

Lance, Book 12

Melissa, Book 13

Nash, Book 14

Owen, Book 15

Percy, Book 16

Quinton, Book 17

Ryatt, Book 18

Spencer, Book 19

Hathaway House, Books 1–3

Hathaway House, Books 4–6

Hathaway House, Books 7–9

The K9 Files

Ethan, Book 1

Pierce, Book 2

Zane, Book 3

Blaze, Book 4

Lucas, Book 5

Parker, Book 6

Carter, Book 7

Weston, Book 8

Greyson, Book 9

Rowan, Book 10

Caleb, Book 11

Kurt, Book 12

Tucker, Book 13

Harley, Book 14

Kyron, Book 15

Jenner, Book 16

Rhys, Book 17

Landon, Book 18

Harper, Book 19

Kascius, Book 20

The K9 Files, Books 1–2

The K9 Files, Books 3–4

The K9 Files, Books 5–6

The K9 Files, Books 7–8

The K9 Files, Books 9–10

The K9 Files, Books 11–12

Lovely Lethal Gardens

Arsenic in the Azaleas, Book 1

Bones in the Begonias, Book 2

Corpse in the Carnations, Book 3

Daggers in the Dahlias, Book 4

Evidence in the Echinacea, Book 5

Footprints in the Ferns, Book 6

Gun in the Gardenias, Book 7

Handcuffs in the Heather, Book 8

Ice Pick in the Ivy, Book 9

Jewels in the Juniper, Book 10

Killer in the Kiwis, Book 11

Lifeless in the Lilies, Book 12

Murder in the Marigolds, Book 13

Nabbed in the Nasturtiums, Book 14

Offed in the Orchids, Book 15

Poison in the Pansies, Book 16

Quarry in the Quince, Book 17

Revenge in the Roses, Book 18

Silenced in the Sunflowers, Book 19

Toes in the Tulips, Book 20

Lovely Lethal Gardens, Books 1–2

Lovely Lethal Gardens, Books 3–4

Lovely Lethal Gardens, Books 5–6

Lovely Lethal Gardens, Books 7–8

Lovely Lethal Gardens, Books 9–10

Psychic Vision Series

Tuesday's Child

Hide 'n Go Seek

Maddy's Floor

Garden of Sorrow

Knock Knock…

Rare Find

Eyes to the Soul

Now You See Her

Shattered

Into the Abyss

Seeds of Malice

Eye of the Falcon

Itsy-Bitsy Spider

Unmasked

Deep Beneath

From the Ashes

Stroke of Death

Ice Maiden

Snap, Crackle…

What If…

Talking Bones

String of Tears

Inked Forever

Psychic Visions Books 1–3

Psychic Visions Books 4–6

Psychic Visions Books 7–9

By Death Series

Touched by Death

Haunted by Death

Chilled by Death

By Death Books 1–3

Broken Protocols – Romantic Comedy Series

Cat's Meow

Cat's Pajamas

Cat's Cradle

Cat's Claus

Broken Protocols 1-4

Broken and… Mending

Skin

Scars

Scales (of Justice)

Broken but… Mending 1-3

Glory

Genesis

Tori

Celeste

Glory Trilogy

Biker Blues

Morgan: Biker Blues, Volume 1

Cash: Biker Blues, Volume 2

SEALs of Honor

Mason: SEALs of Honor, Book 1

Hawk: SEALs of Honor, Book 2

Dane: SEALs of Honor, Book 3

Swede: SEALs of Honor, Book 4

Shadow: SEALs of Honor, Book 5

Cooper: SEALs of Honor, Book 6

Markus: SEALs of Honor, Book 7

Evan: SEALs of Honor, Book 8

Mason's Wish: SEALs of Honor, Book 9

Chase: SEALs of Honor, Book 10

Brett: SEALs of Honor, Book 11

Devlin: SEALs of Honor, Book 12

Easton: SEALs of Honor, Book 13

Ryder: SEALs of Honor, Book 14

Macklin: SEALs of Honor, Book 15

Corey: SEALs of Honor, Book 16

Warrick: SEALs of Honor, Book 17

Tanner: SEALs of Honor, Book 18

Jackson: SEALs of Honor, Book 19

Kanen: SEALs of Honor, Book 20

Nelson: SEALs of Honor, Book 21

Taylor: SEALs of Honor, Book 22

Colton: SEALs of Honor, Book 23

Troy: SEALs of Honor, Book 24

Axel: SEALs of Honor, Book 25

Baylor: SEALs of Honor, Book 26

Hudson: SEALs of Honor, Book 27

Lachlan: SEALs of Honor, Book 28

Paxton: SEALs of Honor, Book 29

Bronson: SEALs of Honor, Book 30

Hale: SEALs of Honor, Book 31

SEALs of Honor, Books 1–3

SEALs of Honor, Books 4–6

SEALs of Honor, Books 7–10

SEALs of Honor, Books 11–13

SEALs of Honor, Books 14–16

SEALs of Honor, Books 17–19

SEALs of Honor, Books 20–22

SEALs of Honor, Books 23–25

Heroes for Hire

Levi's Legend: Heroes for Hire, Book 1

Stone's Surrender: Heroes for Hire, Book 2

Merk's Mistake: Heroes for Hire, Book 3

Rhodes's Reward: Heroes for Hire, Book 4

Flynn's Firecracker: Heroes for Hire, Book 5

Logan's Light: Heroes for Hire, Book 6

Harrison's Heart: Heroes for Hire, Book 7

Saul's Sweetheart: Heroes for Hire, Book 8

SEALs of Steel

Badger: SEALs of Steel, Book 1

Erick: SEALs of Steel, Book 2

Cade: SEALs of Steel, Book 3

Talon: SEALs of Steel, Book 4

Laszlo: SEALs of Steel, Book 5

Geir: SEALs of Steel, Book 6

Jager: SEALs of Steel, Book 7

The Final Reveal: SEALs of Steel, Book 8

SEALs of Steel, Books 1–4

SEALs of Steel, Books 5–8

SEALs of Steel, Books 1–8

The Mavericks

Kerrick, Book 1

Griffin, Book 2

Jax, Book 3

Beau, Book 4

Asher, Book 5

Ryker, Book 6

Miles, Book 7

Nico, Book 8

Keane, Book 9

Lennox, Book 10

Gavin, Book 11

Shane, Book 12

Diesel, Book 13

Jerricho, Book 14

Killian, Book 15

Hatch, Book 16

Corbin, Book 17

Aiden, Book 18

The Mavericks, Books 1–2

The Mavericks, Books 3–4

The Mavericks, Books 5–6

The Mavericks, Books 7–8

The Mavericks, Books 9–10

The Mavericks, Books 11–12

Standalone Novellas

It's a Dog's Life

Riana's Revenge

Second Chances

Published Young Adult Books:

Family Blood Ties Series

Vampire in Denial

Vampire in Distress

Vampire in Design

Vampire in Deceit

Vampire in Defiance

Vampire in Conflict

Vampire in Chaos

Vampire in Crisis

Vampire in Control

Vampire in Charge

Family Blood Ties Set 1–3

Family Blood Ties Set 1–5

Family Blood Ties Set 4–6

Family Blood Ties Set 7–9

Sian's Solution, A Family Blood Ties Series Prequel
Novelette

Design series

Dangerous Designs

Deadly Designs

Darkest Designs

Design Series Trilogy

Standalone

In Cassie's Corner

Gem Stone (a Gemma Stone Mystery)

Time Thieves

Published Non-Fiction Books:

Career Essentials

Career Essentials: The Résumé

Career Essentials: The Cover Letter

Career Essentials: The Interview

Career Essentials: 3 in 1